Once Upon a Camino

Matthew S. Wilson

For Jen & Zack - where my journey begins and ends.

x

June 2010

CHAPTER 1

'Are you crazy?' The Spanish shopkeeper pushed her glasses down her nose. 'Who decides to walk the Camino de Santiago at its end?'

'It wasn't my decision,' said Tom.

'No, then, whose?'

'It's... a long story. I just need to buy a backpack.'

She pinned him with a customs officer's scowl and stepped out from behind her counter. '*Vale, vamos.*'

He followed her deeper into the store, a junkyard of fluorescent clothing and military hand-me-downs. They stopped in front of a row of backpacks held prisoner on the wall.

'Which one you want?'

Tom's idea of camping was staying anywhere without Wi-Fi; he pointed to a green bag. 'Maybe this one?'

'For the Camino de Santiago?' She laughed like a

rooster.

'Too small?'

She glared. 'Too big.'

'What do you suggest?'

'*Aquí* – this one has best quality.'

She pointed to a red pack on the top row. He squinted at its tag; it was also the most expensive. He checked his watch; his flight to the beginning of the Camino departed in an hour.

'I'll take it.'

The shopkeeper magicked a pole from behind a shelf and rescued the bag from the wall into Tom's arms.

'Next, we get *botas*.'

'*Botas?* Tom's Spanish lessons had stalled three years ago in the fruit and vegetable section. Whereas he could comfortably recite the scoreline of a football final from thirty years ago, he'd been unable to retain more than a handful of Spanish words.

'*Sí, zapatos*.' She pointed to his suede boat shoes. 'Walking in these is not possible.' She led him to a display of shoes against the adjacent wall and tossed him a thick leather boot with a high-cut. 'Is best quality and is waterproof.'

The boot seemed chunky, something one might wear climbing the Alps. The city had been full of silver-haired hikers – how difficult could the Camino really be? He pointed to a more modern-looking shoe with a lower cut.

'What about this one?'

'No, is cheap.'

'Yes, but I'm never going to wear them again after the Camino.'

'*Sí*, but do you want blisters?'

It was the type of loaded question volunteers ambushed him with back in London. 'Do you care about the planet, sir?' or 'Do you really support whaling, sir?'

'Fine.' He held up the leather space-boot. 'Do you have them in a UK size 10?'

'Is a EU size 44, no?' She delved behind a curtain and returned with a box. '*Aquí.*'

He started toward the counter; the shopkeeper remained steadfast.

'What now?'

'Your clothes.' She eyed his cream-coloured chinos and the pocket square in his blazer. 'Who dresses like this for the Camino?'

Someone who's trying to get married, not walk across Spain.

'What do you suggest?'

The shopkeeper pulled a pair of beige hiking trousers from a nearby rack and held them against his waist. 'You're tall.' She replaced them with a longer pair of slacks. '*Perfecto.*'

He looked at the trousers' tag. 'One hundred euros? For trousers?'

'*Sí, pero*, these are not just trousers. You unzip here and – *mira* – they are shorts. And look at all these pockets.'

She was right; the trousers were a pick-pocket's delight. He stuffed them into the backpack, and the shopkeeper offered him an identical pair from the rack.

'Why do I need two pairs?'

'You want to wear the same trousers for a month?'

He couldn't tell if she was disgusted or disappointed; he pushed the second pair into the bag.

'*Mochila, botas, pantalones.*' The shopkeeper muttered

her imagined stock-take. 'Ah! *Una chaqueta.*' She marched to a nearby rack and rifled through an assortment of rain jackets and windbreakers. 'The weather is unpredictable on the Camino. Here in Galicia, is always raining.' She held up two coats against Tom: one was black, and the other was fluorescent yellow.

'What's the difference?'

'No difference – is same. Both waterproof, both windproof.'

He inspected the tags of both. 'Then why is the yellow one fifty euros cheaper?'

'Because is ugly, no?'

Tom pointed to the black one and the shopkeeper returned the ugly one to the rack.

'What size are you?'

'Medium.'

The woman slid her glasses down and fixed him with a dubious glare. 'If you are medium, I am twenty-one years old, no?' She laughed so hard, Tom could see the metallic fillings in her teeth.

'Well, sometimes I'm a large,' he said, his voice sounding a little more defensive than he'd intended. He used to be a medium, but, if he were honest, the ten-hour workdays, followed by all the after-work drinks, had caught up with him.

The shopkeeper tossed him a large jacket, which he slid into the pack before following her to the front of the store, catching additional items she threw over her shoulder: a small sports towel, two pairs of hiking socks, a baseball cap and a head-torch. He packed each of them into the bag without objection and followed her to a circular rack next to the counter, where she picked up a bright-green shirt with reflective tape around its collar and cuffs.

'This is sweat-proof and quick-dry,' she boasted as if she'd stitched it herself.

'Why do I need it to dry quickly if I won't sweat?'

'The rain.'

'But I'll have my waterproof jacket.' He pulled the sleeve of the jacket she'd sold him a minute ago. 'Remember?'

'*Si*, but the jacket will make you sweat.'

No wonder Tom didn't hike. He glanced at his watch again. 'I'll take one.'

She frowned. 'Just one?'

'Fine, give me two.'

'*Bueno*.'

As the shopkeeper began scanning the items through the register, Tom noticed a pile of guidebooks on the counter. He flipped through one of them, discovering it contained maps and accommodation recommendations. He held one up.

'Do I need this?'

She paused her search for the jacket's tag. '*Si*, of course. Is *muy importante* for all pilgrims. It guides you along the path.'

'Do you have an English version?'

She rummaged through the rest of the stack like a time-poor librarian. 'German, German, Spanish, German. No English – sorry.' She replaced the books on the counter and recommenced her hunt for the jacket's tag.

'Are there other stores where I can buy it?'

'No pilgrim starts at the end of the Camino.' She didn't bother to hide her judgement. 'Maybe you find one in Saint-Jean-Pied-de-Port, or maybe not. Is a Holy Year, many *peregrinos*.'

'What if I can't find one?'

She shrugged. 'Then, you just walk.'

After being *muy importante* twenty seconds earlier, the guidebook suddenly seemed redundant.

'But how will I know the way?'

'All along the Camino you will see yellow arrows pointing the way to Santiago. Sometimes in the city, you will see this too.' She reached across and pointed to a seashell on the top corner of the book's cover. 'The scallop shell is the symbol of Saint James. If you see this or the yellow arrows, you walk this way to Santiago.'

'Yellow arrows and scallop shells – got it.'

'*Vale*.' She rang up the last item. 'That's seven hundred and twenty euros. How you want to pay?'

Tom checked the total on the cash register to see if he'd understood her correctly. He pulled out his wallet. People were right; getting married was expensive.

Compared with the rest of his Thursday, Tom's journey from Santiago to the beginning of the Camino was uneventful. He'd arrived at Santiago airport early enough to change into his new hiking clothes, helping him blend in with the other hikers strolling around the departure gates. But whereas their clothes looked worn and battle-weary, Tom's were sparkling new and untested. The flight to Bilbao was short; the cabin crew had barely served Tom a packet of nuts before demanding he surrender his wrapper and stow his tray-table. From Bilbao, it was a two-hour bus trip, crossing the border to the French city of Bayonne. He checked his work emails, discovering his inbox already had forty-six new ones. Tom's manager, Alistair, had sent most of them – rightly assuming Tom would be checking his phone. The remainder were the usual requests he received from the team: crunching some data in Microsoft Excel, revamping a ghastly slide deck before a sales pitch, and booking a location for a celebration to mark the end of the financial year. At twenty-eight, Tom was still the youngest member of the bank's foreign markets team. All the mundane tasks slid down to him.

'You're the beating heart of this firm,' Alistair would often say to him, usually after Tom had returned with the team's coffees from the café downstairs.

'They treat you like a dog,' Ana would say during their nightly debriefs on the couch with a bottle of wine. 'Why are we both giving our best years to these companies? We should leave, go someplace warmer.'

But this was simply how London's banking scene worked. 'Your twenties are for learning; your thirties are for earning,' is what everyone said. Tom had been in the role for three years and had calculated they'd hire a new graduate next year. Then it would be their responsibility to fetch the coffees and repair other people's appalling PowerPoint slides. Tom's time was coming; he just needed to wait a little longer. Besides, his job still had its perks: just last week Alistair had issued the entire team the newly released iPhone 4. Admittedly Tom had been the one who'd waited outside Apple's store on Regent Street for nine hours to buy them, but still – most people were stuck with the iPhone 3.

Tom drafted an email to Alistair and explained he'd need to stay in Spain for the weekend, citing an emergency with Ana's grandfather there. He promised to call on Monday morning with an update. He re-read the email before hitting 'Send' and turned his phone to airplane mode to avoid Alistair's inevitable phone call. The excuse had been a stopgap but would grant Tom a few days to formulate a believable explanation for his month's absence. And it hadn't been a lie: Ana's grandfather's behaviour in Santiago absolutely constituted an 'emergency'.

The bus hit traffic on the outskirts of Bayonne, and when it pulled into the train station, Tom had just enough time to buy his ticket and sprint down the platform. He scampered aboard the train, packed with noisy hikers, and spied an empty seat in the back corner of the carriage. He waded through a sea of fluorescent windbreakers, managing to avoid being skewered by the wayward walking pole of a cackling Canadian. He heaved his pack onto the luggage racks above and squeezed into his seat. A conductor slammed the carriage doors shut and blew his whistle, sending the train lurching out of Bayonne and toward the village of Saint-Jean-Pied-de-Port.

Tom took his phone from his pocket and disabled airplane mode. His phone struggled to find a local network, seemingly just as disorientated by all the travel as he was. While he waited, he leaned back into his seat; the vinyl squeaked loudly. He closed his eyes and exhaled the day's disaster from his body.

A voice spoke directly into his ear. 'First time doing the Camino?'

Tom opened his eyes. The man next to him had leaned across with a polite smile. Probably in his sixties, the stranger's baseball cap was as American as his accent.

'Err yeah, first time,' replied Tom.

Tipped off by Tom's own accent, the man's eyes narrowed. 'Where are y'all from?'

'England.'

'England? Well, how about that? We've just come from there.' The man waved toward a middle-aged couple sitting opposite them. The younger man wore a Duke University shirt and enthusiastically chewed gum. The woman – presumably his wife – wore a pair of Oakley wraparound mirror sunglasses, the type exclusively worn by beach-volleyball players.

'Did you hear that? He's from England.'

The woman's bleached eyebrows rose behind her mirrored shades. 'We've just come from there. It was so beautiful; we just loved Buckingham Palace.'

'Yeah, it's great.' Tom never understood the appeal of Buckingham Palace; the Queen didn't even live there. The old man extended his hand.

'I'm Hank.'

'I'm Tom.'

'Well, *buen Camino*, Tom. This is my son, Ed. And my daughter-in-law, Judy.'

Tom nodded to them both, and Ed responded with a particularly energetic chomp of his gum.

'So, are you here for the Xacobeo?' asked Hank.

'Sorry, the what?'

'The Xacobeo, the Holy Year.'

'Someone else told me about a Holy Year. What is that?'

'It's any year where the birthday of Saint James – July twenty-fifth – falls on a Sunday.'

'What's it got to do with the Camino?'

'Well, of course, you know the Camino de Santiago is also known as the Way of Saint James.' Hank had wildly overestimated Tom's knowledge of this hike. 'And the remains of Saint James are buried within Santiago Cathedral. So, on every Xacobeo, or Holy Year, they open a special door in the cathedral called the…' Hank looked to his son for help.

'La Puerta Santa, Pop.'

'Right – La Puerta Santa, which means Holy Door. During a Holy Year, they open this Holy Door to honour him. And it's said if you walk through it, all your sins are washed away.' Hank pointed to the busy carriage. 'Which is why the Camino is so damn busy. I read they're expecting half a million people this year alone. The next one is in 2021, so the kids agreed to do it with me this year.' Hank tapped his leg. 'My knees are starting to go, so I'm not sure I'll be able to do it in another eleven years. The *albergues* will be busy, but I don't mind.' He looked to the kids. 'Slow and steady, right, team?'

'Slow and steady, Pop,' chorused Ed and Judy.

'What are the *albergues*?' asked Tom.

Hank grinned. 'You haven't thought too much about this trip, have you, son?'

Hank had no idea.

'The *albergues* are where we'll all sleep – they're kinda like hostels for pilgrims. You just pay a few euros and sleep in a dormitory with all the other hikers. But you gotta be fast, especially in a Holy Year – they're on a first-come, first-served basis. And make sure you get your passport stamped too.'

'My passport?' Tom glanced to the luggage rack above.

Why hadn't he stored his passport in one of his five pairs of pockets?

'Not your actual passport.' Hank laughed. 'Your pilgrim passport. Ed, what do you call it in Spanish, again?'

'Credencial del Peregrino, Pop. Or you can just call it your *credencial*.'

'Well, I just call it my Pilgrim Passport. Looky here.' Hank unzipped his fanny-pack and pulled out a white document in a zip-lock bag. He unfolded the white card within and handed it to Tom. 'You see, in every *albergue* you stay in, you gotta ask them to stamp it. That way, when you get to Santiago, the stamps you collect prove you walked the whole way. Then they give you a certificate.'

'Compostela, Pop. Compostela.'

Ed seemed to be some sort of Camino aficionado. Tom re-folded the pilgrim passport and handed it back to Hank. The old man held up his hands.

'Why don't you go ahead and keep that?'

'No, it's fine.'

'I insist, I can get another one in Saint-Jean, no problem.'

'Thanks.' Tom slid the *credencial* into one of his thigh pockets.

After finishing his lecture, Hank nestled back in his seat and folded his hands over his paunch. 'So, if you're not here for the Holy Year, why are you doing the Camino, Tom?'

Tom hadn't spun up a cover story yet. 'I'm doing it to propose to my girlfriend, actually.'

Judy clutched her hands to her chest. 'Oh my God, that's so romantic. Is your girlfriend meeting you in Saint-

Jean?'

'Oh, we're not walking the Camino together. She's in London still – it's a surprise. But I'm walking to Santiago to ask her family for their blessing.'

Judy turned to Ed. 'European men are so romantic, aren't they?'

Ed punished his gum, and Judy turned back to Tom, thirsty for more details.

'So, you'll ask her father for his blessing?'

'Ana's parents passed away when she was a girl. I'm actually walking the Camino to ask for her grandfather's blessing.'

'Oh my God, that's so incredibly sweet of you.' Judy's voice wavered, suggesting tears might be forming behind her Oakleys.

Ed wrestled the conversation back to more familiar territory.

'So, you flew in from Heathrow?' he asked.

'No – a bus from Bilbao.'

'And before that?'

'Santiago.'

'As in Santiago in Chile?'

'No – Santiago de Compostela, in Spain.'

The Americans frowned in unison. It fell to Hank to ask the obvious question.

'Now, Tom, why would you walk the Camino to ask for the blessing of your girlfriend's granddaddy if you were already right there in Santiago?'

Tom's phone suddenly chimed, triumphantly announcing it had found a local phone network. He thankfully held it up to the Americans as a series of notifications trickled down the screen.

'Could you excuse me for a second? It's probably the office.'

'Of course,' said Hank.

Judy looked disappointed. Tom angled himself toward the window and scrolled through his messages.

Thurs 20:32 Alistair: I got your voicemail. We have the Van Henning presentation on Monday. I really need you back for that.

Thurs 20:59 Alistair: If you can't get back for Monday, can we have a conference call on Sunday night to brief Phillip?

Thurs 21:03 Alistair: Sorry to hear about your girlfriend's grandfather. Call me.

There was also a text from Ana.

Thurs 21:15 Ana: Hey baby. I'm still here. I have to stay back and help prep for tomorrow's case. I haven't heard from you, so I'm assuming you're still in Manchester. What time does your train get in? We need a holiday lol. How did it go today anyway? xx

Tom drafted several replies to Ana, all of them stuttering to a halt at the part where he'd lied about 'his workshop in Manchester' and had boarded a plane to Spain instead. The lies he'd told Ana in the past had all been minor in comparison – like denying he'd eaten the last chocolate digestive or telling her he'd be home after one more pint – nothing on this scale. He restarted another draft.

Hey babe, you're not going to believe this, but something at work came up, and I'm actually in Spain. I'll call you in a bit to explain. Love you x

His thumb hovered over the Send button. Was he really going to take the next month off and trek across Spain? He pressed Cancel and slid his phone back into his pocket. Of course he wasn't going to go through with this.

Thankfully, Hank and his family had struck up a conversation with another group of Americans across the aisle. The two families lamented how difficult it was to find crispy bacon in Europe. Tom rested his head against the cold glass of the window and closed his eyes. The words of Ana's grandfather rattled through his head and against the glass. This was absurd: he couldn't just drop everything in his life to walk across Spain to prove his love for Ana to her grandfather.

Instead, Tom would check into a hotel in Saint-Jean and book the first flight back to London in the morning. Then he'd email Alistair and tell him the crisis in Spain had been averted and promise to be in the office on Monday. Finally, he'd text Ana and explain his conference in Manchester had finished later than expected and that he promised to be home on Saturday morning. And then, everything could proceed as planned: dinner at the Ritz the following weekend, with the engagement ring nestled among the bubbles of Ana's champagne flute. And after dinner, sitting on their hotel suite's balcony overlooking Green Park, Tom might even tell Ana of his failed mission to Santiago and how close he'd come to walking the Camino de Santiago for her. And she'd laugh, telling him how awkwardly romantic it all sounded, before thanking him for trying.

He smiled at the image and opened his eyes; the French countryside blurred past him like a Monet. He'd briefly considered France for their honeymoon but had settled on the Maldives – no one in the office had been there yet. Tom imagined the turquoise waters of the Indian Ocean, lapping against their private villa, and his eyelids grew heavy.

CHAPTER 2

Clang.

The solitary toll of the cathedral's bell signalled the day had gone a quarter past the midday hour. Tito drained the remainder of his coffee and watched a group of pilgrims leave the cathedral through La Puerta Santa, each smiling with their newfound absolution. The square, the Praza da Quintana, was still rousing itself from another muggy night; the staff from the neighbouring cafés sleepily dragged their tables and chairs into the square while a busker uncoiled her microphone and plugged it into an amplifier resting on a trolley. Her lips were painted like a fire truck, and she wore hooped earrings big enough for parrots to perch upon. Tito hoped she was better than last week's busker: a crooner from Madrid who bleached his hair and exclusively sang Julio Iglesias numbers.

Tito felt a hand on his shoulder.

'*Buenos días*, old man,' said Diego, the bar's tiny owner who – at seventy-three himself – had very few customers he could call 'old'. Diego pointed up to the sun, creeping past the cathedral's spire. 'Another hot one, no?'

'*Sí.*' Tito frowned. 'You're back working already? Your son said it would be another month.'

'It's already been three, and just look at the place.' Diego waved toward the bar in disgust. 'I won't spend my final months watching him send this place to ruins.'

'Final months? It was a hip operation, no?'

'*Sí*, but my heart will be next.'

'The doctors said this?'

'They didn't have to. I could see it in their eyes.' Diego had always found comfort in misery. The little owner pointed to Tito's shopping bag. 'What did you buy?'

'Sardines.'

'Why do you walk to the market every day? There's the new supermarket by the highway now. You can drive there and buy enough groceries for an entire week.'

'How will I know what I feel like eating in a week?'

'Because every day you go to the market and buy the same thing – sardines. It's all you ever eat; you're like a cat.' His woolly eyebrows lowered with suspicion. 'I think you just want to get away from Esmerelda.'

'She likes her television programs.' Tito nodded to the plaza. 'And I like to visit the cathedral.'

'The cathedral?' Diego spluttered out a laugh. 'When did you last step inside?'

It would be fifteen years in September, yet it only seemed yesterday. The details of that fateful day were still scored in his mind. Ana had spilled juice on the dress Esmerelda had bought her. The little girl had howled and wailed, complaining things had needed to be perfect to farewell her parents. The poor girl had only been ten years old; she hadn't understood there'd been nothing perfect about that day. Diego dragged the chair out opposite Tito and sat down.

'Poor Esmerelda. After fifty years with you, who can blame her for watching television all day? At least the television talks, no?' Diego leaned back in the chair and gazed wistfully up to the sky. 'I still remember her, back then. She could have married any of us after her first husband died. Why did she take pity on the mute janitor who worked in an orphanage?'

'I suppose she should have chosen you?'

Diego sat up in his chair. 'Why not? You don't remember what I was like back then.' The little owner ran a hand over his remaining wisps of hair and tugged his waistcoat down over his belly. 'I was slim and handsome. I didn't always look this way.'

Tito nodded to Diego's platform heels. '*Sí*, but you were always that short.'

'A man's height isn't important.' He seemed to sit taller. 'I'd have made Esmerelda a fine husband. Perhaps I'd have worked in the office at her father's shoe factory. Better than running this cursed café.'

'You'd be bored in an office,' said Tito. 'You talk to people here.'

'Psh, customers aren't people.' Diego waved toward a group of tourists. 'The only time they talk is when they ask me for the Wi-Fi password.'

'Well, I'm sure Rosa is happy you didn't marry Esmerelda. You two are blessed to have so many grandchildren.'

'More like infested. Every year, there's another one — they're like rabbits.' He pointed toward a teenager sitting hunched over his mobile phone next to the bar. 'Look at this one, Paco, my son's eldest. His father thought letting him work here for the summer would develop the boy's work ethic. If he sits any longer, he'll develop piles.'

Tito took his cigarettes from his shirt pocket and lit one before offering the pack to Diego.

'My doctor says no more cigarettes,' said Diego.

Tito nodded. '*Sí*, so did mine, but he died at eighty-seven, so I suppose I won in the end.'

The two old men laughed, and Diego eventually succumbed and lit a cigarette too.

'You know,' said Diego, pausing to take a puff, 'I never understood why you and Esmerelda didn't have more children.'

'There was no time. I was already forty-two by the time we married; Esmerelda was thirty-five.'

'I'd had five children by the time I was forty.' Diego leaned closer and lowered his voice. 'I was very potent in my youth, you know?'

'*Sí*, I'm sure. Maybe we would have tried if we'd known what would happen.' If they'd known what would happen, Tito would never have let his son and daughter-in-law drive to that damn restaurant. 'But you cannot predict the future.' He extinguished his half-smoked cigarette in the ashtray, its taste now ruined. 'At least we were blessed with our Ana.'

Diego's face lit up. '*Sí*, how is my Analita? Is she working yet?'

'*Sí*, for a bank.'

'A bank?' Diego frowned. 'I thought she wanted to be

a lawyer, helping those in need.'

'She is a lawyer. She says banks need help too.'

'A lawyer for a bank and living in London? All those books paid off, after all, no?'

Tito wasn't so sure. When Ana had come to live with them after the accident, he'd worried she'd escaped her parents' death within her books. Now, fifteen years later, he still worried his granddaughter had spent her life reading about life instead of living it.

'What about her boy? Is she still with her Englishman?'

Tito nodded.

'And is he a lawyer too?'

'No, an investment banker.'

Diego whistled. 'Investment bankers are loaded, no?' He shook his head as if imagining the bundles of money he'd never see. 'Well, I can't sit around here all day, reminiscing.' He waved at the empty tables around them. 'I have a business to run. You want to pay?'

'Not yet, I'm waiting for someone.'

'Waiting for who? I'm your only friend.'

'I'm meeting the boy; Ana's boyfriend – Thomas.'

'Analita is in Santiago?'

'No, it's just him. He telephoned Esmerelda yesterday and said he was coming to Santiago today – alone. Said he had something important to ask me. Esmeralda organised for me to meet him here at 12:30, while her shows are on.'

'Wait.' Diego slowly leaned forward. 'You don't think he's going to ask for your blessing to marry Ana, do you?'

'*Sí*, maybe.'

'What do you mean, maybe? He's flying all the way here from England, without Ana, to ask you something important – of course he's going to ask for your blessing to propose to her!' Diego clapped toward his grandson. 'Paco, stop making love to your phone and have the kitchen prepare some *pulpo*. And put some champagne on ice, the good stuff in the cellar, not the swill on the menu.'

Tito politely raised his hand. 'No champagne, Diego.'

'Of course champagne; your only granddaughter is getting married – why wouldn't there be champagne?'

'Because…'

'*¿Si?*'

'Because… I'm not sure if I will give the boy my blessing.'

Diego looked horrified. 'Why not?'

'He's not right for her.'

'I don't understand. Does Ana love him?'

'She says she does.'

'But he mistreats her, no?'

'No.'

'He's unfaithful?'

'I don't think so.'

'So what's wrong with him then?'

'Nothing specifically… he's simply not the right man for her.'

Diego rolled his eyes. 'And suddenly you know your granddaughter better than she knows herself, is that it?'

'Ana is just twenty-four. Thomas is the only man she's ever been with – I worry she'll marry him before knowing what she wants.'

'Many girls get married before twenty-four, old man. They don't need our permission anymore; things are not like they once were. If she loves the boy and he has money, that's all that matters.'

'All they do is work. Ana says she works sixty hours a

week; the boy works even more.'

'What's wrong with a man providing for his family? I've worked hard all my life, so have you.'

'And where did it get us? You, breaking your back here at this café, and me, fixing things broken by others. We're hardly the happiest people in the world.'

'Fed and clothed is where it got us, our children too. You can't eat happiness. Since when were you such a communist, anyway? You'd rather Ana marry a bum?'

'That's not what I'm saying. It's just…' He searched for the explanation. 'I still remember the day Ana told us she was going to England to study at university; it was one of the happiest days of my life.'

'Naturally, you were proud of her.'

'We would have been proud of Ana no matter what she'd done. No, I was just pleased she'd be having an adventure. She was finally going to see the world instead of reading about it in one of her books.' He smiled at the thought.

'And she did, you old fool. She went to one of the world's best universities.'

'She might as well have studied here in Santiago. Whenever she called Esmerelda and me, all she ever spoke about were her studies.'

'She was busy becoming a lawyer. Would you have preferred she'd spent her time getting drunk and being chased by boys?'

Tito shrugged. 'Maybe. She was a nineteen-year-old kid living abroad, and I never once heard her tell me about a single party she ever went to.'

'Teenage girls don't tell their grandfathers about the parties they go to, old man. Besides, I thought you said she met her Englishman at a party.'

'It was a dinner party.' Tito wagged his finger. 'It's not the same thing.'

'You're allowed to meet the love of your life sitting around a table; it's called serendipity.'

'More like convenience. Theirs is not a love story, Diego. There's no passion, no chances. The boy lives by his head, not his heart.'

'Heaven forbid Ana marries someone sensible.'

'Sensible is not the same as happy, Diego. Love should be impulsive and spontaneous.'

'Spontaneity?' Diego scoffed. 'From a man who eats sardines every day.'

Tito banged the table. 'Ana deserves a better life than mine.'

'You silly old fool, it's her life to lead, not yours. Don't make Ana pay for your mistakes. Heaven knows that girl's life has been difficult enough. Why invent new hardships for her?'

'Love isn't simply the absence of hardship. Ana will understand my decision.'

Diego stubbed out his cigarette into the ashtray. When he spoke, his voice was calmer. '*Sí*, perhaps Ana will understand your decision, but it doesn't mean she'll ever forgive you. Just let the girl be happy, old man, even if you never were.' The little owner slapped Tito's shoulder and shuffled away. He was halfway back to the bar when he turned. His bushy eyebrows lifted with a courteous enquiry. 'You know, if you're serious about the Englishman, what about my oldest grandson, Javier?'

Tito frowned. 'The baker?'

'No, the baker is Julio. Javier is the plumber.'

'I thought Javier has a fiancée already.'

'*Sí*, he does, but she's not as pretty as your Ana and not as smart. I think he'd change his mind. It's always good to have a lawyer in the family too, no?'

'No, Javier is not what I had in mind.'

The rebuke stung. 'Fine, if you think Ana's too good for Javier, he'll just go ahead and marry the other girl. But don't complain when he starts charging you and Esmerelda every time he fixes your toilet.' Diego waddled back toward the bar, calling out over his shoulder. 'Discounts are for family only.'

Tito returned his gaze to the square. The busker had started to play, singing a slow ballad he'd never heard before. The plaza had continued to fill: pilgrims unloading their enormous backpacks at the cafés in the sun, while the locals favoured the cheaper places in the shade. Tito lit another cigarette and reflected on Diego's words. The little man was right – Ana would be heartbroken if Tito didn't bless her marriage to Thomas. He took a drag of his cigarette and stared at the cathedral. Tito had stopped talking to God the day he'd buried his son, but he now felt tempted to enter the cathedral and pray for the life and love Ana deserved. He would pray for more time. His eyes drifted to the cathedral's clocktower, and he imagined the hands stopping to grant him more time to explain his hopes to Ana or more time for Thomas to prove he was the man Tito wished he was. But Tito was ninety-two, and time had expired. Regardless of his dreams for Ana, what choice did he really have? He had to bless the boy's proposal to Ana.

Clang. Clang.

Thomas arrived shortly after 12:30, more formally dressed than his previous visits.

'*Hola*, Tito,' said the boy, shaking Tito's hand and pointing to the chair opposite him. '*¿Puedo?*'

Tito stubbed his cigarette into the ashtray and nodded.

'*¿Cómo estás?*' asked Thomas, sitting down.

'*Estoy bien. ¿Y tu?*'

'*Estoy bien.*'

They spoke to one another like children; the boy's lack of Spanish prevented anything more sophisticated. There was little evidence of Thomas' supposed Spanish lessons. 'Speak slower,' Ana had always said to Tito and Esmerelda. 'Use smaller words.'

'I ask you an important question,' Thomas said in his broken Spanish. He pulled a piece of paper from his blazer's breast pocket and began reading in Spanish. The boy sounded as nervous as he looked. 'Tito, I have travelled here today for your blessing to marry Ana.'

Thomas described his love for Ana, telling Tito how lucky he was to have her in his life before complimenting her intelligence and generosity. The boy described the couple's future together, including their wedding – 'We'll have two ceremonies, one in England and another in Spain.'

Tito tilted his better ear toward the boy and strained to decipher his garbled pronunciation.

Thomas spoke of his and Ana's plans to buy an apartment in London – 'nothing too big, somewhere close to our jobs', and their hopes of starting a family together one day – 'I know Ana wants to make Associate Partner within her company first, so we'd wait until then.' The boy paid his respects to Ana's parents, as well as thanking Tito and Esmerelda for the job they'd done in raising her. He promised he and Ana would visit them in Spain more often than they had, explaining how busy the two of them had been with work.

'I love Ana deeply, and in asking for your blessing, please know I promise to look after her for the rest of my life. I'll respect her career and allow her to follow her dreams. Being her husband will be my highest priority – everything else will come second. I would do anything for your granddaughter, and I will never fail her. You have my word.'

Tito listened to all of these promises, knowing Thomas could never keep them. The boy hadn't lied; he honestly believed he'd make such sacrifices. But saying the words and proving it were two different things. Thomas eventually looked up from the letter, reciting its final line from memory.

'So it is with the utmost respect when I ask for your blessing to marry your granddaughter, Ana.' He folded the letter and slipped it back into his blazer's pocket, nervously awaiting Tito's decision. The old man glanced helplessly toward the clocktower again, mocked by its unrelenting hands.

'Thomas, I…'

Before Tito could say another word, Diego arrived, carrying a plate of food.

'I brought the boy some *pulpo*.' The bar's owner placed the plate on the table and introduced himself to Thomas, pointing to the dish and undoubtedly explaining its origins. Tito couldn't understand their English conversation, but he'd heard the Spanish version countless times before. It involved Diego spending his summers with his uncle in a small Galician village on the Camino, named Melide.

'My uncles were fisherman,' Diego would be saying. 'And every afternoon, they would return home with buckets of squid. My sisters and I would help our aunties cook it and sell it in the restaurant. We would boil it and serve it with potatoes sprinkled with paprika and salt, all drizzled in olive oil. It was very famous among the pilgrims walking to Santiago. And when I finally took over this bar from my father, I added it to my menu.'

Diego finished his tale by skewering a piece of octopus with a toothpick and handed it to Thomas, watching expectantly as the boy ate it. '*Delicioso*, no?' Diego leaned toward Tito and whispered. 'When you give Paco the signal, he'll bring the champagne.'

'No champagne. I need you to translate something for me.'

Diego frowned. 'Translate? I'm sure the boy knows the Spanish word for "yes".'

'*Sí*, but there's more I need to say.'

Diego eyed him warily. 'Not too much more, I hope.'

'Never fear, I just need him to know my wishes for his and Ana's life together.'

Diego still looked hesitant, so Tito pulled the necessary lever.

'Unless you don't feel confident speaking English?'

'Confident?' Diego's furry eyebrows nearly lifted off his face altogether. 'I've been speaking English longer than he has. Did I ever tell you I learned English as a boy so I could listen to the English football on BBC radio?' Diego had – several times a year. He pointed to Thomas. 'What do you want to say to him?'

Tito pushed his lingering doubts about the boy from his mind and focused on Ana. Her happiness was all that mattered now.

'I want you to tell him…' Tito's voice trailed off as he was distracted by the busker's voice. She was singing a hauntingly familiar song from the other side of the square. He turned to face her, watching her bejewelled fingers strum her guitar. 'This song,' he murmured. 'I haven't heard it in… years.'

Diego shrugged. 'What's so special about this song? "Quizás, Quizás, Quizás"? It's a Doris Day song, no?'

'It wasn't always.'

The busker's voice was mesmerising, a siren's call to passing boats.

'The first time I ever heard this song was when I walked the Camino.'

Diego was taken aback. 'You never told me you walked the Camino de Santiago.'

'It was many years ago.' Tito couldn't take his eyes from the busker; her voice rowed him upstream to another place and time. 'I heard it in a little village, just outside Burgos.' What was its name? 'Hornillos.' He smiled as the word left his lips. 'Sí, Hornillos del Camino. It was a warm summer night, and the locals had strung up carnival lights.' He could still see the buildings, bathed in a soft orange glow. 'A band played music on the footsteps of the church, and the guests danced in the plaza.' He nodded to the busker. 'They played this song.' He smiled as he remembered the touch of her skin. 'And I danced with her.'

'Who? Esmerelda?'

Tito shook Esmerelda's name away. 'No, this was years before Esmerelda. It was a girl I met on the Camino.'

Diego wedged a chair between Tito and the boy and sat down. 'And you're only telling me this now? You've been coming to my bar for forty years. Who was she?'

'Another pilgrim travelling to Santiago. We walked together a part of the way.'

'Forget about the walking, tell me about the dancing.'

Tito could see the reflection of the carnival lights in her copper-coloured eyes. 'It was the happiest moment of my life.'

Diego scoffed. 'How long had you known this girl? A few weeks? It sounds like lust to me, old man.'

'It was love,' snapped Tito, cutting Diego's cackle short. 'Though I didn't know it at the time. The Camino is special, Diego; a stranger you've walked beside for a few days can feel like someone you've known for a lifetime.'

'So if this girl was the love of your life, why didn't you end up marrying her, hmm?'

'One morning, I woke very early and began walking to Santiago without her.'

Diego frowned. 'I don't understand. You just left her behind? Why?'

'I had plans after the Camino, and they never included falling in love. So I followed my head, not my heart.'

'She never caught up to you?'

'I looked over my shoulder every day until I reached Santiago, secretly hoping I might see her again – but I never did. She was gone.'

A tear crawled down Tito's tired cheek, and Diego offered his handkerchief.

'Stop being so dramatic, old man, pull yourself

together. Think of your life with Esmerelda – your son and little Analita – you were right to listen to your head and follow your plans. Chasing after a girl you've only just met would have been crazy. Crazy is good for a week, but it's no way to live.'

The busker finished her song, and the crowd rewarded her with meagre amounts of coins and applause. Tito wiped his eyes dry.

'Her song – it just brought up so many memories.'

'Well, what's done is done; we can't change the past.' Diego nodded toward Thomas. 'Tell me what you want to say to the boy. The poor bastard looks like he's in purgatory.'

Tito tried to recall what he'd been ready to say moments earlier. But after the song, the words felt like a key that no longer fit into its lock.

'Tell him what I just told you: the girl, the dancing in Hornillos, my decision to leave her behind – everything; leave nothing out.'

'What the hell are you talking about? The boy doesn't need to know all that.'

'He does, or he won't understand what comes next.'

'You're speaking in riddles, old man.'

Tito smacked his hand on the table and glared at the owner. 'This is important, Diego – tell him.'

The owner shrank even smaller.

'Okay, okay. I'll tell him.' He turned to Thomas and translated the tale of the girl from the Camino. Tito recognised the name of the village and song. Eventually, Diego turned back to Tito. 'Okay, I've told him.'

'Everything?'

'*Sí* – the song, the town, the girl, everything. He wants

to know what any of it has to do with him.' Diego crossed his arms. 'So do I.'

Tito swallowed. His mouth felt as dry as the desert. 'Tell Thomas if he wishes to marry Ana, he must first walk the Camino de Santiago.'

'I didn't want to believe it,' said Diego, his face crumpled in sympathy. 'But Esmerelda is right – you've finally gone senile.'

'Don't be ridiculous.'

'I'm ridiculous?' Diego's eyes grew as large as the plate of *pulpo*. 'You're ninety-two years old. By the time this boy returns to Spain and walks the Camino, you'll be dead.'

'This is why he must begin walking it today.'

'Today?' The little owner nearly fell from his chair. 'He can't just pack up and leave.'

'A man would walk across a country without hesitation for the love of his life, no?'

'What about his job in England? They'll fire him on the spot. Do you want Ana to marry a bum?'

'I want Ana to be happy. I want her to spend her life with a man who follows his heart, not his head. She needs someone to show her how to live life, not simply think about it.' Tito pointed to Thomas, whose head swivelled between the two old men as if watching tennis. 'He wrote in his letter that he'd do anything for Ana. Anything, Diego! Well, if he wants my blessing for their marriage, he must do this.'

For the first time since he'd known him, Diego looked speechless.

'You're making a colossal mistake,' he finally said.

'I already made the biggest mistake of my life half a lifetime ago. I won't have Ana and Thomas make the same one.'

Diego threw up his hands in resignation. 'Fine, but don't tell Esmerelda or Ana I had anything to do with this. This is your doing, not mine.'

'Tell Thomas I'll be sitting here in exactly one month.' Tito raised a single bony finger. 'And he may ask for my blessing again then.'

Tito lowered his finger, inadvertently bringing Diego's youngest grandson striding toward their table with a bottle of champagne. Diego stood from his chair, his face twisted in horror.

'No, Paco – that's not the signal.'

But it was too late – the boy's thumbs squeezed up on the cork, sending it sailing into the air.

Pop.

A shower of sparkling froth poured out over the table.

CHAPTER 3

Tom jolted from his dream; the train carriage was dark and empty. He peered outside and could see a ghostly white building in the twilight. How long had he been asleep? The sign on the train platform read Saint-Jean-Pied-de-Port. He'd made it to the correct town, but where was everyone else? Why hadn't Hank, or his family, woken him? Tom stood up and reached for his backpack from the luggage rack above. His hand felt nothing but the cold steel of the frame. An ice cube slid down his spine. His backpack wasn't there. He stood up on the seat and shone his phone's torch into the empty shadows.

'Come on… come on… Please be here, please be here.' He waved the light down the length of the rack before checking the other side of the carriage. 'Jesus, Jesus, Jesus.' He dropped to his knees and crawled down the length of the carriage, peering under every seat. His backpack contained everything: his change of clothes, phone charger, toiletries. He froze, paralysed by a horrific thought. Where was his passport? He leaped up and patted each of his five pairs of pockets. He had the pilgrim passport Hank had gifted him, but not the actual passport which would allow him to leave the country.

'Fuck!'

The curse bounced around the abandoned carriage like a squash ball. He remembered stuffing his passport into the top compartment of his backpack when he'd boarded the bus to Bayonne. He'd meant to put it into his trouser pocket later, but he'd become distracted. He collapsed onto the nearest seat and buried his face in his hands. Could this day get any worse?

Tom took stock. The train had been packed, so someone had likely picked up his backpack by mistake, and it was sitting behind the station's Lost Property desk. No hiker wanted to lug a second backpack across Spain.

He composed himself and walked up the platform to the station office. The door was locked, and the windows were shuttered. He checked his watch – 9:24pm; he'd need to try again in the morning.

He took out his phone to find the hostels Hank had told him about. The tiny blue dot in Google Maps lingered in Bayonne. Tom checked his phone's signal. The words 'No network found' appeared in the corner of the screen where the four white bars should have been.

'Are you serious?'

A road's pale outline snaked up a hill to the silhouette of a village. With little choice, he followed the path and arrived at a stone staircase leading through an archway into the town. He passed through it into a narrow, cobbled lane flanked by ivy-covered walls. Tom paused, listening for hikers, but only hearing the wind's rattling of a nearby window shutter. A solemn church bell tolled, and he followed it down the hill to a clump of shops – all of them closed. The church stood opposite; the flickering light behind its stained-glass windows was the only sign of life in the abandoned town. The church's door was ajar, and Tom walked inside.

'Hello?'

His voice echoed around the vaulted ceiling. He walked down the aisle between the pews and looked up to the mezzanine behind him.

'Is anyone here?'

A stand of prayer candles stood next to the altar. Tom walked toward it and tilted his head to read a handwritten message on one of the longer candles.

Annalise. Jamais oublié. 1953–1954.

He thought *jamais* might have meant 'never', but Tom's French was even worse than his Spanish.

'*Qui êtes-vous?*'

The voice startled Tom, and he spun around to see a tall, thin man standing behind him.

'*Bonjour,*' said Tom, thereby using almost a quarter of his French vocabulary.

'*Qui êtes-vous?*' The man was a priest, dressed in a long black tunic with a high collar. He walked toward Tom and lifted an old-fashioned kerosene lantern to inspect his face. '*Que faites-vous ici?*'

'Umm… *Parlez-vous anglais?*' Tom knew the phrase was reviled in France, but it was all he had.

The priest didn't respond; his beady eyes studied Tom in the dim light.

'*Êtes-vous français?*'

'Me, Eng-lish.' Tom tapped his fingers against his chest and spoke louder. '*Ang-lais.*'

'*Vous êtes anglais?*'

'Yes.' Tom nodded his head furiously. '*Oui, oui.* Do you know where the other pilgrims are?' He fumbled for words that sounded similar in both languages. 'Where is the hotel for hikers?' He performed his worst French accent. '*Ho-tel.*'

'*Hôtel, no.*' The priest chuckled and pointed to the crucifix on the front wall behind the altar. '*Église.*'

'Yes, yes, I know it's a church, but where is the *hôtel?* I'm looking for my friends – they are hikers. You know, hikers?' He walked two of his fingers across his palm. 'Walking.'

'*Marcher?*' The priest placed his lantern on the altar and mimicked Tom's hand movement. '*Marcher?*'

'*Oui, marcher.* Do you know where the other walkers are?'

The priest's blank expression indicated their breakthrough had been short-lived. Tom slid his phone out to use Google Translate but still didn't have a signal. As he put it away, his hand brushed against the pilgrim passport Hank had given him. Tom held it up to the priest, whose eyes flashed with recognition.

'*Marchez-vous le Camino?*'

'Camino! Yes!'

'*À Santiago?*'

'*Oui*, I'm walking the Camino de Santiago. I'm looking for one of the *hôtels.*' What had Hank called them? '*Albergue?*'

'*Albergue?*'

Tom's eyebrows lifted to meet the priest's. 'Yes, *oui, albergue.*'

'*Suivez-moi.*' The priest cheerily turned and led Tom up a wooden staircase in the back corner of the church to a set of pews on the mezzanine. A paper-thin mattress rested on the front bench; a folded blanket accompanied it. '*Voilà – albergue.*'

Something had been lost in translation. Tom couldn't sleep here.

'*Pardon, monsieur*, but this is *impossible.*' He winced at how awful the last word had sounded in his faux French accent.

The priest tilted his head, confused. '*Impossible?*'

The old man's smile slid from his face, and Tom suddenly remembered this was still the only open place he'd found in the entire town.

'No, no. It's fine. *Bien.*' Tom sat on the pew and affectionately slapped the mattress, sending up a cloud of dust. '*Magnifique.*'

'*Oui?*' The priest's smile returned. '*Très bon.*' He gave Tom a final encouraging nod and carried his lantern back down the stairs. '*Bonne nuit, pèlerin.*'

'*Bonne nuit,*' Tom muttered to himself, hearing the church doors close behind the priest. He restarted his phone, hoping it might attract a signal, but it didn't. It was almost nine o'clock in London, and Ana would be beginning to worry. He decided against venturing back into the town in search of Wi-Fi. Even if he could get a message to Ana, what the hell would he have said? He removed his boots and socks, sliding them under the pew, and bunched his rain jacket into a makeshift pillow. Despite being summer, the mountain air was cold. He threw the musty blanket over himself and optimistically set his alarm for 6:30, knowing full well he'd not catch a wink of sleep after such a horrid day. He turned his phone to flight-mode to conserve its battery and lay on his side, staring at the flickering candles in the church below. The first one died after ten minutes, the second one three minutes later. By the time the third candle went out, Tom was asleep.

Bells jolted Tom awake and he crashed from his pew onto the hard wooden floor. 'Jesus Christ.' He grappled for his phone in the dark, blindly trying to kill his alarm but immediately discovering the clanging bells belonged to the church itself. He checked the time on the phone's screen – 6:02am – before getting dressed and walking downstairs.

It was still dark outside, and the brisk mountain air caused him to zip his jacket all the way up to his chin. The light shining out of the patisserie opposite the church was the town's first sign of life. The delicious smell of baked goods wafting from its chimney reminded Tom the last thing he'd eaten had been a clammy sandwich he'd bought from a service station during the bus trip to Bayonne. He walked into the patisserie; the little bell above its door sang his arrival.

'*Bonjour,*' called out the woman behind the counter.

She looked up from a basket of baguettes; her face was round and jovial. '*Oui?*'

'*Quatre croissants, s'il vous plaît.*'

It was his most impressive French sentence yet. The woman threw four croissants into a brown paper bag and placed them on the counter without offering a price. He handed the shopkeeper a two-euro coin from his wallet. She furrowed her brow as she inspected it.

'*Non – francs français seulement.*' She slammed the coin onto the counter and folded her arms across her chest.

Tom ignored the woman's slip-up – his dad still referred to Snickers bars as Marathon bars – and held out a ten-euro note. The woman's arms remained folded. Surely she was confused; the French franc had been replaced by the euro in 1999, the same year Manchester United had defeated Newcastle in the FA Cup, 1–0. Tom's middle school had even held a 'Euro Day' where students had dressed as their favourite European currency. Erica Weatherhead from his class had worn a beret and a mini-skirt, representing the French franc. Tom had gone as the German mark, wearing denim shorts and a mullet wig.

'Err, *madame*… no French francs, only euros.'

'*Pas de francs, pas de croissants.*' She snatched the bag of pastries back from the counter and glared at him. He fleetingly searched the counter for a credit card terminal before leaving the store empty-handed. The bell above the door mocked his failure. He stood in the square bewildered, unable to remember a time he'd ever been refused service.

'*Bonjour, pèlerin.*'

Tom looked up to a window above the arch in the clocktower. The priest from the previous night waved enthusiastically down to him. '*As-tu bien dormi?*'

Having not learned any more French in his sleep, Tom simply waved back. '*Bonjour.*'

'*Un moment.*' The priest held up a finger and disappeared from the window, emerging through the church doors a minute later. He carried a canvas haversack, the type a postman might have used half a century ago. '*Avez-vous faim?*' The priest pulled back the bag's flap, revealing half a breadstick and a large chunk of cheese. There was also a small canteen, which splashed around when the priest shook it. '*L'eau.*'

'*Merci*, father. That's very kind of you, but I can't take your food and water.'

The priest pushed the bag into Tom's hand. '*Oui, prenez-le, s'il vous plaît.*'

'Well, at least let me pay you for it.' Tom handed the priest the ten-euro note.

The old man looked at it quizzically before nodding his appreciation. '*Merci.*' The priest handed Tom's pilgrim passport back to him. The first page had been stamped.

'*Merci.*' Tom folded the passport into his pocket, ready to find the other pilgrims. He tried to recall the French word for 'city centre'.

'*Pardon, monsieur*, where is… *centre-ville?*'

'*Centre-ville?*' The priest threw his arms out proudly. '*Ici. C'est le centre-ville.*'

How could this tiny square be the centre of the town? Where were all the other hikers and *albergues* Hank had spoken of? Tom was getting nowhere. He checked his watch; the train station probably wouldn't open for another couple of hours. If he couldn't find where the other hikers had slept, perhaps he could try the only other place he knew they'd be.

'Where is the Camino?'

'*Camino?*' The priest pointed through the arch at the base of the clocktower. '*Le départ du Camino est là.*'

'Okay. *Merci, monsieur.* Thank you.' Tom slung his newly gifted bag over his shoulder and began to walk.

The priest chased after him.

'*Monsieur, monsieur – un moment!*' He opened his cloak, revealing a rope necklace with a seashell attached. He lifted it over his head and slid it over Tom's.

'Oh, that's okay, I don't really wear jewellery.'

'*S'il vous plaît,*' said the priest, holding up his hands to signal he wouldn't take *non* for an answer.

Tom touched the shell dangling on the rope; it was the same type of scallop shell he'd seen printed on the guidebook in Santiago. The priest patted Tom's shoulder and nodded toward the arch.

'*Buen Camino, pèlerin.*'

Tom walked through the arch and over a bridge; the setting moon's reflection shimmered faintly in the canal below. He followed the road past a long row of white houses, each with matching red tiles and window shutters. There wasn't a single *albergue* or guesthouse. He soon arrived at a tall stone wall, signifying the town's end. A crooked wooden sign pointed ahead, reading 'La Porte d'Espagne'. The rising sun's first rays slid out from behind the village, and down the empty road he'd just walked. Hank and the other hikers should arrive any moment, allowing Tom to finally get some answers. He found a dry patch of grass and sat down for breakfast, deciding to eat half of the bread and a third of the cheese – he'd save the rest for later.

Fifteen minutes passed, and Tom had eaten everything.

He got up from the grass and began to pace, glaring back down the street toward the town of Saint-Jean-Pied-de-Port. Tom's time in London was precious, so he got fidgety whenever he felt as if it were being wasted. He tried his phone again – still no network. His lack of phone signal stretched every wasted minute into an hour. Anxiety joined the bread and cheese within Tom's stomach. Maybe the priest had misunderstood, and the town's centre was somewhere else? Perhaps Tom should return to the village for a more thorough search for the *albergues* and pilgrims?

The minutes were punctuated with more checks of his phone's signal until the town's church bells tolled again in the distance. It was now eight o'clock. A new question gurgled to the surface: what if Tom had missed all the other hikers, and they were already walking on the Camino? If Tom's backpack was secure at the train station's office, he could retrieve it at any time. But if another hiker had taken it, maliciously or not, his passport was getting further away from him with each passing minute.

'Jesus Christ.'

He slung the strap of his satchel over his shoulder and followed the path away from Saint-Jean. The trail rose steeply, and he soon arrived at a fork in the road: the road ahead flattened out, while the other climbed steeply to the right. He looked around for one of the yellow arrows the shopkeeper had promised, but could see none. Instead, he noticed a seashell resting on a tree stump further along the path to the right. It was a scallop shell, similar to the one around his neck.

'Here we go,' he muttered, walking up the right-hand trail.

He walked for half an hour, the path climbing ever

higher into the mountains. The farms in the valley below transformed into a quilt of greens and browns. The mountain air was fresh in his nostrils, not the thick and shared air of London. He walked for another hour, never once seeing a yellow arrow, scallop shell or hiker. His fears he'd taken the wrong path in the fork in the road grew with every step.

The jangling of approaching bells gave him hope of finding another church, but when he rounded a bend, he discovered nothing more than a paddock full of cows, large bells rattling beneath their thick black-and-white necks. A farmer hoed an adjacent field; he was the first person Tom had seen since leaving Saint-Jean.

'*Bonjour*,' Tom called out.

The farmer straightened up and squinted toward him.

Tom held up the scallop shell hanging from his neck. 'Is this the Camino?'

The farmer nodded in the direction Tom was walking before resuming his work.

'Nice chatting with you too,' muttered Tom.

The path continued to rise, soon deteriorating to gravel and eventually dirt. Tom scanned the winding trail ahead for hikers, but it remained despairingly empty. After another hour of ascent, he rattled the last drops of water from his canteen down his parched throat and decided to turn back. With no food or water left – and no signs of any of the other hikers – he couldn't keep going. It had been stupid to come this far.

He was about to start his descent when he spotted a thin wisp of smoke rising from the valley ahead. Imagining it might be the first town along the Camino, he decided to investigate. Even if he didn't find the other pilgrims, he could buy more food and water.

The smoke was drifting from the chimney of a long stone building, reminiscent of a ski lodge. The sign hanging above the door read 'Refuge Orisson', and Tom heard the encouraging sound of muffled laughter from within. He placed his hand on the door's handle and hesitated. What was he going to say if he found the person who'd stolen his pack? Tom really didn't want to make a scene, he simply wanted his passport and phone charger back so he could go home. Get in, and get out.

The air inside the Refuge Orisson was heavy with brandy and tobacco. A handful of farmers sat at a long oak table while another couple warmed themselves by the fireplace at the far end of the room. Tom walked toward the bar, scrutinised by a sinewy woman on the other side of it, drying a glass with a rag.

'*Bonjour,*' said Tom. '*Parlez-vous anglaise?*'

The bartender's stare felt like a hot poker pressed against his forehead.

'No? *Parlez-vous français?*' The heat of her gaze intensified, forcing Tom to swallow. 'What about Spanish? *¿Usted habla inglés?*' He held up his scallop shell necklace. 'Have you seen any hikers this morning? Umm, any *peregrinos*? Has anyone passed through here, possibly carrying an extra red backpack?'

She placed the glass on the shelf above her and folded her arms.

'Okay, well, thank you,' said Tom. Thanking people, even those who hadn't helped, was an English affliction. He turned and held out his shell to the farmers at the table.

'What about you, *monsieurs*, have any of you seen

other pilgrims this morning?'

'They no understand you.'

The voice came from near the fireplace. A short girl, no older than twenty, walked toward him. Her mousey hair was styled in an old-fashioned bob, and she had intense emerald eyes. Her khaki-coloured shirt and trousers were free of mud, suggesting she wasn't a farmer. Her lack of fluorescent clothing made it equally unlikely she was a hiker.

'You speak English?' asked Tom.

'*Bai* – yes – only little.' Her accent was thick but understandable.

'Oh, thank God, I'm struggling here. I'm sorry, but I don't speak any French.'

'Why you sorry? This is not France.'

'I've crossed the border into Spain already?'

'This is not Spain either.' She held the gravitas of someone older. 'You in the Basque country now. Here, we speak Basque.'

'I didn't know, I'm sorry.'

She studied him. 'Where you from?'

'England. I was walking the Camino, but my backpack was stolen. I thought another hiker might have accidentally taken it, so I was searching for them. But now, I suppose I'll just walk back to Saint-Jean and call the police.'

'*¿Polizia?*' She looked alarmed.

'I doubt the embassy will re-issue a passport without a police report. I'd call them now, but I still don't have any phone reception.' He took his phone from his pocket and tapped the corner of his screen. 'Do you have signal up here?'

She eyed his phone suspiciously and tentatively

reached for it.

'*Zer da hori?*'

The question came from the girl's companion, the man sitting by the fireplace. He stood up and walked toward them, the floorboards creaking underneath him. He was built like a refrigerator – closer to seven feet than six – with messy dark hair down to his shoulders and a matted beard that dangled to his barrel-like chest. He was older than the girl but dressed in the same khaki-coloured clothes. He took Tom's phone and studied it, a matchbox in his enormous paw.

'*Zer da hau?*'

'He want to know what this is,' translated the girl.

'It's the iPhone 4.' Despite his disastrous twenty-four hours, Tom still had his phone. 'It was released in London last month.'

She relayed this to the man, who turned the phone over in his thick hairy fingers.

'*Zer egiten du?*'

'He asks what it do?'

'It's pretty similar to the iPhone 3, but the camera is five megapixels, and it has a second camera on the front.' Tom pointed to the tiny lens above the screen. 'But it's useless without a telephone network. I haven't been able to access Google Maps.'

She looked confused. 'Maps?'

'Yeah – does this place have Wi-Fi?'

The ill-suited pair didn't respond, turning to one another and conversing in Basque. The girl eventually faced Tom.

'My friend saw the people you searching for.'

Tom's heart fluttered. 'Really? Where?'

'He say they went to the next town – Roncesvalles.'

'How can you be sure it was my pack?'

The question went unanswered. He followed the Basques back to the fireplace as they picked up their bags.

'Was it a red bag?'

'We must hurry,' said the girl. 'They are not far ahead of us.'

'Really?' Tom's excitement was muddled with confusion. 'Were they Americans? Was one of them an old man?'

He trailed them out of the tavern. A fog had blown down from the mountaintop and a chill ran down his spine. This didn't feel right.

'You know what, I think I'll just walk back to Saint-Jean anyway,' said Tom. 'I can always get another passport from the embassy.'

The girl didn't translate this. She simply looked up to her towering companion, who opened his jacket and pulled a pistol from his belt; its dull, scratched barrel pointed at Tom's chest.

CHAPTER 4

'Come on, hurry up!'

It had been less than a week, but Fernando already regretted walking the Camino with Pablo.

'*Jefe*, the Camino is not a race, no?' Pablo stood on the edge of a rocky outcrop, his arms outstretched as if hugging the valley below. 'We're on top of the world here. Mountains as far as the eye can see.'

'*Sí*, and there are many more mountains between here and Santiago. *Vamos*.' Fernando pointed to the path ahead.

The boy scowled. 'You're a real grouch, you know that? Sometimes I can't believe we're both Andalusians.' The boy turned back to the valley and closed his eyes. 'One more minute to bask in this tranquillity.'

While they were both from Andalucía, the towns they lived in could not have been more different. Pablo was from Granada, a beautiful city in the foothills of the Sierra Nevada mountains, renowned for the Alhambra, its spectacular Moorish fortress. Fernando lived in Huelva, a wind-swept port city on the southwestern coast, famous for little more than having Spain's oldest football team and being one of a dozen European cities laying claim to Christopher Columbus' birthplace.

The two men were as different as the cities they lived in. Fernando was thirty-six, with a tall, wiry body burnt and battered from half a lifetime spent fishing the ocean. He kept his dark hair cropped short, with his square jaw clean-shaven. Pablo was twenty-four, squat and portly, with smooth hands that hadn't done a decent day's work in their life. His mass of dark curls fell to his shoulders, and his jaw was imperceptible under a shaggy dark beard. They'd met in Lourdes, a French town made famous for the townsfolk's claims of the Virgin Mary appearing in their lake. Fernando had been smoking a cigarette, watching the crowds bathe in the holy waters when a sopping wet Pablo had approached and asked for a smoke. The young man was talkative and, after discovering they were both destined for Santiago, suggested they walk the Camino together.

'I won't slow you down,' Pablo had promised.

It had only taken a day for the boy's lie to reveal itself.

'That's one minute,' Fernando called out. '*Vamos.* Let's go.'

They continued along the Camino. The boy wailed the same flamenco tune he'd been murdering for the past few days.

'Must you sing?' asked Fernando.

'Cervantes wrote, "He who sings frightens away his woes."'

'*Sí*, but all you frighten away are the birds. You sound like a boar caught in a trap.'

'Cervantes also wrote, "Men of great talents seldom

escape the attacks of those who, without ever favouring the world with any production of their own, take delight in criticising the works of others."'

'What did I say about reciting Cervantes quotes?'

'Miguel de Cervantes Saavedra is the greatest writer in Spanish history, *jefe*. His words can only uplift our pilgrimage, like a sprinkling of salt on a tender steak.'

'And too much salt ruins the meat.'

Pablo threw a mock salute. '*Sí, jefe*.'

'And stop calling me that. I'm not your boss.'

'Of course, *jefe*.'

They walked another hour, eventually outrunning the morning's clouds. The boy pointed down to the sunshine-filled valley below.

'You must confess, it is special, no? Walking across our homeland, like a modern-day Don Quixote and Sancho Panza.'

'Which am I?'

Pablo grinned; a row of perfect white teeth appeared within his woolly beard. 'You're Don Quixote, of course, and I'm your trusted squire, Sancho.'

'Fishermen don't need squires.'

The boy made a face, and a minute later, bent down to pick up a stone from the ground. 'This one is better.' He took a rock from his pocket and tossed it into the valley below. 'The one I brought with me is too jagged; it scratches my skin as I walk.'

Pablo placed the new, smoother stone into his pocket.

'The point of carrying a rock to the Cruz de Ferro isn't for it to be comfortable,' said Fernando. 'You're supposed to carry something weighty to the crucifix.'

'I suppose you have a small boulder packed into your

bag, no?'

Fernando was silent, and the boy grinned.

'Anyway, what sin is so bad it drives a fisherman all the way from Huelva to walk across Spain?'

'I walk to Santiago for the same reason as others.'

'To walk through La Puerta Santa and be cleansed of all your sins?'

The boy's mocking tone made Fernando's jaw clench.

'You don't believe it's true?' asked Fernando.

The boy scoffed. 'Of course not: the Xacobeo, La Puerta Santa, the Cruz de Ferro – nothing but fables to pray on our Catholic guilt.'

'So why walk the Camino if you don't have faith?' asked Fernando.

'I have faith. I fast during Lent and eat fish on Good Fridays.'

'Your acts of devotion are limited to food, no?'

'We all celebrate God in our own way, *jefe*.' Pablo looked indignant. 'But I'm not walking the Camino for absolution. I walk for the same reason as Don Quixote – adventure.'

'A pilgrimage to Santiago isn't supposed to be an adventure, Pablo.'

'Who says? Besides, my journey doesn't end in Santiago. I'll continue all the way to the village of Finisterre.'

'Why, what's there?'

'Nothing but the ocean – that's why they call it the end of the world.' He tugged at his shirt. 'I'll walk there and burn these clothes I've worn across Spain.'

'Why?'

'It's tradition.'

'It sounds like a waste.' Fernando turned to the boy.

'Tell me, how is it you have all this time to be walking across Spain? What is it you do back in Granada?'

'I'm a writer.'

'What books have you written?'

'Well, nothing yet. I've only just graduated university.'

'Did you study Literature?'

'No.' The boy looked unusually coy. 'Dentistry.'

'Dentistry?'

This explained the boy's immaculate teeth.

'Then you are not a writer; you are a dentist.'

Pablo sighed. 'You sound like my father.'

'What does he do?'

'He's a dentist.'

'I rest my case.'

'But just because my father is a dentist, it doesn't mean I am. My friend Jamie studied engineering, yet he writes beautifully. On Friday nights, he recites his poems at the Bodegas Espadafor. You should see it: the entire bar is crammed with beautiful women, all hanging on his every word. It's mesmerising.' The boy smiled at the thought. 'That's what I want.'

'What does your father say about all this?'

'He wants me to be like my older brother, Andreas: work in the family clinic, get married and start a family.'

'Perhaps he is right.'

'Is that what you have?'

Fernando shook his head. 'I was never smart enough to be a dentist.'

'Being a dentist isn't so hard; adults only have thirty-two teeth. I was asking whether you have a family. Is there a wife and some *niños* waiting for you in Huelva?'

'I live alone.'

'Not for the next month.' Pablo flashed his brilliant-white teeth again. 'Who knows what adventures await us on the Camino? Cervantes once wrote: "Destiny guides our fortunes more favourably than we could have expected."'

'What did I say about Cervantes?'

'*Sí, jefe.*'

The path up the mountain steepened, and the boy's Cervantes and flamenco soon yielded to his laboured breathing. The mountain was shrouded in fog, and without any other pilgrims ahead of them, Fernando concentrated on following the trail. By mid afternoon, they crested another slope and arrived at a secluded tavern.

'*Jefe*, look!' Pablo pointed to a pack of boys playing football in a paddock behind the tavern. He unslung his bag. 'Let's play.'

'We don't have time for football,' said Fernando.

'There's always time for football. Do you play?'

'Not since I was a boy in Sevilla.'

Pablo frowned. 'Sevilla? I thought you were from Huelva.'

Fernando paused. '*Sí*, but I grew up in Sevilla.' He pointed to the children. 'If you want to play, hurry up. We still have a long way to walk today.'

Fernando sat on the grass and watched Pablo join the teenagers. His hairy companion chased the ball around like a puppy as the children hollered and whistled while keeping the ball from him. Fernando smiled, reminded of playing football with his brother when they were children.

Their family had lived in Triana, one of Sevilla's poorest neighbourhoods back then. Their two-bedroom apartment was on the second floor of a building sandwiched between a tyre factory and a brewery – meaning it reeked of rubber during the day, and of yeast at night. Fernando had shared a bunk bed with his younger brother, Emilio. Their father had been a large man with a bulged nose, left ruddy from too much drinking. He'd spent his entire adult life as the delivery driver for Vega & Sabina, the local door manufacturer. Their mother had left when Fernando was only five; her dark, waist-long hair had been all he'd ever remembered of her. Whenever Papa had sipped his sherry and read the tale of Odysseus to his two sons, he'd compared their mother to the sirens who'd sung to the sailors from the rocks: beautiful, yet treacherous.

Fernando and Emilio had spent their childhood summers playing football with all the other boys from the neighbourhood on a patch of dirt behind the bottle factory. Being a year and a half younger than Fernando and the other boys, Emilio had always been the last boy selected whenever teams were chosen, sending him onto the pitch enraged. One year, when Fernando was twelve and Emilio was ten, the boy had unleashed a particularly venomous two-footed tackle, nearly breaking another boy's legs. When the brothers had arrived to play the following day, they'd been met with folded arms.

'My mother says Emilio can't play with us anymore,' one boy had said.

'*Sí*, he's too dangerous,' another had called out. 'You can play, but your brother cannot.'

Later that night, Papa had slammed his palm on the table, toppling his brandy glass onto its side. He'd stared at Fernando.

'I work too hard for this nonsense. If you play a sport, so does your brother. Am I clear?'

During the following afternoon's siesta, as their

friends played football and the rest of the neighbourhood slept, the two brothers had walked Triana's empty streets. Fernando had flung a rock onto the baking-hot tin roof of the textiles factory.

'You happy now?' he'd said to his brother.

'There must be other neighbourhoods where we can play,' Emilio had said. 'Why don't we try across the river?'

'Boys on the other side of the river don't play with boys from Triana.'

'Why don't we choose another sport then?'

'Every sport needs a team.'

They'd trudged down the street, kicking stones in front of them, before arriving at the Vega & Sabina door factory where their father worked. A mischievous smile had crept onto Emilio's lips.

'Not every sport.'

He'd led them inside the factory, deserted during siesta, and gathered an assortment of junk: a discarded mop, a broken broom and a few blocks of timber. Emilio had left Fernando clear instructions on fashioning the scraps of wood together with nails and glue before disappearing to the nearby shoe factory. The boy had returned with some thin leather strips, which the brothers had covered in glue and carefully wound around one end of each wooden pole. Nodding with satisfaction, the brothers had emerged from the factory brandishing their makeshift sporting equipment.

'But what good are golf clubs without golf balls?' Fernando had asked.

Emilio had pulled out a pair of large ball bearings, each the size of a golf ball.

'Where did you get those?'

'The bin behind the mechanic. There are dozens of them.'

'Well, we still need a golf course.'

'We have one.' Emilio had placed his ball bearing on the road and pointed down the Calle Alvarado toward a street sign in the distance. 'The first hole is hitting the street sign in four shots.' Without further delay, he'd swung his club and sent the ball bearing sailing through the air toward the Plaza de Chapina.

And just like that, Triana's first golf course had been born.

The brothers had played almost every day that summer, choosing the hottest part of the afternoon when the rest of Sevilla was asleep. Their eighteen-hole course snaked its way around the city in a clockwise direction. Some holes had been short, like the challenging par 3 over the Puente de San Telmo, while the longest hole was a par 5 near the Basílica de la Macarena. It hadn't taken long for Fernando to become proficient in the sport, one week scoring a hole-in-one on the par 3 in the balconied laneways of Santa Cruz. Emilio's progress had been slower, the boy's temperament even less suited to golf than football.

One day on the eighteenth hole, after Emilio had sworn, hissed and cursed his way around the entire city, Fernando had made a proposal.

'Whoever wins this hole wins the entire round.'

'I don't need your charity.'

'It's not charity, it's just to make it more fun. But if you don't think you'll win this hole, Emilio...'

'I'll win it.' His brother had slammed his ball bearing on the ground. 'Just you watch.'

Miraculously, or through some carefully disguised

mis-hits by Fernando, Emilio had won. As they'd walked through the Plaza del Altozano, the boy had been an ungracious victor.

'You see! I told you I'd win. You'd better get a big sleep tonight if you want to beat me tomorrow. You're slipping, brother.'

They'd been stopped by a tourist – a slim American in a sports jacket – who'd spotted them and their makeshift clubs. He'd asked to take their photograph with his Polaroid camera. Emilio had been delighted.

'You see? One win, and I'm already famous.'

Emilio had placed his arm around Fernando's shoulder, and the two brothers had smiled, resting their clubs on their shoulders. The tourist had taken two Polaroids, giving the boys the second one.

Fernando stared down at the photo, faded and creased after twenty years. He gazed at his brother's triumphant smile and wondered what their reunion would be like after so many years apart.

'*Jefe*, help me.' Pablo staggered toward him, bathed in sweat. 'The little monsters have run me ragged. I need water.' He yelled out at his young tormenters, 'Do you hear that? You're all monsters.' He collapsed onto the grass and caught his breath. 'I need to rest, just for ten minutes.'

'We'll leave in five. I don't even know where we are.'

Pablo lifted his head and hollered to the boys. 'Hey, what's the name of this town?'

'Orisson,' one of them yelled.

57

'Why are you doing this?' Tom asked again. 'Is it money? I can get you money; just tell me what you want.'

But the two Basques didn't respond. They simply marched Tom higher and deeper into the fog-shrouded mountains. They hadn't tied his hands, and he scanned the ground for a tree branch to wield as a club before realising he'd need an entire tree to stun the giant behind him. Instead, he decided to wait for a particularly steep section of the mountain where he could sprint ahead and disappear into the fog. But whenever an opportunity arrived, the girl's earlier warning had stifled his courage: 'If you run, he shoot you.' No matter how fast Tom ran, he couldn't outrun a bullet. Finally, after another hour of climbing, the man growled something in Basque.

'Okay, we stop here,' said the girl, pointing to a mound of grass. 'Roncesvalles is no far.'

At least Tom now knew where they were; they were still on the Camino. He sat on the grass and caught his breath, his sweat-drenched shirt clinging to his back. The man barked an instruction to the girl and handed her the gun. What had looked tiny in his hands now looked like a cannon in hers. The giant kneeled by his pack and unstrapped a collapsible shovel, the type used in the army. He extended it to its full size and walked toward the nearby forest. The shovel rested comically, like a toothpick, over his shoulder.

'I need the toilet too,' said Tom.

The girl didn't answer. She simply wrapped her poncho tightly around herself as a cold wind blew down from the peaks above. Tom opened his bag and rattled his empty canteen over his parched mouth.

'Here.' The girl held out her canteen.

'No, thank you.'

'Take it, yours is finished.'

'I don't want it, not from you.'

Her brow furrowed. 'This is not my idea. I no want to do this. I tried to stop him.'

'Sure, you're completely innocent. That's why you're holding a gun.'

'He thinks you a spy for the government.'

'But that's insane. Why would the British government be spying on you?'

'No the British, the Spanish government.'

'That makes even less sense. Why does he suspect I'm a spy?'

'Because of your radio transmitter.'

'My what?'

She pointed to Tom's pocket.

'He thinks I'm a spy because I have the new iPhone?' Tom's stomach knotted. These people weren't criminals; they were insane. 'I'm not a spy, okay? I'm just a tourist. My name is Tom Anderson.'

'T-Toom? Tum?'

He deferred to the name Ana used with her grandparents. 'My name is Thomas. What's yours?'

She glanced toward the forest before answering. 'I am Blanca.'

'Blanca, you need to listen to me carefully: the man you are with is sick, do you understand? He's not well in his head, he's confused.' Tom held up his scallop shell. 'I'm just a pilgrim walking to Santiago. You have to let me go.'

Her brow was creased with indecision, but she shook her head. 'I cannot do this.'

'You can.' He rose to his feet slowly. 'Tell your friend

I ran off.'

'He is not my friend.'

'Then why are you helping him?'

'Because they have my brother.'

'Who does?'

'ATA.' She pronounced it *att-ah*, rather than an acronym. 'Aberri Ta Askatasuna, it means Basque Country and Freedom. They fight for Basque independence.'

'You're a part of them?'

'Never.' She looked behind her to the trees again. 'But Ramon is, and he is taking me to see my brother. Without him, I may never find Felipe again.'

'Come with me, then. We can return to Orisson or Saint-Jean and call the police.'

'There is no *polizia* out here in the country, only the Guardia Civil. They won't help me – I'm Basque.'

'We just need to—'

A whistle pierced the fog, and Tom turned to see Ramon re-emerge from the forest. He waved them over, and Tom gave Blanca one final pleading look.

'Please, let me go.'

Blanca's youthful face strained with doubt, but she eventually waved the gun toward the forest. 'We go.'

Ramon waited for Tom and Blanca to join him by the forest's edge and reclaimed his gun from the girl. The Basque giant grunted something and motioned Tom forward. The three of them left the Camino and walked through the woods, eventually arriving at a clearing the size of a tennis court. A long trench lay in its centre; Ramon's camping shovel was lodged within a pile of fresh dirt next to the hole. Tom nearly vomited with fear.

'No, please.'

Ramon pointed the gun at him and began speaking.

'He say he now ask you questions. He say if you no tell him the truth, he put you in the hole.'

'*Erakutsi gailua.*'

'Show him the device.'

Tom fumbled his iPhone from his pocket. 'Take it, take it. Tell him it's his.'

Ramon snatched the phone from him; his dark eyes narrowed as he studied its screen.

'*Nola bidaltzen ditu bere mezuak?*'

'He want to see how you send transmissions,' said Blanca.

'Transmissions? You mean text messages?'

'*Bai*, tell him how you send your messages.'

Tom reached for the phone, but Ramon tugged it away and sneered something in Basque.

'Tell him to press the home button,' said Tom. 'It's the circle at the bottom of the phone.'

Ramon's massive thumbs pawed at the screen. Suddenly the forest was filled with Beyoncé. Ramon roared.

'No, he's clicked the music app,' said Tom. 'Tell him to press the home button again.'

Ramon pressed the buttons on the side of the phone, and Beyoncé sang louder. The Basque giant flung the phone to the ground and levelled the gun's barrel at Tom's chest.

'He say you try and raise alarm,' said Blanca.

'No, I was only trying to show him.'

Ramon pushed Tom into the pit and howled questions in Basque. Blanca tried to keep up.

'He say he want to know who you work for, Thomas.

He say if you no answer, he will shoot you.'

And to ensure nothing was lost in the girl's translation, Ramon pulled back the pistol's hammer. *Click.*

'There are several ways to prevent tooth decay, *jefe.* For example, the United States has put fluoride into the drinking water.'

For someone who didn't want to be a dentist, Pablo had a lot to say about teeth.

'But the best thing to do is floss. People never—'

Fernando stopped cold, muting the boy with a finger. 'Did you hear that?'

'Hear what?'

'Shh.' Fernando slid his finger to his lips and listened; the leaves rustled in the trees above. 'There!' He looked into the forest. 'Voices.'

The boy tilted his head. 'I hear something, but it sounds like…'

'Music,' they said in unison.

'It must be more pilgrims.' Pablo began walking forward, but Fernando stopped him.

'Wait, something isn't right.'

'Don't be silly. Cervantes wrote: "Where there's music, there can be no evil".'

'There've been no other pilgrims on the Camino today.'

'Perhaps we've caught up to them.'

'Something's wrong. Follow me closely and stay

quiet.' The two of them left the path and walked into the forest. The music grew louder, and it was soon joined by voices. The two of them crouched behind a fallen tree and peered into the clearing. A girl and a very tall man stood, facing the other direction. They seemed to be staring at something on the ground in front of them; their voices sounded angry.

'It's not Spanish,' whispered Pablo.

'It's Basque.'

The man moved, revealing a third person – a ginger-haired man kneeling within a pit before the Basques. His hands were clasped together.

'Is he praying?' asked Pablo, a moment before they both saw the pistol in the Basque man's hand.

'No, he's begging.'

The boy gripped Fernando's shoulder. 'We have to do something.'

Fernando paused before shaking his head. 'Whatever this is, it doesn't involve us. We should go back the way we came and find another way down to Roncesvalles.'

'But, *jefe*, they're going to kill him. We have to help.'

'The Basques might be *policía*. It's best not to get involved.'

The bearded giant screamed louder at the man in the pit.

'Does he look like *policía* to you?' asked Pablo. He nodded to the terrified man on his knees. 'Even if they are, we can't just let them execute him.'

Something dangled around the prisoner's chest. Fernando squinted and made out the familiar shape of a scallop shell. Fernando eventually faced the boy.

'Alright, when I say "go", I want you to run as fast

as you can and tackle the girl to the ground, do you understand? Make sure you've pinned her arms, in case she has a gun too.'

'What do you mean?'

'Go.'

Fernando vaulted over the log and sprinted into the clearing. The man with the gun was twenty yards away, and Fernando was halfway to him before the gunman reacted. Ten yards. The Basque giant began to turn, and Fernando focused on his target, praying Pablo was moving toward the girl. Five yards. The pistol slowly swung up, and Fernando launched himself at the Basque bear; their bodies collided, and they toppled back into the pit. The impact knocked every breath of wind from Fernando's chest, and he gasped for air. Amid a tangle of limbs and groans, the gunman's wild eyes landed on the pistol by the pit's edge. Both of them lunged for it, but the Basque got there first. He pointed the weapon at Fernando, who snatched a shovel protruding from the dirt next to the hole. He swung it toward the gun's barrel.

Bang. Bang.

The clang of metal was followed by bullets thudding into the side of the pit; soil sprayed everywhere. Fernando swung the shovel again, but the Basque caught it like a twig. He gave a toothless grin before wrenching the shovel from Fernando's grasp and hurling it into the forest. Fernando dived at the Basque, sending him staggering backward and toppling over the prisoner. All three men wrestled and writhed against each other in the shallow grave. Fernando desperately tried prising the gun from the bear's iron-like claw. The pistol's barrel jerked back and forward, but the Basque was too strong. It inched steadily toward Fernando's cheek, and there was one final blood-curdling scream.

Bang.

The gunshot echoed through the forest, filling the pit with blood, bone and brain.

CHAPTER 5

Blood dripped down the fair-haired stranger's face and his unblinking blue eyes stared up to the sky.

'Are you alright?' asked Fernando.

The man didn't respond, lying motionless in his grave.

'Hey, are you hurt?'

The stranger finally blinked. Fernando dragged the Basque's massive corpse off him; the hostage's eyes clung to where his captor's head once was.

'Here, give me your hand.' Fernando heaved the man from the pit and handed him his handkerchief, motioning for him to wipe himself clean.

Fernando's final desperate shove had pushed the gun barrel away from his face and directly beneath the Basque's chin. At such close range, the bullet had blown off most of the Basque's face. Fernando looked into the hole at the headless body. He reached into the pit and retrieved the pistol; it was an Astra modelo 400 – old, yet reliable. He tucked it into his belt.

'Get off me, you hairy oaf,' came a shriek from behind them.

Pablo was still atop the Basque girl, his knee pressed firmly into her back.

'I said, let me go.'

Fernando squatted in front of her. She had a broad face, green eyes and short, chestnut-coloured hair.

'What's your name?' he asked.

She stared at him like a caged beast. 'If you're going to arrest me, or kill me, then do it.' She spoke Spanish, but her accent was Basque.

'We're not the *policía*.' He pointed to the pit. 'And we weren't the ones about to execute someone.'

'I was trying to save him.'

'That's not what it looked like to us,' said Pablo.

'So you speak Basque, do you?'

'I don't need to understand Basque to know you are trouble.'

'Says a man who hits women.'

'I didn't hit you, I tackled you.'

'Enough,' said Fernando, waving them both to their feet. 'Let her up, Pablo.'

'But *jefe*...'

'Let her up.'

Pablo hesitated before getting to his feet. The girl stood up, her eyes drawn to the trench.

'Who was your friend?' asked Fernando.

'We weren't friends. I only met him in San Sebastián a few days ago. His name was Ramon.'

'And you were walking the Camino?'

'*Sí*, headed for Pamplona.'

'Pamplona?' Pablo scoffed. 'The path from San Sebastián to Pamplona doesn't pass through here.'

'Ramon said the direct path south had too many Guardia Civil patrols on it, so we walked east and joined the Camino at Irún.'

'Why would the Guardia Civil be looking for you?'

'Because she's a member of ATA,' said Fernando.

Pablo's eyes went wide. 'Holy shit, *jefe*. The terrorists who bombed the *policía* station in Bilbao, no?'

'I'm not a member of ATA,' snapped the girl. 'I would never join them.'

Fernando pointed to the hole. 'What about him?'

She remained silent.

'This is bad,' said Pablo, shaking his head. 'We need to tell the *policía*.'

'No.'

Fernando and Blanca had answered in unison; the boy frowned.

'Why the hell not?'

'Because we still don't know what's happened here,' said Fernando. He pointed to the man they'd saved, still wiping his face clean of blood. 'Who is he?'

'His name is Thomas. He's English,' said the girl. 'He walked into the tavern in Orisson and began asking questions. He said he was searching for people and wanted to go to the *policía*. Ramon panicked and suspected he was a spy.'

'Why?' Fernando eyed the Englishman's clothes: they were too bright to be military, but the scallop shell around his neck didn't seem to fit either.

'Ramon said there were spies in every village we

passed.' She paused. 'And because of that.'

Fernando followed her finger down to a shiny black object lying on the grass. He walked over and picked it up. A woman's shrill voice sang in Spanish; her nonsensical lyrics spoke of humble breasts and mountains.

'What is it, *jefe*?'

The device was slightly longer than a deck of playing cards but slimmer. It was surprisingly heavy, made from smooth black glass, with a thin strip of metal running around its edge. One of the sides had two silver nubs, while the other had a tiny switch. Fernando brought the device to his ear, and the music grew louder. He pressed his thumb against a small dimple on the object, and a colour photograph suddenly appeared. His mouth fell open, and Pablo walked around to inspect the device for himself.

'*Jesucristo.*'

They studied the photograph trapped beneath the glass. It showed two people: a beautiful girl with dark wavy hair and smooth, olive skin, and a man with ginger hair and dull, blue eyes.

'It's him.' Pablo pointed to the man they'd rescued. 'The Englishman is in the photograph.'

Fernando turned the metallic object over in his hands. 'What is this machine?'

'The Englishman called it a telephone,' said the girl.

Pablo pointed to it. 'But there are no lines or wires.'

The Englishman walked over and reclaimed the device, and moved his fingers across it. The music stopped.

'*Gracias*, my name is Thomas.'

The Spaniards stared at him. His mangled pronunciation made his Spanish barely recognisable. Pablo stepped forward with his hand on his chest as if making first contact with a lost tribe.

'I am Pablo, and this is Fernando.' He pointed to the shiny object in the Englishman's hands. 'What is this thing?'

The girl rolled her eyes. 'Yelling louder in Spanish won't make him understand you. We don't have time for this.'

'I agree,' said Fernando. 'We need to bury the body and leave.'

'Bury the body?' Pablo was horrified. 'We can't leave; only guilty people run. We need to walk down to Roncesvalles and telephone the *policía*.'

'There's no *policía* in these mountains,' said the girl, 'only Guardia Civil. What will you tell them?'

'The truth. We were walking along the Camino and stopped two members of ATA from executing the Englishman. One of the terrorists died in the scuffle.'

'You think they'll believe you?'

'It's the truth.'

'That's not what I asked. The Guardia Civil are not like the *policía* in the cities; they enforce the law, but they do not obey it themselves. They're just as likely to arrest you both as co-conspirators: Andalusian separatists working with the Basques, and now, an English spy.' She pointed to Fernando. 'They'll probably charge him with murder.'

The boy looked to Fernando for reassurance. 'By hiding the body, we incriminate ourselves, no? We didn't murder anyone; we saved the Englishman.'

'The girl's right,' said Fernando. 'The Guardia Civil may see events here differently.'

'This is all my fault.' The boy's shoulders slumped. 'I was the one who said we should help.'

'And if we hadn't, the Englishman would be dead.' Fernando squeezed the boy's shoulder. 'He's alive because of you, but now we must save ourselves, no?'

Pablo's face was twisted into a knot, but eventually, he nodded. 'You may be right.'

Fernando slapped him on the shoulder. 'I'll bury the body. Find some branches and leaves to conceal the grave.'

The boy walked into the forest to gather camouflage, and Fernando took the pistol from his belt and tossed it into the hole. He picked up the shovel and began filling in the dirt.

The girl hovered behind him.

'What will you do now?' she asked.

'Hide the body and leave.'

'No, I meant will you continue your pilgrimage to Santiago?'

'*Sí.*'

'You'll stay in Roncesvalles tonight and aim for Pamplona tomorrow night?'

'Probably. Why?'

'Take me with you.'

He looked to see if she were joking.

'I have to reach Pamplona,' she explained. 'My meeting with ATA is in two days. It's my only chance to find my brother.'

'Then continue walking to Pamplona. I'm not stopping you.'

'I can't do it alone. If there really are Guardia Civil patrols, an unaccompanied woman will arouse suspicion – especially a Basque one.'

'Why would we allow you to join us if you already admit it will only make our journey more perilous?'

'Please. My family hasn't seen Felipe in four months, not since the bombings in Bilbao. The Guardia Civil keep visiting our house looking for him. I have to find him before they do.'

'If your brother chose to join ATA, perhaps he doesn't want to be found.'

Her desperation switched to anger. 'You think Felipe chose this? We're Basque; we have no choice. The government has taken everything from us – our traditions, our flag, our language. They want us to disappear. If Felipe joined ATA, he only did it protect our people.'

'By bombing the innocent?'

'After the war, my father was arrested by the Guardia Civil for teaching Basque children their own language. Uniformed men pulled him from his bed and drove him away; we never saw him again. Wasn't my father innocent?'

Her shimmering eyes gave Fernando pause.

'I'm sorry, but we can't take you with us. It's too dangerous.' He plunged the shovel back into the dirt and moved another pile over the body.

'What if I made you a deal?' she asked.

'A deal suggests you possess something I want – you don't.'

'Not even my silence?'

'About what?'

'I saw how quickly you rejected your friend's suggestion of going to the *policía*.'

'Like you said, I killed a man.'

'No, you killed a Basque separatist; the Guardia Civil would likely pin a medal on your chest.' Her eyes narrowed. 'No, there's some other reason you don't want them involved. You're running from something, aren't you?' She smiled. '*Sí*, that's it. Don't worry, whatever you're hiding is not my concern. If you accompany me to Pamplona, I won't say anything to your friend.'

He studied her. She was cunning for someone so young – also braver than most.

'We'll walk you to Pamplona, but no further.'

She looked satisfied.

'And don't mention this to Pablo.'

'Not a word.' She pointed to the Englishman. 'What do you want me to tell him?'

'You speak English?'

'*Sí*, my father fought alongside the International Brigade in the war. He taught them the Basque countryside and language, they taught him English and how to make bombs.'

Fernando looked at the man, standing alone in his shock. 'It's too late in the day for him to walk back to Saint-Jean. Tell him to walk with us to Roncesvalles. We'll stay there tonight.'

'I'll try.' She sighed. 'If he'll forgive me for kidnapping him.'

'Tell him what you told me about your brother and your father. He'll see you did what you must.' Fernando shovelled another heap of dirt into the pit. 'He's had a traumatic day; he just needs a good night's sleep.'

Tom couldn't sleep. Every time he closed his eyes, Ramon's face screamed at him over the barrel of the gun. Tom shuddered and wiped his face again, still somehow able to feel the Basque's blood dribbling down his face. He rolled over in the bunk; the mattress coil wedged into his lower back groaned its relief.

When they arrived in Roncesvalles, Tom had expected they'd stay in the *albergue* with all the other pilgrims from the train. Instead, they'd come to a turreted monastery where a frail man leaning on a cane had greeted them. Blanca had shepherded Tom downstairs to the bathroom, where he'd scrubbed his face with hot water until his fingers were sore. A monk had served supper in the empty dining hall, ladling bean stew over steaming bowls of rice. Feeling as if he might vomit after only a spoonful, Tom had excused himself back to the dormitory to rest. The coils of the mattress had attacked his body regardless of the sleeping position he'd adopted. Somehow, the dormitory bed in the monastery was less comfortable than the previous night's wooden church pew.

Pablo, asleep in the bunk above Tom, had no such qualms. The Spaniard hadn't moved, the only proof of life being the constant roar of his snoring, punctuated by the occasional fart courtesy of the beans. Although Tom couldn't understand the Spaniard, Pablo seemed a jovial type, freely using his hands as he talked. In contrast, Fernando was older and more reserved – there was a surliness to him. They were an odd coupling, and Tom didn't recognise either of them from the train to Saint-Jean. Blanca said the pair had started their pilgrimage somewhere in the south of France. It was a miracle they'd arrived when they had.

Tom had never even heard of the Basques until yesterday, let alone ATA. One time he and Ana had flown to Madrid for the weekend, and Tom had pointed out some mugshots plastered on the airport's walls. She'd explained they were a group responsible for some bombings in the north of the country, but Tom was sure they'd been called ETA, not ATA.

Blanca had apologised repeatedly on the walk down to Roncesvalles, explaining she'd only wanted the safe return of her brother, who'd become mixed up with the group. Her remorse seemed sincere, but he'd still been too numb to accept or decline her apologies. When they'd arrived at the monastery, Tom had asked Blanca if they would report Ramon's killing to the police. She'd said the monastery didn't have a telephone. When he'd suggested they use one of the Spaniards' mobile phones, her face had tightened.

'Is not the same as England; going to the *policía* only causes problems. Problems for my brother, for you and for me.' She'd pointed to the Spaniards. 'But especially for them. They saved you, Thomas. They saved us both.'

While Tom was grateful for the men's help, leaving Ramon's death unreported felt wrong; everything about this trip did. He rolled over and turned on his phone – 4:06am glowed in the darkness. As soon as it was light, he'd walk back to Saint-Jean and check for his bag at the train station. He wanted to get back to London as quickly as possible, putting Spain, and this entire trip, behind him.

He must have eventually fallen asleep because pale light crept through the dormitory's windows when he next opened his eyes. Tom's bunk began to shake as Pablo climbed down the ladder, a final fart escaping upon his descent.

'*Perdone*,' grumbled the Spaniard, scratching his way toward the bathroom.

Tom got dressed and walked down to the dining hall. Blanca and Fernando were sitting at the table, eating the modest breakfast the monks had prepared.

'*Buenos días*, Thomas,' said Blanca, pouring him a cup of coffee. 'How you sleep?'

'Fine.' He accepted the mug and took a sip; it was bitter without milk.

'You return to Saint-Jean today, no?'

'Yes, I'll catch a train back to Bayonne and book a flight to London from Bilbao.'

She frowned. 'Bilbao? A bus from Pamplona to Bilbao is better.'

'But my bag is at the train station in Saint-Jean.'

'You are certain?'

'No, but if there's no telephone coverage here, I'll have to walk back to check.'

'The abbot said the next town is bigger; there will be a telephone. It is an hour's walk. You come with us.'

Tom was getting progressively further from his bag and passport. But the six-hour walk to Saint-Jean would be wasted if his backpack wasn't there. He ran both scenarios through his head and agreed to walk with the Spaniards to the next town. Pablo sat down at the table and inhaled half a loaf of bread and two cups of coffee, speaking joyfully between each mouthful and sip. Fernando eventually stood and lifted his bag to his shoulder.

'*Vamos.*'

'This means, we go,' Blanca translated to Tom.

'I know,' he said. 'Nadal says it every time he wins a big point.'

'Who?'

'Rafa Nadal – the tennis player.'

She looked puzzled but said nothing.

The four of them filed out of the monastery and into the cold mountain air. Tom buried his hands into his jacket's pockets and followed the Spaniards past a sign proclaiming: 'Santiago de Compostela – 790 kms'. He felt a pang of embarrassment: he'd failed Tito's challenge at the very first step.

Fernando led them off the road and onto a faint track behind a barn. Tom couldn't see any yellow arrows or scallop shells, but the Spaniard seemed sure of the way. After a half hour of silent walking, the sun had fully risen. They passed through a birch forest and a tall crucifix with ornate decorations carved into the stone. Fernando kissed a small cross on the chain around his neck before tucking it back into his shirt. The path emerged into an expanse of paddocks; a trio of tan-coloured horses stood and stared at the canvas of pinks and purples on the horizon behind Tom. Pablo picked up a stone and compared it with another he took from his pocket. Eventually, he handed one of them to Tom.

'*Por la Cruz de Ferro.*'

Blanca translated. 'He say you should carry this to the Cruz de Ferro, in Galicia. The rock is your sins.'

Not wishing to appear rude, Tom slid the stone into one of his thigh pockets. After another half hour of walking, the road brought them to the outskirts of a town.

'This is Auritz,' Blanca told Thomas.

Pablo seemed to understand and shook his head. He pointed to a sign which read 'Burguete', and the two argued in Spanish. Exasperated, Blanca turned back to

Tom.

'Typical Spanish, constantly changing Basque names. When the Romans conquered Spain, they renamed our towns in Latin. Iruña became Pamplona, Gasteiz became Vitoria, and Auritz became Burguete.'

By the time they reached the middle of the town, Blanca and Pablo still hadn't agreed on its name. Tom rechecked his phone, but neither Burguete nor Auritz had phone reception. Fernando pointed to a shop with legs of jamón hanging in its window and said something in Spanish.

'He get some food for us,' explained Blanca.

Tom looked up the street for an internet café or *albergue*, and his eye fell on a brightly covered farmhouse. A sign above its door read 'Hostal Burguete'. It was the first hotel he'd seen since starting the Camino.

'I'm going to check for Wi-Fi.' He hurried across the street and opened the hostel's door.

'Hello?'

The reception desk was unattended. All was silent, save for the ticking of an unseen clock.

'*¿Hola?*'

Meow.

A filthy ginger cat appeared from behind the counter, inspecting Tom with its yellow eyes, before sauntering off. He followed it down the hallway and arrived at the hostel's restaurant: a room with lime-green wallpaper and a handful of wooden tables and chairs – all with non-matching cushions. A modest fire crackled in the fireplace, and a battle-weary piano rested against the far wall. An old man sat at one of the tables, absorbed in his newspaper. Tom knocked politely on the doorframe.

'*Perdone, señor.*'

The man looked up, surprised. He resembled a retired sea captain, his round face framed by his receding white hair and bushy, white beard. His maroon turtle-neck jumper was stretched over a sizeable paunch. '*¿Sí?*'

'*Perdone, señor*, but do you have Wi-Fi?' Tom hoped the Spanish word for Wi-Fi was simply Wi-Fi; he couldn't fathom a hand gesture to symbolise the internet. The man shook his head.

'*No lo sé.*'

Tom changed tack. 'Do you have *un teléfono?*' He pretended his hand was a phone and moved it up to his mouth.

The old man winced, looking completely adrift.

'Kid, either your Spanish is bad, or mine is.'

Relief poured over Tom. 'You speak English?'

'Sure I do, I'm American.'

'I'm English, my name's Tom. Is this your place?'

'This is Juan and Elena's place; I'm only a guest. People call me Papa.'

The name suited him; he looked like a cuddly grandfather.

'Are Juan or Elena here?'

Papa pointed to the grandfather clock, standing against the wall. 'It's just gone past eight; they'll be up soon.'

'Well, do you know if they've got Wi-Fi?'

'What in Sam Hill is that?'

'It's the internet.'

The American shrugged. 'Beats me, I haven't been here in thirty years, but I don't think so. Elena does a half-decent vegetable soup, though.'

Tom took out his phone and checked for a nearby network. A warning announced he had only twenty per cent left of his battery.

'I don't suppose you've got a phone charger?' he asked.

'A what?'

Tom held up his phone. 'A power cable for your cellular phone.' He used the American term. 'I haven't been able to get a signal since Saint-Jean, and I need to call home.'

Papa stroked his beard. 'Juan has a telephone in his office. If you need to send any correspondence to London, your best bet is the wire in Pamplona.'

The hairs stood up on the back of Tom's neck. 'The wire?'

'Yeah, there's a post office near the Paseo de Sarasate. My editor sends me notes on my manuscripts there, and I reply via telegram.'

The room tilted, and Tom steadied himself on the closest chair. The sound of the ticking clock got louder.

'Did you say… telegram?' The nagging doubts in the back of Tom's mind came rushing up to the surface: the missing pilgrims, the lack of mobile phone reception, the look on the Spaniards' faces as they inspected his phone. There were so many clues he'd ignored: the missing yellow arrows, the shopkeeper insisting on French francs.

Papa stood up.

'Are you okay, son? You look like you've seen a ghost.'

Tom's eyes were drawn to the old man's newspaper. 'Is that today's paper?'

'It's from a couple of days ago. Why?'

Tom wobbled toward it as if aboard a turbulent flight. It was in Spanish. He searched for the masthead at the top of the page.

Jueves 10 de junio de 1954

It couldn't be right; it had to be a dream or a prank. The grandfather clock ticked louder. *Tick, tock, tick, tock.* He re-read the date.

Jueves 10 de junio de 1954

1954? What was happening? He turned to Papa to see if this was all a sick joke. The American's lips were moving, but his words were drowned out by the sound of the clock. *Tick, tock, tick, tock.* The room started to contract; its walls and ceiling warped inward, and the furniture began to slide across the room. *Tick, tock, tick, tock.* The clock was deafening now; the glasses and cutlery rattled on their tables with each second's tick. *Tick, tock, tick, tock.* The floor gave way, and Tom began to fall. He reached for Papa, but the American's round face was now a thousand feet above him. *Tick, tock, tick, tock.* Tom fell through the floor and into a bottomless, dark chasm.

CHAPTER 6

Tom heard whispers and the sound of shuffling feet. He blinked his eyes open and the two-headed silhouette standing over him sharpened into focus.

'*Hola*, Thomas,' said Pablo. He reached down and helped Tom to his feet.

The room wobbled. Blanca hurried Pablo away and helped Tom onto a chair.

'How you feel?' she asked.

'Dizzy.' Tom looked around. Fernando sat on the piano stool on the other side of the room. 'What happened?' he asked.

Blanca pointed to an old man with a snowy beard. 'This man come and find us.'

'You gave me one hell of a scare, kid,' said the American, whose name Tom suddenly remembered was Papa. 'You hit your skull on the chair pretty good.'

Tom rubbed a lump on the back of his head. His eyes returned to the newspaper on the table.

Thursday, 10th June 1954.

The clock grew louder. *Tick Tock. Tick Tock.* Tom clenched his eyes closed in a bid to wake himself from his nightmare. But when he opened them, Papa and the Spaniards remained. Their faces were full of pity.

'What year is it?' asked Tom.

Everyone stared at him, even the cat.

'I think you've got a concussion, son,' said Papa.

'Just tell me – what year is it?'

The old man looked at the others before replying. 'It's 1954.'

The walls rippled, and Tom gripped the table to steady himself. 'I'm still dreaming, aren't I?'

'Why do you say that, son?' asked Papa.

'Because it can't be 1954.' He laughed at how specific the dream felt. 'It's 2010.'

The clock momentarily stopped ticking, casting the room in absolute silence. Blanca translated Tom's statement into Spanish, and Fernando stood up and joined the others.

'*Está loco,*' Pablo breathed out the side of his mouth.

Papa eyed Tom warily. 'I think you kids better get him to the hospital,' he said.

'*Sí,*' said Blanca and Pablo in unison, finally agreeing on something.

'I'm not concussed,' said Tom. 'This is all just some crazy dream.'

But everyone ignored him, and Papa turned to face Blanca. 'There used to be an old hospital by the River Arga in Pamplona.'

How did people usually wake themselves up from their nightmares? Tom curled his hands into fists and dug his fingernails into his palms. He stared at the divots his nails had formed in his skin. If this was a dream, it was unlike any he'd had before. The Spaniards whispered among themselves. Could Tom really be dreaming in a language he didn't speak?

Blanca walked over to him.

'Thomas, we think you should come with us to Pamplona to see a doctor.'

'This isn't a concussion. Things had already turned strange long before I passed out. I'm telling the truth – I'm from the future.'

Their faces echoed the woman's from the patisserie in Saint-Jean – a combination of fear and pity. Tom suddenly had an idea. He pulled his wallet from his pocket.

'Here, I'll prove it.' He held up a fifty-euro note. 'If I was concussed, how do you explain this?'

Blanca took the note and studied it. 'What is this?'

'It's called a euro. This is the money used in the future.'

She eyed it suspiciously and passed it to Pablo and Fernando, who took turns inspecting it.

'It's used all across Europe,' explained Tom. 'France, Germany, Italy…'

'*¿Inglaterra también?*' asked Pablo, turning to Blanca to translate.

'He asks if England uses it too.'

'Well, no.'

'Why not? England is not part of Europe in the future?'

'No, it is.'

'Then why not use the same currency?'

There wasn't time to explain Tony Blair's 'five economic tests' for Britain adopting the euro. Instead, Tom tapped the date on the note's upper edge. 'You see here? This note was issued in the year 2008.' Everyone peered at it. 'So this proves I'm from the future.'

They completed their inspections before handing it back to Tom.

'You need rest, Thomas,' said Blanca, sounding as unconvinced as the others looked. 'You come with us to Pamplona.'

Tom took his phone from his pocket and held it up. 'Okay, what about this then? I saw the way you all looked at it in the forest yesterday. You don't know what it is, do you?'

'Ramon said it was a government radio transmitter.'

'*Una radio para la música,*' said Pablo.

Tom swiped away another low battery warning and opened the camera app. 'Can a radio transmitter do this?' He toggled it to video mode and pressed record, slowly panning the camera across each of their confused faces.

'*¿Qué está haciendo?*' asked Fernando.

'*Está jodidamente loco,*' replied Pablo.

Tom stopped recording and placed the phone on the table. He pressed play, and the Spaniards watched themselves on the screen, their jaws dropping when they heard their voices played back to themselves.

'Is a television or radio?' asked Blanca.

'It's both,' replied Tom. 'It's called a mobile telephone. In the year 2010, everyone has one.'

They stared at him uneasily, their puzzled faces suggesting they still didn't believe him. His voice surrendered to panic and frustration.

'Look, I know I must sound crazy – I don't understand any of this either – but you have to believe me. I'm telling the truth. Somehow, someway, I've travelled back in time. I don't know how or why it's happened, but I'm begging you to believe me. I need your help to get home.'

The Spaniards huddled together, deliberating Tom's fate in hushed voices. Papa offered a reassuring smile as Tom awaited his fate. Blanca delivered the verdict.

'Okay, we help you,' she said. 'But you must come to Pamplona with us. It is Navarra's capital city and our best chance to help you return home.'

'So, you believe me?'

Blanca glanced at the other two, their faces still uncertain.

'*Sí*, we no understand, but we believe you.'

'Do you really believe him?' Blanca asked as Fernando led them out of Burguete and back to the Camino.

'Of course not,' laughed Pablo. 'But *el americano* was right – nobody can help him in this tiny village.'

'What about the money he showed us?'

'Fake,' said Pablo. 'It had to be.'

'Why would he fake such a thing?'

'Why does a rabid dog bark at the moon? Some people talk crazy for attention, no?'

'*Sí*, but time travel? There are simpler ways of gaining attention. And what about the device?'

'Probably just a trick. If it's really a telephone, why

is Thomas walking with us to use a telephone in the next village? It makes no sense.'

'But it played music. It captured our faces and voices.'

'Maybe Ramon was right; maybe he is a spy. But let me now ask you a question: do you really believe he travelled back in time?'

Blanca glanced back to Thomas, trailing twenty yards behind them. 'I don't know what I believe. What about you, Fernando, what do you think?'

'I think the sooner we get him to a doctor, the better,' he said.

'So you don't believe he's a time traveller?'

'I believe people act strangely after knocking their heads or nearly being executed.' He caught the girl's eye; she wasn't blameless in the Englishman's condition. 'Anyway, we've lost two hours.' He nodded toward the sun, now high in the sky behind them. 'It's another thirty kilometres to Pamplona; we need to walk fast if we want to get there tonight.'

Clear of the Pyrenees, the Camino flattened. It snaked its way through sheep-littered farms before reaching the next village. Blanca pointed to a wooden sign, which bore the name 'Espinal'.

'Its real name is Aurizberri.'

'Then, why does it say Espinal?' asked Pablo.

'Because some people bend their knees more freely than others. You of all people should know this.'

'What's that supposed to mean?'

'You're from Andalucía – a region with its own culture, traditions and flag – yet you seem very comfortable with Franco and the Nationalists.'

'Why? Because we don't blow up police stations?'

'Enough,' yelled Fernando, silencing the feud. 'We're going to pass through a dozen villages on our way to Pamplona. Let's not revisit this debate in each.'

'*Sí, jefe.*'

'*Sí, jefe,*' mimicked the girl. 'You see? Bending the knee.'

Espinal was a mirror of Burguete: rows of white farmhouses, each with bougainvillea overflowing from their windowsills above. The pilgrims filled their canteens in a fountain in the square and continued on. A series of scallop shells etched on the sides of the houses guided them through the town and back to the Camino. Once again surrounded by farmland, they passed a herd of white cows lazily grazing in a paddock. Pablo pointed to a solitary black bull, standing defiantly in the neighbouring field.

'Do you think he's been bred especially for San Fermín?'

'Perhaps,' said Fernando. Pamplona's famed fiesta would occur in a few weeks.

The boy walked over to the field and stood on the fence. He marvelled at the enormous black beast.

'Can you imagine having those horns chasing behind you? They say the Plaza del Toro in Pamplona holds twenty thousand people.' He looked back to Fernando. 'Do you attend the bullfights in Huelva?'

'No.'

'Never?' The boy looked shocked. 'What about when you were a boy in Sevilla? The Real Maestranza is amongst Spain's most beautiful arenas, no?'

'I've been inside once, but never for a bullfight.'

'Perhaps we can see a bullfight in Pamplona?'

'We don't have time.' Fernando nodded back to the Camino. '*Vamos.*'

'What's the point of walking across Spain if we don't stop to see any of it?'

Pablo's question went unanswered.

As the foursome travelled west, Fernando's mind drifted south once more. Visiting Sevilla's bullring – the Real Maestranza – had been one of the happiest days of his childhood. When he'd turned fifteen, Fernando had left school to work with his father at the door factory, Vega & Sabina. The job had been tedious: sweeping up the factory floor and carrying timber scraps to the bins. But on Fridays, Fernando had accompanied his father on his delivery run around Sevilla. Most of the deliveries were nothing more than dropping pallets of doors to building sites across town – but their delivery of new gates to La Maestranza had filled him with anticipation.

While boys his age had all cherished football, matadors had been the true heroes of his neighbourhood. On the days of the bullfights, Fernando and Emilio often ran across the river to sit with their backs pressed against the stadium's white-and-yellow walls. They'd felt the roar of the crowd vibrate through their scrawny bodies and imagined their heroes dancing with the bulls on the arena's burnt-orange sand: famous matadors like Manolete, Joselito and Fernando's favourite, Juan Belmonte. Belmonte had been born in Triana, just a few streets from where their family had lived. He'd become a matador at sixteen. His technique had been unique, not relying on the exotic flourishes and twirls of the other bullfighters. Instead, he'd stood like a statue, waiting for the perfect moment to strike.

Fernando's father had driven the lorry through the

gates and onto the arena, and Fernando had leaped down, staring up at the majestic stadium encircling him. He'd imagined the crowd above, showering him with flowers and applause.

That night at supper, Fernando had recounted the excursion to Emilio. The boy had been on the verge of tears as he'd looked to their father.

'Why does he get to go to La Maestranza?'

'Your brother was working,' Papa had said, pouring another tumbler of whiskey. 'It wasn't for fun.'

'So when I turn fifteen, am I allowed to work at the factory too?'

'No, you've got too many brains to waste away in a damn factory. Your teacher says you're smart enough for a scholarship to the university.'

'But it's not fair. I want to see these special places too.'

Papa had necked the whiskey. 'I'll make you a deal: if you continue working hard at school, I'll bring you on our next special delivery.'

Emilio hadn't studied hard, but he hadn't needed to. His grades had remained high, despite him spending more time reading Papa's newspaper than his textbooks. So when Fernando and his father had delivered new doors to the Ministry of Finance in the Plaza de España at summer's end, Emilio had joined them.

'Are we going inside the palace?' Emilio has asked, staring wide-eyed at the long row of buildings curved around the plaza's semi-circular forecourt.

'It's not a palace, Emilio. These are the offices of the Andalusian government – Finance, Defence, Planning – this is where all the decisions are made.'

Emilio had pointed to a line of men being ushered

onto a bus.

'Who are they, Papa?'

'The army.'

'They don't look like normal soldiers.'

Emilio had been right; these soldiers had looked different. They'd worn distinctive khaki-coloured caps with red tassels, and their tight, short-sleeved shirts bulged around tattoo-covered arms and chests.

'They are the Spanish Legion.' Their father had nodded to a line of scruffy men boarding the bus. 'Every summer they recruit volunteers to fight the rebels in Morocco.'

'Why would anyone volunteer to fight in a war?'

'Because some men are desperate, Emilio. Many who join the legion are escaping the law.'

'But can't the *policía* arrest them when they join?'

Their father had shaken his head. 'Once a man signs his papers, the next five years of his life belong to the legion. No one can touch him – not even the *policía*.'

Fernando's father had driven the lorry up to the gates of the government buildings, where a uniformed guard checked a clipboard before waving them through. Fernando had helped Papa carry the doors up several staircases, while Emilio had brought the ladder. The uniformed officer had led them down corridors with polished floors, past bustling offices to the Ministry of Finance. When Papa had realised they'd left the toolbox in the lorry, Fernando had offered to retrieve it.

'No need.' Papa had slid up the leg of his overalls, revealing a screwdriver and a small mirror tucked into his sock. 'To hang a door, all a good door-man ever needs is a screwdriver and a mirror.'

When the job was done, Fernando had raced Emilio

back to the truck. The two brothers had leaped down the stairs, two or three at a time, startling the staff as they rocketed past them.

'That wasn't fair,' Emilio had complained as he'd arrived at the truck, breathless. 'There were people in my way. Let's race again – you won't beat me again, you'll see.'

Now, eighteen years later, Fernando realised his brother had been right. Their race through the offices of the Plaza de España had been their last; everything had changed the following year.

'*Jefe*, shall we stop?'

Pablo's voice dragged Fernando back to the present. They'd arrived in the next village.

The boy pointed to a fountain. 'We should stop for water, no? And wait for him.' Pablo pointed behind them to Thomas, labouring toward them in the distance. 'Maybe forty kilometres is too far for him today, especially after his fall, no?'

Fernando squinted toward the Englishman. 'He'll be fine; we'll make it.'

Tom was falling apart. His earlier relief of the Spaniards believing him had worn off, and he trudged behind them, wrestling with the same unanswerable question: what in the actual fuck was going on?

Was this a nervous breakdown? Had Tito's unwillingness to bless Tom's marriage to Ana induced a prolonged panic attack, triggering a series of hallucinations? Was that even possible, given he was self-aware enough to even consider the possibility?

As Tom stumbled along, his next thought had been he was still asleep on the train to Saint-Jean, and all of this was a hyper-realistic dream. After all, things had only grown strange after he'd woken up. It had to be a dream. Ordinarily, Tom's dreams jumped around: one moment he'd be playing squash with a long-lost school friend, the next he'd land at the birthday party of an ex-girlfriend's mother. But all of this was too coherent to be a dream. Everything in the past thirty-six hours had been painfully linear; he hadn't seemed to skip a single step of the past thirty kilometres he'd walked. And even if he was asleep, why couldn't he wake himself up?

And this definitely wasn't a concussion. Hank's disappearance and the shopkeeper's insistence on the French francs had occurred the day before Tom had bumped his head. Nor was it a prank. Ignoring the question of why anyone would play such an elaborate trick, the logistics would have been impossible, the cost astronomical. He reluctantly shifted his thinking to the last remaining possibility: time travel.

When he was younger, Tom had a keen interest in astrophysics, finding comfort in its laws and dependence on numbers. He might have followed a career in it had he not calculated a corporate life would be more profitable, and therefore happier. He still remembered the general gist of time-travel theories, though; they explained time and space being fused together in a concept called 'space-time'. Astrophysicists had hypothesised space-time could theoretically fold onto itself, creating portals named 'wormholes'. He still remembered the diagram of two connected funnels. If a person, or object, passed through a wormhole, it would be instantaneously transported from one part of space-time to another. Time travel. But all of this was only theoretical; no one had ever proven it.

Tom followed the others up onto the road. The hard ground stabbed at his left foot. So much for the expensive boots preventing blisters.

'¡*Oye!* ¡*Thomas!*'

He looked ahead to the three Spaniards waving toward him.

'I'm okay.' He pointed to his foot and gave a thumbs up. '*Bueno.*'

Blanca hurried toward him but the wind swallowed her words. She pointed frantically behind him, and Tom turned to see an approaching car in the distance with a plume of dust trailing behind it. It was only when he saw the flash of its lights and wail of its siren that he understood what Blanca had been screaming.

She'd been yelling for him to hide. It was the Guardia Civil.

'Say as little as possible.' Fernando directed the instruction at Pablo; the girl would know to keep quiet.

The jeep pulled off the road and onto the gravel, killing its lights and siren. A man emerged from the vehicle's passenger side; he was tall and slim, with a face as crisp as his dark-green uniform. He swept his wavy brown hair back and pulled on his *tricornio* – the traditional three-cornered hat of the Guardia Civil.

'*Buenos días.*' He walked toward them. 'My name is Capitán Javier Aznar. Are you the pilgrims who stayed in the monastery in Roncesvalles last night?'

Fernando stepped forward. '*Sí.*'

'And left from Saint-Jean yesterday morning?'

'No, Lacarre. We started our pilgrimage from Lourdes.'

Aznar took a notebook and pen from his jacket's pocket and scribbled a note. 'But you took the Jacobian path through the mountains yesterday, no?'

'*Sí,* we did.'

'And did you see anything unusual?'

'No, *señor*, the Camino was quiet yesterday.'

Aznar wetted his finger and flipped his notepad to the previous page. 'On my patrol this morning, the abbot said he'd heard gunshots in the woods yesterday.'

When the abbot had asked them the same thing yesterday, Fernando had suggested the old man must have imagined it. 'We heard nothing.'

'Gunshots in farmland aren't uncommon, no?' asked Blanca.

Aznar faced her. 'Who are you?'

Fernando waved toward her. 'She is…'

'… his sister,' said Blanca, recounting the same lie they'd fed the abbot.

Aznar scribbled something down.

'We're searching for Basque separatists who may be disguising themselves as pilgrims on the Camino de Santiago.'

Aznar's hand slid to his hip, and Fernando momentarily tensed. The capitán pulled out a handful of photographs: the first showed a bald, middle-aged man with a grey beard.

He wore a pair of black-framed spectacles. 'This is Enrico Vasquez, a member of ATA. We believe he masterminded an attack in Bilbao several months ago.'

Vasquez looked more like an accountant than a revolutionary. Aznar held up another mugshot and Fernando's heart paused.

'This is Ramon Ochoa.'

The photo was old – taken when the man's hair was shorter and his beard neater – but it was the same brute they'd buried in the forest.

'Ramon is Vasquez's chief enforcer, used to intimidate locals into supporting their cause. He was in Bilbao the night of the bombing too, along with this boy.' Aznar held up the final image, a sketch instead of a photograph. It showed a younger man with light skin and eyes. 'Witnesses saw this boy parking a lorry next to the barracks. We believe it was filled with explosives.'

Blanca's trembling lip nearly betrayed her.

'No, *señor*, we haven't seen these men,' said Fernando. 'As I said, the Camino has been quiet.'

Aznar studied them a moment longer before slipping the pictures back in his pocket. 'If you see anything, report it to the nearest *policía* station or church; these men are killers.' He slid his notebook back into his pocket as well and nodded curtly. '*Buen Camino.*'

Aznar walked back to the jeep. The pilgrims exhaled quietly and turned to rejoin the Camino.

'One moment.'

They froze, stopped by the raspy voice of another man. The pilgrims turned slowly, and the driver stepped out from the vehicle. His uniform was the same as Aznar's, but everything else was different. Approaching fifty, the driver was short and barrel-chested, like a uniformed boulder. His cropped black hair was peppered with silver, and his black eyes were as shiny as his knee-high boots.

'*Buenas tardes*, pilgrims, my name is Brigada Esteban Ramos.' He strode toward them. The winged *tricornio* atop his head was as faded as the chevron and star on his arm. 'Before you go, tell me your names.'

'I am Fernando Morillas.'

Unlike the younger officer, Ramos didn't carry a notepad. 'Where are you from, Morillas?'

'Huelva.' Fernando pointed to the girl. 'This is my younger sister, Blanca.'

'Your sister has much lighter skin than you.'

'Our mother is unwell,' said Blanca. 'I spend my days indoors tending to her.'

'A good daughter.' Ramos nodded to Pablo. 'You're from Huelva too?'

'No, *señor* – Granada. I am Pablo Martínez.'

'And him?'

Everyone faced Thomas.

'He doesn't understand; he's from England,' said Blanca. 'We met him yesterday.'

Ramos cocked an eyebrow toward Fernando. 'You said you met no one on the Camino yesterday.'

'Just him. He was lost.'

Ramos' gaze lingered on Fernando before slithering to the Englishman. 'Show me his papers.'

Blanca spoke to Thomas, who pulled his wallet from his pocket and removed a thin, plastic card. Ramos snatched it.

'Tho-mas An-der-son. Hamp-stead, Lon-don.' Ramos inspected the pink card. It bore a small photograph of the

Englishman's face on it. 'Where is his passport?'

'He says his bag was stolen in Saint-Jean-Pied-de-Port,' said Blanca. 'We are helping him reach Pamplona to return to England.'

'You speak English?'

'*Sí*, a little.'

'That must be invaluable for tending to your sick mother in Huelva.' Ramos' gaze loitered on her a moment before he nodded to Thomas' satchel. 'You said his bag was stolen.'

A pause.

'It was,' replied Blanca. 'But he was given another.'

Ramos clicked his fingers toward it. 'Show it to me.'

Thomas seemed to instinctively surrender his bag, and Ramos rummaged through it.

'What's this?' He held up Thomas' shiny black radio transmitter.

Fernando's neck prickled beneath his collar.

'Well?' snapped Ramos. 'What is it?'

Blanca spoke to Thomas in English while Ramos turned the device over in his hands. Fernando held his breath, terrified the photograph within it would appear beneath the glass. The device remained idle.

'He says it's a shaving mirror,' said Blanca.

Ramos stared at his dull reflection in the dark glass before nodding to the Englishman's unshaven chin. 'Not a very good one, no?'

'His razor was in his stolen bag,' said Fernando.

Ramos remained silent; his eyes burned into Fernando's. Eventually, the heat of his gaze moved to Fernando's arm and he tugged Fernando's rolled sleeve higher. 'A tattoo of a musket, crossbow and mace.'

Fernando hastily rolled down his sleeve. 'All fishermen have tattoos.'

'*Sí*, but not all of them carry the insignia of the Spanish Legion.' Ramos' black eyes narrowed to slits. 'Morillas… your face is familiar, even if your name is not.'

Capitán Aznar re-emerged from the passenger seat of the jeep. 'Brigada, Comandante Besteiro has radioed for us to return to Bilbao, at once.'

'*Sí*, Capitán.' Ramos stared at Fernando, a pit bull deprived of its bone.

'That's an order, Brigada,' said Aznar.

Ramos turned and stalked back to the jeep. It was only after the engine started that Fernando finally exhaled. They watched the jeep drive off. Blanca turned to Fernando, her face filled with terror.

'I was right, they're searching for Felipe.' Her voice began to tremor. 'If they think he bombed those people, they won't arrest him – they'll kill him.'

'They don't know who he is,' said Fernando.

'But they know his face; how long until they have a name to match? I have to find him before they do.'

Fernando nodded westward. 'Pamplona is still twenty kilometres away. If we hurry, we'll still reach it tonight, ready for your meeting with ATA tomorrow.'

They followed the road back toward the Camino, and Fernando's mind returned to their encounter with the Guardia Civil. The recognition in Ramos' eyes had chilled him. Fernando's past had never felt so close.

'My father oversees more than two-thirds of Spain's rail network.' Aznar leaned back in the seat and smoked his cigarette. 'He's had a personal audience with El Caudillo.'

Ramos kept his eyes on the road. They'd only been driving for fifteen minutes, and the capitán was already talking about his family. Names were important in today's Guardia Civil, especially for officers. Names led to status, and status led to promotion. It was Ramos' first look at his new commanding officer. Already a capitán at twenty-five, Aznar's trajectory was steep. But to make comandante, an officer must eventually leave the comforts of Madrid and serve on the frontline. Ambition had lured Aznar to Bilbao.

'And you? How long have you been in the Guardia Civil, Ramos?'

'Eighteen years in total, *señor* – the first two in the army.'

'Eighteen years?' Aznar shook his head in awe. 'I was only a boy. Things were different then, no?'

'*Sí.*'

'Some of the other officers in the stations have told me about your service in the war. You hunted out the traitors and deserters, no?'

'I did whatever was asked.'

'The stories I've heard are…'

'Just stories, Capitán. You should pay them no mind.'

'*Sí,* of course.' He blushed. 'So, what made you enlist?'

'There were no other jobs; the Republicans had ground our economy to a halt. Then, one day, a truck stopped in our village and a man in uniform offered bread and soup to any man willing to serve. My wife and daughter hadn't eaten in two days, so I held out my bowl with the rest of the men.'

'*Sí,* and because of men like you, Spain is respected again. The Americans now see how useful we are against the Soviets. Next year we'll join the United Nations – the European Council will surely follow. Comandante Besteiro calls it a new Spain.'

'*Sí,* I've heard the comandante speak of progress. People seem eager to forget the war.'

'Not forget – but it's time to focus on the future, rather than dwelling on our past.'

'Time stands still out here, Capitán.' Ramos nodded to the steep hills on both sides of the winding road. 'These villagers do not care about your new Spain. They don't see themselves as Spanish; they have their own language and traditions. They don't want progress. They want things to return to how they were, and they'll stop at nothing to achieve it. They proved this in Bilbao. You say the war is over?' Ramos scoffed. 'Not out here.'

Ramos pulled off the highway and navigated them through the city's bustling streets. It wasn't until they'd arrived at the station that Aznar noticed their change of destination.

'This isn't Bilbao. Where are we?'

'Pamplona.' Ramos got out of the jeep and put on his *tricornio.*

'Pamplona?' Aznar scrambled out of the car and hurried after Ramos. 'But the comandante's orders were for us to return to Bilbao.'

Ramos stopped at the stairs leading up to the station. 'No, his orders were for us to find the Bilbao bombers.'

'I don't understand. You suspect the bombers are here in Pamplona?'

'Not yet, but they'll likely arrive tonight or tomorrow.'

A pause while Aznar caught up.

'The pilgrims? You suspect the three Andalusians are somehow linked to ATA?'

'Two Andalusians – the girl was Basque. Her accent alone should have told you that.'

The young officer stuttered to recover. 'Just because she's Basque, it doesn't prove she's ATA.'

'*Sí*, but her lies prove she has something to hide. She also matches the description of the girl seen with Ramon Ochoa in Hernani.'

'But that was days ago. Besides, if it's really the same girl, where is Ochoa?'

'I don't know, but the girl is somehow connected to Vasquez. I'm certain of it.'

'We should brief the comandante.'

'Brief him on how you allowed the Bilbao bombers to slip through your fingers, Capitán?'

Aznar's cheeks burned red, and he pointed to the jeep. 'Let's drive back and arrest them now.'

Ramos slid a cigarette into his mouth and lit it. 'Have you ever worked on a farm, Capitán?'

'No.'

'When I was a boy, I spent my summers at my grandmother's farm. One year, she handed me a machete and told me to clear a field of heather. While clearing the undergrowth, I discovered a viper. I'd never seen a snake so beautiful – it had a dark-brown stripe running down its centre, with patches like black opals on either side. Rather than kill it, I pushed it into a bucket and brought it back to the house.'

Ramos took a deep drag of his cigarette and exhaled.

'I realised I must eventually feed it. The surrounding fields were crawling with mice, but they were difficult to catch. So one night, I placed the bucket with the snake in the middle of the field and dropped a piece of cheese into it. Next, I built a little wooden trap over the bucket, so when a mouse crawled up the ramp for the cheese the trap would send it down to the snake.'

'Did it work?'

'The following morning, the snake was dead.'

'How come?'

'Because mice are attracted to the sound of other mice in distress. After the first mouse fell into the bucket, its squeaks and squeals attracted all the other mice from the surrounding fields. One by one, they climbed up the ramp and fell into the bucket.' Ramos took his final drag of the cigarette and tossed the butt onto the ground.

'And the viper, starved of food for days, ate so many mice that it exploded.' Ramos smiled at Aznar's repulsed face. 'So that is what we will do with ATA. Rather than catch one mouse, we will use the girl to catch them all.'

CHAPTER 7

They woke early and left the village of Irotz before it was light. The Spaniards had hoped to reach Pamplona the previous evening, but Tom had been in too much pain. He'd inspected his feet in the dim light of the barn's kerosene lantern and discovered several blisters on the ball of his right foot, as well as emerging ones on his left. His hopes of them improving by the morning had been mislaid. Every step felt like fire.

After half an hour of walking, the sun had risen fully behind them, and the surrounding woodlands were bathed in a soft peach glow. Tom couldn't remember the last London sunrise he'd seen. He was awake early enough, but was usually too busy scanning his work emails on his phone, sandwiched between others doing the same: a tin of pin-striped sardines rumbling beneath London. He winced and waddled behind the others, his left foot now hurting more than his right. He was relieved to see the others stop by a bridge.

'This the outskirts of Pamplona,' said Blanca. 'There will be more people; keep close.'

Across the river, farmland surrendered to suburbia, and any hope that Tom wasn't trapped in the 1950s dissolved: men in suits and hats smoked cigarettes and read newspapers in the street; a queue of women, with their hair pinned beneath hats, waited to use a payphone; Spanish crooning wafted from a gramophone perched outside a bar. When the pilgrims stopped at an intersection, a vintage, electric-blue Aston Martin road-tourer cruised past them, gleaming as if it had driven straight out of the factory. This was not 2010.

They continued toward the city, and the streets became increasingly crowded. A group of teenage boys ahead of them laughed and clapped. Each was dressed in white, with a red sash tied around their waists or necks. Tom looked around and noticed more boys dressed similarly.

'Why is everyone dressed like that?' he asked Blanca.

'They wear this for the San Fermín fiesta – is tradition.'

A group of Tom's university friends had gone to the running of the bulls a few years ago, but he was certain the festival occurred in July, not June. The pilgrims walked over a stone bridge and through a manicured garden. More of the antique cars sparkled past them, their drivers merrily honking their horns and waving red scarves out of their windows. Pablo pointed across the road to a ramp leading up to a medieval gate.

'Pamplona.'

The city's lowered drawbridge carried them across a grassy ditch, which must have once been a moat. A banner hung from the gate's ramparts, similar to the Spanish flag Ana had pinned to the wall of their study in London. It had the same red-and-yellow stripes, but a menacing black eagle had replaced the coat of arms. Tom stayed close to the others as they emerged into the city's old quarter. A sharp whistle pierced the noise. A teenage boy clung halfway up a lamppost and waved them over. When they approached, he climbed down. Grimier than a chimney sweep, the boy handed Blanca a note before disappearing into the crowd. She unfolded the letter and read it.

'What is it?' asked Tom.

'Is from Vasquez. He say the Guardia Civil is searching the city for a Basque girl travelling with two Andalusians and an Englishman.' She looked up nervously before continuing. 'Vasquez has moved the meeting. He wants to meet tomorrow, at noon, in a village called Eunate. He say he has urgent news about my family.'

Blanca spoke with the Spaniards before turning back to Tom.

'You stay with the Spaniards. They will get you out of the city and safe.'

'What about you?'

'I find my own way, now.' If she was scared, she didn't show it. 'Sorry to involve you in this, Thomas – truly.'

'I hope you find your brother.'

'*Gracias.*' She smiled, and for that brief moment looked like any ordinary nineteen-year-old girl. '*Buen Camino.*' She turned and walked back the way they'd come, swallowed by the oncoming wave of locals.

Pablo tapped Tom's shoulder.

'*Vamos.*'

Tom followed the Andalusians deeper into the city.

The shopfronts were boarded up with plywood, and the people in the balconies above looked down with anticipation. Anticipating what? The running of the bulls should be weeks away. Perhaps this was another festival. Somewhere a clocktower tolled, sending the masses of young men around them into raptures. Fernando looked uneasy.

'*Rápido, rápido.*'

More boys entered the street, their youthful bodies wedging between Tom and the Andalusians. The crowd pushed forward, squeezing people between a tall building and a raised platform. Families leaned over a railing above and clapped wildly. Tom desperately tried to keep sight of Pablo and Fernando, but the stretch of white-and-red between them increased. Fernando turned and yelled something. He pointed to a flight of stairs leading to the church above.

'*Allí, allí,*' Pablo yelled, his ever-smiling face looking unusually panicked. '*Rápido,* Thomas.'

Tom fought his way through the crowd toward the stairs. 'Excuse me, *perdone, perdone.*'

The church bells tolled – eight strikes. An ominous hush swept over the street. Suddenly, a high-pitched scream ripped through the silence. A dark projectile launched into the sky and froze in mid air before exploding in a shower of sparks. Cheers erupted from the balconies above, and the boys around Tom slowly edged backward – toward the direction he'd just walked from. Tom heard a deep rumbling, accompanied by the clanging of distant bells. He looked at Pablo, still wrestling his way toward the stairs.

'Pablo? What's going on?'

The crowd was retreating faster now; some of the younger boys had begun to run. Men who'd been singing and dancing moments earlier looked frightened. The cobblestones under Tom's feet began to tremble. Waves of oncoming bodies repelled him further from the stairs. Fernando moved toward Tom, the Spaniard's face filled with alarm. He pointed to the road ahead of him, toward the growing rumble.

'¡*Toros*! ¡*Toros*! ¡*Toros*!'

It was one of the few Spanish words Tom understood. It meant 'bulls'.

The street reeked of fear and alcohol. Fernando had tried to get them through the city before eight o'clock, but they hadn't made it. The tide of people had been too strong, sweeping them down Calle Carmen and into the worst possible position: the beginning of the *encierro*.

Fiesta de San Fermín – and its running of the bulls – wasn't supposed to start for another month, but a local walking near them on their entry into the city had told them the fiesta had been moved forward for the Xacobeo.

'There's going to be bulls on these damn streets all month, man.'

The *chupinazo* rocket fizzed up into the sky and crackled into a shower of sparks – the bulls were loose. There would be twelve in total: six steer and six bulls. The bells hanging around the necks of the lighter-coloured steers made them easier to hear and elude, but the bulls were the real danger. They weighed six hundred kilograms each and could run as fast as a horse. These were the ones who killed. Fernando looked for a sign of escape and spotted some stairs leading to the balconies above.

'Pablo, get to the stairs.'

The boy nodded, and Fernando searched the sea of red-and-white for the Englishman.

'Thomas! Thomas!'

He pointed to the stairs, and Thomas seemed to understand, but the receding crowd began sucking him back down Calle de Santo Domingo. Fernando caught his eye, desperate to tell him what was coming.

'Bulls! Bulls! Bulls!'

The high-pitched hiss of the second firecracker announced the animals had left the corrals and headed toward them. Fernando fought through the crowd and reached for the Englishman. Their fingers briefly touched before a swell of bodies swept Thomas further down the street. Fernando heard the bells clanging and turned just in time to avoid a pair of steers thundering past. He glimpsed Thomas, now thirty metres away, running with a group of boys in the middle of the road. Fernando sprinted after him. Screams rang out from behind, and a black shadow burst through a group of locals and past him. The heaving bull was transfixed on a clump of runners ahead – Thomas was among them.

'Get to the side!' screamed Fernando. 'Against the walls!'

The bull charged toward the group, lowering its head and flinging one of the local runners against the wall like a bag of kindling. The sound of fractured bones was followed by a gasp from the watching crowd above. The bull continued past Thomas in pursuit of a screaming boy ahead. Fernando ran down Calle de Santo Domingo and into the Plaza Consistorial, where a second bull was carving a path through the crowd like a hot knife through butter. Fernando zig-zagged around the fallen bodies and past the town hall. He surveyed the chaos before him and saw Thomas standing in the far corner of the sharp bend leading into Calle de la Estafeta. Fernando sprinted toward him.

'Don't stop,' roared Fernando. 'Keep running!'

He grabbed a fistful of the Englishman's jacket and slung him out of the corner. They ran down Calle de la Estafeta, and there was a deafening sound of a collision behind them. Fernando glanced back. One of the bulls must have run wide on the bend; its horns had splintered the plyboard barricading where Thomas had stood moments earlier. Fernando gripped the back of Thomas' jacket.

'Hurry.'

The screams of runners behind them were followed by the sickened groans from the balconies above. Eventually, they reached the final stretch into Pamplona's famed bullring, the Plaza de Toros. Inside the arena, pandemonium reigned: hundreds of delirious young men dodged and danced around the bulls, each thinking they were Belmonte himself.

'There.' Fernando pointed to a gate on the other side of the bullring and led Thomas past the crowd of drunken matadors. They were nearly there when Thomas cried out.

'Fernando!'

He followed the Englishman's gaze to a colossal black bull charging toward him, its head lowered in preparation to strike. With no time to dodge, Fernando braced for impact. But rather than being hit from the front, he was knocked over from behind. He crashed into the arena's yellow sand and rolled over just in time to see the bull's right horn pierce Thomas' shoulder. The beast lifted the Englishman into the air like a wet rag before chasing its next target.

Fernando scrambled over to Thomas, who was lying face-down on the blood-soaked sand.

CHAPTER 8

'Hello?'

Her voice startled Tom. It was close, yet somehow distant. Everything was dark, or were his eyes closed? He tried to open them, but his eyelids felt like suitcases. He waited for her to speak again, wondering if he'd imagined her.

'Hello, can you hear me?'

There she was again – her voice was so familiar, but he couldn't attach it to a face.

'Are you awake?' she asked. 'Can you hear me?'

He felt a hand on his arm – the skin was soft and warm. His eyes flickered open, just long enough to glimpse a faceless silhouette hovering over him.

'It's okay,' she said. 'It's over. You're safe now.'

She placed her hand on his forehead, and Tom suddenly realised where he was.

'Ana?' He tried to open his eyes again, desperately resisting the blinding sunlight behind her. 'Ana?'

He reached out to her, and she took his hand and leaned forward. Ana came into focus: her light-brown eyes, a dark curl of her hair falling across her forehead, the freckle on her left eyelid. It was her; it was Ana.

'You'll never believe what I just dreamed.' He wasn't sure if he'd said the words aloud or simply thought them. He tried to sit up, but fatigue pushed him back down. 'I met Tito in Spain.' He had to tell her everything before he forgot it. 'And he made me walk to Santiago – except it was in the past. I travelled back in time, and I met some Spaniards named Fernando and Pablo.'

He tried to sit up again, but Ana gently guided him down.

'You need to rest, Thomas.'

He wanted to argue, but his head fell deeper into the pillow. He always forgot his dreams; he didn't want to lose the details of this one. He'd tell her everything when he woke. The important thing was he was home, and it had all been a dream after all.

'Will he be alright?'

The nurse stood up from Thomas, who was still unconscious on the fold-out bed. '*Sí*, he'll survive, but he lost a lot of blood.'

The hospital was small. When Fernando had arrived with the unconscious Englishman over his shoulder, every bed had contained some other blood-soaked casualty from the bull-run. The nurses had ushered Fernando upstairs into an old office doubling as a storeroom – a desk stood in the corner, covered in bottles of bleach and piles of sheets. The nurses had dragged a temporary bed into the room.

'Your friend was lucky; it was a clean wound.' The nurse pointed to Thomas' shoulder. 'The bull's horn missed the joint.'

The woman was in her late twenties. She was shapeless underneath the multiple flowing layers of her pale-blue uniform and the navy-coloured shawl she wore over it. Her dark hair was tied beneath a bonnet, and her eyes were hazel.

'Will he need a doctor?' asked Fernando.

'Why? Do you doubt I can care for him?'

'No, I…' Fernando felt as if he were in school again.

'A doctor will check him before he can be discharged. Until then, your friend needs rest.' She pointed to Thomas' blood-soaked jacket on the floor. 'You did this?'

'*Sí.*' Fernando had tied it tightly around Thomas' arm to stem the flow of blood.

'You might have saved his arm. Are you a soldier?'

'No – a fisherman.'

Her eyebrows lifted with surprise. 'My father is a fisherman, but I've never seen him apply a tourniquet to a fish.'

'There can't be many fishermen in Pamplona. The Bay of Biscay is one hundred kilometres away, no?'

'I'm from Valencia.'

'Valencia? Why are you here then?'

She nodded to Thomas. 'Because of fools like him. The hostess at my hospice said the hospital was overwhelmed.'

'You didn't travel to San Fermín for the bullfights?'

'Fights?' She spat the word out like poison. 'Only when the bull is given a sword will I call it a fight. Until then, it's a barbaric slaughter.'

'The *encierro* is tradition in Pamplona.'

'Since when did cruelty become a tradition? There's nothing noble about torturing innocent animals.'

'The meat from the bulls is used to feed the poor.'

'Then feed the poor; you needn't parade the bulls through the streets before slaughtering them.' She folded her arms across her chest. 'Do you have any idea how terrified those poor animals are? And don't tell me this is for the locals – half the people here aren't from Pamplona.' Her eyes suddenly narrowed. 'Where are you from? You said yourself, there are no fishermen in Pamplona.'

'Huelva.'

She rolled her eyes. 'Ah, an Andalusian. Why am I not surprised?'

Fernando felt a match flare within him. 'Why do you say that?'

'Andalusians are obsessed with murdering bulls. You travelled across Spain to prove you are a man too, no?'

'No.' He took the scallop shell hanging around his neck from beneath his shirt. 'We're pilgrims travelling to Santiago.'

'And I suppose it was merely luck you passed through Pamplona during San Fermín?'

Fernando pointed to Thomas. 'Given he nearly died, I would say it was unlucky, no?'

She went to speak and paused. When the words finally came, her tone had cooled.

'Well, you might have told me you were pilgrims

earlier. I'm travelling to Santiago as well.'

'You're walking the Camino?'

'Not walking, driving. I'm volunteering at an orphanage in Santiago for the remainder of the summer. I'm travelling with a priest who is delivering sermons along the Camino.'

'You're his nurse?'

'No, his interpreter. He's English.'

'Ana?' Thomas' mumblings interrupted them. 'Ana, wait.'

The nurse held her palm against his forehead. 'The morphine will ease his pain, but he'll remain drowsy. He might say nonsensical things when he wakes.'

'He does that already.'

The girl frowned. 'He's English, no?'

'*Sí.*'

'Well, from what I've seen so far, all Englishmen are a little crazy. Even their priests.' She buttoned her lips to trap any further blasphemy. 'Who is Ana, anyway? His wife?'

'I don't know. I only met him on the Camino two days ago.'

'Yet you carried him to the hospital?'

'Well, if it wasn't for him, it would be me lying on that bed.'

She seemed to read his face as if deciding whether to believe him.

'Well, there are plenty of other crazy men downstairs to tend to,' she eventually said, heading to the door.

'May I stay here with him?'

'Suit yourself.'

'*Gracias*, Sister.'

'Sofia.'

'Pardon?'

She stopped at the door and looked over her shoulder. 'My name is Sofia. "Sister" makes me sound like a nun.'

'I'm Fernando.'

'I know.' She nodded toward Thomas. 'He muttered something about two Spaniards from the Camino: Pablo and Fernando. You don't look like a Pablo.' She smiled briefly before closing the door behind her.

Fernando returned his attention to Thomas. He couldn't leave the unconscious Englishman alone in the hospital, but he needed to continue his journey. He picked up Thomas' bag and pulled out his wallet. He thumbed through the slippery paper the Englishman had claimed as futuristic money before studying a plastic card with a long number embossed across it. There was another piece of cardboard with several holes punched through it and a tiny drawing of a coffee cup. Suddenly, the door to the room swung open, and Sofia reappeared.

'Hide,' she hissed.

'What?'

Fernando heard heavy footsteps in the hallway. He slid under the bed and watched two pairs of black leather boots enter the room. He held his breath.

'We have orders to arrest this Englishman,' said a man's voice, his legs dressed in the dark-green trousers of the Guardia Civil.

'This man's French, not English,' said Sofia.

'You're certain?'

'Of course I am. He was speaking to me in French when they admitted him.'

A pause.

'Wake him,' said the voice of the second guard. 'We need to question him.'

'I can't, he's sedated. You're welcome to question him when he wakes. Do either of you speak French?'

Another pause.

'Your matron told us he was English and was carried here by an Andalusian,' said the first voice.

'Our matron is old and easily confused. The men you are talking about were taken to the auxiliary ward.'

'The auxiliary ward?'

'*Sí*, it's downstairs. Let me show you.'

Sofia's feet walked to the door, but the guards' boots remained steadfast.

'What if he wakes? One of us should remain here.'

'He'll be asleep for at least another hour, maybe two,' replied Sofia.

The boots reluctantly followed Sofia to the door.

'Lock the door after us,' commanded one of the soldiers.

'I told you, he won't wake.'

'It's not a choice, Sister.'

Fernando heard the door close behind them, followed by the turning of the lock. He waited for their voices and footsteps to fade down the hall before sliding out from under the bed.

'Thomas, wake up.' He shook the Englishman's uninjured shoulder. 'Quickly!'

Thomas mumbled something in English and rolled onto his other side. Fernando heaved him into a seated position on the bed and swung the Englishman's legs down to the floor.

'We're in danger, do you understand? Danger. Put

your shoes on.'

Sofia had sliced off Thomas' blood-soaked shirt when she'd treated his shoulder. Fernando pulled out the spare shirt from his own bag and handed it to Thomas.

'Put this on.'

Fernando crept over to the door and put his ear against it. Hearing nothing, he twisted the doorknob – it was definitely locked. He raced to the windows on the opposite side of the room and looked down to the alley below. They'd break their legs if they jumped. He then noticed a pipe running from the building's gutter to the ground. Climbing down it was their only chance of escape. He looked back to see if Thomas was ready.

'*Ay Dios mío.*'

The Englishman was fast asleep again, with one boot on his foot and the other still in his hand. Fernando jammed the remaining shoe on Thomas' foot and pulled the shirt onto him. It was snug, but it would do.

'Come on, wake up, Thomas.'

He didn't stir. Fernando picked up a vase from the desk and threw the dead flowers in it to the floor. He emptied the vase's murky water over Thomas' head.

'*Farc.*'

The Englishman lurched forward, and Fernando yanked him from the bed. He slung their bags over his shoulders and led Thomas to the window.

'You see this?' He pointed to the gutter's downpipe. 'We need to climb down it.'

Thomas looked down to the alley and blankly back to Fernando.

'I'll go first,' said Fernando. 'You watch me.' He climbed out of the window and gripped the pipe, wedding his foot to the bracket connecting to the wall. 'You see? Just like this.' He carefully climbed down to the alley, jumping the last five feet to the ground. He looked up to Thomas. 'Okay, now your turn.'

The Englishman looked as if he was about to vomit. He shouted something down in English, and Fernando held his finger to his mouth.

'Quiet,' he hissed. 'The Guardia Civil are searching for us. Climb down.'

'Ana?'

'If you climb down, we'll find Ana.'

Repeating the girl's name seemed to work. Thomas lifted his leg over the windowsill and leaned out to grip the pipe.

'Good. Now place your foot onto the bracket.'

The Englishman swung his body out of the window and tried to rest his foot on the pipe, but slipped. He yelped as he slid down the tube, and Fernando lunged forward to catch him. Thomas crashed onto Fernando and the pair collapsed into a heap on the ground.

'Okay, okay, let's go,' Fernando groaned as he climbed out from beneath Thomas.

He helped the Englishman to his feet, and they walked up the alley and away from the hospital. They arrived at a square filled with locals enjoying the day's last hour of sunshine. Fernando scanned the crowd for the dark-green uniforms of the Guardia Civil.

A hand gripped his shoulder.

'Fernando.'

He turned to discover Blanca, now dressed in the same white-and-red clothing worn by the rest of the city.

'What are you doing here?' he asked. 'I thought you'd

left for your meeting with Vasquez.'

'The Guardia Civil has locked down the city. They're searching for us.'

'*Sí*, they came to the hospital too. We must find Pablo.'

'He's not with you?'

'No, we were separated during the bull-run.'

'That was hours ago; he could be anywhere.'

A group of locals in the square had linked their arms around one another and begun to sing.

'Where is the busiest part of Pamplona during San Fermín?' asked Fernando.

Blanca shrugged. 'Probably the Plaza del Castillo. Why?'

'Because I think I know where Pablo is.'

Tom's dream turned ever more surreal. After escaping a hospital, Fernando and he had followed Blanca through the crowded streets of Pamplona to a bar-lined square. His shoulder throbbed and he rubbed it through an unfamiliar shirt that didn't appear to be sweat-proof. Despite this, he felt inexplicably elated. He followed the Spaniards through the revellers toward a bar with music wafting from it. Blanca swiped an armful of unattended beer bottles and offered them to Tom and Fernando.

'I'm fine,' said Tom.

She pressed the bottle firmly into his hand. 'We must blend in.' She took the red bandanna from her neck and tied it around his forehead. '*Perfecto.*'

Inside the bar the crowd clapped and cheered a man atop a table. He had his head thrown back and his mouth opened wide as a second man emptied a bottle of gin down it. When the last drop of liquor had disappeared, the crowd erupted.

'¡*Olé*.'

The man on the table stood upright and basked in the drunken applause. Tom immediately recognised him.

'Pablo!' He waved up at the Spaniard, who squinted toward his name.

'¡*Oye* – Thomas! ¡*Mis amigos!*

The sea of drunks parted and Pablo leaped down and ran toward the three of them. The Spaniards hugged and spoke excitedly amongst themselves while Tom scanned the bar for Ana. Where had she gone?

Pablo eventually turned admiringly toward Tom and prodded his aching shoulder. The bearded Spaniard lifted a bottle of wine into the air and addressed the crowd.

'*Todos, propongo un brindis...*' Pablo waved toward Tom as if unveiling a new car. '¡*El matador de Londres!*

'¡*El matador de Londres!* echoed the crowd before each took a healthy slug of whatever drink they held in their hand.

While Fernando and Pablo spoke, Blanca turned to Tom.

'Pablo say he has friends who will help us escape the city.'

The four of them left the bar and crossed the plaza to a more subdued tavern. A table of young men drank tall, frosted glasses of beer; a pile of enormous papier-mâché heads lay on the ground beside their table. The men welcomed Pablo with clinks of their glasses and warm embraces.

'Are these friends of his from Granada?' Tom whispered to Blanca.

'No, he only meet today.' She pointed to the heads on the floor. 'These are called "Los Cabezudos de Pamplona" and are very famous in San Fermín. Every morning, these men wear the paper heads in the parade. Is great honour.' She nodded to one of the heads, a distinguished-looking man with a moustache. 'This is Concejal, you call him Councillor, no? The one with beard is the Mayor, and lady with grey hair is Abuela.'

'Grandmother?'

'*Sí.*'

Tom pointed to the last two heads. 'Those ones look Asian.'

'*Sí*, they are the Japanese heads.'

'Why are they Japanese?'

She shrugged. 'Is tradition.'

A young man wearing a beret stood up from the table and shook Pablo's and Fernando's hands. Two other men from the table rose and lifted the moustachioed head of the Councillor toward Tom.

'What's happening?'

They placed the head upon his shoulders. He peered through a thin slit in the Councillor's mouth and watched the other men set the Mayor's head on Blanca while Fernando and Pablo were each given a Japanese mask to wear. The young local removed his beret and lifted Abuela's head onto his shoulders.

'*Vamos,*' said the grandmother, waving them out of the tavern and into the plaza. The waiting crowd applauded them. As the odd procession of alien heads bobbled across the plaza, drunken locals fell in behind them, singing and dancing merrily. Tom swayed under the mask's weight. By the time they reached the city gates, Los Cabezudos de Pamplona had attracted a long tail of rowdy followers. The Guardia Civil officers at the city's gates looked overwhelmed and simply waved the surreal convoy through.

The road out of the city soon turned to dirt; Tom spied a scallop shell through the slit of his mask. The pilgrims had somehow found their way back to the Camino. Tom concentrated on remembering every minute detail; he couldn't wait to tell Ana all about his impossible dream when he woke. The round, wobbling head of the Concejal hid a smile that stretched from ear to ear.

CHAPTER 9

The cocking of a nearby rooster announced a new day. Fernando looked around the barn and saw Pablo and Thomas asleep on opposite corners of the floor. Their *cabezudos* grinned from a wall, still proud of the role they'd played in the pilgrims' escape the previous night. Fernando got dressed quietly and walked out of the barn. Blanca sat outside on a tree stump, lacing up her boots.

'*Buenos días*,' said Fernando.

'*Buenos días.*'

The sun had woken too, its first rays casting the surrounding paddock into a purple haze.

'You woke early,' he said.

'*Sí*, I can't be late meeting Vasquez.'

'The meeting is at noon, no? The locals said Eunate is only three hours' walk from here. If you wait for us, we'll walk with you.'

'Our deal was to walk to Pamplona together, no further.'

'*Sí*, but it's on our way.'

Her eyes lifted from her boots; she looked tempted to accept. 'No need.'

He sat on a log opposite her. 'What will you say when Vasquez asks where Ramon is?'

'That Ramon suspected the Guardia Civil were searching for us in Pamplona and he decided we should split up.'

'What if someone has found the body?'

'There was nothing in the newspapers, and the Guardia Civil said nothing of a body when they questioned us. You hid it well.'

'When Ramon never turns up, Vasquez will eventually suspect you.'

'Maybe – but I'll blame it on the Guardia Civil. It will be no different to what they did to my father. Besides, Felipe and I will be far away by the time Vasquez comes after us.' The crack in her voice betrayed her confidence.

'It's a dangerous game,' said Fernando. 'You don't have to go through with this.'

'How else can I save Felipe?'

Fernando trod carefully. 'Have you considered your brother doesn't want to be saved?'

'Felipe wants Basque Independence – we all do – but he's not a murderer.' Her green eyes shimmered. 'If he was in Bilbao during the bombing, it's only because Vasquez misled him.'

'Let us walk with you to Eunate – just to ensure Vasquez arrives.'

She hesitated. 'Then, you'll leave?'

He nodded, and the girl looked satisfied with their revised deal.

A screen door of the nearby farmhouse banged open, and a middle-aged woman in a fluffy housecoat emerged. She carried a steaming pot across the paddock toward them.

'*Buenos días*, pilgrims.' She rested the pot by their feet and handed some bowls to Fernando. 'I have brought you porridge. The mornings in Navarra are cold, even in June.'

'*Gracias, señora.*' Fernando handed a bowl to Blanca. 'And thank you for allowing us to sleep in your barn last night.'

'As if I had a choice. I wake up, and my drunken son tells me there are four pilgrims in the barn – what am I supposed to do? Refuse?' She tutted. 'I'll be standing before Saint Peter soon enough; perhaps offering porridge and shelter to some pilgrims might be enough for him to send me up the stairs, not down them.' She turned and trudged back toward the farmhouse, calling back over her shoulder. 'When you reach Santiago, remember to tell Saint James that Maria Lopez de Morentin from Cizur Menor fed you.'

Fernando and Blanca ate their breakfast in silence. Eventually, Pablo staggered from the barn and collapsed on the ground next to them.

'I feel dead.'

'If we hadn't found you, you might have been.' Fernando offered him a bowl. 'Have some porridge.'

'Porridge?' The boy gagged. 'I want fried eggs and ham on a toasted baguette, soaked in olive oil with salt sprinkled over it. I need something greasy to soak up all this alcohol.'

'More for us.'

Blanca dug her spoon back into the pot, but Pablo glumly claimed his bowl. Thomas walked out of the barn a few minutes later. Pablo pointed and laughed.

'He looks worse than I do.'

'*Sí*, but his wounds are not self-inflicted.' Blanca offered her seat on the stump to Thomas and served him a bowl of porridge, speaking to him in English.

'How is his shoulder?' Fernando asked her.

'He says it hurts, and he still wants to return to England. He says he will walk back to Pamplona.'

Pablo nearly choked on his porridge. 'He can't go back – the Guardia Civil are looking for him too.'

'Pablo's right,' said Fernando, turning to Blanca. 'What's the next biggest town on the Camino?'

'Logroño is three days from here, maybe two.'

'In La Rioja region, no? It's further from the border, so there will be less Guardia Civil. Tell Thomas that Pamplona isn't safe. We will walk him to Logroño and help him get home to England.'

'I'll try.'

After what sounded like a debate, Thomas eventually agreed. They finished their breakfasts and began their day's journey; the cloudless dawn signalled the beginning of another hot day.

After an hour of walking, the rocky ground rose steeply toward a mountain that filled the horizon. Their conversations were soon replaced by laboured breathing. After another twenty minutes of gruelling progress up the hill, Pablo wheezed something between breaths.

'*Jefe...* look.' The boy pointed to a long trail of walkers ahead of them. They soon caught up to the caravan of travellers, a family of ten. Some rode on horseback; the remainder walked. A middle-aged man, who might have been the family's father, tipped his hat toward them. '*Buen Camino.*'

'*Buen Camino,*' replied Pablo, pointing to the scallop shell on one of the horses' saddlebags. 'Travelling to Santiago?'

'God willing, although this is already our sixth day since starting in Roncesvalles.' He nodded to an elderly woman atop a donkey in front of them. 'My wife's mother is travelling with us.'

'If you didn't want me to come, you should have said so,' snapped the old woman.

The man smiled wearily. A little girl ran up the final stretch of the ascent and turned to face them, an enormous smile painted across her young face.

'Papa, I made it, I made it!'

'*Bravo,* Amelia, you've conquered the Alto del Perdón – the Mountain of Forgiveness.'

The little girl threw up her arms in triumph. 'Does this mean Mama forgives me for breaking her vase?'

The man's wife shook her head.

'You'll still need to pass through La Puerta Santa in Santiago, little one,' said the man.

The pilgrims were met at the summit by fierce winds. Fernando turned to the others. 'We'll rest here for a few minutes.'

Pablo trudged toward some shrubs on the far side of the peak; his miserable face had turned from green to grey. 'I need to get rid of last night's gin.'

Fernando looked back over their morning's route. The city of Pamplona now looked tiny, and the Pyrenees, which had taken days to conquer, were a misty blue outline painted on the horizon. Someone whistled, and Fernando turned to see a man standing on the mountain's apex.

'*Buenos días*,' called out the stranger, waving Fernando over. 'Could you lend me a hand, *amigo?*'

Fernando walked over. The man, who wore thick-rimmed spectacles, stood beside some form of scientific instrument atop a tripod. Another man sat on the ground beside him, scribbling into a notepad.

'*Gracias.*' The man with glasses smiled. 'Could you hold this steady while I take some readings? The wind is ferocious today.'

Fernando gripped the tripod and inspected the instrument upon it.

'What is this thing?'

'An anemometer,' said the man, pointing to a flickering dial on the device. 'It measures the speed of the wind.'

'You need a machine to tell you it's windy?'

'An anemometer tells me how much electricity could be generated from the wind. My name is Miguel, and this is my brother, Roberto. We're scientists from Pamplona.'

'Miguel is a scientist,' said the boy on the ground. 'I'm an artist.'

He held up his notebook; it bore a sketched profile of the family of pilgrims climbing up the mountain. Fernando noticed the drawing even included him and the others at the convoy's tail.

'*Sí*, if it were up to my brother, this mountaintop would bear one of his sculptures,' said Miguel, hunched over his machine.

'It's better than defiling it with your silly windmills.'

'Not windmills – turbines. And if we had enough of

them, we could someday power the entire city.'

Roberto stood up and closed his notebook. 'That's my brother – chasing tomorrow's wind.'

'It's better than stuck in today, lost in the stars.'

'Let's see, shall we?' Roberto turned to Fernando. 'Which would you rather have seen climbing the mountain, *amigo*: windmills for your free electricity or a statue to inspire you to continue your ascent?'

Both brothers stared at Fernando.

'Perhaps there's room on this mountain for both, no?'

Dissatisfied, Miguel hunched back over the anemometer. Roberto reopened his pad and scribbled a caption above his sketch.

'Where the path of the wind crosses that of the stars,' he murmured, signing it with a flourish.

There was another whistle; this time it was Blanca.

'Good luck to both of you,' said Fernando. '*Adiós*.' He returned to Blanca and Thomas. 'Where's Pablo?'

The boy emerged from the bushes; his face had returned to its usual hue. 'I'm here – physically and now, spiritually too. The gin was more enjoyable going in than coming out.'

They followed the Camino down the other side of the mountain, taking extra care upon the loose stones. It eventually levelled out and wound pleasantly through grassy paddocks and patches of almond trees. They arrived in Eunate a little before noon; a tree-lined avenue led to a squat building in the middle of a field.

'There's the church,' said Blanca.

The octagonal sandstone building resembled a military outpost more than a church. The simple iron crucifix atop the building's bell tower was the only clue it was a place of worship.

'Well, I suppose this is it,' said Blanca.

Fernando scanned the surrounding fields. A gentle breeze shook the poplar trees lining the road. The girl noticed his frown.

'What's wrong?' she asked.

Why would Vasquez choose this place? Pamplona had made sense: if the authorities had arrived, there'd been a maze of laneways to disappear down. But here, a church in an empty field, there was no escape.

'It doesn't feel right,' said Fernando. 'We're coming in with you.'

Blanca must have shared his doubts, for she didn't argue. They walked to the church, passing through the stone porch encircling it. The heavy wooden door was ajar, and Blanca gave one final look to Fernando before pushing it open. They followed her inside. The church was sparsely furnished: its eight stone walls and domed ceiling were bare. A simple white altar stood before half a dozen pews. Fingers of light poked through the window slits dotted around the walls. There was no one here yet.

'*¿Hola?*' Blanca's shaky voice circled the church's walls. They walked toward the altar.

'Perhaps we are early?' said Pablo.

The door clattered closed behind them; a young man, no older than twenty, stood against the wall behind it. He had a wispy beard and a flat cap crookedly pulled over his dark curls. He cradled an old bolt-action rifle – a Spanish Mauser – in his arms.

'Who are you?' asked Blanca. 'Where's Felipe?'

A door beside the altar opened, and two more boys with guns emerged from an antechamber. They were followed by a short, balding man with a beard and dark-rimmed spectacles.

'You must be Blanca,' said the man. 'Felipe has told me much about you. I am Vasquez.' He looked older than the photograph they'd been shown; his beard was now streaked with white and dark bags hung beneath his eyes. Vasquez walked over and kissed each of Blanca's cheeks before placing his hands on her shoulders. 'I feared the Guardia Civil captured you in Pamplona.'

She nodded toward Fernando and the others. 'They helped me escape.'

'*Gracias, amigo.*' Vasquez shook Fernando's hand; his grip was firm, but his hands felt smooth.

Blanca looked eagerly to the antechamber. 'Is Felipe here?'

'Come and sit, child.'

Vasquez led her to the first pew, and they sat.

'Has something happened to Felipe? Is he safe?'

Vasquez patted her arm reassuringly. '*Sí*, of course he is.'

'Can I see him?'

'Soon, I promise.' He smiled politely. 'But first, tell me: where is Ramon?'

The girl recited the story she'd rehearsed on Fernando earlier. Vasquez listened intently, only speaking when she had finished.

'So you haven't seen him since Pamplona?'

'No, not since yesterday,' said Blanca. 'I thought he would have found you. Do you think he was captured?'

'There's been no word of his arrest.'

'Perhaps he is lying low until the Guardia Civil leave Pamplona?'

Vasquez stroked his beard. '*Sí*, perhaps.'

'When can I see Felipe? Our mother is worried. The Guardia Civil came to our house. They accused Felipe of being involved in the Bilbao bombing.'

He peered over his glasses at her like a school principal. 'And you believe them, after everything they have done to your family?'

'The newspapers say it too.'

'The newspapers?' Vasquez scoffed. 'They are even worse – at least the Guardia Civil wear uniforms. The media disguise Franco's lies as news; they aim to turn us against one another.'

'So Felipe didn't murder those men?'

'Murder?' The word raised Vasquez to his feet. 'What we did in Bilbao wasn't murder, child – it was self-defence. These were not innocent civilians; they were invaders of our country – combatants in the war.'

'The reports said a woman and child were killed by the blast; they weren't soldiers.'

'Neither were you. When the Nationalists took your father, your mother was left to raise you and your brother alone.'

'So Felipe was there?' Blanca's voice threatened to crack.

'Felipe did his duty for his people,' said Vasquez. 'He would have made your father proud.'

'No, our father wanted Basque independence. Aberri Ta Askatasuna – ATA – stands for "Basque Homeland and Liberty".'

'ATA?' Vasquez snorted. 'True Basques laugh whenever they hear these words – *aberri* means "duck" in half our people's dialects.' He pointed to the boys behind him.

'These men and your brother are part of a new movement, one which Franco cannot ignore. Euskadi Ta Askatasuna.'

'ETA?'

Vasquez nodded proudly. 'ETA will not be so easily dismissed. It will become the axe that lops the head off the serpent of Spanish politics.'

Blanca's voice now trembled. 'When can I see Felipe?'

'Soon. But first, tell me... where is Ramon, really? My friends in the villages you passed through all saw you walking with two Andalusians and an Englishman.' Vasquez's eyes glanced toward Thomas before drilling into Blanca's. 'But no one has seen Ramon in days.'

Blanca's face drained of colour as Vasquez stepped toward her.

'What happened between Orisson and Roncesvalles?'

'What do you mean?'

Vasquez slapped her hard across the cheek, sending the girl to the floor. Fernando lunged forward, but the two gunmen lifted their rifles toward him. Blanca clutched her face, and Vasquez loomed over her.

'Don't you dare lie to me!' He hauled her up to her feet and wrapped his smooth fingers around her throat. 'Our man in Roncesvalles said Ramon wasn't with you when you arrived at the monastery. Ramon wasn't in any of the villages between there and here.' He tightened his grasp. 'What happened?'

'I told you, already... when we got to Pamplona... we saw a Guardia Civil patrol and...'

Vasquez squeezed her throat tighter.

'You're lying,' he hissed.

'Please... I... can't... breathe.'

'What did you do to Ramon? Is he dead?'

Blanca slapped at Vasquez's hand, but his grip stood firm. The girl's green irises rolled up to the ceiling as she started to suffocate.

'Let her go,' yelled Fernando.

He stepped forward, and the boys slid their fingers to their triggers.

'I killed Ramon, not her.'

Vasquez released his grip and Blanca collapsed to the ground, coughing and gasping for air. The Basque glared at Fernando.

'You? Why would you kill Ramon?'

'It was an accident. We were walking through the forest and discovered Ramon about to execute the Englishman.'

'Why would he do that?'

'Because he'd gone mad,' gasped Blanca from the church floor. 'Ramon thought he was a spy.'

'Shut your mouth.'

Vasquez kicked her in the ribs, and the girl cried out in pain. He leaned over her.

'You expect me to believe you, after all your lies? Is this why you sent me your little note? To summon me here and feed me your lies?' Vasquez pulled a pistol from his belt and pointed it at her.

'Wait,' shouted Fernando. 'What note?'

'The note she had her messenger boy deliver to my men; the note to lure me all the way out here.'

Blanca clambered to her knees. 'I never sent you a note.'

Vasquez pressed the gun against her forehead. 'Of course you did; it's right here.' He pulled a crumpled piece of brown paper from his pocket and threw it down to her.

She picked it up and read it; her eyes widened.

'I didn't write this.'

Vasquez's finger slid to the trigger. 'You've told your last lie, girl.'

'I swear to you, I didn't write it. It's identical to the note you sent me.' She frantically retrieved the message the boy had given her in Pamplona and held it out to Vasquez. 'You see? They're the same.'

He snatched the two notes and compared them. 'I never sent this.'

Fernando stepped forward. 'If neither of you sent them, who did?'

Vasquez shot a look at the boy at the back of the church. 'César, check outside.'

The boy in the crooked cap carefully opened the church door and peered out into the courtyard. He stepped out onto the gravel and swept his rifle across the surrounding paddocks before turning back to Vasquez and shrugging.

'It's all clear, boss.'

A faint crack of a whip turned the boy's head to the west. A second later, his head exploded against the church's door.

CHAPTER 10

'I said a warning shot,' hissed Aznar.

Ramos glided the crosshair of the rifle's scope past the blood-spattered door in search of another target. An unseen set of hands pulled the fallen gunman inside the church, and the door slammed shut. Ramos lifted his cheek from the rifle butt and pulled back its bolt. The expended shell casing tumbled into the dirt.

'*Sí*, and now they are warned, Capitán.' Ramos stood up and surveyed the church from the edge of the field. 'Let us capture the others.'

'The comandante's orders were to simply observe the Basques until reinforcements arrive.'

'By which time, the separatists will have escaped.' Ramos strode into the field toward the church. 'You saw it as well as I did, Capitán; the Basques are attempting to flee.'

The three men from the Pamplona station fell in step with Ramos. Their sergeant, a wiry man named Molina, had served under Ramos before transferring to Pamplona. The scar running down Molina's cheek was proof of the man's patriotism. The four of them fanned out into a straight line and advanced toward the church. Aznar trailed at a safe distance.

'How can you be sure they won't escape through the door to the south, Ramos?' called out the officer.

'Because the key to the antechamber door is secure within my pocket. They have nowhere to run.'

The church had been Molina's idea. He'd suggested the surrounding fields offered uninterrupted views of all the building's approaches, making it ideal for an ambush. The priest was young and eager to demonstrate his value, handing over the key without question. Some simple subterfuge with the two fake notes had been all that was needed. The mice had fallen into the trap.

A flash of light from one of the church's windows was followed by a crack and thump. A bullet thudded into the hip of the corporal to Ramos' left. The boy crashed into the dirt and screamed.

'Take cover,' roared Ramos.

Sargento Molina sprayed the church with a burst of gunfire while the others dragged the fallen officer to the safety of the church's stone porch. Ramos dropped his rifle and pulled his pistol from its holster. He peered out from behind one of the pillars and saw the church door swing open. A man ran out into the courtyard and fired a volley of shots. Bullets slammed into the stonework, and Ramos waited to hear the boy reload before swivelling out from behind the pillar. He fired twice: the first bullet missed, but the second flew through the boy's left eye. The separatist dropped instantly. Capitán Aznar crawled his way up to join them behind the stone balcony.

'Brigada Ramos, stand down, that's a direct order. We have them surrounded. We'll wait for the reinforcements to arrive.'

The church door slammed shut again, Ramos reloaded his pistol. He waited for Molina to take up his position on the other side of the doorway before arching his head up toward the church's nearest window slit.

'Enrico Vasquez, this is Brigada Ernesto Ramos of the Guardia Civil. We've already killed two of your men and we have you surrounded. You can either leave this place in handcuffs or in a box – the choice is yours.'

He strained to hear a response over the wind tearing across the field; none came.

'Don't be a fool, Vasquez. There's no reason you or the others should die. Come out without your weapons, and you'll live.' He scanned the windows for movement. 'If you haven't surrendered by the time I count to ten, my men and I will lob grenades through those windows and kill everyone inside it. Is that understood?'

More silence. Ramos nodded to one of Molina's corporals, who unfastened a grenade from his belt. Grenades weren't standard issue in the Guardia Civil anymore, but wars weren't won by those who operated within the confines of the law.

'*Uno…*'

'*Dos…*'

Pablo turned to Fernando, his face drained of all its colour.

'It's him – it's Ramos. He found us. What do we do?'

While Vasquez and his last remaining gunman tended to their fallen comrade, Fernando led Pablo and Thomas into the antechamber. Blanca stayed in the church, shell-shocked. The antechamber was simply furnished like the rest of the church: an oak desk stood against the wall with a bookshelf alongside it and a Moorish rug lay on the dusty floor.

'*Tres…*'

Fernando tried opening the door leading outside, but it was locked.

'We need to find the key. Check the desk, check the bookshelf – it must be here.'

Thomas must have understood, for he began rifling through each of the desk's drawers. Pablo tipped the Bibles from the bookcase and ran his hands over the shelves, feeling for the key. Fernando returned to the church. Ramos' raspy countdown continued from outside.

'*Cuatro…*'

Vasquez took the pistol from the boy's corpse and walked toward Fernando.

'Andalusian – we must work together to survive.' The Basque offered Fernando the pistol. 'We outnumber them; we can still fight our way out. Join us.'

'*Cinco…*'

Fernando shook his head. 'This is your fight, not ours,'

'This fight is all of ours. Until we join together and rise up, we'll never rid Spain of the fascists; we'll never be free.' Vasquez shook the gun. 'Take it. After we escape, I'll take the girl to her brother. You have my word.'

'*Seis…*'

The two men stared at each other.

'*Siete…*'

Vasquez spat at Fernando's feet. 'Fucking coward.' He levelled the pistol at Fernando's chest. 'Bootlickers like you are the real enemy.' His finger slid to the trigger. 'If I'm going to die, at least I'll know I took one more of Franco's servants with me.'

'*Ocho…*'

'Stop it,' screamed Blanca, tears trickling down her cheeks. 'If you swear to take me to Felipe, I'll help you. Don't kill them, please.'

Vasquez reluctantly lowered the gun and handed it to her. They joined the last remaining gunman by the church door.

'*Nueve…*'

Pablo emerged from the antechamber.

'*Jefe*, the key's not here – what do we do?'

Fernando got on his knees and clasped his hands in front of him. 'We pray.'

The gunman placed his hand on the door's handle and looked to Vasquez for his signal. The gun trembled in Blanca's hand.

'*Diez.*'

The door swung open.

'*Diez.*'

Ramos nodded to the corporal, who tugged the pin from the grenade and reached up toward the window. Suddenly, the church's door flung open, and gunfire erupted. Bullets thudded into the corporal's chest, hurling him backward. The grenade slipped from his fingers and dropped into the gravel.

'Down!' roared Ramos, diving back behind the porch's stone wall.

An explosion of dust, shrapnel and rock ripped apart the courtyard; for a moment, the world was fire and silence.

Ramos stumbled to his feet, his ears ringing. He saw the fallen soldier's charred remains through the clearing smoke. Then, somewhere, the soft popping of balloons. Ramos turned to see a Basque boy running across the courtyard. Molina shot him through the neck, and the boy collapsed into the dirt. The sergeant walked over to him and fired another bullet into the separatist's head; red mist sprayed over the earth. More muffled shots came from another of Molina's corporals. Ramos followed the boy's aim to two figures running through the fields toward the trees.

'Alive,' came Capitán Aznar's muffled voice. 'We need Vasquez alive.'

The corporal fired another round, clipping Vasquez's leg and sending the old Basque into the dirt. The soldier trained his rifle on the girl.

'Leave her,' screamed Aznar. 'Vasquez is the target.'

Ramos snatched the rifle from the corporal and brought it up to his shoulder. He trained the crosshair on the middle of the girl's back, took half a breath in and paused.

Bang.

The bullet missed. Ramos chased the girl with the gun's barrel, but the forest swallowed her. He tossed the rifle back to its owner.

'Your weapon isn't sighted, Corporal. Arrest Vasquez, and then bring me that girl.'

Aznar looked as if he might vomit.

'The girl isn't our priority.' His voice was barely audible. The young officer pointed to the wreckage around them. 'L-Look at what we've done.'

'You should be pleased, Capitán; you've brought the Bilbao bombers to justice. Perhaps you'll be next to have an audience with El Caudillo, not simply your father, no?'

Ramos met Molina at the open doorway of the church; both men drew their pistols.

'Pilgrims,' barked Ramos. 'Surrender now, or suffer the same fate as the Basques.'

Receiving no response, they entered the church. Their guns swept around each of the temple's eight walls, immediately resting on the closed door to the antechamber.

'There's nowhere to run,' said Ramos, stalking down the central aisle toward the door. 'No more countdowns – surrender now, or die.'

Ramos nodded to Molina, who kicked the door open. They burst into the room with their fingers on their triggers. The antechamber was empty too – the contents of its desk and bookcases upended over the floor. Ramos stepped over the Bibles and tried to open the door – it remained locked. He unlocked it with the key from his pocket and stepped outside; the fields behind the church lay empty.

'They must be hiding in the church,' he said, pointing Molina back inside. 'Find them.'

His order was met by the sound of arriving vehicles, their tyres skidding to a halt in the courtyard's gravel. Ramos and Molina walked back through the church. Swarms of guardsmen emerged from the vehicles, each of their sergeants barking orders. A tall man exited the passenger seat of the last jeep, the golden stars on his shoulders glinting in the sun.

'What the hell's going on here?' Comandante Besteiro's baritone voice demanded. 'Where in God's name is Aznar?'

'I'm here, *señor*.' Aznar ran over to the comandante and snapped a salute. Besteiro's dark eyes sliced ribbons off his young officer.

'I explicitly ordered you to wait for my arrival, Capitán.'

'*Sí, señor*, but my assessment of the situation was—'

'I don't give a damn about your assessment; you disobeyed a direct order.'

Ramos walked over to rescue the young officer. 'Comandante Besteiro, the Basques discovered our presence and launched an attack. If it were not for Capitán Aznar's ordering us to storm the church, I fear more of us would now be dead.'

Besteiro's eyes could hardly contain his rage. He'd never hidden his disdain for Ramos or the Spain he'd represented, but the comandante's hands were tied: men like Ramos remained necessary weapons. Besteiro turned to Aznar.

'Have Vasquez loaded into my jeep. We'll interrogate him in Bilbao while the rest of the men attend to the crime scene.'

'*Sí, señor.*' Aznar ran into the field, where one of the men was attending to Vasquez's wound.

Ramos turned toward the church.

'And where do you think you're going, Brigada Ramos?'

'To clear the church, Comandante.'

'Negative, you'll be driving us back to Bilbao. I'll need your statement.'

'My statement, *señor*?'

'For the investigation.' Besteiro nodded toward the bodies littering the courtyard. 'I'm well aware of your military record in the war, Ramos. I'll not tolerate the savage methods you employed in Castilla y León. Is that clear?' The comandante's tone suggested he didn't expect an answer. 'Things are not like they used to be, Ramos – this is a new Spain.'

Tom couldn't tell if they'd been walking for ten minutes or an hour. The last time he'd been somewhere so dark had been a 'dining in the dark' restaurant he'd taken Ana to in Soho. The only hint of light was the faint glow of the lantern carried by the man who'd saved them.

'Where's he taking us?' Tom whispered.

'*Silencio,*' hissed the stranger.

Tom had nearly screamed when the old man had appeared out of nowhere in the antechamber. Tom had initially thought the stranger was another of Vasquez's men. But the old man had looked more like a vagrant:

wrapped in a brown cloak, he wore a floppy wide-brimmed hat over long, matted hair. The stranger had pointed to the floor; the room's rug had been peeled back to reveal an open trapdoor. As gunfire and explosions erupted outside, the cloaked stranger had disappeared into the church and returned with Fernando and Pablo.

'Where's Blanca?' Tom had asked.

'*Silencio*,' the old man had whispered before ushering them all down the ladder and pulling a trapdoor closed behind them.

They'd stood in the darkness and listened to boots stalk across the floor above them. Tom had pressed his hands against his chest, fearing the thumping of his heart would betray them. The sound of vehicles had soon followed, and a platoon of feet had trampled over them. The old man had lit an oil lantern hanging from the wall and ushered them down a tunnel. They'd been following him ever since.

When the tunnel finally ended, the stranger passed the lantern to Fernando and climbed up a set of invisible footholds built into the wall. He inched open a hatch in the ceiling, and a needle of sunlight pierced the darkness. He then silently observed the surface for an entire minute before throwing open the hatch.

'*Vamos.*'

Tom followed the others out of the hole and found himself in a forest. The old man closed the metal trapdoor and kicked leaves across it before leading them away into the woods. Here in the dappled sunlight, Tom could now see the man was likely in his sixties. His rosy cheeks and pale-blue eyes, combined with his dishevelled clothing, gave him the appearance of a derelict Father Christmas.

Tom tapped Pablo on the shoulder and nodded to their guide.

'Who is he?'

'*No lo sé.*'

After an hour of slow, careful walking through the forest, they arrived at a path.

'*El Camino,*' said Pablo.

Voices approached, and the old man motioned for the pilgrims to hide behind a fallen tree. The man crept to the edge of the path and pulled back his cloak, revealing a scabbard hanging alongside his leg. Tom's eyes widened.

'Wait, is that a…'

The stranger slid an enormous broadsword from the scabbard, the type of weapon Tom had only ever seen in museums or films. Their guide gripped the hilt of the sword with both hands and waited for their pursuers to reveal themselves. The voices grew louder, but rather than a Guardia Civil patrol, a middle-aged man wearing an eye patch appeared. He was accompanied by a small boy. The cloaked stranger sheathed his blade and warmly greeted the man and his son. Tom followed the Andalusians out onto the Camino. He tried to follow the animated conversation around him, but the words flew by too quickly. The pilgrims and their saviour eventually followed the local man and his boy down the hill to their village. With the sun directly over them, the town's residents had withdrawn to their siestas; the cobbled streets were empty. As they passed a church, the man with the sword dropped a coin beside a man kneeling on the pavement. The beggar looked up.

'*Muchas gracias, Santo Gutierre. Dios te bendiga.*'

The cloaked stranger tapped his floppy brim and

continued on. Further along the cobble
nursed her baby on a balcony above. She le.
blew a kiss toward the pilgrims.

'*Buen Camino, Santo Gutierre.*'

The old man took off his hat and no   an
acknowledgement up to her, responding in a deep,
commanding voice, '*Buen Camino, señorita.*'

A bridge, its sandstone bricks glowing orange in the
afternoon heat, led them across a river and out of the town.
They walked up a gentle hill to a farmhouse on the other
riverbank. A woman with flour-dusted cheeks and rolled-
up sleeves welcomed them. She ushered everyone through
the house to a backyard that resembled a thriving farmer's
market. Juicy tomatoes glowed on their vines, while the
bushy leaves of lettuces, cabbages and carrots all competed
for space in the soil. An apple tree dominated the yard's
centre, its branches sagged with ripe fruit. A procession of
screaming children ran out of the house and toward the
silver-haired stranger.

'Santo Gutierre, Santo Gutierre!'

The children clung to his legs until their mother
shooed them back inside and steered the pilgrims to an
outdoor washbasin next to an outhouse. Tom and the
Andalusians took turns splashing their necks and faces
with the cold water. When they were finished, they sat
at a table on a wisteria-shaded terrace. Tom turned to the
Andalusians.

'Where's Blanca? Did the police arrest her and
Vasquez? Did she escape?'

The Spaniards shook their heads, either not
understanding the question or not knowing the answer.
Their hostess arrived with her children, each carrying

...tes of food. The table soon groaned beneath platters of bread, roasted peppers and stuffed olives. The man with the eye patch emerged from the house, joined by the bearded stranger who'd saved them. Everyone found a seat around the table and bowed their heads as the oldest child said grace. When she was finished, the children's father clapped his hands together.

'*Comamos.*'

The bread was still warm from the oven – but Tom's appetite had abandoned him. He pushed the food around his plate and tried deciphering the conversation, occasionally snatching familiar words like 'Guardia Civil' or 'ATA'. His thoughts eventually drifted back to the church and how close they'd all come to dying. The realisation brought his fork clattering to his plate, and he clasped his hand over his mouth to quell the rising vomit. The conversation stopped abruptly; all eyes snapped to him. Pablo lowered his glass from his lips.

'Thomas? *¿Qué tal?*'

Tom held his hand to his mouth until the nausea passed. 'I'm fine. I just need to get some air.'

'*¿Qué?*'

'Air.' He stood up and pointed back toward the river. 'I need to take a walk.'

Fernando stood up as well, but Tom gestured for him to continue eating. 'I'm fine, I just need a walk. *Bien. Estoy bien.*'

Fernando reluctantly sat. Tom walked back through the house and returned to the bridge they'd crossed earlier. He climbed down to the riverbank and sat with his back against the bridge's stone foundation.

'Breathe,' he whispered to himself. He hung his head

between his legs. 'Just calm down and breathe.'

He'd never had a panic attack, and the realisation this was his first only made him more anxious. He lifted his eyes and tried to focus on the water, pushing away his fears for Blanca and thoughts of time travel.

'Slow down,' he told himself. 'Slow down and breathe. In and out, in and out.' A leaf floated past him, and Tom imagined it was him: drifting down the river, past countless unnamed villages and eventually out to the ocean. 'In and out, in and out.'

When Tom roused from his trance, it was dusk and cicadas sang their familiar lullaby to the departing sun. He ran his hand across his chest; it was no longer tight. The smell of tobacco made him look up. The stranger who'd saved them in Eunate leaned on the bridge's railing above, smoking a pipe. Tom scrambled up the riverbank to the bridge. The man was now dressed in a simple white smock and trousers, his ragged silver hair in a long ponytail. The scabbard and sword were gone.

'*Hola*,' said Tom.

'*Hola*.' The man nodded toward the river. ''Tis a beautiful night.'

Tom's eyes widened. 'You speak English?'

'Of course, lad – I'm Scottish.'

'Scottish?' The word sounded alien. 'But you speak Spanish so fluently.'

'Aye, well, I've lived in Spain for many years.' The man's thick Scottish accent was now unmistakable. 'Are you alright, lad? Your companions were worried about ye.'

Tom's cheeks reddened. 'Yeah, I'm fine. I just needed some air.'

'Aye, 'twas an eventful day.' The man took a puff of his

pipe before pointing to the river; a ghostly reflection of the bridge shimmered beneath the moonlit water. 'Well, you picked a tranquil place to sit. 'Tis called Puenta la Reina, or the Queen's Bridge. 'Twas built to provide safe passage to pilgrims like yourself across the River Argo. 'Tis where this town bears its name.'

'Do you live here?'

'Here? Nay.'

'But all the locals seemed to know you.'

'Aye, I've passed through many times.'

'Which part of Spain do you live in?'

'No one place, lad. I spend my days walking the Camino. Home is wherever my feet carry me on any particular day.' He nodded to the town across the river and offered a roguish smile. 'Tonight, home is here.'

Tom felt himself blush; he'd always felt guilty for how little he did to help the homeless. 'How many times have you walked the Camino?'

'Which one?'

'There's more than one?'

This produced a deep full-bellied laugh. 'Aye, lad, there's many caminos. We're on the Camino Frances, the most popular, to be sure, but not the only one. The Camino Norte snakes along the Bay of Biscay, and the Camino Via de la Plata emerges from the south.'

The knight pointed to the scallop shell hanging around Tom's neck. 'You see how each of your shell's grooves lead to the same single point at its base? Santiago is the same. All the different caminos eventually lead to Saint James.'

'So that's what the shell means?'

'Aye, some believe that. Others believe that after his beheading in Jerusalem, the ship containing James' body was lost in a ferocious storm. They say his body 'twas eventually washed ashore in Galicia, covered in scallop shells, untouched.'

'Which is true?'

The man chuckled. 'Both of them, I suppose – or neither. There are no absolute truths on the roads to Santiago.'

In Tom's job, there were never two correct answers; one investment was always better than the other.

'How many times have you walked the Camino Frances?' asked Tom.

The Scot gazed out to the river and chewed his pipe. 'You know, I've never stopped to count. Whenever I reach Santiago, I always just turn around and walk back the other way.'

'How long have you been doing that?'

'Oh, around eleven years, now.'

'Eleven years?' Somehow, Tom actually believed him. 'Don't you ever grow tired of it?'

'Never – the same man never walks the same path to Saint James.' The old man regarded Tom. 'What's your name, lad?'

Tom held out his hand. 'I'm Tom. Tom Anderson. I heard the children call you Santo Gutierre?'

'Aye, that's what the Spanish call me, but my real name is Sir Walter Samuel.' If the old man was joking, he didn't smile. He wrapped Tom's palm in a handshake built of oak. 'Pleased to meet you, Tom Anderson.'

'You too… Sir Walter.' The phrase sounded odd, but the man didn't correct him. 'And thank you for saving us today.'

''Tis our duty to protect the pilgrims.'

'Your duty?'

'Aye, for almost nine hundred years, the Templars have patrolled the Camino, providing safe passage to pilgrims travelling to the tomb of Saint James.'

Tom frowned. 'The Templars? As in the Knights Templar?'

'Ah, you're a scholar, I see. So you've heard of the Templar Order?'

'Only what I've read in *The Da Vinci Code*.'

Sir Walter stroked his beard. 'I'm unaware of this Code of Da Vinci you speak of.'

'Never mind.' The reference was fifty years too early. The old man didn't linger.

'The Church of Santa Maria in Eunate is an old Templar outpost,' said Sir Walter. 'The tunnel we escaped through was originally built for times of siege.'

Was all of this some ruse, or did the old man really believe he was a Templar knight?

'I'd slept in the church last night,' continued Sir Walter. 'When I heard a car approaching, I hid beneath the antechamber's trapdoor. I heard voices above. 'Twas the new priest conspiring with the Guardia Civil to trap and arrest Basque separatists. They also spoke of capturing pilgrims.'

Regardless of the man's insanity, Tom and the others owed their lives to him.

'Thank you – I don't know what would have happened if you hadn't helped us.'

The two of them fell quiet, watching the river grow dim.

''Tis getting late, Tom Anderson,' said the old man. 'Isabella has prepared beds for you and your companions back at the house.'

'What about you?'

The knight started walking across the bridge back to the town. 'Oh, I'll find a wee space for myself in the church.'

Tom watched the old man walking back across the bridge, still filled with unanswered questions. 'Are you really a Templar knight?'

The Scot turned and smiled like an understanding grandfather. 'Aye, lad. 'Tis more common in my time than yours.'

The choice of words felt magnetic. 'What do you mean, your time?'

'I'm not from here, Tom Anderson.'

'Not from Spain?'

'No, lad – I mean, I come from the twelfth century.' Time slowed, and Tom's skin broke into goosebumps. 'I'm what you might call a time traveller.'

CHAPTER 11

'Don't burden yourself, Sofia,' said Padre Price from the car's passenger seat. 'We'll still arrive make our meeting with Archbishop Carreño. Have faith, child.'

She smiled from the backseat, but said nothing – unsure she could trust her tongue. As their car finally escaped the suburbs of Pamplona – two days later than scheduled – her mother's words returned to her.

'Men cannot be trusted, Sofia.'

The English priest must have sensed her displeasure and turned around.

'We couldn't simply have left Pamplona in the middle of San Fermín, could we? Not with all the bulls and music and parades. So much culture, Sofia.' By culture, Padre Price meant wine. 'Pedro will get us to Burgos in time. Won't you, Pedro?'

Pedro nodded from the driver's seat. '*Sí, Padre.*'

Sofia fired a glare into the back of Pedro's head. The unkept driver claimed he didn't speak a word of English yet seemed to have little trouble recommending lavish restaurants and hotels. Padre Price had hired Pedro as his personal driver back in Valencia. At first glance, Pedro looked like a professional chauffeur, dressed in a black jacket and cap. But upon closer inspection, the coat was two sizes too large, and the hat was an army officer's cap that had been painted black. Even his car, which Pedro proudly described as a 'limited edition Bentley', looked suspiciously like a FIAT with a Bentley's hood ornament crudely affixed to its front. In short, Sofia didn't trust the driver.

'Anyway, cheer up,' said the priest. 'Pedro has booked us into a lovely little hotel in Los Arcos tonight, and another in Logroño tomorrow.'

'Logroño? But Padre, we must be in Burgos tomorrow night. Our meeting with Archbishop Carreño is at noon on Thursday. We mustn't miss it.'

'Pedro will have us there in time, Sofia.' The old man waved a dismissive hand. 'Besides – I'm sure it will be nothing more than a cup of tea.'

'Burgos Cathedral is one of Spain's largest. You'll need to have your sermon prepared.'

'It's no larger than my congregation in Manchester. And it's not as if I have to speak Spanish – I'll have you there to translate, remember?' The priest pointed to the rows of grapes out the car window. 'And it would be a travesty to miss spending at least one night in La Rioja. So much culture.'

She crossed her arms and looked out the window.

'Men cannot be trusted, Sofia.'

She could almost see her mother saying the words now, shaking her head while pegging wet clothes onto the line of their apartment's balcony in Valencia.

'You may love them, you may marry them – but you must never trust them.'

As a girl, Sofia must have heard her mother's foreboding warning a thousand times. One time Sofia had asked her mother if Papa could be trusted. Her mother's laugh had been maniacal.

'Of course not. Your father promised me a life of love and comfort, but all he delivered was fish and poverty. Beware men bearing promises; they'll only disappoint you.'

Sofia's father was a kind man; it was difficult to imagine he'd wittingly deceived Mama. Sofia's happiest childhood memories remained those early mornings of just her and Papa on his boat in the calm turquoise waters of the Balearic Sea.

'Patience, Sofia, patience,' Papa would say every time Sofia had reeled in her line to check whether a fish had taken her bait.

'But how will I know if a fish has bitten?'

'You'll feel it, but you have to be patient.'

While sitting on their rented boat, her father had shared his dreams of opening a seafood restaurant on one of Valencia's white-sanded beaches.

'It will begin as a beach shack,' he'd say, his eyes twinkling as he held his fishing rod. 'We'll serve grilled fish, the freshest in all of Valencia. When enough people come, I'll buy a boat of my own and hire some boys to do the fishing while I build the restaurant. There will be an outdoor deck where guests can sit right on top of the ocean. I'll work the grill while you and Mama prepare the paella.'

Sofia's father still spent his days fishing alone on that same rented boat. He didn't seem to mind he'd never caught his dream; he'd accepted his lot in life. Sofia's mother had been less satisfied, not abandoning the idea of the comfortable life she'd been promised. Every Sunday, on their walk home from mass, she'd remind Papa of his obligations.

'Alejandra and Julio are moving into a bigger house next month – three bedrooms, not two. And did you see the automobile Marian rode past in? Her husband is a rice farmer, yet even they have a car. Look at us, walking home from church in the gutter like dogs.' When her complaints were exhausted, Mama's glare would invariably shift to Sofia. 'And what about you? Conxita is about to become a grandmother – Elsa is pregnant. She's younger than you, no? When are you going to find a husband?'

'Soon,' had been all Sofia had ever answered. But 'soon' hadn't been soon enough, and Sofia's mother had drawn up a list of available suitors.

'What about Matías? I always thought you secretly liked him.'

'When I was eight.'

'His mother tells me he works at the abattoir, now. She says he brings home the freshest meat, Sofia – the freshest! Or Federico and Clara's youngest boy – what's his name – José? He works at the quarry, but he doesn't smash the rocks himself, like some rock-smashing animal. He supervises the rock smashers, Sofia. I even checked with his mother. A supervisor is very respectable, no?'

Throughout the summer, each of Mama's candidates

visited their apartment and was served a plate of shallow-fried fish. After each interview, Sofia's mother had closed the door and immediately rounded on her daughter.

'Well?'

Sofia was always polite in her rebuffs. 'He was very nice.'

'*Sí*, and handsome too, no?'

'*Sí*, handsome too.'

'So?' Her mother would creep closer.

'… there's no spark.'

'Spark?' Her mother had boiled like a kettle. 'You're closer to thirty than twenty, Sofia. It's a little too late to insist on a spark, no? Do you want to die a spinster?'

Sofia had shrugged. 'It's like Papa used to say when he'd take me fishing – I'll know it when I feel it.'

Sofia's mother had stabbed her finger into Papa's chest. 'You! This is all your fault. You and your cursed fish have ruined us.'

Years later, when Sofia started her apprenticeship as a nurse at the local hospital, her mother had dreamed her daughter might fall in love with a doctor. She'd had no way of knowing all of the hospital's blood, vomit and faeces had left little room for romance.

Thoughts of the hospital immediately reminded Sofia of the two pilgrims she'd treated in Pamplona. She'd flipped through the newspapers the previous day, searching for any mention of the two escapees or the nurse who'd abetted them. The Englishman had been lucky – if the bull's horn had been two inches to the left, his injury would have been fatal. If the Andalusian had any sense, the two of them would have stopped to rest.

The steep morning climb allowed little conversation between the pilgrims and a thick fog brought an eeriness to their ascent. Fernando stopped and looked back to Thomas; the Englishman's limp had worsened.

'I told you we should have left him with Luis and Isabella,' said Pablo, wiping sweat from his brow.

The Andalusians had tried convincing the Englishman to stay in Puenta La Reina, but the Englishman had insisted he continue. By decoding his garbled Spanish, it seemed Thomas wanted to find the old man who'd saved them.

'I think he is saying Santo Gutierre can take him home,' Pablo had said.

Before leaving, the two Spaniards had asked their hosts for the old man's whereabouts.

'He slept in the church,' Luis had said. 'But he'll have already set off on the Camino by now; Santo Gutierre is an early riser.'

'Who is he?' Pablo had asked. 'He is a little odd, no?'

Luis' uncovered eye had hardened, and he'd pointed to the apple tree in the centre of the yard. 'Do you see that tree? Ten years ago, Santo Gutierre passed through town. He must have seen how poor we were, with Isabella pregnant with our eldest. He gave us some pesetas, a basket of eggs and a small sack of apples. The tree which grew from those apples' seeds has fed our children ever since.' Luis had looked sternly at Pablo. 'People are quick

161

to mock Santo Gutierre for how he speaks or dresses. I don't know if the rumours of him being a knight are true, but I know he helps all who need it.' With his point made, Luis had nodded toward Thomas. 'There's an old Templar church in the village of Torres del Rio; tell your friend he may find Santo Gutierre there.'

Luis was right: the pilgrims would have died if Santo Gutierre hadn't saved them. Fernando's thoughts had drifted back to the church. Why had Ramos ambushed them? Was he only after the Basques or something else? Luis had said his neighbours had seen the Guardia Civil convoy heading north to Bilbao the previous evening.

'And the Basque girl escaped,' Luis had said. 'A friend said she made it to Obanos. Some locals agreed to drive her back to the north.'

Fernando hoped Blanca would make it home to her mother. He wondered if she'd ever see her brother again.

Thomas eventually arrived, and the Andalusians walked alongside him at a snail's pace. The morning's cloud finally lifted, revealing rows of vineyards on either side of the Camino. The first sign of La Rioja – Spain's famed wine region – lifted Pablo's spirits, and the boy broke into song. After another half an hour of slow walking, they decided to break for lunch. They settled under the shade of an oak tree at the edge of a vineyard, and Pablo divided the bread and cheese Isabella had given them. A farmer emerged from the vines, carrying a large sack of wooden pickets. Pablo waved, and the man walked over.

'*Hola, peregrinos.*' The farmer placed the pickets on the ground. 'It's a hot day to be walking to Santiago, no?'

'*Sí*, and too hot to be working in the fields,' said Pablo.

'It's never too hot for a man to work, especially one

with young children to feed.'

Pablo nodded to the bag. 'What are you building?'

'A fence for the winery.' The man turned and pointed to a spire rising up behind the vineyard.

'It looks more like a monastery.'

'*Sí*, it was once the first hospital for pilgrims to Santiago. The King of Navarra donated its surrounding vineyards to the monks. It's privately owned now.'

'Is the wine any good?'

The farmer offered a sly grin and pulled an unlabelled bottle of red wine from his bag. 'See for yourself.'

'Only if you'll sit and share our bread and cheese.' Pablo gestured for the man to join them.

Before Fernando could point out they weren't staying long, the farmer had sat down.

'Do you have a corkscrew?' asked Pablo.

The farmer laughed. 'This is La Rioja; what good is an unopened bottle of wine?'

Pablo removed the cork and took a swig. 'Mmm, *delicioso*.'

He passed the bottle to Thomas, and the three Spaniards watched in wonder as the Englishman tilted, swirled and sniffed the wine before eventually taking a sip. He gurgled and swished it around his mouth, finally swallowing.

'Tempranillo?' he asked.

The farmer nodded, impressed. 'Your friend consumes it bizarrely, but he knows his grapes.'

Pablo snatched the bottle back from Thomas and took another swig. '*Sí*, I thought the same.'

The farmer offered the bottle to Fernando. 'And no wine for you, *amigo*?'

'*Gracias, señor*, but no.' Fernando held up his water canteen. 'Only water.'

'He doesn't drink.' Pablo looked embarrassed.

The farmer eyed Fernando suspiciously. 'In La Rioja, this is considered a sin. Even Jesus drank wine; it's good for the soul.'

'*Sí*, but not always good for the head.'

'Nonsense,' said Pablo, reclaiming the bottle. 'Wine, taken in moderation, never does any harm.'

The farmer frowned. 'Cervantes?'

'You know him?'

'Of course, Spain's greatest novelist.'

The boy looked triumphant. 'Finally, a man of culture.'

The following thirty minutes were lost to talk of literature and grapes. When the wine was finished, the farmer rose to his feet.

'If it were up to me, I'd gladly share another bottle with you – but alas, it's up to my wife.'

The pilgrims packed up their belongings. Fernando shook his empty canteen and asked the farmer where the nearest fountain was.

'The village of Ázqueta,' said the man, picking up his bag of pickets. 'It's not far.'

They thanked him for the wine and started back on the Camino. The man called out after them.

'Perhaps once I have finished this fence, I shall build a fountain for pilgrims to fill their canteens with water.'

Pablo turned and grinned. 'Or better yet, a fountain for them to fill their canteens with wine.'

The farmer laughed. 'Perhaps both. *Buen Camino, peregrinos.*'

The farmer had been right; Ázqueta wasn't far. The

three pilgrims filled their canteens in the fountain and splashed their faces with cold water. Fernando rolled up his sleeves in anticipation of the afternoon's unforgiving sun. Pablo pointed to his arm.

'Is that really a Spanish Legion tattoo?'

Fernando tugged down his sleeve and led them toward the nearest scallop shell. '*Vamos.*'

'I've never known anyone who served in the Spanish Legion,' said Pablo, trailing closely behind. 'What was it like?'

'I don't remember; it was a long time ago.'

Fernando quickened his pace, but the boy matched it.

'*Sí*, but you must remember something about it, no? Did you serve in Morocco?'

'*Sí.*'

'Really?' The boy's eyes widened. 'What was it like? Was it dangerous?'

'It was hot.'

'What about the rebels? Did the Berber tribesmen fight as fiercely as the newspapers described? In school, they taught us of the amphibious landing at Alhucemas.'

'We outnumbered the Berbers ten to one.'

'Still – we stormed the beaches, *jefe*. Those men were heroes; they defended Spain.'

'Morocco isn't Spain.'

Pablo's eyes widened. 'You sound like the insurgents.'

'They can't be insurgents in their own country. We should leave Morocco when France does.'

The boy shook his head. 'I don't understand. If you're so opposed to our occupation of Morocco, why did you join the Spanish Legion?'

'I didn't have a choice.'

'You were conscripted?'

'No, but…'

'Then you chose to join.'

The boy's smug smile heated Fernando's blood.

'Not all of us have the luxury of deciding whether we shall become a dentist or a writer, Pablo.'

The comment stung the boy. This time, when Fernando lengthened his pace, Pablo fell behind. As the distance between them grew, so did Fernando's anger. How could he have been so careless to reveal the tattoo again? He'd made more mistakes in the last two days than he'd made in the previous two decades. He needed to concentrate. His annoyance only deepened, knowing Pablo was right: it had been a choice to join the legion.

It had been the last days of summer in 1935, and Fernando was only seventeen years old. It had been an especially hot summer and he and Emilio had spent their evenings in the plaza, listening to their father and their uncle talk with the other men from the neighbourhood. Their uncle was a bricklayer, with a face even redder than their father's.

'This country has gone to the dogs,' Tio Bernardo had said, shaking his head. 'The rest of Europe is flourishing while we Spaniards remain on our knees.'

'This is what happens when our president is a lawyer,' Emilio had said, only fifteen. 'Alcalá-Zamora is more interested in compromise than following the will of the people.'

'Exactly – all the best land is still owned by a small percentage of elites.'

Papa had glared at their uncle. 'You're corrupting my son, Bernardo. What other boy his age speaks of politics?'

'Bah.' Their uncle had thrown his hands into the air. 'The boy is smart; he sees what is happening to this country. If the government doesn't remember they serve the workers, we'll all suffer the war the Fascists are promising.'

'And the clergy is not free of blame either,' Emilio had offered. 'Why should we fill the church's coffers while the bellies of the people remain empty? We must do what the Russians did and take back our country.'

Their conversation had attracted glances from others, and Fernando had tried to change the subject.

'I've got another delivery to the Plaza de España tomorrow.'

Papa had beamed and slapped their uncle on his back. 'Did you hear that? Two years working at the factory, and my boy has already stolen my job.'

'Let him,' Tio Bernardo had said. 'You're too old and fat to be carrying doors around the city anymore, brother.'

'*Sí* and there are lots of stairs, Papa,' Fernando had said. 'It's replacing the door we hung there the last time; it's rotted.'

'That's not all that's rotted and in need of replacement in that building,' Emilio had said.

Papa had banged his hands on the table. 'Enough, Emilio! Help your brother deliver the door tomorrow.'

'I can't; I'm going to the university to help plan the protest for the minister's upcoming visit.'

Papa had rolled his eyes. 'When I said you'd one day

Once Upon a Camino

attend university, I never intended you wasting your time there planning those damn political rallies.'

Emilio had spent every spare minute volunteering at the university: handing out leaflets and painting placards for the Communist and Trade Unionist associations. So when he'd appeared at the factory the following morning, Fernando had been surprised.

'I thought you had a rally to prepare for?'

The boy had shrugged. 'Papa said he'd lash me if I didn't help.'

The brothers had driven along the golf course they'd created as boys. When they'd arrived at the Plaza de España it looked identical to their visit two summers earlier. Fernando had shown his manifest to a uniformed guard, who'd waved them through the gate. The brothers had unloaded the replacement door and carried it up the same staircase they'd raced each other down previously. Emilio had returned to the truck to fetch the ladder and after an hour the boys had swapped the door and loaded everything back on the lorry.

'*Gracias*, boys,' the overweight guard had said with a smile.

He'd waved the gates open, and Fernando had started the engine. Suddenly, there'd been shouts from behind.

'Close the gates, close the gates!'

Fernando had checked his mirror and saw a pair of uniformed officers running toward them.

'Did you forget the ladder?' Fernando had asked.

Emilio's face had been as white as milk. 'Just drive.'

'What do you mean? What's going on?'

'Drive.' Emilio had lifted his shirt to reveal a brown folder tucked into his jeans.

Fernando had snatched it from him. 'What's this?' He'd flipped it open; the word '*SECRETO*' had screamed at him in red ink. 'Emilio, what have you done?'

Tears had flooded his brother's eyes. 'Please, just drive.'

The gates had closed in front of them; the guards grew larger in the mirror.

'Wait until they're distracted,' Fernando had said, 'then use the ladder to climb the fence.'

Emilio had looked confused. 'Distracted by what?'

There'd been no time to explain. Carrying the folder, Fernando had opened the door and sprinted from the truck. He'd made it halfway up the chain-link fence on the opposite side of the courtyard when a sea of hands had yanked him to the ground. A knee had slammed into his spine as a guard barked orders.

'Find the other one; he can't have gone far.'

With his cheek pushed against the concrete, Fernando had spied the ladder resting against the fence by the truck. At least Emilio had escaped.

The guards had dragged Fernando upstairs into a windowless office and thrust him onto a metal chair. A staff sergeant, who'd smelled of sweat and tobacco, had sat opposite him. He'd slid a map from the brown folder and held it up.

'The details of the security protection for the minister's visit next week. Radio communication frequencies and codes. The parade route.' The sergeant had slammed the folder onto the desk. 'Who are you working for?'

The sergeant had interrogated Fernando for two straight hours, citing an endless list of names from Andalucía's Communist and Unionist parties. When he still hadn't uncovered Fernando's handler, the staff sergeant had changed tack, offering a sympathetic smile.

'Look, I know who you are.' He'd pointed to the delivery manifest on the desk. 'I know a couple of kids from Triana didn't plan all this by themselves. So why not make this easy on yourself. Tell me who asked you to steal the folder.'

Fernando's eyes had burrowed into the desk's scratched surface.

The sergeant had eventually sighed and screeched his chair back.

'Well, I tried to help you – I really did – but if you don't give me what I want, you and the other boy will go to jail.'

'He had nothing to do with it.'

Fernando's reaction had produced a satisfied smirk from the sergeant.

'Then it's even more selfish of you. The theft of classified documents is treason. Pray your friend forgives you for sending him to jail for twenty years.' The sergeant had risen from the desk. 'I'm going to call the *policía* now and have Triana torn apart for your friend. While I'm gone, I suggest you think about what happens to little boys like you and him in prison.'

As soon as the door had locked behind the sergeant, Fernando had leaped to his feet. His father's words had left an impression on him two years earlier, and he had reached into his boot and pulled out the spare screwdriver he'd tucked into his sock. He'd quickly removed the door's hinges and prised it from its frame – just enough to squeeze through – and had crept down the corridor. He'd made it to the ground floor and seen the ladder still resting where Emilio had left it. There'd been shouts from the floors upstairs while Fernando had climbed the ladder over the wire fence. He'd then pressed himself against a wall and scanned the forecourt for an escape path.

Voices had rung out behind him. Guards had streamed out of the buildings, howling instructions to one another as they fanned out across the plaza. A tiny gap had opened between the guards near the river, but Fernando had remained frozen. Even if he managed to return to Triana, it would have only brought the *policía* to his family's doorstep. Fernando had realised he couldn't go home; for Emilio's sake, he'd need to disappear. He'd slid behind a passing family, walking among them toward the green bus parked in the middle of the plaza.

'Who are you?' the legionnaire at the steps of the bus had grunted from behind his clipboard.

Fernando had given his name, and the legionnaire had scanned his clipboard before shaking his head.

'You're not on the list. Where're your papers?'

Sweat had trickled down Fernando's temple. He'd pointed to the driver. 'I gave them to him.'

'You know this kid?' the legionnaire had asked his comrade behind the steering wheel.

The driver had pointed to the guards spreading out across the forecourt. 'They're locking down the plaza; we can sort it out in Malaga.' The bus' engine had rumbled to life. 'Let's go.'

The legionnaire with the clipboard had narrowed his eyes at Fernando. 'How old are you, kid?'

'Eighteen, last week.'

The driver had revved the engine. 'Come on, come on.'

The legionnaire had nodded up the stairs. 'Get on

board.'

Rows of luckless eyes had watched him walk down the aisle of the bus to an empty seat. The bus door had squeaked closed, and they'd driven past the guards and out of the plaza. Fernando had had no way of knowing it was the second-last time he'd ever see Sevilla.

CHAPTER 12

Tom wasn't going to make it another thirty kilometres to Logroño; the pain from his feet had become unbearable. He'd inspected them in the morning and discovered a trail of blisters running down the soles of both. The throbbing of his shoulder was nothing compared to the hot coals searing him within his boots. He hobbled onward, falling ever further behind the Spaniards, driven only by the thought of finding Sir Walter again.

Tom hadn't known how to react when Sir Walter had confided he was also a time traveller. He'd simply dismissed the old man's claims as yet another sad attempt for attention. But as he'd lain awake that night, Tom had analysed the available evidence. Sir Walter did dress in a very peculiar way, even for 1954. And while an enormous hat and cloak didn't prove the man was a knight – he could have just as easily been a wizard – the broadsword hanging by his hip was less easily explained. But more than his appearance, it was Sir Walter's demeanour that had been amiss. The Scot recounted events from past centuries as if they'd happened only yesterday. And Sir Walter's confession about time travel had been entirely unsolicited. Coincidences happened – people read the same book on trains, ordered identical meals at restaurants, even named their children alike – but when had two strangers ever independently admitted to being time travellers while walking the Camino de Santiago? By morning, Tom had convinced himself: the time-travelling Templar knight was his only lead on how to travel home.

Pablo and Fernando had suggested the knight may be found in the village of Torres del Rio, but when they arrived all they found were crumbling houses with barren flower boxes. They discovered an octagonal-shaped church, nearly identical to the one in Eunate. The Spaniards spoke with a nun who indicated that Santo Gutierre had passed through the town hours earlier. Tom had decided to continue with the others to Logroño; there was little alternative.

The afternoon's walk had been flat, but Tom's progress remained slow. The only thing slower were the hands of his watch. He tried to distract himself with the view. Vineyards stretched across rolling hills on both sides of the path, making it one of the most beautiful sections of the Camino yet.

After another hour, they finally reached the outskirts of Logroño, a city as seemingly large as Pamplona. Fernando and Pablo crossed a bridge and entered a park next to the river. They then stopped walking and were deep in discussion when Tom caught up to them.

'What's going on?' he asked. 'Is this Logroño?'

Pablo nodded. '*Sí, Logroño.*' He then unleashed a flurry of Spanish.

'Slow down, I don't understand.'

Pablo took a breath and pointed to himself and Fernando. '*Iremos al albergue.*' He nodded to Tom before gesturing to the river and rubbing his hands over his chest. '*Quédate aquí y báñate en el río.*'

Tom decoded the message. 'You two are going to the *albergue*, and you want me to bathe in the river?'

Pablo flashed his blinding smile. '*Perfecto.*'

'No, I'll come with you to the *albergue*.'

Pablo pointed to Tom's feet and wagged a finger. '*Nosotros volveremos.*'

Tom couldn't shake a feeling the Spaniards had finally decided to rid themselves of him, but he was too sore and tired to argue. 'Okay, fine – *adiós*, then.'

'*No es un adiós.*' Pablo's eyes locked with Tom's. '*Hasta luego.*'

Tom silently translated the words: Until then. Pablo was saying this wasn't a farewell – that the men would return.

'*Hasta luego,*' repeated Tom.

Pablo beamed.

The Spaniards disappeared down the path and Tom sat beneath a shady tree on the riverbank. He removed his boots and carefully peeled off his socks; sweaty wool clung to each pustule. Whatever skin hadn't yet been blistered was now red and inflamed. He stood and unzipped the bottom of his trousers, converting them into shorts the way the shopkeeper had shown him, and limped into the river. The cold water extinguished his burning feet and he groaned, half with relief and the rest in pain. Tom slipped off his shirt and tossed it onto the riverbank before dunking himself beneath the waterline. He scrubbed away the caked-on sweat and dirt that had survived his feeble attempts to wash in each of the *albergues*. Then, when he felt as clean as he would possibly get, he floated on his back. Dappled light trickled through the leaves, and his chest rose and fell beneath the waterline with every breath.

The clouds hanging over Logroño reflected Sofia's mood.

Their car pulled up to the kerb outside the hotel. A boy with an untucked shirt hurried from the entrance and collected their bags from the trunk. Sofia stepped out of the vehicle, but Padre Price didn't follow, instead rolling down his window.

'Pedro will have me back to the hotel later this evening.'

'What do you mean?' asked Sofia.

'Well, you see, Pedro knows of a fabulous little winery up in the mountains. Apparently, they have the most wonderful cellar with wines dating back to 1862.'

Her rage must have been self-evident, as the priest stammered when he continued.

'I did think of inviting you, of course, but you didn't seem interested in the wines of Pamplona.' He nodded to the hotel. 'Pedro says the hotel has a lovely little restaurant, so go ahead and eat whatever you like for dinner and I'll settle the account in the morning.'

'Won't you need me to translate for you?'

'Oh, I shouldn't imagine there'll be much to translate. *Vino tinto* is red wine, and the white is *vino…*'

'*Blanco.*'

'Yes, *blanco*, quite right.' The priest's face turned the colour of Rioja. 'I prefer a good red anyway.'

Pedro got back behind the steering wheel and started the engine.

'Alright, well, we must be off – enjoy your evening, Sofia. *Adiós.*'

She didn't wait for the FIAT/Bentley to make it around the corner before storming into the hotel. The concierge – a wiry man with a pencil-thin moustache – walked out from behind his counter to greet her.

'Welcome to Hotel Marqués de Viejo, *señora.*' His cologne smelled like the disinfectant they used in the hospitals. 'Your acquaintances have reserved our finest room for you, and our restaurant opens at nine.'

Sofia's stomach growled alongside her temper. She checked into her room, and the boy carried her suitcase up to the second floor.

'*Gracias,*' said Sofia, closing the door behind her. She sat alongside her case on a bed better suited to a couple on their honeymoon and undid her bonnet. Her hair tumbled to her shoulders. A grandiose mirror stood against the wall; the girl sitting within it looked tired, fat and foolish. Her mother's voice echoed through her mind: 'You see? What did I tell you about trusting men?' Sofia snatched up the room's key and walked downstairs. She ignored the concierge's warnings of impending rain and stepped out into the street.

Logroño had stirred from its siesta and locals meandered from their beds back to their jobs. She weaved past them, walking without thought. The late afternoon's thick, humid air did little to cool her temper; her uniform and shawl clung to her warm skin. She found herself in a park and walked alongside the river, hoping the sight of the water would calm her as the ocean often did back in Valencia.

It wasn't Padre Price's unannounced excursion to the winery that had angered her; it was the fact she'd trusted the English priest to get her to Santiago. What would she do if she didn't make it to the orphanage in time?

The clouds above darkened, their watery reflections in the river beside her. Sofia's thoughts were interrupted by the sight of a man floating on his back in the river ahead. She stopped walking and watched him from afar as he stood up in the water and shuffled onto the grassy riverbank, wearing nothing but a pair of shorts. She walked closer. The man looked oddly familiar. He had the same strawberry-blonde hair and pale skin as her English patient in Pamplona. He lay down on the riverbank and closed his eyes. Sofia warily approached. The man's left shoulder was bandaged.

'It's you,' she said in English. 'I know you.'

The man looked up at her, shielding his eyes from the sun. 'Who… who are you?'

'I did that.' She pointed to his shoulder. 'Your friend carried you into the hospital. Your name is Thomas, no?'

The Englishman got to his feet. 'You're the nurse from Pamplona?'

'*Sí.*' Sofia looked around. 'Where is Fernando?'

'He and Pablo went to find an *albergue.*'

'I can't believe it is really you. How did you escape the Guardia Civil?'

'Some locals helped us, although I can't remember much.'

'*Sí*, you were heavily sedated. How is your shoulder now?'

Thomas stepped forward and grimaced. 'Not as sore as my feet.'

'Show me.' It was the same tone she used in the hospital – a polite yet firm demand.

Thomas sat on the grass and stretched out his legs. She kneeled and lifted one of his feet onto her lap.

'*Dios mío.*' There was more skin with blisters than without. She prodded the bubbled skin with her thumb.

Thomas winced.

'You cannot walk on these. You must rest in Logroño until they heal.'

'I can't. I have to keep going.'

'A few extra days to reach Santiago will not matter.'

'You don't understand, I'm looking for someone. If I stop, I'll lose him.' He looked at her pleadingly. 'Is there nothing you can do? Please.'

Sofia inspected his other foot and sighed. '*Vale*, let me see.' She took a cigarette lighter from her purse; she felt the Englishman flinch. 'I am not going to burn them off.' She took out a needle and thread from her bag. 'I must sterilise the needle.' She threaded the needle before holding its tip in the lighter's flame. 'You will feel a little prick.'

Sofia pierced the first blister with the needle and ran the thread through before cutting the cotton with her small pair of scissors. Thomas' eyes were glued on the needle as she repeated the process on the next blister.

'So, who are you searching for?' she asked, distracting him as if he were a child receiving an injection. 'A friend?'

'No, I don't even know him, really. He's a Scottish man who walks the Camino. He calls himself Sir Walter. I think he can help me get home.'

'You are not continuing to Santiago?'

'Not anymore.'

'Why?'

'It's… a long story.'

She nodded toward his feet. 'We have time.'

His silence suggested his reasons for abandoning the Camino caused more discomfort than his feet.

'My girlfriend, Ana, is Spanish,' he said finally.

'*Sí*, you called out to her in the hospital.'

'Well, I'd originally come to Spain to ask for her grandfather's permission to propose to her. He said he'd only bless our marriage if I walked the Camino de Santiago.'

She frowned. 'How do you mean? Like, a test?'

'I suppose so.'

'So this is why you walk to Santiago?'

'Originally, but I'd already decided against walking the Camino while on the train to Saint-Jean.'

'So you no longer wish to marry Ana?'

'No, of course I do. It's just…' His face tightened. '… things have changed.'

'What things?'

'Well, for one thing, my bag with my passport was stolen.'

'*Sí*, but you do not need a passport to walk to Santiago. Why not continue?'

'It's not that simple.'

She could feel him want to pull his foot away from her and escape.

'The whole thing is ridiculous, anyway. How would walking across Spain possibly make me a better husband? It doesn't make sense.'

'Perhaps this was the point of the test, no?'

'Well, none of that matters anymore. All I want to do is return to my own time.'

'Your time?'

His face caught aflame. 'I mean my life back in London. Anyway, what about you? Why are you here if you live in Pamplona?'

Sofia told Thomas about her job at the orphanage in Santiago and her trip with Padre Price. After puncturing the last blister, she wiped the needle on her uniform. Thomas gingerly ran his hand over the cotton threads hanging out of them.

'When do I pull them out?'

'Not for a few days. They will stop the blisters from reforming and push the fluid out as you walk.'

He got to his feet and shifted his weight onto each foot. 'Thank you.' He gave a sheepish grin. 'You've patched me up twice, now, and I don't even know your name.'

'My name is Sofia, and you are welcome.'

Two men approached along the path. One was round and hairy; the other was more familiar.

'Sofia!' said Fernando. 'What are you doing here?'

She nodded toward Thomas' feet. 'Fixing your Englishman – again.'

Fernando's companion looked confused. 'Wait, you know this girl, *jefe*?'

'This is Sofia, the nurse who helped us escape the

hospital in Pamplona,' said Fernando. He motioned to his friend. 'This is Pablo.'

'I helped us escape from the city,' said Pablo, as if it had been a competition.

'I was worried you'd be in trouble for helping us,' Fernando said to Sofia.

'No, I just kept walking the guards around the hospital in circles. By the time they returned to your room, I'd disappeared back to my hospice.'

'Thank you – it was very courageous.'

Pablo interrupted again. 'What about when we wore the *cabezudos* and I led us past the guards? That was brave too, no?'

Fernando ignored him, perhaps not for the first time. Unfazed, Pablo stripped down to his underwear and waded into the river. He groaned as if shot.

'*Jesucristo*, it's cold.'

Sofia picked up her purse. 'I should be getting back to my hotel. We are leaving early for Burgos. Where are you headed tomorrow?'

'Azofra.' Fernando pointed to Thomas. 'Will he be able to walk?'

'Better than he would have. I told him to rest, but he says he's searching for someone to help him get home.'

'*Sí*, a wanderer from Britain, named Santo Gutierre.'

'Another crazy British man?'

They smiled at their shared joke; Fernando's face looked different, free of its scowl.

She pointed to Thomas. 'Ensure you change his bandage.'

'I will,' said Fernando. 'Good luck in Burgos.'

'And good luck with these two.' She nodded to

Thomas and Pablo. 'Try and stay out of trouble.'

Sofia walked back along the river, still astonished her path had intersected with the pilgrims once more. She re-entered the city and, in no rush to return to an empty hotel room, walked through Logroño's cobbled lanes. Locals stood around wine barrels in taverns, each picking at tapas and drinking wine. By the time Sofia returned to the hotel, it was dark; drizzle fell.

'I told you it was going to rain,' said the concierge, a smug grin on his face. He held up a slip of paper. 'A message for you.'

Sofia took the note and read it – twice. She scrunched the paper tightly within her fist and walked up the stairs to her room. Her mother's words screamed within her once more. Men were not to be trusted.

Tom silently ate his dinner as Spanish conversation rattled around him. Five pilgrims from Madrid sat at the dining table with them. Pablo looked pleased to have new people to entertain, talking excitedly between mouthfuls of stew. A pilgrim wearing glasses introduced himself to Tom.

'My name is Marcos,' he said in heavily accented English. 'I once worked on a British cargo ship.' He lit a cigarette and offered one to Tom.

'No, *gracias*,' said Tom.

The man frowned. 'You no smoke?' He held his fingers to his lips, simulating a cigarette. '*¿Por qué?*'

Tom patted his chest. 'It's not good for the lungs.'

Marcos relayed this to the rest of the group. Pablo said something in Spanish, and everyone laughed.

'Your friend asks if people smoke the cigarettes in the future,' said Marcos, looking bewildered.

Tom's cheeks reddened while Pablo continued talking.

'He wants me to ask you what the future is like,' said Marcos.

All eyes turned to Tom, who shook his head.

'I shouldn't say.'

'*¿Por qué?*' asked Pablo on behalf of the other smirking faces.

'Because telling you about the future might change it,' said Tom, his temper beginning to fray. 'It's called the butterfly effect.'

'Butterfly?' Marcos turned to the others and pressed his thumbs together, fluttering his fingers like butterfly wings. '*Mariposa.*'

'*¿Mariposa?*'

Pablo and the others mimicked the hand gesture, filling the dining room with imaginary butterflies. Everyone spoke at once.

'There are no butterflies in the future?' translated Marcos, grinning.

'It's just an expression,' said Tom, swatting the imaginary butterflies away. 'It's a metaphor for how something small – like the flapping of a butterfly's wings – can result in something huge, like a tornado.'

'This is a lie; butterflies no cause tornadoes.'

'It's just an example. Like if I told you tobacco causes cancer, you might…'

'Tobacco causes cancer?' Marcos looked alarmed and

relayed the claim to the others.

Their faces became angry.

'¡*No*! *Eso es una tontería.*'

'Is this true?' asked Marcos. 'Cigarettes cause the cancer?'

Tom squirmed, pinned between an ethical dilemma and changing the course of human history. 'Yes, tobacco causes lung cancer.'

Once translated, the Spaniards around the table glanced nervously toward the cigarettes they each held between their fingers. Pablo asked another question.

'He asks if the cigarettes still exist in the future,' said Marcos.

'They still exist, but…'

Marcos translated the first half of Tom's reply, and Pablo clapped his hands triumphantly. He spoke excitedly to the others, and relieved faces appeared around the table. Marcos took a thankful puff of his smoke.

'Your friend is right,' said Marcos. 'Why would people of the future smoke if they know it causes cancer?'

Tom excused himself from the table and went back to the dormitory room. Later, lying in bed and listening to the rain hammering down upon the *albergue's* tin roof, he sighed. The Spaniards didn't believe him, after all. They thought he was crazy. Tom felt more alone than ever.

He closed his eyes. The sound of rain on the roof reminded him of Ana – it was her favourite thing to fall asleep to. What must she be feeling? It had been a week since he'd last seen her – the longest they'd been parted in the five years they'd been together. Was she just as scared and worried as he was, or had the butterfly effect already rewritten the future? Suddenly panicked, he pulled out his phone and turned it on. Ana's smiling face glowed in the darkness; she still existed. He ran his thumb across her cheek before switching the phone off to conserve the last of its battery.

Tom woke to the rustling of the other pilgrims getting dressed and leaned over to peel back a curtain; the sun was barely visible behind a veil of rain. He climbed down the ladder and got dressed, running a hand over his thread-covered feet before sliding on his socks and boots. When he walked out to the dining room, the pilgrims from Madrid had already left. His companions sat waiting for him at the dining table.

Pablo handed him a mug. '*¿Café?*'

It felt like the Spaniard's way of apologising.

'*Gracias.*'

The coffee was lukewarm but strong; the caffeine would help him confront the waiting rain.

The path out of Logroño was a slow and steady incline. After thirty minutes of climbing, Tom realised he was keeping pace with the Spaniards. Both feet felt much better. They still ached, but the intense burning of the previous days had disappeared. He promised himself if he ever saw Sofia again, he'd be sure to thank her.

'*Mira.*' Pablo pointed to a solitary figure plodding up the hill ahead of them. They had their head bowed against the rain and carried a suitcase by their side. '*¿Peregrino?*'

It didn't appear to be one of the pilgrims from Madrid. They caught up to the lone hiker quickly, and Tom realised he wouldn't have to wait long to fulfil his promise.

The pilgrim with the suitcase was Sofia.

CHAPTER 13

'Padre Price had an accident.'

Sofia's cheeks were wet; Fernando couldn't tell if it was from her tears or the rain.

'He slipped and fell on the stairs of a cellar at a winery. Our driver said he was taking him to the hospital in Pamplona. They think he dislocated his knee.'

After finding her on the Camino, the pilgrims had convinced her to take shelter in a nearby barn with them while they waited for the rain to pass.

'The poor old man.' Pablo shook his head, his sopping curls straightened by the rain. 'My Aunt Juanita says her knee injury was agony.'

'He was probably drunk.' Sofia sounded bitter. 'All he ever did was drink, and our driver only encouraged him.'

'Why are you out here, though?' asked Fernando. 'Can't the priest's driver come for you?'

'*Sí*, but he'll only drive me back to Valencia. I'm expected at the orphanage in Santiago in three weeks.'

Pablo pointed up the mountain. 'So, you're going to walk?'

Sofia folded her arms. 'You don't think I can make it?'

'No, I...' For once, the boy was lost for words. 'I simply mean, wouldn't you be better catching a train?'

'Trains and buses cost money. The entire point of travelling with Padre Price to Santiago was because it was free.'

'But it's—'

'A long way to walk?' Sofia glowered at the boy as if she were a hot brand. 'I know precisely how far it is, which is why I can't be standing here, wasting my time.' She wrung some of the rain out of her cloak before throwing it back over her shoulders.

'At least wait until the storm passes,' said Fernando.

'Some storms never pass.' She picked up her suitcase and set off, back into the downpour.

They watched her shuffle up the hill, one hand clutching at her hood, the other carrying the case.

'She's crazy,' said Pablo.

'Come on, let's go.'

They caught up to Sofia, and Fernando reached for her case.

'No, I can manage,' she said, wrenching it away from him and slipping. Her knee landed in the muddy red clay of the Camino. '*Mierda.*'

He offered his hand to her, but she knocked it away.

'I don't need your help.' She pulled herself back up to her feet and attempted to brush her cloak clean, but her soiled hands smeared more mud across it. She glared at

Fernando. 'Well, what are you waiting for?' she snapped. 'The three of you are clearly faster than me – get moving.'

'Let us help you.'

'I don't need your help,' she repeated.

'Don't be silly,' said Pablo. 'The Camino is no place for an unattended woman.'

'I'm not unattended.' The girl shot up her left hand.

Fernando was surprised to see a ring on it.

'I'm engaged to be married, so I don't need you, or any other man, as a chaperone.'

Pablo frowned. 'Well, then, where's your fiancé?'

'Where's yours?'

The boy blushed. Fernando rescued him.

'I think Pablo means it will be better if you walked with us.'

'Better for who? I'm tired of people telling me what's best for me.'

The wind and rain lashed them. Pablo tugged his sodden poncho around him tighter.

'Come on, *jefe. Vamos.*'

The boy and Thomas walked up the hill. Sofia faced Fernando.

'I appreciate your concern – truly. But I prefer to walk alone.'

Fernando didn't want to leave her, but he didn't have permission to stay. He nodded defeat. '*Buen Camino*, Sofia.' He walked up the hill and caught up to the others.

'Jesus, *jefe*, what a bitch, no?'

'She's upset. Her trip is ruined.'

'Well, it wasn't our fault. We were only trying to help, but she's too damn stubborn to accept it.' The boy glanced back at her. 'See how pitiful she looks.'

Fernando watched Sofia trudging up the mountain alone, her head bowed against the wind and the rain.

Pablo tutted. 'Cervantes wrote: "All women are good – good for something, or good for nothing."'

Fernando glared at the boy. 'No more Cervantes today.' He took a final look at Sofia battling up the hill. She didn't look pitiful to him; she looked courageous.

Beneath her hood, Sofia fumed. The days since leaving Valencia had all had bright, clear skies. But today, as she walked up Spain's steepest mountain, God had decided to flood the Earth again.

She bowed her head against the sheets of rain. Each time she glanced up, Fernando and the others were farther ahead, until one time she looked up and they'd disappeared altogether. Good, she didn't need them. Thomas and Fernando were harmless enough, but the arrogance of the hairy one, Pablo, was infuriating. He reminded her of the doctors in her hospital in Valencia. They breezed in and out of the ward, dismissing the nurses' observations and leaving an illegible tangle of notes to unravel. One day on a cigarette break, Sofia had asked the other nurses whether there'd ever been a female doctor in the hospital.

'Here?' The others had laughed out clouds of smoke. 'Never. The closest was Abigail, but she was only screwing one of the surgeons.'

Undeterred, Sofia had enquired about studying medicine at the local university, but the fees had been exorbitant. When she'd mistakenly mentioned her visit to her parents, Sofia's mother had been alarmed.

'Is it even legal for a woman to become a doctor? I don't think I'd feel safe with a female doctor. Anyway, you already have a good job as a nurse, Sofia. What do you want to be a doctor for? Perhaps you could marry a doctor; that would be much easier, no? Or what about Sergio? He's still at the abattoir. It's the freshest meat, Sofia.'

Sofia had abandoned her dreams of studying medicine until a staff meeting at the hospital several months later. Professor Calatrava, the hospital's head of physicians, had addressed the ward. He'd waved forward a slim man in his early thirties with wavy dark hair.

'I'd like to introduce our newest addition to the hospital. Doctor Hector González studied at Oxford University in England, one of the world's finest medical schools, with a full scholarship. He's spent the past year in his hometown of Barcelona and joins us as the new Registrar for General Medicine, replacing Doctor Costa. I'd ask all of you to help him find his way around the wards and to make him feel welcome.'

The other nurses had whispered amongst themselves. Doctor González had been dressed in a grey suit and wore glasses with tortoise-shell frames. He'd looked handsome, in a bookish sort of way.

The prospect of studying medicine at Oxford University with a full scholarship had intrigued Sofia. Several weeks later, after her shift, she'd waited for the young doctor outside the hospital.

'Excuse me, Doctor González?'

'¿Sí?' He'd walked toward her with a vague smile.

'My name is Sofia Lozano. I'm one of the nurses here

at the hospital.'

'I see. How may I help?'

'Professor Calatrava said you studied medicine at Oxford University in England.'

'That's right.'

'Well, I'm interested in applying for the scholarship.' The young doctor had frowned and Sofia had quickly explained, 'It's for my younger brother; he wants to become a doctor.'

With the clarification, Doctor González had been extremely helpful, patiently telling Sofia the subjects covered in the scholarship's entry examination, while she'd diligently scribbled in her notebook.

'And of course, the test is in English. But I'm assuming your brother already speaks English, no?'

Sofia had laughed. '*Sí*, of course he does.'

The next day, she'd visited a second-hand bookstore behind the university and bought a dusty set of English textbooks and an anatomy book heavier than a sack of potatoes. She'd soon discovered the English language was infinitely more complicated than medicine. Whereas the human body consisted of two hundred and six bones and seventy-nine organs, there were boundless meanings of the word 'run'. The English used things called 'prefixes', making them 'dishonest' instead of 'unhonest' or 'non-honest'. Some words contained letters that were written but never spoken. Or cowardly vowels that fled whenever a word was joined by the letters 'ing'.

The hardest part of preparing for the entrance examination had been hiding it from Mama. For months, Sofia had studied alone in her room at night, often by candlelight, to avoid attracting her mother's suspicions. But this became untenable, and as the entrance examination had neared, Sofia had told her parents she'd agreed to work night shifts at the hospital.

'Working day and night?' Mama had asked. 'When will you sleep?'

'At the hospital for a few hours between my shifts,' Sofia had lied. 'It's only for a few months, and then I can focus on finding a husband.'

She'd felt guilty toying with her mother's emotions, but it had worked. Mama had begrudgingly accepted the deal and Sofia had spent her evenings studying in the staff room's library. And while the library was strictly reserved for use by the hospital's doctors, the staff room had remained empty in the evenings, granting her access to its comprehensive collection of medical books. As a result, Sofia had enjoyed several hours of undisturbed study before safely escaping to one of the spare beds on the ward ahead of her next day's shift. But those long days and nights had eventually caught up with her.

'Sister Lozano, what in God's name are you doing in here?'

Sofia had sat bolt upright, sucking in the drool from her open mouth. Sunlight had streamed through the windows, and Professor Calatrava had glared at her from across the staff room. The entire cohort of the hospital's doctors had stood behind him, ready for their 8am faculty meeting.

'I'm sorry, Professor Calatrava… I was just…' She'd frozen. Excuses had eluded her, both in Spanish and English.

'Sister Lozano was helping me, Professor.'

The roster of doctors had parted to reveal Doctor

González, pushing his tortoise-shelled glasses up the bridge of his nose.

'As you know, I've been running some extra tuition for our junior doctors on the topic of dementia, and I'd asked Sister Lozano to assist in preparing some notes for me.'

The elderly professor had been unimpressed. 'Doctor González, this is highly irregular. The library is reserved for my physicians.'

'*Sí*, I understand, *señor*. My apologies.'

An awkward silence had followed. Professor Calatrava had eventually waved Sofia away, and she'd gathered her belongings and staggered out of the room as quickly as possible. She'd been halfway down the hall when a voice had called after her.

'Sister Lozano.'

Sofia had turned to see Doctor González walking toward her. Her cheeks had turned crimson.

'I'm so sorry, Doctor González. I lost track of time, and I haven't been sleeping well lately, and I suppose I… well, I must have fallen asleep. It won't happen again.'

Doctor González had simply held up the textbook she'd drooled on moments earlier.

'Tell your brother to memorise the diagrams in Chapter 10; it will most certainly be on the entrance examination.'

'*Gracias*.' She'd been too stunned to say anything more.

'You're welcome.' He'd smiled. 'And my name is Hector.'

The rain kept tumbling, and the Camino turned muddier beneath Sofia's feet. She finally made it up the hill, emerging out of a pine forest to a reservoir where the raindrops splashed onto the water's surface like artillery. She looked in the nearby trees, half expecting to see Fernando and the others, but she was all alone. The rain poured harder, and the Camino rose again. Sofia tightened her cloak around her and walked on.

'I don't think it's going to get any softer.' Pablo pulled his hand back in from under the tree. 'Maybe we should start walking again, *jefe*?'

'Five more minutes.'

The boy huffed before lighting another cigarette. 'It's nearly been an hour; the crabby nurse will catch up to us soon.' Pablo's ring of smoke was snuffed out by the rain. He grinned slyly toward Fernando. 'Unless that was your plan?'

'Don't be foolish.'

A dentist's grin appeared through his bushy beard. 'Admit it, *jefe*, you like her.' His smirk widened. 'It's only natural to yearn for a woman. Jamie and I are mobbed by women during our poetry readings in Granada.'

'And you sleep with them all, I suppose?'

'Tsk, tsk.' Pablo wagged a teasing finger. 'A gentleman never tells.'

'You don't have a special girl back in Granada then?'

'One? Cervantes wrote: "A wise man does not trust all his eggs to one basket". It's like walking into an ice-cream parlour with all these delicious flavours and being told you may only eat chocolate for the rest of your life. Maybe one day I'll want strawberry or vanilla or—'

'*Vamos*,' said Fernando, cutting the boy short before he'd recited all the other flavours. He led Pablo and Thomas out from beneath the tree back to the Camino.

A chain-link fence ran alongside the path, and Pablo pointed to the cars cruising along the highway on the other side.

'Maybe we should hitch-hike?'

Thomas said something in English and pointed behind them. A lone pilgrim toiled their way up the mountain, dragging a waterlogged suitcase.

'I told you she'd catch up to us,' said Pablo.

Fernando handed his bag to Pablo. 'Wait here.'

'There's no point; she doesn't want our help. We're men, remember? She hates us.'

Fernando slipped and slid down the muddy path to Sofia.

'Here, give me your case,' he called to her over the rain.

She stared at him defiantly from beneath her hood. 'I told you already, I don't need your help.'

He pulled the suitcase toward him, and Sofia yanked it back.

'Leave it,' she shrieked.

He tugged the case's handle toward him. 'Let me help.'

'I don't need it. Just leave me alone.'

Sofia yanked again, and the wet handle slipped from both of their grasps. The case toppled to the ground and landed on its latches, causing the bag's lid to spring open. Sofia's clothes slid down the muddy mountain.

'No!' she cried.

Fernando scrambled after the suitcase. More of its contents tumbled out and into the mud as he lifted it. Sofia collapsed onto her knees to rescue them. Fernando tried to help, but she threw a menacing finger into his face.

'Don't.'

Flames flickered in her amber eyes, and Fernando retreated to watch her repack the muddy clothes into the case. Suddenly, she stopped, and her eyes brimmed with tears.

'What's wrong?' he asked.

She reached into the case and pulled out a green ceremonial gown and what appeared to be the black cassock of a priest.

'These were being crushed in Padre Price's luggage, so I offered to pack them in my case.' Tears raced the raindrops down her cheeks. 'When I spoke with Pedro on the telephone, I was so angry that I forgot I still had them. I'm so stupid; I should have checked.' She let the garments fall back into the case and buried her face into her hands; her shoulders trembled with each sob.

Fernando walked over and placed a cautious hand on her shoulder. 'It will be alright.'

She looked up, the fire in her eyes now extinguished by tears. 'How? Now I'll have to walk all the way back to Logroño and wait days for Pedro to pick them up. I'll never make it to Santiago in time.'

Thunder rumbled in the blackened sky; they couldn't stay where they were.

'The next town isn't far,' said Fernando. 'You can arrange for the priest's driver to pick them up from the church.'

'I can't just leave them in one of these towns; the robes are priceless.'

'Didn't you say he was due to deliver a sermon in Burgos? We'll be there in a few days. His driver can pick them up from there.' Fernando pointed to the grim clouds above. 'You can't stay here; the storm is getting heavier. Walk with us to Burgos.'

He held out his hand to her, and to his surprise, she took it. They crammed the remainder of the sopping clothes back into the case and made their way up the slippery path to the others. Pablo and Thomas emerged from the shelter of a tree.

'Looks like you needed our help after all,' said Pablo.

Sofia looked ready to slam her suitcase into the boy's pretty white teeth. Fernando pointed ahead.

'*Vamos.*'

'Now?' Pablo threw his arms up to the heavens. 'It's the heaviest it's been; we'll drown!'

Fernando searched the sodden ground at his feet. He leaned down and picked up two strips of bark.

The boy scoffed. 'It's too late to build an ark.'

Fernando knotted the pieces of bark together into a makeshift crucifix and looped it through the chain-link fence. He crossed himself and mouthed a silent prayer before slinging his bag onto his shoulder.

'What the hell did you pray for?' asked Pablo.

Fernando nodded to the sky. 'The sun.'

Pablo looked appalled. Sofia placed her case down and picked up another two pieces of bark from the mud. She tied an identical crucifix and threaded it through the fence next to Fernando's; Thomas added a third. Pablo stared at the three makeshift crosses, all rattling in the wind.

'I thought Thomas was the only crazy one.' He bent down and made a cross of his own, tying it next to theirs. 'Dear God, save us from drowning.'

Their prayers went unanswered at first; the rain continued assaulting them as they slipped, slid and stumbled down the muddy slope. They eventually arrived in the village of Navarrete, where an old woman with a bent spine waved them into her house. Shedding their cloaks and jackets, the four pilgrims huddled around her stove and accepted warm cups of coffee. They patiently listened to the woman's complaints about each of her neighbours, and by the time they returned to the Camino, the rain had stopped. On the climb out of the town, the clouds stretched apart like cotton wool, and they finally felt sunshine on their faces. Pablo looked sheepish.

'This isn't because we tied some sticks to the fence, okay?'

An hour later, the Camino was once again bathed in sunshine. They eventually came to Ventosa and made their way toward the town's church, where a stork had built its nest in the building's spire. The pilgrims draped their damp cloaks over the church's picket fence to dry before sitting on a pair of benches in the courtyard. Sofia reached into her suitcase and pulled out some mandarins.

'Mandarins for lunch?' Pablo looked horrified.

'I didn't realise this violated any laws.'

'Not laws.' Pablo gestured to Fernando and Thomas. 'But we always have bread and cheese for lunch.'

'Then eat bread and cheese; I'm not stopping you.'

Sofia peeled a mandarin for herself and ate one of its segments, while Pablo divided the bread and cheese amongst the others.

'So why isn't your fiancé with you?' Pablo asked Sofia.

'He's working.'

'Is he a nurse too?'

'A doctor, actually.'

The boy's snigger was cut short. 'You've done well for yourself, no? Catching yourself a doctor.'

'I didn't catch him; he's not a fish.'

'So, how did you meet?'

'He was helping me to study.'

'For what?'

'I was studying for a scholarship to study medicine at Oxford University.'

'Oxford?' Pablo choked on his bread. 'Whatever made you think you could study there?'

Sofia's eyes blazed, and the boy hastened to recover.

'Well, it's probably best you weren't accepted; medical school takes many years. I'm sure your fiancé wants to start a family.'

'I'm confused: is it female doctors you object to, or mothers older than thirty?'

The boy looked to Fernando to toss him a life-ring before he drowned. 'Neither, it's just…'

'What about you then?' asked Sofia. 'Are you married?'

'No.'

'You'd best hurry up; no child wants an old father.'

'The women in Granada bore me,' said Pablo casually. 'My friend Jamie and I are spending next summer in Paris. French women are more sophisticated than Spanish girls.'

'*Sí*, I can see what an intellectual giant you are.'

Sofia shook her head and ate her last segment of mandarin. Pablo watched her drop its peel into the nearby bin.

'Is that all you're going to eat?' he asked.

'*Sí*, why? Does that break another of your rules?'

'We still have an entire afternoon of walking before us; you'll need more than a mandarin.'

'Well, it's all I have. I'll buy more food tonight.'

Pablo took his remaining cheese and a hunk of bread over to her. 'Here.'

'It's fine; I'm not hungry anyway.'

'Don't be silly.'

She eyed the food and reached for her purse. 'At least allow me to reimburse you.'

Pablo laughed. 'We didn't buy it.' He dangled his scallop shell in front of her. 'The locals gave it to us. Catholics don't need a starving pilgrim on their conscience.'

'But I'm not a pilgrim.'

He pointed to her muddy uniform. 'You could have fooled me.'

By the time they'd finished eating, their jackets and cloaks were almost dry. A series of scallop shells directed them back to the Camino, and they followed it through the vineyards and farms of the sun-baked countryside. Pablo's attention remained on their newest member.

'So, Sofia, have you read Cervantes' *Don Quixote de la Mancha*?'

'Well, I'm not as sophisticated as a French girl, but *sí* – I've read it.'

'And?'

She shrugged. 'I always preferred Cervantes' *La Galatea*.'

'*La Galatea*?' The words gashed the boy. 'But there's no story; it's all just flowery words.'

'Sometimes it is enough for writing to just be beautiful,

no?'

'No – it's not; *Don Quixote* is his best work.'

'I didn't say *La Galatea* is his best, I said it was my favourite.'

'You're wrong.'

'How can I be wrong about which I enjoy the most?'

'Because you are.'

They agreed to stay the night in Azofra, finding an *albergue* behind the church. Fernando sat on the bench outside and waited for Thomas to arrive while Pablo trudged inside, announcing he had a headache.

Sofia watched him disappear and sat next to Fernando. 'I think I finally broke him about Cervantes.' She wore a triumphant smile. 'How long have you been walking with him?'

'Over a week.'

She shook her head in wonder. 'How have you not gone mad?'

'I'm used to it – my brother was the same when we were boys. He would talk, and I would listen.'

'Is he a fisherman too?'

'Emilio?' Fernando smiled at the thought. 'No, he'd make a terrible fisherman. No patience.'

'My father said the same thing about me. Are you the older brother?'

Fernando nodded before pulling his wallet from his pocket. He slid out his photograph and handed it to her. Her smile lit up her face.

'How old were you here?'

'I was nearly fourteen, Emilio was twelve.'

'You two look like trouble.' She grinned and handed back the picture. 'This was in Huelva?'

'No, Sevilla.'

'Do your parents still live there?'

'My father is dead now, and our mother left us when I was still young. It was only ever Papa, Emilio and me.'

'I'm sorry.' Her smile faded. 'Do you live near your brother?'

'No.' It felt rude keeping a secret from her. 'I haven't seen him in many years. The truth is, after Santiago, I will return to Sevilla to put things right between us.'

'That's as good a reason to walk the Camino as any, no?'

There was a pause, and Fernando pointed inside the *albergue*.

'There is a telephone inside. You can call Pamplona and tell your English priest we will leave his robes in Burgos.'

'*Gracias.*' When he didn't respond, Sofia looked into his eyes. 'I mean it. Thank you for rescuing me on the mountain.'

'It was nothing. You saved Thomas and me in Pamplona.' He shrugged. 'Do not withhold good from those to whom it is due when it is in your power to act.'

She rolled her eyes. 'Don't tell me you're reciting Cervantes too.'

'It isn't Cervantes.' He studied her face, unsure whether she'd been joking. 'It's the Bible.'

Tom's feet were improving. Despite all the miles they'd covered since Logroño, the cotton threads had prevented the blisters from reforming. It was nice having a nurse within their group, especially one who spoke English. With his feet and shoulder healing, Tom's focus shifted back to finding Sir Walter. It had been four days since he'd stood with the knight in Puente La Reina, and his hopes of finding the old man were beginning to fade. In every town they visited, the locals said Santo Gutierre had already passed – sometimes by only a few hours.

The pilgrims arrived at the medieval town of Santo Domingo de la Calzada, with the merciless midday sun at its peak. Upon reaching the town's square, Tom made his familiar declaration to Sofia.

'I'm going to ask if anyone has seen Sir Walter.'

The interior of the town's cathedral was cold and dimly lit. It was identical to most of the other churches and cathedrals they'd visited on the Camino.

'Hello?' he called out, walking down the central aisle toward the altar.

Bok, bok, bok.

Tom spun around. 'Is someone there?' His eye fell on a statue of a bearded saint, dressed in a robe and carrying a staff. The statue's feet were flanked by a pair of bronze chickens.

Bok, bok, bok.

Tom followed the peculiar sound to a dimly lit enclosure in the back corner of the cathedral. A fat, white cockerel stood proudly within it, accompanied by a plump, brown hen. The chickens stared back at him.

'Ah, I see you've met the locals, Tom Anderson.'

The voice made him jump, triggering a boisterous

laugh from Sir Walter. The knight walked toward him with a boyish grin.

'Oh, I dinna mean to frighten you, lad; I apologise.' He nodded toward the enclosure. 'Do you know the story about these here chickens?'

Tom was still too startled to answer.

'The locals say many years ago, a family passed through this town, on their way to Santiago. 'Tis said a local lass took a liking to the family's eldest son but was rebuffed by the pious lad. Scorned, the slighted lass planted a silver cup in his bag and accused him of pilfering. The town's sheriff had the boy hanged on the outskirts of the town. His heartbroken parents continued to Santiago, desperate to find meaning in their son's death.'

The knight's tale had turned darker than Tom had expected. Sir Walter continued.

'When the parents passed through the village on their return journey, they discovered their son, still hanging in the tree, yet somehow still alive.' The knight's eyes twinkled. 'They ran and found the sheriff, interrupting his dinner, and pleaded for the release of their boy. 'Tis said the sheriff told them their son was as dead as the roasted chicken on his plate. At which point, the chicken miraculously sprang to life and walked up and down the dining table. The sheriff had the lad cut down, and the family was free to go.' He nodded toward the glass enclosure. 'And there've been chickens in this here cathedral ever since.'

Sir Walter tilted an eyebrow toward Tom. 'But why do I sense you've got more than chickens on your mind, Tom Anderson?'

'I've been looking for you.'

'Me?' Sir Walter's face grew serious. 'Whatever for,

lad?'

'It was something you said to me in Puente La Reina.'

'About the Templars?'

'No – about being a time traveller.'

'Oh.' The old man looked embarrassed. 'You should ignore me, lad. 'Twas nothing more than the ramblings of a tired, old fool.'

'I don't think it was. I think you were telling the truth.'

'And why would you think that? We all know such things aren't possible.'

'Because… I'm a time traveller too.'

Bok, bok, bok.

Tom ignored the chickens' jesting. 'I'm from the year 2010. You see, I was on a train to Saint-Jean, and I somehow woke up in 1954. At first, I thought it was a dream, or that maybe I was going crazy, but then you said you were a time traveller too. If this is real – you're the only person who can help me.'

'How could I possibly help, lad? I'm not a sorcerer.'

'If you tell me how you travelled forward in time, it might help me understand how I can return home.'

The knight shifted uncomfortably in his boots. ''Twas so long ago, I'm not sure I can remember.'

'Please, I'm desperate. If there's anything you can remember – even the tiniest detail – it could help both of us get home.'

The knight eventually nodded and motioned to a nearby pew. 'Aye, I'll try.'

The two of them sat.

'What happened when you travelled forward in time?' asked Tom.

''Twas the year 1193, returning from Richard the

Lionheart's campaign to retake the Holy Land from Saladin and the Moors. I believe the people of today call it the Third Crusade. I had ridden the Via de la Plata, north to Santiago, and began travelling east along the Camino Frances when an unnatural storm appeared.'

'What do you mean – unnatural?'

''Twas like nothing I'd ever witnessed. One moment the skies had been clear; the next, they were as black as coal. High-pitched screams rang down from the heavens, followed by deafening claps of thunder – so loud, they made my teeth chatter.' His face creased as he strained to remember. 'Enormous balls of flame flew high into the night sky. My horse reared up and tossed me to the ground. I heard my wife and our sons calling my name, and I staggered toward them. Blinded by the ash, I followed their cries deeper into the abyss until I eventually fell. 'Twas as if I'd fallen into a bottomless cavern.' He stared at the church floor, as if it might crumble too. 'And then everything turned black. When I woke, it was late afternoon. The storm had disappeared, as had my horse. I heard a peculiar noise above. I looked up into the sky and saw a giant bird flying higher and faster than any creature I'd ever encountered. It seemed to glint in the sunshine and moved without so much as flapping its wings. I turned and walked back down to Santiago, noticing the city had somehow grown taller. Indeed, the city I soon arrived in was not the one I'd left hours earlier. The dusty road I'd ridden out of had been replaced with black stone, and men rode in metal carriages, no longer pulled by horses. I stopped a man in the street and asked him what day it was; he replied it was the year 1943.'

'And you've walked the Camino for the last eleven

years?'

'Aye.'

Tom stood up and paced. He scoured the details of Sir Walter's journey for commonalities with his own.

'What's the link?' he murmured to himself.

'How do you mean, lad?'

'Well, at first, I thought it might be a specific location, but we were on opposite sides of the country when we travelled through time. And there wasn't a storm when I was on the train.'

Tom turned to the numbers. His entire life was numbers: scores from meaningless football matches, stock variations in throwaway companies, travel routes with the shortest journey time. Every problem had a mathematical solution.

'I travelled fifty-six years into the past, yet you travelled from 1193 to 1943.' He silently did the arithmetic. 'That's seven hundred and fifty years into the future. What's the link?'

'Who says there is one, lad?'

'It's not leap years,' he muttered. Those coincided with European Cup years, and the last of those was in 2008 – where Spain defeated Germany in the final, 1–0. He turned to Sir Walter.

'Is there anything special about 1954?'

'How do you mean?'

'Something significant, like an eclipse or the passing of a comet?'

Sir Walter shrugged. 'Nothing except the Xacobeo, of course.'

'Of course – the Holy Year.'

'Aye, but I'd hardly call that a phenomenon – the last

one was in 1948.'

'And the one before that?'

The knight stroked his beard. 'Must have been 1943.'

'The year you arrived?'

'Aye.'

'That's it.' Tom clapped his hands, causing the chickens to flinch. 'In my time, 2010 is a Holy Year, and so is 1954. That's the pattern! We can only time travel through the Holy Years.'

'I dinna understand, lad.'

Either did Tom, really. But if wormholes existed, then perhaps Holy Years were the intervals at which they opened. If time travel was like travelling on the London Underground, the Holy Years were the stations where people could get on or off.

'You said your wormhole appeared near Santiago?' asked Tom.

Sir Walter looked bewildered. 'What is the worm's hole, lad?'

It was a fair question. Theoretical physics hadn't existed in the Middle Ages.

'Think of it as a gate through time,' said Tom.

'A Time Gate?'

'Exactly, a Time Gate. I think there might be two Time Gates: the one you passed through near Santiago, which sent you forward in time, and the one I passed through on the train near Saint-Jean, which sent me back in time.'

His theory offered the first rays of hope in over a week.

'Can you remember precisely where the storm appeared?' Tom asked Sir Walter.

'Aye, 'twas a mountain just east of the city – the Monte del Gozo.'

'Right, well, if I pass through the Time Gate at Monte del Gozo, I should travel forward in time. And if you pass through the Time Gate near Saint-Jean, you'll travel back in time.'

Sir Walter frowned. 'But when I passed through the Time Gate, I was sent many hundreds of years into the future. Won't the same thing happen to you, lad?'

Sir Walter was right: how could Tom be sure he'd travel forward to 2010? His theory was incomplete.

The church door squeaked open, and Pablo's scruffy silhouette stood in the doorway.

'Thomas, *comamos.*'

'It appears your lunch is ready, Tom Anderson.'

Tom couldn't leave, not with the answers to his questions within reach. Sir Walter smiled as if detecting Tom's hesitation.

'Go with ye companions; I'll not be far away. Keep travelling west to Santiago, and I'll do the same. By the time we reach the Time Gate atop Monte del Gozo, we'll have unlocked its secrets, I promise.'

Drowning in uncertainty, Tom clung to the knight's vow like driftwood. He followed Pablo back to the others and ate his lunch in silence. The wormholes and Holy Years felt like crucial pieces in an impossibly complicated jigsaw. The Camino hugged the side of the highway for most of the afternoon, and after they passed the village of Grañón, a crooked signpost announced they were leaving the region of La Rioja and entering Castilla y León. After several monotonous hours along the flat, straight path, Pablo began to grumble.

'*Odio el suelo plano. Es tan jodidamente aburrido.*'

'He says he prefers the mountains,' translated Sofia.

Pablo's wish was granted the following day when the Camino veered back up into the hills. By mid morning, with the sun beating down on them, Pablo groaned something else.

'*Maldita sea, odio las montañas.*'

'He says he hates the mountains,' said Sofia.

Each gruelling ascent was followed by an equally punishing descent; Tom walked in zig-zags to avoid running down the mountain. Whereas his lungs would feel close to bursting during the climbs, the descents attacked his knees and ankles. Pablo and Sofia struggled as well, and it was only Fernando who negotiated each mountain with ease. Finally, after stomping down yet another hill, they arrived at a stream. Tom's heart sank as his eyes followed the trail over a wooden bridge, where it rose steeply again on the other side of the water. Sofia, red-faced and breathless, seemingly shared his view.

'*Mierda.*'

Ana said something similar whenever anyone scored against Spain in the football. Fernando pointed to some pine trees, and the four of them rested in the shade. A few minutes later, a woman walked down the same mountain they'd just descended. She was middle-aged and wore a long dress; she carried nothing but a small bunch of wildflowers. Pablo waved to her.

'*Buenas tardes, señora.*'

The woman looked at them but said nothing. She continued toward the stream before leaving the path and walking into a clearing. She placed the flowers carefully onto the ground and bowed her head in prayer. When she was finished, she crossed herself and walked back along the Camino toward them. She stared at them with haunted eyes.

'*No deberías estar aquí. Esta es tierra santa.*'

Fernando held up his hand. '*Lo sentimos, señora.*'

The Spaniards rose to their feet and packed their canteens back into their bags. Tom instinctively did the same and followed the others over the footbridge. As they climbed the next mountain, Tom caught up to Sofia.

'What did that woman say back there?'

'She said we were sitting on holy ground.'

'What does that mean?'

Sofia glanced around the empty fields before answering. 'They call it the Terror Blanco – the White Terror.' She kept her voice low. 'When Franco took power, the Nationalists arrested anyone who opposed them: the socialists, communists, the masons, anyone who would offer a differing view. Some were made to work in the camps, but many were simply rounded up and disappeared forever.'

'Disappeared?' Tom looked back to the unmarked clearing; the small bouquet of flowers on the ground rustled in the wind. He remembered what Blanca had told him about her father. 'Why did no one intervene?'

'Because Spain and the Americans have a mutual enemy in the communists; Franco is a useful ally against the Soviets. No one wishes to lift the bandages around our country.'

'What about the church? Couldn't they have done something?'

'Franco used the clergy to legitimise his cause; he called it the defence of Christendom. Some priests even spied for the Nationalists, using what they learned in confession to help the government identify the traitors.'

'They betrayed their people?' Tom thought of the smiling priests and nuns who'd fed and housed them along the Camino.

'Not all of them, but many saw the war as an opportunity for power. Even today, they watch the people closely. Those who do not attend church regularly have their names passed to the government.'

'But they're supposed to serve God, not the government.'

Sofia smiled sadly. 'In Spain, it is the same thing.'

CHAPTER 14

The terracotta tiles of San Juan de Ortega's monastery glowed in the fierce afternoon sun. A weary-looking priest sought refuge in the shade of the church's bell tower.

'*Buen Camino*, pilgrims.'

Fernando waved to the old man. '*Buenos días, Padre.*'

'I suppose you've come to visit the monastery?' The priest didn't wait for an answer; he sighed and picked up his cane.

Sofia and Fernando followed him inside, while Pablo and Thomas went to fill everyone's canteens. The church's interior was modest, the only notable embellishment being the intricate stone carvings of Bible stories around its columns.

'Saint John the Hermit built this monastery with Saint Domingo de la Calzada in the twelfth century.' The priest sounded more bored than proud. He led them down a narrow set of stairs into the crypt, and they followed him along a narrow corridor. 'This is his tomb.' The priest waved toward a stone case lying on the ground. It was flanked by two candles, and a statue of a bearded saint stood behind it. 'Saint Domingo is the patron saint of hospice keepers, children and, of course, barren women.' His glassy eyes fell to Sofia. 'Good luck to you both.'

'No, we—'

The old man didn't wait for Fernando's protests.

'Come up when you're done.' He shuffled back through the passage and disappeared up the stairs.

The tomb's stale air became thick with discomfort. Fernando faced Sofia, his cheeks red with embarrassment.

'Ignore him,' he said. 'He's senile.'

Sofia didn't say a word; she simply stood and stared at the saint's statue. Each silent second weighed heavier. When she eventually faced Fernando, her eyes glistened in the candlelight.

'Do you ever think about having children?'

'Me?' The question unbalanced him. 'Once, maybe.'

'But not anymore?'

'I'm too old.'

'Men can father children into their fifties.'

'Not without a wife.'

'You don't think you'll ever marry?'

'No.'

'How can you be so certain? Have you ever been in love?'

'Of course.' His neck prickled under his collar, the way it always did when he lied. 'What about you? Do you and your fiancé want to start a family?'

'No, Hector and I...' Sofia's voice choked with tears,

and she turned to face the tomb.

A pit opened within Fernando's chest.

'Sofia… I'm sorry.'

Silence suffocated the tomb once more. The priest had been right after all: Sofia couldn't bear children. Knowing he couldn't offer any comfort, Fernando wished he could disappear; his presence felt like an invasion. Paralysed, he looked at the curved edges of the stone tomb, smoothed over the centuries by the hands of helpless women.

'It's unfair,' he said without thinking. 'Thousands of women have come here praying for a baby, yet my mother abandoned her two.'

'Did your father ever say why she left?'

'He didn't have to; she just didn't love us anymore.'

'You don't know that. Perhaps she had a reason.'

'What reason could anyone have for abandoning their children?'

Sofia stared at the tomb; silent tears trickled down her cheeks. The hushed minutes seemed to stretch on for years. She eventually took a deep breath and dried her eyes.

'It's funny, isn't it?' she said. 'The different saints people pray to. My father prays to Saint Andrew – the patron saint of fishermen – and my mother prays to Saint Joachim – the patron saint of grandparents. She's always wanted grandchildren.' Her eyes brimmed with tears again, but she unexpectedly laughed.

'What is it?' asked Fernando.

'It's silly.' She seemed to try to shake the thought from her mind, but her smile only broadened.

'Tell me.'

'Well, when I was a little girl, I always laughed at Saint

Drogo. He was the patron saint of many things: the sick and unwell, shepherds – even the patron saint of coffee-house owners.'

'Shepherds and coffee-house owners also need someone to pray to, no?'

'*Sí*, but Saint Drogo was also the patron saint of…' She clapped her hand over her mouth to stifle her laughter. 'I'm sorry, I cannot say it.'

'Please do.'

She leaned toward him and whispered, 'Santo Drogo is also the patron saint of the ugly.' She exploded into unexpected laughter; her entire body shuddered beneath its various layers.

Her melodious cackle was contagious, and Fernando soon cracked a forbidden smile. His blasphemous grin only made her laugh harder, and Fernando began to chuckle too. Soon, the entire crypt was filled with unrestrained laughter.

Bang. Bang. Bang.

Fernando and Sofia froze, their eyes immediately drawn to Saint Domingo's tomb on the floor.

Bang. Bang. Bang.

When they realised the thumping had come from the priest in the church above and not from the saint himself, the pair laughed harder. Sofia clutched Fernando's arm to steady herself as she howled and shuddered against him.

Bang. Bang. Bang. Bang. Bang. Bang.

The priest's incessant pounding on the floor chastised them back up the stairs and into the church; his beady glare from the church's pulpit expelled them out into the afternoon heat. They sat on the bench in the shade; Sofia wiped her tears from her cheeks and smirked.

'So, you do laugh.'

Fernando nodded. His cheeks felt sore. '*Sí*, occasionally.'

Their eyes met, and Sofia looked ready to say something more but was interrupted by Pablo and Thomas reappearing from the corner.

'For such a small village, you'd think the locals would be friendly.' The boy stopped dead. 'What's happened? Have you two been crying?'

'Laughing, actually,' said Sofia.

'About what?'

'None of your business.'

Pablo's eyes narrowed toward Fernando. 'Wait – you've been laughing too? While Thomas and I battle the village's *abuelas* for water from their precious fountain, you two are sitting here laughing? What were you joking about?'

Fernando stood up and took his and Sofia's canteens from the boy. '*Gracias*.'

'*Gracias?* Is that all you're going to say?' The boy looked hurt. 'Why do you wait until I'm gone to laugh? I like to laugh. In fact, I love it.'

Fernando pointed ahead to a scallop shell. '*Vamos*.'

Undeterred, the boy trailed closely behind. 'Friends shouldn't keep secrets from one another, *jefe*.'

'I'm not.'

'Oh, no? You said you were from Huelva, but you're really from Sevilla. Now you two are laughing about some secret joke.'

'It's not a secret, and I already told you: I live in Huelva, but I grew up in Sevilla. I'm not keeping secrets from you, Pablo.'

'Really? Then why won't you tell me about the war then?'

'What war?' asked Sofia.

'In Morocco,' said Pablo. 'Fernando served in the Spanish Legion. I've been asking him about it ever since Navarra.' The boy walked backwards in front of them. 'Come on, *jefe*, just one story.'

'There's nothing to tell.'

'I don't believe that.' The boy looked to Sofia. 'Do you know what people called the Spanish Legion?'

'Leave it, Pablo,' said Fernando.

'*Novios de la muerte*,' said the boy, in an ominous voice. 'The grooms of death.'

'I said, stop it.'

But the boy grinned toward Sofia. 'I bet you didn't know you were walking alongside a trained killer, did you?' He frowned at Fernando. 'Is that why you're walking the Camino, *jefe*? For all your murders?'

Fernando punched Pablo in the face, and the boy collapsed to the dirt.

'Get up.'

Fernando loomed over him, aching to slug the boy again. He reached down and pulled Pablo to his feet. A set of hands grabbed Fernando from behind; the fingernails dug into his flesh. He spun around and instinctively raised his fist.

'Fernando!'

Sofia cowered behind her hands; her eyes were wide with terror. Fernando lowered his fist. He picked up his bag from the ground and walked away.

'*Jefe*, I'm sorry,' called out the boy. 'I was only joking.'

Fernando didn't slow to hear the boy's apologies; he

marched toward the scallop shell at the end of the street and followed it out of town. Why couldn't Pablo keep his mouth shut? He had no right to tell Sofia that Fernando had served in the legion.

The image of her fear-stricken face flashed before him. It was an expression he'd not seen in decades; it was a look of terror.

Terror was a legionnaire's primary weapon; it had been the first lesson of his basic training. Thoughts of this time in his life immediately reminded Fernando of tobacco and sweat; the recruiting bus to Cádiz had been filled with both. Fernando had stared at the bus floor for the entire hour of the journey from Sevilla, scared that if he'd looked out of any of the windows he might have seen the *policía* in pursuit. When he and the other recruits had finally emerged onto the parade ground, they'd been lashed by the sand-filled winds from the gulf. Flocks of dirty seagulls had hovered overhead, inspecting the new recruits for any sign of food. A sergeant had stood and waited for them to organise themselves into rows. His skin had been as tough as an old piece of leather.

'My name is Company Sergeant Geraldo Mendoza.' His voice had shaken the recruits like leaves. 'But you miserable bastards may call me Santo Geraldo because one day the Catholic Church shall anoint me a fucking saint.' Mendoza had slowly paced down the line of recruits, a wolf surveying a flock.

'To become a saint, a man must complete two miracles. My first one shall be a prophecy.' He'd walked past Fernando, smelling of gun oil. 'I predict the next three months will be the worst of your pitiful lives. Each of you will feel unimaginable pain, and all of you will

Matthew S. Wilson

consider quitting; the smarter ones will go. The dumber ones – which looks like most of you – will persevere. A handful of you may still even be here to witness my second miracle.' Mendoza had returned to the front of the parade ground, choking them with his stare.

'Whereas Jesus turned water into wine, I shall transform a handful of you terrified sacks of shit into the fiercest warriors on God's green earth. The looks of dread on your vile faces will soon be on those of our enemies.'

It hadn't taken long for the men to consider quitting. Hours before dawn, the corporals had dragged the recruits from their beds – motivating the slowest among them with punches and kicks. The corporals had marched the recruits around the base at breakneck speeds, dumping them back to their barracks as the sun had risen. The recruits were then allowed to eat, shave, shower and shit – or as many of those things as could be achieved in fifteen minutes – before attending the first lesson of the day.

'Today, you will learn how to stand,' a wardrobe-shaped sergeant had growled on that first morning. 'You may think you know how to stand but you know nothing. Is that clear?'

'*Sí, Sargento.*'

'You worms only know what I teach you, is that clear?'

'*Sí, Sargento.*'

'When I call you to *atención*, you will lift your right leg ten inches off the ground and curl your hands into fists by your sides – thumbs to the front. A half breath later, you will drive your right foot down into the ground so hard you shatter the earth.'

For those recruits who hadn't executed the movement correctly, their knees, knuckles or stomachs had received

221

stinging rebuttals from the drill sergeant's baton. When multiple recruits had failed, the entire platoon had been ordered to run to the flagpole and back. Fernando had favoured the latter punishment until he'd seen the flagpole perched atop the hill overlooking the base. After their fourth trip around it, under a relentless Andalusian sun, the recruits' ability to stand at attention had miraculously improved. The next day they'd been taught to march. The day after that they'd been shown how to salute. The drill sergeant had delivered each lesson with the same teaching aids: the baton or the flagpole.

But as menacing as the sergeants had been, they hadn't scared Fernando half as much as his comrades. His father had warned him the legion was full of thieves and murderers. Their older, sullen faces had all borne a hardened edge absent from Fernando's youthful one. Fernando had been too frightened to fall asleep in those first few nights, convinced one of the other men might slit his throat.

As it turned out, he'd needn't have worried – there'd been little time for sleep. Their long days of marching and drills had always finished with Company Sergeant Mendoza's nightly inspection of the barracks. If Mendoza found nothing, the recruits had earned the right to sleep. But Santo Geraldo always found something.

'Hernández, your shirt has more creases in it than my ball sack. Duarte, your bed looks like a barn of pigs spent the night fucking in it. Suarez, I know you left the shit floating in the latrine because I saw you stuffing your face with corn cobs in the mess hall.'

And so the remainder of their nights had been filled with cleaning every inch of the base. From the comandante's vehicle to the bathroom faucets – the recruits had scrubbed and polished every conceivable surface. By the time they'd eventually collapsed into their beds, the barracks' doors had been kicked open by the corporals again, signifying the beginning of a new day.

Mendoza's prophecy had been realised quickly; each morning on the parade ground, there'd always been another man who'd decided to quit, choosing whatever dire consequences awaited them in the outside world over another day of hell within the legion. Fernando had considered leaving too. Sometimes, amid the endless hours of marching, his mind had drifted back to Sevilla. He'd replayed that fateful day in the Plaza de España a thousand times, wondering if the staff sergeant's threats of prison had been real or merely intended to extract a confession from a scared boy. He'd imagined Emilio telling Papa what had happened and their father scouring the streets of Sevilla for his eldest son. Fernando had enviously watched the other recruits quit and ached to return home. But every time he'd come close to leaving, he imagined what might become of Emilio if he reappeared in Sevilla. As hard as life in the legion was, it couldn't be worse than what might await his brother in prison. Fernando could survive this type of punishment; Emilio couldn't.

After three months of hell, Mendoza's second miracle had also come true.

'Look at you magnificent sons of bitches.' A smile had almost escaped Santo Geraldo's stone face as he'd surveyed the twenty hopeless souls who'd survived the torturous three months. 'They send me sheep, and I return them wolves.'

Fernando had felt proud as Mendoza had issued him

his *chapiri* – the traditional khaki-coloured cap with red hanging tassel worn by the legionnaires. Fernando had signed his enlistment papers and marched into the town of Cádiz with the rest of the graduating recruits. After three months without liquor or women, the old city of Cádiz had offered an abundance of both. Fernando had followed his older comrades from bar to bar and eventually into a tattoo parlour. When everyone had the legion's insignia carved into whatever bare skin they had available, Fernando had rolled up his sleeve.

'Legionnaires, to fight; legionnaires, to die!' he'd yelled, as the rest of his comrades had repeated the legion's motto after him.

Once branded, the soldiers had all bounded back out to the street in search of the nearest brothel. Fernando had accidentally barrelled into a passing family and the father's eyes had widened in anger.

'*Lo siento, señor,*' Fernando had said.

The father had protectively wrapped his arms around his wife and children.

It was only then that Fernando realised the father's eyes hadn't widened with anger. It had been the same look on Sofia's face back in the village.

It had been fear.

The afternoon's walk had been hot and dusty, with Pablo walking silently beside Sofia, and Fernando remaining well ahead. Despite the searing afternoon heat, things had remained icy between the Andalusians. Sofia was relieved when they decided to stop in the town of Orbaneja Riopico.

A stern-faced woman waved them into her farmhouse opposite the church, and they followed her down the cool hallway.

'The girl can sleep here,' said the woman, pointing to a small room on the left. 'And the men sleep in the room on the right. There's a sink and clothesline outside for you to wash your clothes in. Stew is served at seven o'clock.' She eyed Pablo. 'If you're not at the table at seven, your stew goes to the dogs. Lights out at eight o'clock – no exceptions.'

Once inside, Sofia dragged one of her room's two empty beds in front of the door. Safe from intrusion, she got undressed and lay naked on the other bed, spreading out her sticky limbs like a starfish. She closed her eyes and must have eventually drifted to sleep, for the slamming of a nearby door woke her. She considered going back to sleep, but the pile of sweat-soaked clothes on the floor dragged her to her feet. She changed into her spare uniform and carried her laundry outside. Fernando was scrubbing his clothes over the sink.

'I'm nearly finished,' he said. They were the first words he'd said all afternoon.

Sofia placed her soggy clothes on the bench next to him. 'You shouldn't have punched him, you know.'

'He shouldn't have said anything about the legion. It wasn't his secret to tell.'

'That may be true, but you still can't punch people, Fernando.'

His scrubbing slowed, and he turned his head ever so

slightly toward her. 'I'll apologise to him tonight.'

His concession had taken her by surprise. She nodded curtly. 'Good then.'

He turned to face her fully. 'And I'm sorry I frightened you. I was angry; I didn't want you to know.'

She frowned. 'What does it matter what I know?'

Their eyes met briefly before Fernando turned back to the sink. He resumed his washing.

'People look differently at those who served in the legion,' he said. 'They know the horrors we committed.'

'Wars make men do terrible deeds – but they were orders, not choices.'

'Soldiers tell themselves this, but following orders is still a choice.' He scrubbed his clothes with renewed vigour.

'It must be difficult,' she said, 'carrying such a heavy burden. Do you ever speak about it?'

'To who?'

'Your brother?'

'Like I said, we haven't spoken since the war. Besides, what good would come of it? What's done is done; we cannot change our pasts.'

'No, but talking about it might bring you some peace.'

'Any time I've tried, the words get stuck in my throat. Some truths are too dark to be unburied.'

'You need to start with the happy parts of the story first.'

'What if there aren't any?'

'There are always happy parts.' She smiled. 'It's like the old men in my ward. Some of them are very ill, but they simply blame their wives for being dramatic whenever a doctor asks what is wrong. So when I speak to them, I ask them about their lives, not their illness. Their eyes light up as they tell me their stories, sometimes happy but often sad. And after they trust me with their pasts, they often confide their illnesses to me.' She caught Fernando's eye. 'If you like, I'll listen to your stories too – the happy ones or the sad.'

His lips parted, but no sound came out. Sofia's eyes silently urged him to share some small detail with her, but Fernando turned and gathered his wet clothes instead.

'I should hang these to dry.' He left her alone with her thoughts.

Sofia scrubbed the day's sweat from her uniform. Had she overstepped her boundary with Fernando? Probably, but she'd sensed his yearning to open the locked rooms of his past. When her clothes were as clean as she could expect, she pegged them on the line in the courtyard; hopefully, they'd be dry enough to ruin again the following day.

Their hostess had been faithful to her word, placing a steaming pot of stew on the *albergue's* dining table at precisely seven o'clock. Sofia sat between Fernando and Thomas. Another pair of pilgrims sat opposite them: two brothers who'd started their pilgrimage from the medieval city of Ávila. The hostess stared at the empty chair beside the brothers.

'Where's the hairy one?'

The door swung open, and Pablo casually entered with his hands behind his back.

'*Buenas tardes, señora.* Apologies I'm late, but I couldn't seat myself at your table with an unwashed face.' He leaned over the pot and inhaled the steam wafting from it. 'Mmm, *delicioso*. Beef?'

The sinewy woman glared. 'Lamb.'

227

'Ah, lamb stew and bread.' Pablo nodded toward the stale-looking loaf on the table. 'Cervantes once said, "All sorrows are less with bread".'

'Wash the dishes when you're done,' said their hostess, leaving a kettle of hot water before heading to the door. 'Lights out in an hour.'

'*Sí*, of course, *señora. Buenas noches.*' Pablo waited for the door to close before sliding his arm out from behind his back and placing a bottle of red wine on the table. 'And to drink – *vino.*'

'Where did you get that?' asked Sofia, ladling the stew into the bowls.

'A local.' Pablo found some cups in the cupboard and began to pour the wine. 'And all it cost me was half an hour listening to him complain about his suffering crops.'

The brothers from Ávila gratefully accepted the wine, but Fernando pulled his empty cup away from Pablo.

'None for me.'

The smile fell from Pablo's lips, and Sofia stamped her heel down hard on Fernando's foot beneath the table. He looked up at her, stunned; she glared at him like the sun.

'Actually, Pablo' – Fernando slid his cup back toward the boy – 'I will have a little.'

A luminous smile spread across Pablo's face. '*Sí*, of course, *jefe*, of course.' He filled Fernando's cup before filling his own. 'This calls for a toast, no?' Before anyone could protest, Pablo raised his glass. 'As Cervantes wrote: "Man has to have friends, even in hell". So, I propose a toast to my friends.'

'To friends,' everyone echoed, tapping their cups together.

The wine was too bitter for Sofia, but the lamb was

surprisingly good. She helped herself to a second ladle as Pablo swapped tales from the Camino with the brothers from Ávila. After dinner, he suggested they finish their wine in the little square outside the church.

'I'm tired,' said Sofia. She gathered the empty bowls from the table and carried them to the small sink in the corner. 'I'll wash these, and then I'm going to bed.'

Fernando stood up. 'I'll help.'

Pablo herded the others out to the courtyard, and Fernando cleared the rest of the table. He held up Sofia's wine.

'Do you want the rest?'

She shook her head and he poured both their wines into the courtyard's drain.

'You didn't like it either?' she asked.

'The only reason I said yes was to avoid having a broken foot.'

They grinned at each other.

'Here – you can dry.' She tossed him a rag and filled the sink with hot water from the kettle. 'So you never drink alcohol?'

'Rarely more than a glass.'

'The fishermen in Huelva are different from those in Valencia; one-third of my father is rum.'

Fernando took a clean bowl from her and dried it. 'The other fishermen in Huelva drink plenty. Just not me.'

'Ever?' She frowned. 'So you've never been drunk?'

'Not for a very long time.'

'How long?'

He tilted his head. 'December…'

'That's less than a year.'

'…1935.'

Sofia's mouth fell open. 'Nineteen years? You haven't been drunk for nineteen years?' She scoffed. 'Did something traumatic happen?'

'In a way.' He placed the dried bowl in the cupboard and waited for the next one. 'It was my first night in Morocco. Back then, the legion sent many of its recruits down there to patrol and protect Spain's territory. I was posted there with another boy from my basic training, named Jiménez.'

'How old were you?'

'Almost eighteen.'

'You were only a boy. Weren't you scared?'

'Scared? I nearly soiled my uniform.' He ignored her smirk. 'When Jiménez and I arrived at the base, the sergeant major told us the rest of the men had organised a surprise for us in the sergeants' mess. When we walked into the mess, we found the entire company – almost one hundred men – had prepared an enormous feast to welcome us.'

'That's very nice, no?'

'*Sí* and not only that, but the corporals told us they'd arranged for the following day to be a rest day. They said they wanted us to get acclimatised to the Moroccan heat. As a welcome gift, they presented Jiménez and me with a bottle of gin each. And when every drop was drunk, and all the food was eaten, we linked arms with our new comrades and sang long into the night.'

'You sing?' She grinned. 'Now this I have to see.' She passed him another bowl to dry. 'So you drank so much you never wanted to drink again?'

'The problem wasn't the drinking and eating in the night, but the training the next day.'

'But you said you had a rest day.'

'The other men had lied. At five o'clock the following morning, I woke to the sound of a bugle and the sight of the sergeant major standing at the foot of my bed. The rest of the men were stood at attention, already dressed in their uniforms. All except for Jiménez and me. It had been a prank on the new recruits.'

Sofia covered her mouth in shock. 'What did you do?'

'We got dressed and ran outside to join the others for a twenty-mile march.'

'*Ay Dios mío.*'

'The other men had sipped the same drinks all night; Jiménez and I had been too drunk to notice. So after fifteen minutes of marching, all of the food and beer poured out of us. By the time we finished, the sun was up. The forty-degree heat baked the sweat and vomit into our uniforms.'

'But you could have died.'

'*Sí*, I wish I had.'

Something about the way he'd said it made her laugh, and she tried to stop herself. 'I'm sorry – that's awful.'

He grinned and dried another bowl. 'So that's the reason I rarely drink.'

They finished the washing up in silence, each with a smile on their face. After hanging their dishcloths on the rack to dry, Sofia turned to Fernando.

'*Gracias.*'

'They were all of our dishes, not just yours.'

'No – *gracias* for sharing your story.'

Their eyes met, and this time neither of them looked away.

The *albergue's* door squeaked open, and Pablo's face appeared.

'Another local has invited us to try his homemade sherry. Come and have a drink with us.'

'I'm going to bed,' said Sofia, nodding to Fernando. 'But I'm sure he'll have a glass, maybe even two. Tomorrow is a rest day, no?' She walked to her room with a smile on her face.

The following morning's walk into Burgos was flat. The Camino ran parallel with the highway until it was eventually swallowed by it completely. On the city's outskirts, cars and trucks rocketed past them. They arrived in the Plaza Mayor as the clocktower chimed eight o'clock and decided to sit at one of the square's cafés for breakfast. Their waiter brought them coffee and fresh bread. Sofia's stomach growled as she smothered the bread, still warm from the oven, in butter and jam. As she ate, she watched families walk across the square, each of them impeccably dressed.

'It's Sunday, today, no?'

'*Sí*,' said Fernando. 'Why?'

'Padre Price and I were supposed to deliver today's sermon at the cathedral here.'

'This morning?'

'*Sí.*' Sofia smiled to herself. The days had become a blur on the Camino. It had only been five days since Padre Price's accident, yet it felt like a lifetime ago. She was distracted by Pablo, who waved his crumpled *credencial* to the rest of them.

'That miserable cow from last night's *albergue* didn't stamp our *credencials*.'

'Missing one day won't matter,' said Fernando.

'When they inspect our stamps in Santiago, they'll see an eighty-kilometre gap. They might not issue us our Compostela if it looks suspicious, no?' Pablo pointed to a stately-looking building on the opposite side of the square. 'We can get it stamped at the town hall.'

They finished their breakfast and paid the bill, their scallop shells not drawing the same generosity found in the countryside. A pair of Spanish flags hung beneath each of the town hall's twin clocktowers. Inside, the front desk was unattended. Pablo slapped his palm down on the brass desk-bell, and its ding echoed around the empty room. A door behind the counter opened, and a man appeared. He was young, with broad shoulders, dressed in the dark-green uniform of the Guardia Civil.

'*¿Sí?*'

Sofia clenched at the sight of the uniform. Pablo tentatively stepped forward with their papers.

'*Perdóname, señor*, could you stamp our *credencials* for Santiago?'

The guard took the papers. Without smiling, he flipped through them.

'Granada.' He stamped Pablo's *credencial* and scribbled the date beneath it. 'And Huelva.'

Fernando and Pablo collected their papers just as the door behind the counter opened again. Another Guardia Civil officer stepped out. He was older and stockier than the first guard, and he wore three stripes on his sleeve.

'I'm going to the market,' he said, walking out from behind the counter toward the front doors.

The first guard picked up Thomas' *credencial* and his brow furrowed.

'*Sargento?* Do you remember the dispatch we received from Bilbao?'

The sergeant paused in the doorway. 'About the

pilgrims?'

'*Sí*. Where were they from, again?'

'Andalucía, I think. The other one was Irish, no? Or English. Why?'

Ice trickled down Sofia's spine as the guard's eyes flicked to Thomas. Fernando stepped forward.

'Is there a problem, Corporal?' he asked.

The guard's face grew as serious as a storm. He looked to his superior. '*Sargento*, I think this is them – the pilgrims.'

The sergeant frowned; his thick body blocked their escape. 'Is this true? Are you the pilgrims who fled from the Basque terrorists in Navarra?'

None of them knew what to say.

'Answer me,' he barked, his once cheerful face now grave. He clicked his fingers and held out a fleshy hand. 'Show me your identification – all of you.'

The silence sucked the air from the room; Fernando and Pablo looked to each other for the right lie to tell. Sofia was as surprised as anyone when she was the one to speak.

'Very well, *Sargento*.'

She hoisted her suitcase up onto the counter and unfastened its latches, pulling out an envelope. The sergeant snatched it from her.

'What's this?' He pulled a piece of paper from within it.

'Our identification.'

His lips vibrated as he quietly read, his eyes momentarily flashing toward Thomas halfway through.

'Is this real?' the sergeant eventually asked.

'Look at the seal and signature,' said Sofia. 'In

addition to fleeing a crime scene, are you also accusing us of forgery?'

'No… of course not, but…'

'But what?'

Flustered, the sergeant looked at Thomas. 'He looks so young.'

'How old are you, Sergeant?'

'Thirty-eight.'

'And yet you look fifty-two. Judging an apple from its appearance alone is fraught with danger, no?'

His mouth flapped like a fish, and Sofia pressed her advantage.

'And I suppose you think these are fake too?'

She threw back the suitcase's lid, and the sergeant's face drained of colour.

'*Jesucristo.*' The sergeant's fat cheeks blushed with blasphemy. He stared at Thomas. 'Please forgive me.'

'We don't have time for this,' snapped Sofia. 'You saw the letter's date and time. We must reach the cathedral immediately.'

'I'll escort you there myself.' He pointed to the door behind the counter. 'You can get changed in my office.'

'That won't be necessary,' said Sofia.

'I insist.' The sergeant ushered them behind the counter and through the door into the hallway. As they followed him to his office, Thomas turned to Sofia with confusion.

'What's going on?' he asked in English.

How was she going to translate all of this?

CHAPTER 15

Tom looked ridiculous. Father Price's black trousers were far too short, yet loose around his waist, and he was practically drowning in the priest's flowing black cassock. Even the high white collar sagged, clearly intended for a meatier neck. There was a knock on the door, and Sofia appeared.

'We must go; we only have ten minutes.'

'This will never work.' He held up his arms to show the billowing sleeves of the cassock. 'I look ludicrous.'

She walked in and tugged down his sleeves and trouser legs before straightening his collar. She nodded her satisfaction. '*Bueno.*'

'I can't just pretend I'm Father Price.'

'Why not?'

'Because it sounds like he's forty years older than me for starters; we don't look anything alike.'

'*Sí*, but the archbishop wrote he was looking forward to meeting Padre Price, so they've never met. Archbishop Carreño has no idea how you're supposed to look. All he's expecting is an Englishman.'

'But you'd already telephoned the cathedral and told them about the accident. Won't it be suspicious when I unexpectedly arrive, fully healed?'

She threw her hands up with exasperation. 'Pretend you have a limp. We had no other option, Thomas.'

There was a knock on the door, and the Guardia Civil sergeant's voice came through the door. '*Diez minutos, Padre.*'

Sofia reached into her suitcase and wrapped Father Price's shimmering emerald-coloured ceremonial robe around Tom's shoulders. She stepped back to inspect her creation. '*Vale*, now you are a priest.'

The two Guardia Civil officers led the four of them through the town hall's arches and down a tree-lined boulevard. Locals stared at their strange procession as the sergeant issued repeated heartfelt apologies to Tom.

'*Lo siento, Padre, lo siento.*'

They passed through a city gate resembling a turreted castle and emerged into another plaza; the cathedral loomed opposite. The enormous rosette window on the cathedral's Gothic façade reminded Tom of Notre-Dame in Paris. The officers rushed them past the queue of worshippers filing into the church; Fernando and Pablo drifted into the crowd at the rear.

While the cathedral wasn't as big as Saint Paul's in London, hundreds filled it. Sofia and Tom left the red-faced officers behind and walked up the central aisle; he remembered to limp halfway down.

'Ready?' asked Sofia.

'Not really.'

They ascended some red-carpeted steps onto the chancel – the raised platform between the congregation and altar. A tall, thin priest dressed in crimson robes greeted them. Sofia spoke to him in Spanish before introducing Tom.

'And Padre Price, may I present to you the Archbishop of Burgos Cathedral, Padre Alonso Carreño.'

Tom shook Archbishop Carreño's hand; the priest's slender fingers were cold and adorned with rings. Carreño's hair was jet black, despite the man being in his seventies, and parted directly down its middle. His skin was as pale as fresh snow.

'*Mi secretario me dijo que estabas herida, padre.*'

Sofia translated. 'Archbishop Carreño says his secretary had informed him you wouldn't be attending today's mass on account of your accident.'

Tom offered an embarrassed smile. 'Please apologise to the archbishop on my behalf. I'm afraid the doctors overreacted; it was nothing more than a muscle sprain.' He tapped the right knee he'd limped on.

Carreño's dark, unsmiling eyes surveyed Tom. '*Parece joven para un sacerdote. ¿Cuándo fue ordenado?*'

'He says you look very young to be a priest,' said Sofia. 'He asks when you were ordained.'

Tom remained vague. 'Not long, a couple of years.'

Carreño listened to Sofia's response without removing his eyes from Tom. He spoke to Sofia at length; his voice was as cold as his fingers had been. Sofia turned back to Tom to relay the priest's words.

'Archbishop Carreño says there are many dignitaries

and government officials attending today's mass to hear your sermon.'

Tom noticed a row of uniformed men in the front pew.

'The Archbishop asks which passage you will recite today.'

Tom's mouth dried to sandpaper. 'Well, that's very kind, but please tell him I'm quite happy to be a spectator today.'

Sofia didn't relay the message.

'Why aren't you translating?' he asked.

'Because it will look suspicious if you do not perform a sermon.' She spoke as if she were a ventriloquist. 'You cannot simply watch.'

'*Un momento*,' said Tom, smiling politely at the archbishop. He pulled Sofia to the other side of the chancel. 'I can't deliver a sermon,' he hissed at her.

'Why not? Recite the sermon from the last mass you attended.'

'It was a funeral.'

'It doesn't matter.'

'It was a year ago.'

'You don't attend mass?' She frowned. 'But you are Catholic, no?'

'No, I'm an atheist.'

'What is this word... *atheist*?'

He leaned closer and lowered his voice to the softest whisper. 'Someone who doesn't believe in God.'

'You don't believe in God?' She'd said it loud enough for several of the congregation to look up. She shot a look back to the archbishop, to ensure he hadn't understood, before responding. 'What kind of a pilgrim doesn't believe in God?' Sofia looked scared. 'Oh, Thomas, this is bad, this is very bad. What do we do?'

Archbishop Carreño cleared his throat and stepped toward them.

'*¿Quizás puedas recitar Romanos Trece?*'

'He suggests you recite Romans 13,' translated Sofia. 'You can read from Padre Price's Bible – it is in English.'

Tom smiled politely at the priest. '*Muchas gracias.*'

Tom turned back to Sofia. 'What's Romans about?'

The cathedral's pipe organ burst to life, and the worshippers rose to their feet as a procession of altar boys advanced down the central aisle. A robed steward appeared and guided Tom and Sofia to two high-backed chairs toward the chancel's rear. Tom used the edge of his robe to mop his brow.

'Relax,' whispered Sofia, watching the procession advance toward them. 'I will be alongside you to translate, remember?'

The organ stopped, and Archbishop Carreño glided to the pulpit and motioned for the congregation to sit. Tom and Sofia took their seats, and Sofia retrieved Padre Price's Bible from her suitcase.

'Here.'

Tom opened the cover to the contents page; it was the first Bible he'd held since he was a boy. His finger ran down the names of the stories he'd daydreamed his way through in his childhood – books like Genesis and Exodus. Like many others in England, his family had loosely been Christian – christenings, weddings and the occasional Easter mass.

'*Buenos días, damas y caballeros.*'

Carreño's shrill voice rang out through the amplifier

at the foot of the pulpit. As the archbishop started the service, Tom rummaged through the Bible's pages to the Book of Romans.

'Which chapter did he say?'

'Thirteen,' replied Sofia.

Tom eventually found the page, just as he heard his new identity mentioned.

'*Y desde Manchester, Inglaterra, por favor dé la bienvenida al Padre Price para pronunciar el sermón de hoy.*'

'It is time,' whispered Sofia.

Tom stood and walked toward the pulpit, his stomach churning as if he'd drunk a pint of curdled milk. He rested the Bible on the lectern and looked out over the cathedral. An ocean of expectant eyes stared up at him as he leaned toward the rounded, chrome microphone.

'*Buenos días.*'

A shriek of feedback made the audience wince. Sofia stepped forward and nudged the microphone further from his mouth. She smiled her encouragement, and he tried again.

'My name is Father Price, and I'm from Manchester, in England.' He gave Sofia room to translate, hoping no one knew what a Mancunian accent really sounded like. He then gestured to their host. 'I would like to thank Archbishop Carreño for his kind invitation to be here with you this morning. I've enjoyed my time on the Camino de Santiago very much. Spain is a wonderful country, filled with warm and welcoming people.'

The stone-faced officials in the front row gave unsmiling nods at Sofia's translation. Tom lifted his Bible.

'I'm going to read from the Book of Romans this morning.' He cleared his throat and began. 'Let every soul be subject to the governing authorities. For there is no authority except from God, and the authorities that exist are appointed by God. Therefore, whoever resists the authority resists the ordinance of God, and those who resist will bring judgement on themselves.'

Tom stepped back to allow Sofia to translate. The congregation's heads were lowered in prayer as they listened. He resumed reading the passage.

'For rulers are not a terror to good works, but to evil. Do you want to be unafraid of the authority? Do what is good, and you will have praise from the same. For he is God's minister to you for good. But if you do evil, be afraid; for he does not bear the sword in vain; for he is God's minister, an avenger to execute wrath on him who practises evil.'

Sofia completed the translation, and Archbishop Carreño returned to the pulpit.

'*Gracias*, Padre Price.' The priest smiled like an executioner. '*¿Quieres leer otro pasaje?*'

'He asks if you wish to read something else,' said Sofia.

Tom shook his head, and the archbishop politely gestured them back to their seats. Tom and Sofia sat back down, and Carreño's spidery fingers curled around the sides of the lectern as he studied his parishioners.

'*¿Qué podemos aprender de los escritos de Pablo?*'

Sofia leaned across to Tom. 'He asks what we may learn from this passage,' she whispered. 'He says through faith in God, Spain has prospered. Spaniards now live in peace, free of bloodshed; those who want to work have jobs; our economy grows; food is now bountiful. We are living in a golden era of Spanish history.'

The archbishop gestured toward Tom as Sofia

continued her translation.

'He says, even those from countries who once denounced Spain, now travel here to marvel at our achievements.'

Tom felt uneasy with the unintended endorsement his presence had offered. Carreño hammered his hand down upon the pulpit as he continued. Sofia struggled to keep up.

'He says Spain must remain vigilant. Like weeds growing through cracks in the cement, we must watch for Leftist and Marxist sentiments. He says we must rip them up from their roots before they may spread their seeds. Spain's struggle is a crusade; as soldiers of God, we carry with us the evangelism of the world.'

Carreño's shrill voice rose; spittle flew from his thin lips. The officials in the front nodded fervently with each impassioned sentence. The eyes of the families in the pews behind them remained lowered. Tom suddenly realised the locals' heads weren't bowed in contemplation; it was in submission.

'The archbishop implores the people to remain watchful,' continued Sofia. 'He reminds them they are being watched – not simply by their neighbours – but by God himself.'

When Archbishop Carreño finished, the cathedral was as quiet as a tomb. Tom stared at the defeated faces of the locals. The archbishop had bent and twisted the words from Tom's reading to his own devices. Tom suddenly realised Padre Price's visit had been just another propaganda exercise, a way of legitimising Franco's dictatorship. He looked at the Bible in his hands. The words within were supposed to offer these people hope, not be held to their throats. Tom had been used; his presence here would hurt people. A match ignited within him, and he stood up.

'Wait.'

Archbishop Carreño's eyebrows lifted with surprise. '*¿Sí?*'

'Thomas, what are you doing?' asked Sofia.

Tom held up the Bible and walked toward the pulpit. 'I do have something more to say.'

The archbishop turned to Sofia for an explanation before reluctantly surrendering the lectern. Sofia followed Tom to the microphone.

'We should go, Thomas.'

'Not yet.'

Tom rested the Bible on the pulpit and searched the contents page for the story he'd seen earlier, quickly finding the correct page. He looked up at the congregation.

'My best friend back in England is Spanish,' he said into the microphone, 'and she misses Spain terribly.' As Sofia translated, looks of curiosity appeared on the faces below. 'I'd always assumed it was the food or weather she missed, but after walking the Camino, I now know it's the people.' The men in the uniforms looked up with intrigue. 'There's a tremendous spirit in the Spanish people – a certain joy and belief. Belief is powerful; it can turn despair into hope, and hope is a contagious force. But for anyone who has lost their belief, I have one more passage I'd like to read before I leave.'

Tom turned to the Book of Samuel and read.

'And the Philistines stood on a mountain on the one side, and Israel stood on a mountain on the other side: and there was a valley between them. And there went out a champion out of the camp of the Philistines, named

Goliath, whose height was six cubits and a span. And he had a helmet of brass upon his head, and he was armed with a coat of mail; and the weight of the coat was five thousand shekels of brass.'

Sofia translated Tom's words. Her concerned eyes never left him as he read the story of David and Goliath. The bowed faces of the congregation began to lift as they listened to the story of the shepherd who faced the giant, armed with nothing more than a sling and five smooth stones.

'And David put his hand in his bag, and took thence a stone, and slang it, and smote the Philistine in his forehead, that the stone sunk into Goliath's forehead; and he fell upon his face to the earth.'

Sofia's lip began to tremble as she spoke; more faces lifted.

'And when the Philistines saw their champion was dead, they fled. And the men of Israel and of Judah arose, and shouted, and pursued the Philistines, until thou come to the valley, and to the gates of Ekron.'

Nobody moved when Sofia completed her translation – not even the fidgeting children. Archbishop Carreño stood from his chair and stepped toward the microphone, his face now paler than before. His black eyes flicked from Tom down to the uniformed men. He leaned toward the microphone and wet his thin lips, ready to issue a retraction of everything Tom had just said.

'*Damas y caballeros*—'

Carreño was interrupted by a slow, deliberate clap. Tom scanned the cathedral for its source, discovering it was a woman sitting in the middle of the congregation. She was middle-aged with dark hair and eyes and had the same solemn defiance of the woman they'd seen laying flowers on the unmarked grave by the stream outside San Juan. Carreño's eyes locked on her. Like a hawk hovering over a mouse, he looked ready to strike out at her when another clap rang out – this time from an elderly man sitting in a pew to the left. A third clap came from a younger woman near the front, then another by the elderly couple to her right. The archbishop released his grip on the microphone; applause spread through the congregation like a spilled glass of red wine on a white tablecloth.

Sofia leaned toward Tom. 'We must go.'

He yanked the microphone toward himself. '*Gracias*, for hosting me. And *buen Camino*.'

'*Buen Camino*,' echoed several of the congregation.

Tom and Sofia hurried down the stairs and up the central aisle. The cathedral stood and clapped in unison, farewelling the priest from Manchester with resounding applause.

It was only after they'd crossed the river and left Burgos completely that Sofia's heart finally slowed.

'I think we're safe,' said Fernando. 'Let's rest a moment.'

The group sat on a patch of grass beside the river and caught their breath.

'What should we do with these?' Thomas asked Sofia, slipping out of the emerald ceremonial robes.

'*¡Dios mío!*' Sofia's shoulders slumped. 'I told Padre

Price I'd leave them at Burgos Cathedral.'

Even in English, Pablo recognised the city's name.

'We can't go back, now,' he said in Spanish. 'We were lucky to get out of there at all. Why did you have Thomas impersonate a Catholic priest? We were lucky not to be arrested in the cathedral.'

'We'd have been arrested earlier for your silly stamp. I didn't exactly have a lot of time to think of a better solution, Pablo.'

'Well, we can't return to Burgos now. Thomas sounded like he was inciting a revolution. Why did you translate all of that?'

'Next time, you can translate, okay?'

'There's little point in fighting,' said Fernando, facing Pablo. 'Sofia is right; we'd all be arrested by now if she hadn't intervened. She and Thomas saved us.' He turned to Sofia. 'And Pablo is right too; we can't go back.'

'So what do we do with the robes?' she asked.

He paused to think. 'We're supposed to pass a monastery soon. We can leave them there, with a note to return them to England.'

Sofia's sense of duty to Padre Price had expired. They left the robes and tunic neatly folded on the front pew of the abbey of Santa María la Real de Las Huelgas. A small note asked for the garments to be returned to the Catholic Church of Manchester, England.

After two more hours walking through flat farmland, they arrived at the village of Tardajos, its squat roman church shimmering in the late-morning sun.

'Let's eat,' said Pablo. 'I'm starving.'

'You were starving two hours ago,' said Fernando.

'Evading arrest makes me hungry, *jefe*.'

'Well, we've run out of food, and it's Sunday. Nothing will be open in a village this small.'

Fernando was right; the town's store was closed. Pablo futilely knocked on its door anyway before spotting an elderly woman spying on them from a nearby balcony.

'*Señora*, is there nowhere in this village for some hungry pilgrims to eat?'

'No,' said the woman, ignoring the boy's hints at being fed. 'The next village is Rabé.'

'How far is it?'

'Half an hour.' The woman eyed Sofia. 'Maybe longer.'

Sofia glared at the woman. 'Let's go – there's an unpleasant smell in this town.'

They reached Rabé de las Calzadas in an hour. To Pablo's delight, a small bar was open and served food and drinks. The four of them sat at a table against the wall, shielded from the midday sun by a faded umbrella. Fernando gathered their flasks to fill at the fountain while Thomas searched for Santo Gutierre. A waitress appeared and handed menus to Pablo and Sofia. She looked as if she were not yet twenty; her bronzed skin and big brown eyes made her uncharacteristically glamorous for such a forgotten village. She smiled at Pablo, with teeth as straight and white as his.

'Do you know what you want?'

Pablo scanned the menu. 'How is the tortilla?'

'It's the best in Castilla y León; my mother cooks it.'

Pablo nodded his approval and handed back the menu. 'Then we'll have half your tortilla, a little jamón and some bread.'

'No wine?'

'Sadly, no. My friends never drink during the day.'

'Perhaps you should get new friends.' She offered a playful smile and took their menus without ever glancing toward Sofia. 'I'll be back.'

The waitress sauntered inside, and Sofia stared at Pablo.

'What?' he asked.

'She was flirting with you.'

His eyebrows rose with surprise. 'Really? I didn't notice.'

Sofia rolled her eyes. 'How could you not? She's stunning.'

Pablo craned his neck and looked into the bar. '*Sí*, she's cute, I suppose.'

'Cute? Any woman would kill for her figure.' Sofia studied Pablo's face, surprised by his nonchalance. 'Ever since I've met you, you've bragged about all your conquests back in Granada. Yet, here you are – faced with an exotic beauty on the Camino – and you're indifferent.'

'Well, even if she was flirting, it's hardly practical, is it? I live in Granada, and she lives in…' He checked the sign above the bar. 'Rabé de las Calzadas.'

'I thought your Camino was an adventure. What could be more exciting than a fleeting romance with a beautiful girl from a distant village?'

'Perhaps she's not my type.'

'Nonsense – she's every man's type.'

He shrugged again, seemingly putting the matter to rest. But Sofia couldn't let it go.

'So what is your type, then? Do you prefer short and curvy women, or tall and athletic?'

'There's no single type.'

'There must be some woman you're attracted to. What

of all those nights where you and your friend drunkenly chased after the women of Granada. Were they all just stories?'

'No, they were real. Partly, anyway.'

'What do you mean?'

She looked into his eyes and noticed they were shimmering with tears.

'I wasn't there for the girls.'

'What do you mean?' But as soon as she'd asked the question, she realised she already knew the answer.

'Pablo, I…' She gathered her thoughts, unsure if he was saying what she thought he was saying. 'So you and Jamie…'

'Were friends in the beginning. We did everything together: spending our days studying and our nights getting drunk, discussing literature.' His voice wavered. 'But somewhere along the way, it became something more. Something… unnatural.'

It was the word everyone used – her parents, their priest – but here it sounded misplaced. Sofia stood up and sat next to him.

'There's nothing wrong with you, Pablo.'

'Of course there is – everyone says so.' His voice finally cracked. 'My father says it's one of life's vilest sins.'

'He knows about Jamie?'

Pablo sniffed and nodded. 'My parents drove to Córdoba for the weekend last month, but my mother fell ill, and they returned early. My father discovered Jamie and I asleep in bed together.' He looked embarrassed, ashamed. 'My father screamed at us and dragged Jamie out of the house.' An unwilling tear trickled down his cheek. 'I haven't seen Jamie since.'

'You left for the Camino soon after?'

'*Sí*. My father said walking to Santiago during the Xacobeo would cleanse me of impurity.' He scoffed. 'God, I wish he'd been right.'

Sofia remained silent, searching for the words to match her feelings. Pablo gave a rueful sigh.

'I never expected the Camino to alter who I'm attracted to, but I'd hoped it would offer me some answers.'

'What kind of answers?' she asked.

'About how I feel about Jamie or whether I should follow my dream of writing. But the Camino hasn't solved anything. We're halfway to Santiago, and I'm even more confused than when I started. I was a fool to think a trek could answer such things.'

It felt wrong to see such a joyful person hurting so much.

'Well, if you're foolish to think such things, you're not alone,' Sofia eventually said. 'The Camino hasn't offered me the answers I wanted either.'

'No?'

'Not a single one.'

The pair looked glumly at each other, recognising the disappointment they saw in the other.

'It appears we were both lied to about all the epiphanies,' said Pablo.

'Perhaps they will arrive in the second half of our journey.'

They shared a smile.

'*Gracias*, Sofia. I didn't have anyone else to tell.'

'Don't be silly.' She placed her hand upon his. 'I'm sorry I don't yet have the right words to say, Pablo. But there's nothing wrong or sinful about you.' She squeezed his hand. 'You've got a good soul.'

Her words summoned tears to his eyes, and he squeezed her hand. 'I just wish I was normal, you know? Life would be so much simpler if I was normal.'

His anguished plea made her own eyes water. 'The only thing I'm certain of is there's no such thing as normal, Pablo. We feel how we feel; we love who we love.'

'*Gracias.*'

He leaned across and hugged her tightly; she could feel his body quiver against her. When he eventually pulled himself away, his cheeks were shiny with tears. He wiped them dry.

'So, what were the questions you wanted answering by the Camino?' he asked.

But before Sofia could respond, the waitress returned with their food.

'So, we have the tortilla, the jamón and some bread.' She placed the dishes on the table before resting a hand on one of her beautifully rounded hips.

'Do you want anything else?' she asked, smiling sweetly toward Pablo.

'Nothing else,' said Sofia.

The disappointed girl returned inside; Pablo began attacking the food.

'Mmm, *delicioso*,' he said, between mouthfuls of tortilla. 'If this girl's mother cooked this, perhaps I should marry her after all, no?'

They both laughed, and Sofia cut a slice for herself. Pablo's chewing paused and his face grew serious.

'Sofia?'

'*¿Sí?*'

'Don't tell *jefe* about any of this, okay? I don't think he would understand.'

Sofia wasn't so sure but nodded. 'I won't say anything, I promise.'

After the service, Archbishop Carreño stormed back to his chambers and notified his stewards he wasn't to be disturbed. He retrieved the correspondence he'd shared with Padre Price from his filing cabinet and re-read both letters at his desk. The first had arrived before Christmas the previous year. The Englishman had introduced himself as the dean of Saint Christopher's – Manchester's second-largest Catholic cathedral – and explained he would be undertaking a pilgrimage to Santiago in the summer. Price went on to say he'd heard of Burgos Cathedral's vast collection of tapestries and had enquired whether he might be extended a private viewing. Carreño had broached the request with Burgos' mayor in their weekly meeting. The mayor – an overweight man, perpetually perspiring – had been intrigued by the Englishman's request.

'Europe has long shunned us, Padre. Alliances within Britain's clergy could only aid Spain's submission for entry into the United Nations.'

The potential publicity of such a visit wouldn't have gone unnoticed in Madrid – perhaps even remembered when the next cardinal was appointed. As such, Carreño had immediately replied to Price. But rather than offering a tour of the tapestries, he'd invited the Englishman to deliver a sermon in their cathedral. Price had graciously accepted in his second letter a few weeks later and had suggested a date of Sunday 20th June. Carreño had written a final letter proposing the two men meet on Friday 18th for a private tour of the cathedral and to prepare their joint sermon.

Archbishop Carreño placed the letters next to one another on his desk. Neither suggested Price should have been an older man, yet the archbishop found himself unsettled by the English priest's youthful appearance. In Spain, a priest of forty was considered exceedingly young, yet Price hadn't looked a day beyond thirty. It wasn't impossible to have finished the required studies by such a tender age, but it was irregular. In fact, the priest's entire visit had been odd. Days earlier, the archbishop's secretary had received a telephone call from Price's driver, notifying him the priest had suffered a fall and would be unable to deliver Sunday's sermon. Carreño had immediately telephoned the mayor, who had flown into a rage down the line.

'Have you any idea how many party members I've organised to attend? All the generals will be there.'

So Carreño had been shocked when the youthful Englishman had limped up the stairs of the cathedral. There'd been something improper with the boy, but the cathedral's front pews had already been filled with senior party members – what other choice had there been? In hindsight, it had been a mistake to defy his intuition.

Price's reading of David and Goliath had been problematic. The implication – however slight – that Spain was Goliath was inappropriate, at best. At worst, it was treason. And while Carreño was still the head of the archdiocese, he wasn't beyond reproach. He'd seen how the party officials had shifted uncomfortably in their seats during the Englishman's remarks; Carreño had half expected the mayor to be waiting in his chambers following the sermon.

A knock at the door startled him.

'*¿Sí?*'

The door opened, and one of the cathedral's stewards, Brother Vedruna, appeared in the doorway. '*Perdóname*, Archbishop, but you have a visitor.'

'Is it the mayor?'

'No, Padre.'

'I explicitly told you no visitors today. If it's someone seeking a private counsel, they're welcome to make a donation for next Sunday.'

'They aren't here for confession, Padre.' Brother Vedruna glanced behind him into the hallway. 'And I'm afraid they're insistent they see you.'

'Who is it?'

'It's Padre Price.'

Archbishop Carreño frowned. 'The Englishman? He's returned?'

'Not quite.' Vedruna looked distressed.

Carreño stood and strode toward the door. An elderly priest sat on the plush red couch in the hallway. He was stocky and mostly bald, with grey wisps of hair clinging to his head. He wore thick-rimmed glasses, and one of his legs was in a cast.

'Who is this man?' asked Carreño.

Brother Vedruna smiled uncomfortably. 'He says his name is Padre Benjamin Price.'

CHAPTER 16

When they arrived in the village of Hornillos del Camino, it was late afternoon. The day's walk across the flat and empty plains of what the locals called the Meseta had been punishing, offering few opportunities for water or shade. Fernando checked the position of the sun. If they pushed on, they'd make San Bol by dusk.

'Let's fill our canteens and keep going,' he said.

The town's fountain was on the edge of the village square; its bowl was shaped like a scallop shell. As the pilgrims filled their flasks, Pablo pointed to a crowd of people emerging from a nearby church.

'Look, it's a wedding.' He edged toward it. 'Let's go and look.'

Fernando pointed to the dipping sun. 'We should keep going.'

'Just a quick look.' The boy walked toward the church.

Fernando turned to Sofia and Thomas for support, but they shrugged helplessly and followed Pablo.

'Fine,' he sighed, trailing behind.

A young couple exited the church and were showered with confetti and cheers from the crowd. Pablo leaned forward and tapped a local woman on her shoulder.

'*Perdóname, señora*, but who is getting married?'

'That's my nephew, Sergio.' The woman's cheeks nearly burst under the strain of her smile. 'And his beautiful bride, Ella.'

'Congratulations!' Pablo hugged the woman and kissed both of her cheeks.

She eyed the rest of them. 'But who are you?'

'We're pilgrims, bound for Santiago.'

The woman's eyes grew wide as saucers. 'This is a sign. You've been sent here to bless the wedding.'

'We're not staying, *señora*,' interjected Fernando politely. 'We're merely passing through.'

The woman mustn't have heard him. She climbed up the steps to the church's veranda and clapped her hands together.

'*¡Oye!* Listen, everyone, listen!'

The crowd froze, and she pointed down to the pilgrims.

'Saint James has sent four pilgrims to bless Sergio and Ella's wedding.'

A boisterous cheer erupted, and fistfuls of confetti rained down upon the pilgrims. The little woman climbed down the stairs toward them, beaming. Fernando tried to be respectful.

'*Señora, gracias* for the invitation, but—'

She swatted his formalities away. 'Please, everyone

calls me Tia.'

'Tia, we are grateful for your invitation but we cannot stay. We're aiming for San Bol tonight.'

'San Bol is a dusty little hole in the ground! The four of you will join our celebrations and stay here tonight.'

'We'll need to find an *albergue*.'

'You've found one.' She pointed to the stone building beside the fountain.

'But it's closed.'

'Of course it's closed – everyone is here. But don't you worry.' She pulled out a ring of keys worthy of a jail warden. 'I'll open it.'

'We're too tired for a wedding. We've walked all the way from Burgos this morning.'

'Then you'll be hungry. My husband, Benito, is cooking his suckling pig; it's the best in Spain.' Tia turned to Sofia. 'Is he always this miserable?'

'Always.' Sofia grinned.

Pablo nodded enthusiastically. '*Sí*, always.'

Tia jingled toward the *albergue*, and the pilgrims followed. She ushered them inside and pointed them to their rooms.

'I'll return with hot water for you to wash your faces and dirty clothes in.'

Their host disappeared back outside, and Pablo turned to the group.

'Let's go and get some of that pig.'

'I'll wait for the hot water,' said Sofia. 'You three go ahead.'

Fernando followed Pablo and Thomas outside, where they took turns splashing themselves clean in the fountain before joining the festivities. They were greeted by a man with a thick black moustache and an enormous belly.

'Welcome, pilgrims, welcome! I am Ignacio, Ella's uncle. *Muchas gracias* for blessing my niece's wedding.' Ignacio held out three bottles of beer.

Thomas took one, and Pablo took the other two.

'My friend doesn't drink,' explained the boy.

Fernando prised one of the beers from Pablo. 'I drink – just not as readily as my friend here.'

'This is good.' Ignacio laughed, raising his beer toward them. 'We all drink tonight, no? *Salud.*'

Their bottles clinked against his. The ice-cold beer slid easily down Fernando's throat, and it wasn't long before each of their bottles was drained. Ignacio led them across the square to an enormous chest filled with beer and ice. Pablo fell to his knees before it.

'Our pilgrimage is over, *jefe*. We have arrived.'

He filled his arms with bottles, and Ignacio shepherded the pilgrims through the crowd to the rest of his family, who greeted them with raised glasses.

'*Salud.*'

The clinks of their bottles were chased down by more swigs of beer. Another family waved the pilgrims over for a toast, followed by another and another. It seemed all of Hornillos stood waiting to drink with their guests of honour. After their third beer, Pablo assumed the role of toastmaster.

'To Sergio and Ella,' he bellowed, hoisting a newly replaced bottle into the air.

'*Salud*,' chorused the crowd.

A toast to the village was soon followed by a heartfelt toast to the entire region of Castilla y León. Feeling the beer's effects, Fernando walked back to the chest of drinks, searching for a flask of water.

'Looking for the gin?'

He spun around and nearly didn't recognise Sofia at first; she was wearing a long, flowing, white summer dress, with her blue shawl wrapped loosely around her. Her dark hair, usually tied up beneath her nurse's bonnet, hung by her shoulders, still wet but already starting to curl in the warm evening air.

'Um… no,' he stammered. 'Can I get you a drink?'

'*Sí*, just a little.'

Finding a bottle of red wine, he poured them a glass each. She nodded toward the square.

'I see Pablo is popular with the locals.'

'*Sí*, he is a celebrity.'

She smiled and continued to eye the crowd. 'The bride and groom look happy, no? She looks beautiful.'

'So do you.'

Her eyebrows lifted with surprise; his cheeks glowed with embarrassment. He hurriedly raised his glass to rescue them from the silence.

'What shall we drink to?'

'How about the Camino?' She seemed to enjoy how flushed he was. 'And the friends we make along the way.'

'*Salud.*'

They touched their glasses together and sipped their wine. Fernando remained silent, mistrustful of his loosened tongue. Thankfully, Tia arrived with a pile of plates.

'Hey, you two had better see Benito before the pig is gone.' She pointed to a man toiling over a flaming spit on the other side of the square.

Fernando and Sofia each took a plate and walked over; Benito carved them massive hunks of meat and guided them to a table laden with potatoes, beans and bread. With their plates stacked, they found a bench on the lawn overlooking the flat, empty fields of the Meseta. What had been punishing to walk across in the afternoon now looked tranquil in the twilight.

'Well, this beats soup and bread in an *albergue*,' said Sofia.

Tia hadn't lied; the pig was so succulent, it melted in Fernando's mouth. The two of them enjoyed their dinner in silence as the night's first stars twinkled to life above them. When they'd finished their meals, Fernando took their empty plates and cutlery over to a sink by the church. An old woman with a toothless smile snatched his dirty dishes and shooed him away. While walking back to Sofia, rows of carnival lights flickered to life overhead, bathing the square in a soft orange glow. A trio of musicians stood on the church's porch, tuning their instruments.

'Looks like there's going to be a band,' he said, sitting back down on the bench.

Sofia didn't respond, cradling her wine in her hands and staring into the distance.

'Are you alright?' he asked.

She stirred from her thoughts. 'You said there was a band?'

'*Sí*, near the church.'

Applause rippled from the square behind them as the band began to play. Sergio led his bride into the middle of the courtyard.

'Let's go and watch,' said Sofia.

They joined the other guests at the plaza's edge and watched the young couple's first dance as husband and wife. Fernando studied Sofia's face under the warm glow of the lights. She was smiling, yet her eyes glistened. As the band continued to play, men led their wives or girlfriends into the square to dance. Tia plucked the wine glasses from Fernando and Sofia's hands.

'What are you waiting for? Dance with your wife.'

'Oh, no, we're not married,' protested Fernando. 'Sofia's engaged.'

'*Sí*, I have a fiancé.'

Tia's initial confusion turned to joy. She wrapped her arm around Sofia's shoulder and nodded to Ella, still dancing with Sergio. 'So this will be you soon, no?'

'*Sí*, soon.'

'And then you'll be married and have lots and lots of babies.' Tia clutched her hands to her chest as if she was gaining grandchildren of her own.

Benito arrived, temporarily relieved of his pig-carving duties, and led his wife into the square to dance. Fernando faced Sofia; tears had begun trickling down her glowing cheeks. His thoughts returned to her mournful expression in the tomb of Santo Domingo.

'Sofia, Tia couldn't know; she was only being nice.'

Sofia turned and hurried off in the direction where they'd eaten dinner. He waited, debating whether to afford her time and space. He eventually followed her to the bench. She lay crumpled upon it, sobbing into her hands. He placed his hand on her back; her body shuddered beneath her shawl.

'Tia couldn't have known about you and Hector.'

Sofia lifted her slippery face from her hands. 'There is no Hector and I anymore…' Her voice was little more than a whisper. 'I lied to all of you, Fernando. I'm not engaged.'

'What?' His head whirled. 'I don't understand. You made up Hector?'

'No, Hector is real – and we were engaged to be married, but…' Her voice trailed off and her eyes filled with tears. 'I'm sorry I lied. It's just when Pablo asked me if I was married, I felt angry and ashamed. I didn't want to admit to him I was alone.'

She slumped back onto the bench, and he sat down beside her.

'What happened?'

She swallowed back her tears. 'A month ago, Hector and I had a horrible fight, and we called off the engagement.'

'I'm so sorry.' He felt powerless. 'Fights are often temporary.' He pointed to her hand. 'You still wear the engagement ring; perhaps you'll still mend things, no?'

'Married women attract less attention than unmarried,' she said. 'There's no way to repair things between Hector and me. When some things break, they are broken forever.' She paused as if deciding how much she should share. 'The truth is, a few months ago—'

'There you two are!' Pablo bounded over to them, his sweaty curls clinging to his forehead. 'I've been looking for you everywhere. Sofia, come dance.'

And before she could decline, the boy dragged Sofia from the bench and back to the square. Fernando followed slowly, still processing the discovery that Sofia wasn't engaged to be married. It shouldn't have mattered to him, but his entire body pulsed.

Back at the courtyard, the band played an upbeat tune. Sofia – crestfallen a moment earlier – laughed hysterically at Pablo, who gyrated and orbited her like a drunken moon. Fernando leaned against the church's wall and smiled as he watched. He felt a tap on his shoulder, and Thomas handed him a glass of wine. The Englishman's gentle sway suggested he was just as drunk as Fernando.

'*Salud.*'

They clinked glasses and drank. When the song ended, Pablo wobbled over to them.

'*Jefe*, I need to piss.' He pulled Fernando into the square toward Sofia. 'You two dance, I'll be back.' The boy stumbled off toward the nearest paddock.

Fernando shook his head. 'He's crazy.'

'*Sí*, but he's fun,' said Sofia, catching her breath.

The band started to play a song Fernando had never heard; it had a slower Latin-American feel. All of the couples around them began to slow dance. Sofia must have seen how helpless Fernando felt.

'Don't worry, you don't have to dance with me.' She turned to leave, but Fernando took her hand.

'No, I do.'

The alcohol made him sound more confident than he felt; he placed his other hand lightly on her hip. The guitar's strumming was slow and staccato, almost remorseful. As the singer's husky voice rang out across the square, Fernando looked into Sofia's eyes, the carnival lights reflected in them. He realised her hazel irises had flecks of green within them; they were beautiful. The singer purred the chorus; the song's title seemed to be 'Quizás, Quizás, Quizás'. Fernando kept his dancing simple, doing little more than gently swaying to the song's slow beat. A lock of Sofia's hair tumbled onto her forehead, and he felt the urge to stroke it back behind her ear. He could still see the tracks of her earlier tears on her cheeks, and he followed them down to her lips; they looked so soft.

His eyes darted back to hers, fearful she'd detected his attraction. She merely looked back at him; her eyes felt warm and comforting. His thumb rubbed against the back of her hand, but he couldn't be sure if he'd moved his hand or she'd moved hers. The song finished too soon, and he reluctantly released Sofia's hand to applaud the band. He looked up to the musicians, desperate for them to play another slow song.

'Okay, okay, I'm back,' said Pablo, swaying his way through the crowd. 'And look what I found?' He held up a bottle of bourbon.

'I should go to bed,' said Sofia. 'It's been a long day.'

'Bed? That's no fun. What about you, *jefe*? Fancy a little nightcap?'

Fernando looked at Sofia. 'I don't think…'

'Come on,' moaned Pablo. 'It's a wedding, for heaven's sake. Can't we have just one night to enjoy ourselves?'

'*Sí*, you should stay,' said Sofia. 'Tia will be upset if we all leave early. I'll see you all in the morning. *Buenas noches.*'

'*Buenas noches,*' said Pablo, ushering Fernando over to Thomas by the church.

Fernando looked back over his shoulder for Sofia, but she'd already disappeared into the night. The band started playing its next song.

'Thomas, get rid of that swill.' Pablo didn't even attempt to speak English, throwing the remainder of the Englishman's wine to the ground before refilling his glass with bourbon. He poured some more into a nearby tumbler and passed it to Fernando before raising the bottle into the air. 'I propose a toast – let us drink to love.'

Fernando clinked his glass against Pablo's bottle, but

Thomas' glass remained by his side. Pablo frowned.

'What's the matter, Thomas? You don't like bourbon?'

The Englishman didn't respond; he didn't even look at Pablo. Instead, his face was drained of colour, and his pale eyes were transfixed on Fernando. It was as if Thomas had seen a ghost.

CHAPTER 17

As the carnival lights flickered to life over the square, Tom felt a strong case of déjà vu – as if halfway through a film, he'd realised he'd seen it before. The words of Diego – the waiter who'd translated for Tito in Santiago – inexplicably returned to him.

'Before he blesses this marriage, the old man wants me to tell you a story,' Diego had said. 'He says he walked the Camino de Santiago many years ago. One night he stayed in a small village named Hornillos del Camino. He says it was a warm June night, and the locals had strung up carnival lights over the square.'

Tom gazed up at the lights, and music began to play. A small band stood on the church's veranda; two men strummed acoustic guitars while the female singer tapped a tambourine against her hip. A romantic-sounding ballad poured out from their fingers and voices.

'There was a band playing on the footsteps of the church,' Diego had said. 'Everyone danced in the plaza.'

Tom watched the groom lead his bride into the middle of the square. The smiling crowd gathered to watch the newlyweds share their first dance. Tom felt an urge to escape but was powerless to leave. Locals gradually joined the newlyweds in the square; couples danced. The band continued playing, eventually moving to a faster-paced rock song. Pablo hauled Sofia into the courtyard, and Fernando leaned against the church, watching the pair dance. Tom poured two glasses of wine and walked over to offer one to Fernando.

'*Salud.*'

The song ended, and Pablo breathlessly staggered over to them. He'd pulled Fernando from the wall and into the square. The band played their next tune; the guitar's strumming immediately triggered Diego's voice again inside Tom's head.

'This is the song,' Diego had said, pointing to the busker in Santiago. 'Its name is "Quizás, Quizás, Quizás". Tito says the first time he ever heard it was the night he danced with the love of his life in the village named Hornillos.'

The singer's voice drifted through the evening air; it was the same song the busker had played in Santiago. Before this trip, Tom had only ever heard its English version – 'Perhaps, Perhaps, Perhaps'. He watched Fernando and Sofia gently sway against one another, lost in each other's eyes.

'He says he's never loved a woman like he loved her,' Diego had told Tom. 'Including Ana's *abuela* – Esmeralda.'

Tom wanted to look away – as if refusing to turn a book's page might protect him from the dark twist that awaited. But he couldn't stop staring. The man Sofia was dancing with was Tito.

Fernando was Ana's grandfather.

Even when the music stopped, Tom couldn't stop staring at Fernando – searching for the old man he'd sat opposite in Santiago nearly a fortnight earlier.

'*¿Qué pasa, Thomas?*' asked Pablo, with his bourbon bottle raised in the air and a puzzled expression on his face. '*¿No te gusta el bourbon?*'

Later, lying in his bed in the *albergue*, Tom's brain fought to disprove what his heart already knew to be true. Fernando was tall and athletic, with thick dark hair. Tito was hunched and gaunt, with only a few silver strands clinging to his bald head. Even with half a century separating them, it was difficult to imagine they were the same man.

As always, Tom deferred to the numbers. Tom and Ana had travelled to Santiago in 2008 to celebrate Tito's ninetieth birthday, meaning Tito would have been thirty-six in 1954. The ages loosely matched, yet their names didn't. Ana's grandfather was Tito Hernández, not Fernando Morillas. Perhaps all of this was an enormous coincidence after all.

Tom must have fallen asleep clinging to this hope, for when he opened his eyes, it was morning. He got dressed and stepped outside, the drooping carnival lights across the bottle-littered square the only sign of the previous night's festivities. Tia served the pilgrims a breakfast of fried eggs and sausages. Back on the Camino, Tom spent the morning walking behind the others, silently observing Fernando and Sofia from a safe distance. If Fernando truly was a younger version of Tito, the situation was perilous.

The butterfly effect meant Tom's every action or word could have disastrous consequences on his future, no matter how innocuous.

By mid afternoon, Sofia had seemingly noticed Tom's wariness.

'Are you alright, Thomas?' she asked, slowing to walk alongside him.

'I'm fine.'

'You seem quiet today.'

'It must have been all the wine from last night. I'm fine.'

They walked in silence until a question burned its way into his mouth.

'Sofia, do Spanish people ever abbreviate the name Fernando?'

'What do you mean, abbreviate?'

'Well, for example, my name is Thomas, but in England, everyone calls me Tom. Do Spanish people ever do that with the name Fernando?'

She tilted her head. 'No – Fernando is only ever Fernando. Why do you ask?'

'Well, I have a friend – back in London – some people call him Fernando, but others call him Tito.'

'Tito?' She shook her head. 'No, they are different names.'

Tom wasn't sure if he was relieved or disappointed.

'Perhaps it is a nickname?' suggested Sofia.

'Perhaps.' She stopped walking and looked at him, her face full of concern.

'Are you sure you are okay, Thomas?'

'I'm fine.'

She looked unconvinced.

'I just have a lot on my mind, is all. I probably just need some time to myself to work through it.'

She nodded politely. '*Sí*, of course. If you ever need to talk to someone, I am here.'

'Thank you.'

Tom watched her walk ahead to rejoin the others, and his mind returned to Santiago.

'What happened to the girl?' he'd asked Diego.

'The old man says he betrayed her.'

'How?'

Diego had shrugged. 'He didn't say. All he said was it is the biggest regret of his life.'

In the following days, the Camino remained tediously straight. Outside of Frómista, Fernando pointed to an oak tree, the only shade they'd seen in the past hour. They sat and sipped water from their flasks, waiting for Thomas. Sofia nodded back toward the Englishman.

'I'm worried about him.'

'He's fine,' said Pablo. 'It's probably just more blisters.'

'No, it's not that. Thomas has been different recently – ever since Hornillos.'

'Different how?'

'He's quieter – more guarded. It's almost like he's become scared of me.' She turned to Fernando. 'And he's scared of you too. You must have noticed it, no?'

Fernando lit a cigarette. 'No.'

In fact, Fernando had noticed. He'd caught Thomas

staring at him throughout the day, with the scared expression Sofia had described. The previous evening in the *albergue*, Thomas had said very little and retired to bed early.

'He's likely just homesick,' said Fernando.

She waved ahead to the empty path before them. 'Then why does he keep chasing after this mysterious Santo Gutierre? There are dozens of boats a day that could carry him back to England.'

'*Sí*, but none of them will take him back to the future,' said Pablo.

Fernando stared a dagger at the boy, but it was too late.

'What do you mean?' asked Sofia.

'Nothing,' mumbled the boy, suddenly transfixed on a rock by his foot.

'Pablo?' Sofia folded her arms across her chest and pinned him with a glare. 'What do you mean, get home to the future? What aren't you telling me?'

Pablo gave one last helpless look toward Fernando before his body deflated like a balloon. 'Alright, fine. The day after we met Thomas in Navarra, he collapsed. When he woke' – the boy winced – 'he told us he was from the future.'

'The future?'

'*Sí*, he said he was from the year 2010.'

'Did he have a concussion?' She rounded on Fernando. 'Why didn't you take him to a hospital?'

'I did,' he protested.

'*Sí*, with a punctured shoulder. You never said anything about time travel.'

'Well, he's been better since then.'

'*Sí*, he's hardly mentioned the future at all since then,' agreed Pablo. 'He's been normal.'

'Normal?' Sofia's eyes flashed with anger. 'He spends every waking moment searching for a man dressed as a knight. Does that seem normal to you?'

'It does if Santo Gutierre is also a time traveller,' said Pablo. 'I told *jefe* I think Thomas wants the old man's help returning to the future.'

Sofia's eyes lashed Fernando. 'So this is what you talk about when you stay up smoking cigarettes?'

'No,' said Fernando.

'Sometimes,' conceded Pablo.

Her nostrils flared. 'And neither of you told me?'

'It wasn't intentional,' said Fernando. 'I didn't want to worry you unnecessarily.'

She shook her head with angered disbelief. 'And I thought I could actually trust you.'

'You can.'

She gave an angry scoff. 'Clearly not.'

She started walking, and Fernando tried to follow.

'Sofia, wait.'

'No.' She spun around and thrust a blameful finger toward him. 'You two stay here; I want to be alone.'

The flames within her eyes told Fernando it wasn't negotiable. As they watched her leave, Pablo lit a cigarette.

'Cervantes wrote: "Truth will rise above falsehood, as oil above water."' He exhaled a plume of smoke. 'I bet she'll have forgotten all about this by nightfall.'

The afternoon crept like sap down a tree trunk; the Camino remained flat, straight and dusty. Sofia walked ahead of them for the rest of the day. The monotonous countryside allowed Fernando's mind to wander. Sofia was right: it had been wrong to keep Thomas' secret from her, especially after she'd entrusted Fernando with the truth about Hector.

They arrived in the town of Carrión de los Condes at dusk. Rain spat on them as they reached the town's central square; a plaque on the wall read 'Plaza del Generalísimo Franco'. A local directed them to an *albergue* a few blocks away. When they arrived, they found the last beds had been taken by a rowdy group of Catalonians.

'You can try the church of Santa Maria,' the *albergue's* owner had said, wearily looking down his hallway to the sound of raucous singing. 'The nuns may still have some beds.'

The church wasn't far, and they knocked on its door just as the clouds unloaded. A nun waved them inside.

'Come in, come in – you arrived just in time, no?'

The pilgrims entered and shook themselves dry.

'I'm Sister Ava,' said the nun. She had a kind face; her chubby cheeks and dark bushy eyebrows were framed by her white headdress. 'Follow me; I'll show you to the dormitories.'

She led them down the hallway, pointing Sofia to a room on the left. Fernando tried to catch Sofia's eye, but she pulled the door closed behind her. He followed Pablo and Thomas into the men's dormitory, where a bearded stranger slid down from a bunk bed.

'*Hola, amigos*, my name is Enzo,' he said in Spanish, with a musical Italian accent. 'I'm from Roma.'

Pablo made the introductions on their group's behalf before the two of them partook in the usual banter between pilgrims.

'Where did you start your pilgrimage?' asked Enzo.

'In Lourdes,' replied the boy.

'Lourdes was beautiful, no?'

'You started your pilgrimage there too?'

'No, I started in Roma.'

'You're walking all the way from Rome to Santiago?'

'And back again.'

Pablo's mouth fell open. 'You're mad!'

Enzo laughed. 'The pilgrims of the past commenced their pilgrimages to Santiago from their homes.'

Pablo turned to Fernando, concerned. '*Jefe*, is this true? Should we have walked from Andalucía?'

'Next time,' said Fernando.

The rain prevented them from doing any laundry. Instead, they took turns using the shower; its lukewarm trickle made Fernando consider washing in the cold pouring rain instead. When they walked to the kitchen for dinner, Sofia sat at the table already. She didn't look up; her mood remained as dark as the clouds outside.

The stew was bland but hot. Pablo and Enzo cheerfully continued to swap stories from the Camino while everyone else ate in silence. Fernando imagined the explanation he might eventually offer Sofia if she permitted him to try. When everyone had finished eating, Sister Ava and a younger nun arrived to clear their bowls.

'That was delicious,' said Pablo, slapping his belly contently. He peered toward the window. 'It's getting heavier out there. I hope it clears by morning.' The boy's gaze fell on a guitar leaning against the wall. 'Whose guitar is that?'

'It belongs to Mother Superior,' said Sister Ava.

'Does anyone here know how to play it?'

'Oh, yes, Sister Ava plays it beautifully,' said the

younger nun.

Sister Ava shot the girl a sharp look. 'Mother Superior only allows us to play it under her supervision,' said the older nun.

'She's not here?' asked Pablo.

'No, she's in León, tending to her ailing mother.'

'I see.' Pablo stood up from the table and picked up the instrument. 'So if she's not here, then perhaps we could have a little music, no?'

'She'd be very furious if she found out.'

'But who is going to tell her?' He gave the guitar a little strum and held it out to the nun. 'I mean, it's just one song. There's no harm in that, is there?'

Sister Ava looked at the guitar and chewed on her bottom lip. She placed the dirty bowls back on the table. 'One song, only.'

She took the guitar, and the younger girl disappeared up the hallway. She returned with two elderly nuns; the three of them smiled like mischievous schoolgirls. Pablo pulled his chair away from the table and offered it to Sister Ava. She sat down and rested the guitar on her lap before adjusting its tuning pegs.

'What shall I play?'

'"Be Thou My Vision",' the young girl blurted.

Her elder sisters nodded their agreement.

Sister Ava softly began strumming the guitar, and the room filled with the nuns' sweet voices. Fernando had sung the hymn on his childhood Sundays, but he'd never heard it performed quite as beautifully. The melodic harmony of voices, accompanied by the unblemished joy on the nuns' faces, stirred something within him. Despite all the churches they'd entered, this was the closest he'd felt to God upon his pilgrimage. The scallop shell around his neck hung heavier.

When the hymn was finished, everyone applauded.

'*Bellissima*.' Enzo clapped. '*Brava, brava*.'

The nuns fought to conceal their smiles.

'We demand an encore,' said Pablo. 'Won't you sing us one more to help these weary pilgrims sleep? *Por favor*.'

The nuns each looked expectantly to Sister Ava.

'Just one more.'

As the nuns chose their next song, Sofia stood up.

'Forgive me, Sisters, but I'm very tired. *Muchas gracias* for the food and the music. Both were beautiful. *Buenas noches*.'

The nuns bade Sofia good evening, and Sister Ava started playing the first chords of 'Oh, Amor de Dios'. The nuns' voices lifted Fernando to his feet, and he followed Sofia down the hallway.

'Sofia?'

She paused in the open doorway to her room.

'I wanted to explain about earlier,' he said, stopping behind her. 'I just…' His thoughts caught in his throat, and she turned to face him.

'Fernando, I'm tired.'

'*Sí*, I know. It's just… this isn't easy for me.'

'What isn't?'

'This.' He motioned to the space between them. 'Talking – I've always been better at listening.'

'I'm not asking you to be a poet, Fernando. I just want you to be honest with me.'

'I didn't lie to you.'

'But you didn't tell me the truth, either.' She sounded hurt more than angry. 'How do you think it made me feel, being excluded like that? After what I'd shared with you in Hornillos, why didn't you tell me the truth about Thomas?'

'Because it's crazy. There's no such thing as time travel.'

'Of course there isn't – but you still should have told me. If Thomas is unwell, we should get him help.' Her voice was flat. 'I'm tired of secrets.'

'You know about Thomas, now.'

'Only because I discovered it myself. And what about your other secrets?'

'I don't have any.'

'No?' She locked onto his eyes. 'Then why are you really walking to Santiago?'

'I told you: to see my brother.'

'You needn't walk across Spain for that. What's the real reason?'

The scallop shell tugged on his neck. After so many years, could he finally admit the truth to someone? Could he admit it to himself?

'I'm scared if I tell you, you'll think less of me.'

'You know me well enough to know I wouldn't do that.'

'But you don't know what I've done.'

'You're right – I don't.' She touched his hand. 'So why don't you tell me?'

'I want to.' His throat tightened, and his eyes glistened. 'But I don't think I can.'

'You can.'

She squeezed his hand and, in that moment, he thought he could tell her anything. He took a deep breath in, preparing to unveil the horrible truth.

'It was during the war…'

The silence stopped him. Sofia noticed his change of expression.

'What's wrong?' she asked.

'The music has stopped.'

He turned and walked back down the hallway. When he arrived in the dining room, the nuns and Pablo were crowded around the windows.

'Trucks,' said the boy. 'Lots of them.'

Fernando walked out of the *albergue's* front door and into the lane. He squinted through the rain to the square at the end of the street; a group of army trucks stood parked. A jeep drove up the alley behind him, and Fernando moved aside to let it pass. As it zoomed toward the plaza, he realised he'd been wrong. The insignia on the side of the jeep hadn't been that of the army; it was the crowned insignia of the Guardia Civil.

Ramos stepped from his jeep. He strode into the middle of the plaza and barked orders to his men.

'I want checkpoints at every road in and out of the town. If the pilgrims run, they'll head west along the Camino. Close the bridge. Keep them on this side of the river.'

His men had erected speakers around the square, their cables snaking back to the rear of the jeep where Sergeant Molina was hunched over the radio.

'Is it ready, Sergeant?' asked Ramos.

'Two minutes.'

The last of the jeeps pulled into the square. A familiar figure exited the passenger side and cowered beneath an umbrella.

'Ramos, what are you doing?' asked Capitán Aznar. 'I said we could conduct a preliminary search for the pilgrims, not lay siege to the entire town. We don't even know they're here.'

'They're here, Capitán. The locals in Frómista saw them leaving town after midday. They won't have tried to make Calzadilla tonight.' He looked up; the cold rain showered his face. 'Not in this storm.'

'Regardless, after Eunate, we need to be cautious. Commandante Besteiro and I won't tolerate another calamity.'

Ramos bit his tongue. Eunate had been a victory: Vasquez was in a cell and ATA was crippled, yet Ramos had been rewarded with threats of suspension. The assault on the church hadn't been in line with Comandante Besteiro's 'New Spain'.

Thunder rumbled in the heavens above.

'I mean it, Ramos,' warned Aznar. 'I won't have my men out here all night in the pouring rain, chasing after some Englishman who played a prank in Burgos Cathedral.'

'Impersonating a Catholic priest is hardly a trivial matter, Capitán, nor is desertion from the army.'

'You really believe Morillas is some deserter you hunted twenty years ago?'

'It's him.'

'Why, because he has the Spanish Legion on his arm? Thousands of men bear that same tattoo; it doesn't make Morillas your deserter.'

'I spoke to the station chief in Huelva, and he questioned some of the men on the docks.'

'You telephoned another jurisdiction without my authority?'

'I served with him in the war. Besides, you and the comandante were preoccupied with your investigation, Capitán.' Ramos enjoyed seeing the officer's perfect face creased with anger. 'The Huelva station chief said Morillas is a loner – no friends, no family – he appeared out of nowhere during the war.'

'So?'

'One of the legionnaires I hunted deserted his post in July 1936 – six months before Morillas appears in Huelva.'

'Coincidence isn't the same as evidence.'

Ramos removed a folder from within the back of the jeep and handed it to Aznar. 'Is this enough evidence for you?'

The officer passed the umbrella to Ramos and flipped open the file.

'What is this?'

'The personnel file of the missing legionnaire.'

'This isn't Morillas. It says his name is Tito Hernández.'

'Look at the second page.'

Aznar turned the page and squinted at the small black-and-white portrait.

'Two decades on the ocean may have burned and cracked the boy's skin, but the eyes are the same, Capitán. It's the man we questioned in Navarra. It's Fernando Morillas.'

Aznar gave one final inspection of the photograph before handing it back to Ramos. 'I cannot have a repeat of Eunate, Ramos. Is that clear? Good men died.'

'Good men always die in war.'

'The war is over, Ramos.'

'Don't be naive.' Ramos stowed the file back into the jeep. 'This war will never be over.'

'Brigada Ramos, we're ready,' Sergeant Molina called out.

Ramos snatched the handset from the sergeant and lifted it to his lips.

'Citizens of Carrión de los Condes.' His voice echoed from the speakers dotted around the waterlogged square. 'My name is Brigada Esteban Ramos, of the Guardia Civil. Some of you may remember me. Regrettably, I have returned searching for more of Spain's enemies. We hunt four persons – three men and one woman – posing as pilgrims to Santiago. Do not be deceived – they are dangerous criminals. Their leader uses an alias of Fernando Morillas, but his real name is Tito Hernández. He is a deserter from the Spanish Legion, now colluding with Basques in the north and spies from abroad. My men have sealed every exit of your town and are now sweeping its streets. All of you are to remain in your homes and await inspection. If any of you know the whereabouts of the traitors, you are to notify my men at once.'

Ramos nearly returned the handset to Molina but lifted it again to issue one final warning. 'Those of you who remember me will also remember I punish co-conspirators with equal vigour. Anyone sheltering these traitors shall share their fate.' He released the pressel switch and handed the handset back to Molina.

Aznar looked disturbed. 'You've been here before?'

'One of the neighbouring villages, years ago.'

'What did you mean when you said they'll remember

you?'

'It was during the war, Capitán.' Ramos slid a cigarette into his mouth and lit it. 'And I know how much you detest looking back at Spain's past.'

'This is madness. I'm calling off the search.'

'We're not leaving without the pilgrims.'

'Need I remind you of my rank, Brigada? I'll not have you harassing these people, all to appease some personal obsession of yours. Terror no longer works.'

Sergeant Molina stood up from the radio and drifted behind Aznar; Ramos caught his eye. Suddenly, raised voices echoed from a laneway; a guard dragged a man across the plaza.

'He says he saw them,' said the guardsman.

Ramos stamped out his cigarette and examined the man. He was in his sixties and kept his eyes at his feet.

'Where are they now?' he asked.

'In the *albergue, señor*.' The local's words were strangled by fear.

Ramos smiled toward Aznar. 'You see, Capitán? Terror always works.'

CHAPTER 18

Nobody spoke; everyone's eyes were on Fernando. Eventually, Pablo broke the silence.

'Is it true? Is your name really Tito Hernández?'

Fernando nodded, unable to voice his confession.

The boy's face crumpled with disbelief. 'I don't understand. All this time, you had us believe you were someone else?' His confusion gave way to anger. 'Why did you lie to us?'

'I didn't lie to you on purpose.'

'You lied accidentally?'

'I haven't been Tito Hernández in almost twenty years, not since—'

'Not since you fled from the war.' Pablo's disgust was obvious. 'And all this time, I thought we were friends.'

'It was too dangerous to tell people the truth.'

'*Sí*, and now you've endangered all of us by hiding it.'

He was right.

'I'm sorry.'

'You're sorry?' Pablo scoffed. 'That's it, you're sorry?'

Sofia placed her hand on the boy's arm. 'We need to concentrate on how to get out of here.'

'We can't!' cried Pablo. 'You heard Ramos – they're searching every house. We have to surrender.'

'No, you're all going to wait for the guards to be distracted and then find a way out of the city,' said Fernando.

'Distracted by what?' asked Pablo.

'I'm going to surrender.'

'No, you're not,' said Sofia. 'We're escaping together.'

Fernando shook his head. 'If the city is truly sealed, you'll need a distraction to get past the patrols.'

'We're not leaving you.'

'Ramos wants me, not you. If I surrender, the three of you still have a chance.'

Bang. Bang. Bang.

The thump on the door startled them. Fernando turned to Sister Ava.

'I'm sorry for endangering you, Sister. Please help my friends. They've had no part in this.'

Her scared eyes studied his face before she turned to the other nuns.

'Take them through to the church and down to the crypt.'

'*Muchas gracias*, Sister.'

'No,' said Sofia, gripping his sleeve. 'You don't need to do this.'

Bang. Bang. Bang.

'*Sí*, I must.' He unhooked her fingers from his arm

and looked into her shimmering hazel eyes. 'There isn't time to argue. Go with Pablo and Thomas.' He looked over her shoulder to Pablo. 'Go with the nuns.'

Bang. Bang. Bang. Bang. Bang. Bang.

Pablo coaxed Sofia away, and the nuns led the pilgrims up the hall toward the church. Fernando turned back to the door and opened it. A solitary old woman stood in the rain, cowering within her shawl; a fork of lightning illuminated her gaunt face.

'Are you the pilgrim?' She pointed down the road. 'My husband is leading them away, but it will only earn us a few minutes. I will hide you and your friends.'

Fernando paused. Was this another of Ramos' traps?

'Hurry, we haven't much time,' urged the woman.

Footsteps approached from the hallway, and Pablo reappeared with the nuns.

'Pablo, what are you doing?' asked Fernando.

The boy walked past him and stood next to the woman in the rain. 'We're getting out of here.'

'*Sí*, all of us,' said Sofia, ushering Thomas past Fernando and out into the lane.

The local woman waved Fernando forward urgently. 'Come, we must hurry.'

The stranger led the pilgrims along the street to a nondescript farmhouse and down into a basement filled with barrels and hay. She lit an oil lantern hanging from the ceiling.

'You'll need to be quiet when they come.'

'We've put you and your husband at too great a risk, *señora*,' said Fernando. 'Is the river shallow enough for us to wade across?'

'Not in this storm. Besides, Ramos will have thought

of that. He'll have men on the other riverbank waiting for you.'

'You know him?'

'*Sí*, he came to my family's village – not far from here – during the war. Ramos was only a corporal back then.' She spat the name out like venom. 'He will tear this town apart for you and your friends.'

Fernando shook his head. 'I can't endanger the town like this; I have to surrender.'

'If you surrender, you'll die.'

The statement silenced the pilgrims; ominous thunder growled outside. The woman's eyes pierced Fernando's.

'When our village fell in the war, some surviving communists fled into the surrounding forests. Those men eluded the Nationalists for months, conducting raids and then disappearing back into the woods. Then, one day, the Guardia Civil arrived. They rounded up the wives and children of the guerrillas into the main square. Ramos pointed a megaphone toward the forest and ordered the rebels to surrender by nightfall, or he'd execute the men's families. He held the megaphone to the children's lips and ordered them to call out to their fathers, begging for their lives.'

'Did they surrender?' asked Pablo.

'*Sí*. All nine men walked into the town at dusk with their hands held high.' The woman's eyes glistened in the lamplight. 'Not that it mattered.'

'What do you mean?'

'That night, Ramos loaded the men and their families into a truck and drove them into the woods. When he returned the following morning, the truck was empty.'

Sofia gasped. 'He executed them? Even the wives and

children?'

The woman simply nodded.

'Why wasn't he investigated?' asked Pablo. 'Even the Nationalists have their limits.'

'Ramos isn't a fool. He drove those families into the forest alone; there wasn't a single witness.'

'What about the bodies?'

'We searched those woods for months but never found a single bone. Many of those villagers now live in Carrión. We know what Ramos did, but he's the only person who could ever prove it.' The woman turned to Fernando. 'So you see, Ramos will not show you any mercy if you surrender. He'll only use you to capture your friends.' She picked up a crowbar and pointed to the barrels. 'If you hide, perhaps you live.'

Pablo began prying the lids from the barrels while Sofia relayed the woman's story to Thomas. Fernando shook the old woman's hand.

'*Gracias* for helping us, *señora*. I'm sorry we've involved you and your husband.'

'You didn't involve us.' The woman's eyes glistened. 'Ramos did – the night he drove my son and his family into the forest.'

Ramos stormed up the street. His men dragged the old man behind them.

'Forgive me, *señor*,' the local called out. 'My wife said the *albergue*, not with the nuns.'

Ramos ignored his lies and strode up the laneway to

the brick building clinging to the rear of the church. He thumped his fist on its sodden door; muffled voices came from within. He unclipped his revolver from his holster. The lock turned, and the door crept open. A fat-faced nun with thick eyebrows stood in the doorway.

'¿Sí, señor?'

Ramos pushed past her and strode into the room. 'Where are they?'

'Who?'

He clenched a fist by his side. 'The pilgrims.'

'Those you seek aren't here, señor.'

He snapped his fingers to his men. 'Search the dormitories.'

The guards disappeared down the hallway while a nearby clock counted the wasted seconds. His men returned with an Italian man.

'They're not here.'

The nun offered an apologetic smile. 'It's too wet for many pilgrims tonight, señor. Perhaps they are staying in the *albergue*?'

Ramos scanned the room, his eye catching the dining table. He walked toward it and pointed to a pile of empty bowls.

'That's a big appetite for one pilgrim, no?'

She paused.

'Those… were from the other nuns, señor.'

Her stammer, however slight, had been enough. Ramos turned and walked out into the lane, pointing to the man who'd led them here.

'Bring him.'

The guards dragged the old man through the rain up to the square. Ramos seized the radio's handset from

Molina and lifted it to his lips.

'Citizens, it appears I wasn't clear before, so allow me to remind you what happens to those caught assisting the traitors.'

The guards pulled the man before Ramos.

'What is your name?' Ramos said into the microphone before holding it to the man's mouth.

The man's lips remained pursed. Ramos nodded to one of the guards, who wrenched the man's frail arm behind his back. The villager cried out in pain.

'Your name?' shouted Ramos.

'Rodriguez,' he whimpered into the handset. 'Francisco Rodriguez.'

'*Muy bien.*' He stared up at the square's shuttered balconies as he spoke into the handset. 'Citizens, Señor Rodriguez mistakenly attempted to be heroic. Instead, he made a grave error. Fortunately, as a Catholic, I'm a merciful man. If Morillas and his accomplices surrender by the time Señor Rodriguez counts to sixty, he'll live.' Ramos took his pistol from its holster. 'But if they do not, he will die.'

Ramos lifted the handset to the man's mouth. Instead of counting, Señor Rodriguez scowled before spitting at the ground.

'I won't say a damn word.'

Ramos smiled. And spoke into the radio.

'It appears Señor Rodriguez wishes to delegate his responsibility.' He turned to one of the guards. 'Go to his house and retrieve his wife. If it's empty, bring me his neighbours.'

The guards turned to leave.

'Wait!' Rodriguez cried.

Ramos held the microphone to the local's trembling lips and waited.

'*Uno... dos...*'

Fernando walked up the stairs and into the house. Sofia chased after him.

'You can't surrender,' she said, following him through the farmhouse's door and into the rain.

The voice of the woman's husband echoed down the laneway.

'*... veinte... veintiuno... veintidós...*'

'You heard the woman's story from the war,' pleaded Sofia. 'Ramos won't arrest you; he'll kill you.'

Fernando pointed toward the square. 'He's going to kill that man.'

The local woman had followed them outside. 'I'll go. You and your friends get to the river; follow it south as far as the Iglesia de Villanueva del Río. The priest there is a good man; he can help you.'

'I won't let you and your husband suffer because of me,' said Fernando.

'And I'm not letting my husband die alone.' The woman's voice had grown impatient. 'There isn't time to argue; don't let our sacrifice be for nothing. Go!'

They watched her walk through the rain toward the sound of her husband's voice.

'*... treinta y tres... treinta y cuatro... treinta y cinco...*'

Pablo pointed in the opposite direction. 'She's right. We should go while Ramos is distracted.'

They ran away from the square, keeping to the side streets as they weaved toward the river. Suddenly, the man's counting stopped; a peculiar calm befell the town's drenched streets.

'Perhaps she convinced Ramos to release them,' said Pablo.

A gunshot rang out like a clap of thunder. Everything froze, even the rain. The pilgrims stared at each other in horror until the counting resumed. This time, the voice of the woman who'd saved them echoed through the town.

'*Uno... dos...*'

The others moved forward, but Fernando stood still. Pablo looked back with pleading eyes.

'*Jefe*, we need to hurry.'

Fernando shook his head. 'How many more people must die because of me?'

'*... ocho... nueve...*'

Sofia walked back to him. 'No, you're coming with us. We're all leaving together.'

'I'm sorry, Sofia. I can't.'

She slammed her fists against his chest. 'Stop saying that. Of course you can. We're all going. You promised me you'd get me to Santiago.' She thumped her fists harder into him. 'Do you remember? On that hill in the mud? You promised me, Fernando. You promised.'

He caught her wrists and looked into her moist eyes. 'If I go with you, Ramos will keep chasing all of us. And I can't let anything bad happen to you.'

Her lip began to tremble, and he placed his hand on her cheek.

'I'm sorry.'

She collapsed against him. He wrapped his arms

around her, resting his chin on top of her wet hair and closing his eyes. If only he could stop time forever.

'... *veinte... veintiuno...*'

He reluctantly pulled away from her. Thomas began babbling in English, and Fernando used the distraction to take Pablo aside.

'Do as the woman said: use the smaller streets to get to the river; travel south to the church. Stay off the Camino from now on, do you understand?'

'*Sí*, I'll try.'

Fernando shook the boy roughly by his collar. 'Can I trust you or not?'

The responsibility hardened the boy's face. 'I won't let you down. I'll keep them both safe.'

'I'll give you as much time as I can.' He embraced the boy. '*Buen Camino, amigo.*'

'*Buen Camino.*'

Fernando turned and faced the square.

'Wait,' cried Sofia, running up and gripping Fernando's shirt. 'Thomas thinks there might be another way.'

The local woman's ominous count continued.

'... *cuarenta y cinco... cuarenta y seis...*'

The woman's eyes remained fixed on her husband's corpse on the ground.

'Don't slow down.' Ramos pressed the gun to the woman's temple. 'Or you'll be joining him sooner than you think.'

'*… cuarenta y nueve… cincuenta…*'

Ten seconds left. Ramos would shoot the woman and find the next accomplice to interrogate – perhaps the nuns who'd sheltered the traitors in their hostel. They were nuns, but they'd lied. A betrayal of Spain was also a betrayal of God. Examples must be made.

'*… cincuenta y cinco…*'

'Ramos!'

Everyone's eyes and rifles swung toward a silhouette emerging from the alley.

'Hold your fire,' barked Ramos. 'It's him.'

Two guards ran across and frisked the Andalusian for weapons before dragging him toward the jeep. The traitor didn't resist.

'Fernando Morillas, the modest fisherman from Huelva.' Ramos smiled. 'Or is it Tito Hernández, the cowardly legionnaire who fled from the war?' He paused for a reaction, but none came. 'Where are the others?'

'We separated after Burgos.'

'A lie. The four of you were seen together in Frómista. But, fear not, we'll soon find your friends.'

Capitán Aznar, still hiding beneath his umbrella, stepped out from the shadows.

'We've got what we came for, Ramos. Let's go.'

'We're not leaving without his co-conspirators.' Ramos faced the Andalusian. 'Where are they?'

Morillas stayed silent.

Ramos scoffed. 'You think this town will shelter them? They'll give your friends up soon enough.'

'Not after what you did to them following the war. I know about the village.'

Aznar stepped forward.

'What's he talking about, Ramos?'

'Nothing, Capitán.' Ramos' gaze hardened on Morillas before sliding to the local man's body on the ground. 'Just peasants spreading lies.'

'Where did you hide them, Ramos?' asked Morillas. 'Where did you bury the children?'

Ramos unsheathed his baton and smashed it across Morillas' jaw; the traitor crumpled onto the wet cobblestones. Aznar marched forward.

'Stand down,' cried the officer.

But Ramos ignored him and took a fistful of the Andalusian's hair. He dragged the traitor away from the others and into the centre of the plaza.

'You think you have the right to judge me?' he hissed into Morillas' ear. 'A coward who betrayed his people?'

Morillas coughed up blood as he croaked a weak reply. 'There's no bravery in murdering innocent people.'

'Innocent?' Ramos smashed the baton into Morillas' nose; blood spurted like a geyser. 'Those men were like you – traitors.'

The Andalusian's face was covered in blood. 'Were their children traitors too?'

Ramos squatted and kept his voice to a whisper. 'It was only a matter of time. Their parents had infected those children with an entitlement to freedom.'

Some of the locals had cautiously left their homes and hovered around the edges of the plaza. Ramos waved his bloody baton toward them while whispering to Morillas.

'These people yearn for their beloved freedom, yet when they had it, their bellies were empty. We lifted this country up from its knees.'

'This is how you justify your crimes?'

Ramos stood up and kicked Morillas in the ribs before looming over him.

'You think I've lost a minute's sleep over what I did? I'd kill those men and their families again tomorrow if it meant protecting Spain from the Marxists.'

'If you're so proud, why not tell them?' Morillas nodded his bloody face to the growing crowd of locals. 'Tell them what you did for Spain.'

Ramos smirked. 'This was your plan? To bait a confession from me?' He kneeled back down and put his lips to Morillas' ear. 'Shall I tell you how I drove those men and their families into the woods and put bullets into each of their heads? Or how I started with the children, to prevent their high-pitched squeals being heard in the town.' He inched closer. 'The reason no one found the bodies was because I buried them in a mass grave leftover from the war. Those villagers never thought a Catholic would defile the graves of his fallen comrades. But they underestimated what a patriot would do for his country.'

'You'll never get away with it.'

'It's been fifteen years; I already have. There's only one other person who knows the truth.' Ramos grinned down at Morillas. 'And dead men can't testify.' Ramos stood and walked to the jeep, lifting the radio handset back to his mouth.

'Citizens, the leader of the insurgents has been captured.' His voice echoed through the speakers; more locals edged out of their homes and into the square. 'He has confessed to an imminent attack on your town. While my men find the other members of his terrorist cell, it falls to me to exact swift justice on their leader.'

Ramos threw the handset back into the jeep and

strode back to Morillas. Aznar trailed behind.

'What are you doing?'

'Our duty, Capitán.'

He pulled Morillas up to his knees for everyone to see his bloodied face. To see that this was where defiance led. Ramos pulled his pistol from his holster and pressed it against the back of the Andalusian's head.

'Fernando!'

A woman pushed through the crowd and collapsed in front of Morillas, flinging her arms around him; it was the interpreter. Ramos scanned the direction from which she'd appeared, recognising the other Andalusian and Englishman close behind her.

'Arrest those two,' he snapped, pointing them out to his men. Ramos pulled the girl from Morillas. The three traitors were dragged toward the back of the jeep, and Ramos smiled down at Morillas' broken face once more. 'Fear not – your friends will join you shortly.' He levelled the gun at Morillas' head again and slid his finger to the trigger. '*Buen Camino*, traitor.'

'*It was only a matter of time. Their parents had infected those children with an entitlement to freedom.*'

Ramos lowered the gun and stared at each of the speakers. The voice ringing out across the square was familiar. It was his.

'*These people yearn for their beloved freedom, yet when they had it, their bellies were empty. We lifted this country up from its knees.*'

Ramos spun around. The girl looked to have passed the Englishman something which he held up to the radio's microphone.

'What's going on?' called out Ramos. 'What's he

doing?'

'*You think I've lost a minute's sleep over what I did? I'd kill those men and their families again tomorrow if it meant protecting Spain from the Marxists.*'

'Stop that!'

Ramos walked toward the jeep. The Englishman was holding the same black device he'd carried in Navarra, but this time, it glowed in his hand.

'What is that?' Ramos lifted his gun at the foreigner. 'Step away from the radio.'

'*This was your plan? To bait me into a confession? Shall I tell you how I drove those men and their families into the woods and put bullets into each of their heads?*'

Ramos thrust his gun toward the Englishman. 'I said stop that!'

'*Or how I started with the children, to prevent their high-pitched squeals being heard in the town.*'

Someone in the crowd threw an empty bottle. It missed Ramos by an inch and shattered against the jeep. He swung his gun toward its source.

'Who threw that?'

Another bottle smashed at his feet.

'Murderer!' someone yelled.

'Child killer!' screamed another.

The mob edged forward, their faces twisted with vengeance. Ramos shot his gun into the air, temporarily halting them.

'*The reason no one found the bodies was because I buried them in a mass grave leftover from the war. Those villagers never thought a Catholic would defile the graves of his fallen comrades. But they underestimated what a patriot would do for his country.*'

The crowd continued their advance. Ramos looked over at Aznar.

'Capitán, it's an uprising. Order the men to fire.'

The officer's face was pale. His mouth opened, but no sound came out. More bottles shattered around them, and a protective cordon of Guardia Civil uniforms formed around the jeep. The crowd of locals chanted in unison.

'Murderer! Murderer! Murderer!'

Someone reached for one of the guardsmen's rifles and was beaten back by another guard. The terrified soldiers looked to Aznar for their orders.

Ramos shook the young officer from his paralysis. 'Order them to fire before this entire town tears us to fucking pieces.'

Aznar's eyes widened as more locals poured into the square from the surrounding streets, most brandishing tools or weapons. Finally, the officer wrenched the radio's handset from the Englishman.

'Attention, everyone, attention!' Aznar's voice quivered from the speakers. 'My name is Capitán Javier Aznar.'

The crowd ignored him and continued its surge forward. Finally, Aznar pulled his pistol from his belt and fired two shots into the air.

'I am ordering all of you to disperse immediately. Return to your homes.'

A man pushed his way to the front of the crowd. In his fifties and built like a bear, he wore the greasy overalls of a mechanic. A lead pipe lay in his enormous hands.

'You and your men can leave, but Ramos stays here.'

'Brigada Ramos is a member of the Guardia Civil.'

'He murdered our children and our grandchildren. You heard it yourself.'

Aznar looked flustered. 'I don't... I don't know what I heard.'

'Liar,' screamed a woman.

She was followed by several more shouts. The mechanic pointed the pipe toward Ramos.

'For two decades, we've known what you did in that village. Tonight, we finally heard the proof.' The mechanic faced Aznar. 'Ramos stays here.'

The crowd roared its approval.

'I'm not leaving any of my men behind,' said Aznar.

'He's a murderer.'

'If Brigada Ramos has committed a crime, he'll answer for it in a court of law, not at the hands of a mob.'

'Then you'll arrest him?' asked the mechanic.

The crowd hushed, their eyes burning into Aznar.

'This is ridiculous,' snapped Ramos. 'We don't negotiate with peasants, Capitán. We're taking these prisoners back to Bilbao with us. Order the men to shoot anyone who tries to stop us.'

Ramos moved toward Morillas, but the mechanic blocked his path. Ramos aimed his gun at him.

'Step aside, or I'll shoot you.'

The mechanic looked at Aznar. 'If you let him shoot me, Capitán, you and your men will not leave here tonight.'

More townspeople arrived, each armed with a makeshift weapon. They'd encircled the plaza. A different chant broke out among them.

'Arrest Ramos! Arrest Ramos! Arrest Ramos!'

Ramos kept his gun trained on the mechanic's chest, looking back for Aznar's permission to fire. Sweat trickled down the young officer's temple. When he eventually gave his order, his voice was barely audible.

'Arrest him.'

Ramos reluctantly lowered his gun and waited for a guardsman to seize the mechanic. Instead, a soldier ripped Ramos' pistol from him. Another set of hands wrenched Ramos' hands behind his back and snapped a pair of cold metal handcuffs around his wrists.

'What are you doing? Arrest him, not me.'

Capitán Aznar's shaky voice wavered through the speakers.

'I am placing Brigada Ramos under arrest for the alleged crimes outlaid here tonight. He will be taken back to Bilbao, where these charges will be investigated.'

The crowd cheered. Ramos glared at Aznar in shock.

'Have you lost your fucking mind? I'm not the enemy.' He nodded to the villagers. 'They are.'

One guard frisked Ramos and discovered a second pistol concealed beneath his jacket. The soldier ripped the holster free from Ramos' lower back.

'You fucking coward,' Ramos spat at Aznar. 'Do you have any idea what you're doing?'

Aznar ignored him and faced the man in the overalls. 'Order your people to allow us to leave safely.'

'How do we know you won't release Ramos and return with more troops tomorrow?'

'Brigada Ramos will be investigated; you have my word on that. My men and I will not return; no crimes have been committed here tonight.'

'Then we also have your word you'll not pursue the pilgrims any further?' The man held out an enormous hand.

Aznar paused before shaking it. '*Sí*, you have my

word.'

Ramos tried to wrench himself free of his handcuffs. 'Don't be a fool, Aznar. Morillas is a deserter, and the rest are spies. This is treason.'

The mechanic released Aznar from his grasp. The peasants formed a path for the trucks to leave, and Aznar ordered the soldiers to load everything back into the vehicles. A pair of guards bundled Ramos into one of the trucks, their young faces looking nervously at their prisoner. The trucks rumbled to life, and the crowd watched their convoy snake its way out of the square.

Ramos stared out from the truck's trailer, past the hate-filled faces of the locals, to the traitor, Morillas. The broken and bloodied Andalusian was still kneeling in the middle of the plaza, locked in an embrace with the weeping nurse.

CHAPTER 19

When Tom walked into the convent's kitchen the following morning, he was stunned to find Fernando already seated at the table.

'*Buenos días,*' said Tom.

The Spaniard looked up from lacing his boots. '*Buenos días.*'

Tom had expected they'd stay in Carrión for a few days until Fernando had healed, but he looked ready to continue. Tom pointed to the bandages Sofia had wrapped around the Spaniard's broken nose.

'How is it?'

Fernando frowned, so Tom tried again in Spanish.

'*¿Cómo estás?*'

'*Soy bueno.*'

But there was nothing 'good' about the Spaniard's face. In addition to the bandaged nose, Fernando's blackened left eye was almost entirely closed, and his bottom lip was still swollen. Sofia arrived and unloaded a barrage of Spanish at her patient, seemingly displeased with Fernando's unwillingness to rest. Finally, after more lively debate, Sofia threw her hands into the air.

'He is stubborn,' she said to Tom in English. 'He could have been killed last night.'

Sofia enlisted Pablo's help in convincing Fernando to rest, but with the same outcome. And after Sister Ava served a breakfast of oats and coffee, the pilgrims resumed their journey.

'He worries the Guardia Civil will not honour their agreement,' Sofia explained to Tom as they walked through the town.

Villagers trickled from their houses, offering their gratitude to the pilgrims with breads, meats and cheeses. The four of them rejoined the Camino with bags sagging with the town's generosity.

The Camino was muddy underfoot. A blanket of cloud remained draped over the sky, but the rain looked to have passed – for now. They spent their morning walking through fields of sodden wheat. Tom couldn't shift his gaze from Fernando – or was he supposed to call him Tito now?

Tom took his phone from his pocket and held his thumb against its power button. The screen remained dark. There'd been just enough power left in the battery to capture Ramos' confession and play it back to the crowd. There'd been no other choice: if Fernando was Ana's grandfather and died in 1954, Ana would never exist. But now without any power, Tom couldn't see Ana's picture. He slid his thumb across the screen where her smiling face should have appeared. What if his meddling with Tito's past had already invoked the butterfly effect? What if Ana no longer existed?

The pilgrims walked for a couple of hours, each of them glancing behind for signs of uniformed pursuers. After stopping to eat some of the food the people of Carrión had gifted them, Sofia walked alongside Tom.

'Enzo told Fernando of an alternative path after Calzadilla; it is only used by the locals. If the Guardia Civil returns, we will be harder to find.'

'Will it still take us to Santiago?'

'*Sí*, it rejoins the Camino in the village of Terradillos de los Templarios. Enzo says the village was once a Templar stronghold. Perhaps your friend will be there, yes?'

Tom felt a ray of hope; so much had changed in the week since he'd last seen Sir Walter. Perhaps the knight would have a theory about Tito's role in all of this.

'You really believe he will help you return home?' Sofia asked.

'I hope so.'

'Back to the future?'

Tom looked up, shocked. 'Who told you?'

'None of you.' She sounded unimpressed. 'So is it true? Are you really from the future?'

There was no point in lying anymore. 'I am.'

Sofia seemed more curious than shocked. 'Which year are you from?'

'2010.'

'And how did you travel here?'

'That's what I've been trying to understand. I think I might have passed through a wormhole.' He caught himself. 'A wormhole is like a gate through time; a Time

Gate.'

'And why must you find Santo Gutierre?'

'Because he's a time traveller too. He passed through a Time Gate near Santiago.'

'And this is how you will get home to the future?'

'I hope so.'

She looked ready to say more but didn't. As the silence grew between them, so did Tom's embarrassment. He pointed ahead to Fernando.

'Will his wounds heal?'

'In time.' Her face creased with concern. 'It was a miracle Ramos didn't kill him. You saved his life.'

'No, I just—'

'You did, Thomas. Fernando would be dead if you didn't use your device.'

'Well, I couldn't let anything happen to him. He's too important.'

'Important?'

Pablo called out to them from ahead. He pointed to some rocks peppered along the path. Sofia translated.

'He says these stones are the remains of the original paved road to Santiago. They were laid by the Romans two thousand years ago.'

Tom looked up the dusty gravel path bisecting the wheat fields and imagined the cobbled road which had once existed. He squatted down and pressed his palm against the smooth face of one of the stones, picturing the millions of feet that had smoothed its edges over the centuries: pilgrims searching for atonement in Santiago, armies seeking victory in foreign lands. Had Sir Walter once ridden over these stones on his way to Jerusalem?

After Calzadilla, they joined the alternative path Enzo

had told Fernando about. Tom walked behind the three Spaniards, his eyes never leaving Fernando. Did Ana know her grandfather's history? She'd never mentioned Tito had fought in the Spanish Civil War. Did she know he'd once used the name Fernando Morillas? What would make him revert to his original name, and would this still occur? Tom had likely already inflicted too much damage on history even before his decision to save Fernando. He looked at how closely Sofia and Fernando walked to each other now; their connection had grown stronger. Diego's words from Santiago echoed back to Tom.

'He says she was the love of his life.'

Ordinarily, Tom might have been pleased for them, but this version of history wasn't permitted. Fernando was meant to meet Esmerelda, and the two of them would have a son together – Ana's father. Diego had said Tito had left the girl on the Camino because of a betrayal. But looking ahead, they looked inseparable. Tom ached to see Ana's photograph on his phone. He needed to know he hadn't lost her.

Sir Walter wasn't in the town of Terradillos de Templarios. In fact, there was little sign the Templars had ever existed in the dusty village. A local approached and told them he'd heard of their tale from Carrión.

'He says the village has been keeping watch for us, and also a watch for the Guardia Civil,' Sofia said to Tom. 'He has offered beds in his farmhouse to us for the night.'

The following day, in San Nicolás, a local woman pointed them to a dirt path, snaking into the woods. Sofia told Tom it was another path used by the locals, which would eventually rejoin the Camino. After an hour of walking, a crooked sign announced they'd entered the

province of León, leaving Castilla y León behind. They
arrived in Sahagún two hours later; it was the largest town
they'd passed since Burgos. A woman waved them into her
house, where a table laden with food lay waiting. Pablo
immediately attacked a plate of grilled fish while Fernando
and Sofia spoke with the woman.

'She has been waiting for us too,' said Sofia. 'Her sister
lives in Carrión.'

They left the woman's house with filled bellies and
followed her directions to another local path running
parallel to the Camino. Tom fought off his growing fears
their continued detours might inadvertently carry them
past Sir Walter, but his hopes of finding the old knight
faded with each passing hour.

Later that afternoon, the alternative path rejoined the
Camino at the walled medieval town of Mansilla de las
Mulas. It was the busiest village they'd passed in days.

'Fernando says we should not linger,' said Sofia.

They walked to the town's main square and filled their
canteens in the fountain. Tom scanned the plaza, each
local suddenly an undercover agent for the Guardia Civil.

'*Mira*,' said Pablo, walking back from a park bench
carrying a discarded newspaper.

The Spaniards crowded around it and spoke excitedly
to one another. Dread gripped Tom's heart in its fist.

'What is it?'

Sofia snatched the newspaper from Pablo and showed
it to Tom. As she translated the article, he recognised the
man in the photograph.

'Esteban Ramos, a brigada within the Guardia Civil,
has been suspended from duty,' she read. 'Following an
illegal siege of Carrión de los Condes, Comandante Emil

Besteiro said Ramos' actions were unsanctioned and beyond the Guardia Civil's purview. An investigation continues.'

Tom couldn't believe it. 'Does it say if they're still looking for us?'

Sofia scanned the remainder of the article before shaking her head. 'No, nothing.'

He took a breath, his first proper one in several days. They were finally safe.

'We give up, Pablo; why don't you just tell us?'

'Come on, *jefe*, one more try.'

The pilgrims had departed Mansilla the following morning. After briefly disappearing in the village of Villarente, Pablo had returned, gloating about a surprise he'd organised for them in the upcoming city of León. They'd spent the past two hours trying to guess it, and Fernando's patience had exhausted. The Camino had borne far too many surprises already.

'You're going to stop reciting Cervantes?' guessed Fernando.

Pablo scrunched his face into a sarcastic smile. 'Very funny. Fine, I'll tell you.'

'Don't you dare,' yelled Sofia. She was labouring behind them, drenched in sweat under her various layers. 'This surprise is the only thing getting me up this godforsaken mountain. It had better be worth it, Pablo.'

'It is – trust me.'

They arrived in León two hours later. Fernando pointed to a spire peeking out behind a row of buildings.

'There is the cathedral. Let's find an *albergue*.'

Pablo pointed in the opposite direction. 'But your surprise is this way.'

'We can see it later.'

'No. First, the surprise, then the *albergue*.'

Fernando turned to Sofia, who looked hot and exhausted. 'Well, whatever we do, let's do it quickly,' she said.

'*Bueno*, follow me,' said Pablo. 'It's not far.'

The boy led them through the bursting streets of León, pausing briefly to ask some locals for directions, before arriving at an enormous open square on the bank of the Bernesga River. He beamed and thrust his hands out toward a majestic Gothic church on the far side of the plaza.

'Surprise!'

With its convent running the entire length of the plaza, the church was impressive, yet not quite the surprise the boy had promised. Sofia barely hid her disappointment.

'Let's find somewhere to sleep.'

'But we have somewhere to sleep.' Pablo threw his arms open triumphantly. 'This is our hotel for tonight; this is the surprise.'

Bewildered, they followed him through an arched entrance into a foyer adorned with marble columns and frescoes on its ceilings.

'This is a hotel?' asked Fernando. 'It looks more like a museum.'

'It's both, *jefe*. It has a museum, function rooms, a restaurant and now – a hotel.'

'*Buenas tardes*,' called out the concierge from behind the hotel's front desk. Dressed in a crisp tuxedo, he eyed the flecks of dried mud the pilgrims' shoes had left upon his polished marble floor. 'May I help you?'

Pablo flashed his broadest smile. '*Buenas tardes, señor.* My friends and I have a reservation for two rooms this evening.'

The concierge raised a sculpted eyebrow. 'The name of the reservation, *señor*?'

'Martinez – Doctor Antonio Martinez.'

The concierge's manicured finger ran through a book of reservations before whipping out a sheet of paper.

'You've reserved a suite and another single room, no?'

'*Sí.*' Pablo waved toward Sofia. 'Our female companion will take the single room. These gentlemen and I shall take the suite.'

'I see.' The concierge eyed the group carefully. 'And may I ask how you'll be settling your account with us, *señor*?'

Pablo frowned. 'Is it customary for you to request payment from your guests for rooms they've not yet set foot inside?'

'Apologies, *señor*, but we only received your reservation a few hours ago.' The concierge slid an invoice onto the mahogany counter. 'I'm afraid our policy is to receive an advanced payment for such reservations.'

Fernando peered over Pablo's shoulder at the sum at the bottom of the bill.

'We can't afford this,' he murmured from the side of his mouth.

The boy ignored him and pulled a crumpled cheque from his pocket. He smoothed it down upon the counter.

'May I borrow a pen?' asked Pablo.

The concierge reluctantly surrendered his fountain pen, and the boy made the cheque out to the hotel and signed it with a flourish. The concierge picked it up and examined it.

'Clínica Dental Antonio Martinez, in Granada?'

'*Sí*, I'm a dentist.' Pablo smiled widely, revealing his perfect teeth as evidence. 'Now, my friends and I are weary from our day's travels. So if you'd direct us to our rooms, we'd be grateful.'

The concierge cast one more look at the crinkled cheque before placing a pair of keys onto the counter.

'Both rooms are on the third floor. You'll find the stairs behind you and to the left.'

Pablo scooped up the keys and smiled. '*Gracias, señor.*' He went to turn and stopped. 'Oh, one more thing.' He pulled out their tattered *credencials* from his bag.

'Would you be so kind as to stamp these for us?'

The hotel suite was magnificent, with an enormous sitting room with plush velvet couches and French doors opening out to a balcony over the square below. Fernando had never stood in a room so grand.

'You shouldn't have done this, Pablo. We don't have this kind of money.'

'It's my treat, *jefe*.'

Fernando inspected the second bedroom; a pair of double beds stood next to each other. 'No, it's your father's treat. What will he say when he finds out?'

'It's a loan. I'll pay him back when my first novel is published.'

'Writers can't afford this type of room.' Fernando next opened the master bedroom. An enormous four-post bed stood in its centre, and a walk-in wardrobe led to an en suite. 'Not even Cervantes,' he murmured.

They unloaded their bags and removed their filthy boots. Fernando and Thomas took the room with twin beds, leaving Pablo to snore alone in the master bedroom. Pablo showered first; the tiled bathroom was soon filled with steam and flamenco. Thomas' shower was quieter and faster. When Fernando eventually stepped into the shower, he almost forgot to wash, being temporarily paralysed by the torrent of hot water. When he eventually stepped out, he wiped the steam from the mirror and inspected his face. The swelling had subsided, and his blackened eye was now a shade between green and yellow. He peeled the bandages from his nose, bent forevermore, before wrapping himself in a plush white robe he'd found hanging on the back of the door. As clean as he'd been in weeks, he washed his filthy clothes in the basin and hung them alongside Pablo and Thomas' on the balcony; the luxurious suite soon resembled a makeshift laundry.

'*Jefe*, catch.'

Pablo tossed an object toward Fernando, who reflexively caught it. It was the fountain pen.

'This belongs to the concierge,' said Fernando.

'Not anymore. Think of it as a souvenir.'

'We can't just steal things.' Fernando placed the pen into his bag; he'd return it to the concierge the following morning.

At dusk, the three of them headed to the lobby to meet Sofia. When she walked down the stairs, she was wearing the same white dress she'd worn to the wedding in Hornillos, with her perpetual blue shawl loosely wrapped over her. Her hair was still wet from her shower. As she neared, they noticed her glistening eyes.

'What's wrong?' asked Pablo.

'*Gracias*, Pablo.' She threw her arms around the boy. 'It was the most beautiful bath of my entire life.'

The boy smiled and patted her back. 'You're welcome.'

It was nine o'clock, and León's streets were packed with families strolling to dinner. The pilgrims returned to the city's Old Town; the narrow streets buzzed with bursting restaurants and bars. The pilgrims squeezed themselves into a tavern, securing a cramped corner of the bar. The bartender silently poured four beers and pointed to the menu scrawled on a blackboard behind him. Pablo ordered every item listed.

'Are we expecting guests?' asked Fernando.

'Relax, *jefe*, we've been eating nothing more than bread, cheese and stew for three straight weeks. We deserve a treat, no?'

They clinked their glasses and drank; the beer was ice cold. A procession of cured meats and fish arrived, followed by various cheeses and half a loaf of bread. Thomas took a piece of cheese and reached for the jamón Iberico. Pablo slapped his hand away.

'What's wrong?' asked Sofia. 'Cheese and jamón make a beautiful couple, no?'

'*Sí*, but not the jamón Iberico,' explained Pablo, pointing to the lighter-coloured jamón. 'The Serrano is made from the white pig, high in the mountains. It is very nice, but it has more fat.' He then gestured to the Iberico. 'Jamón Iberico is made from the black pigs, which feed on acorns only. Their meat is cured for a year and a half, making it juicier and richer – much too precious to ruin with cheese.'

Sofia relayed all of this to Thomas, who apprehensively slid some of the jamón Serrano onto his cheese.

Pablo ate a slice of the Iberico and rolled his eyes back in bliss. '*Exquisito.*'

Fried chorizo arrived next, then the *morcilla* or blood sausage. The pilgrims methodically worked their way through every dish, washing each down with their replenished mugs of beer. Sofia mopped up the remnants of the last meatball.

'So, *jefe*, I have an important question to ask you,' said Pablo, wiping his mouth with a napkin and sounding more than a little tipsy. 'Do we call you Fernando or Tito?'

It seemed as if the bar had fallen silent; Fernando placed his beer down. 'No one has called me Tito in a very long time.'

'But it's your name, no?'

'*Sí*, it was once, but...' He ignored Sofia's eyes upon him and studied his frosted glass of beer.

'I don't really care,' said Pablo, sounding bored already. The boy placed his hand on Fernando's shoulder. 'To me, you are just *jefe*, no?' He raised his beer again. 'Which reminds me, to propose another toast. To our saviour, *jefe*.'

They clinked their glasses and drank; Fernando felt the heat of his cheeks starting to cool. The waiter brought them their final dish: the *leches fritas* were warm, deep-fried milk puddings sprinkled with cinnamon.

'So, Sofia,' said Pablo, dunking one of the puddings into the accompanying saucer of milk, 'how long will you work in the orphanage in Santiago?'

'Until the end of the summer, probably. Why?'

'We can visit the tapas bars of Santiago when I return from Finisterre.'

'What's at Finisterre?'

'Pablo is walking there to get naked and burn his clothes,' said Fernando.

'Is tradition, *jefe*.' The boy turned back to Sofia. 'You should come too.'

'Absolutely not.'

Pablo sighed. 'You two are no fun.' He pointed to Thomas. 'Sofia, ask him if he will come with me.'

Sofia asked Thomas in English, whose face folded with confusion.

'*No*,' said Thomas.

'He says no,' translated Sofia.

'*Sí*, I understood,' grumbled the boy.

The four of them finished the remaining desserts before stepping out onto the street; Fernando's belt felt tight around his waist.

'Where shall we go, now?' asked Pablo, clapping his hands together. 'Perhaps a gin and tonic to aid our digestion?'

Fernando's head was already buzzing from the beer. 'I'm going back to the hotel.'

'Me too,' said Sofia.

'The hotel?' Pablo looked hurt. 'Tomorrow, we will be back to sleeping in barns and eating stale bread – we should enjoy ourselves.'

'Exactly,' said Sofia, 'and right now, I want to enjoy a proper bed.'

'Well, Thomas and I are going to have another drink.'

The Englishman looked puzzled as Pablo threw an arm over his shoulder and guided him toward a crowded bar on the other side of the street. Fernando and Sofia turned and started walking back to the hotel.

'They say León Cathedral is one of the most beautiful in Spain,' said Fernando. 'Shall we walk past it on our return to the hotel?'

'Okay.'

They walked up the Calle Anche, where locals sat at outdoor tables and smoked cigarettes with their coffee. A side street curved around to the cathedral – its Gothic tower glowed from the orange light beneath it. Sofa looked entranced.

'Oh my God.'

'*Sí*, it's beautiful, no?'

'No, look.' She pointed to a small trolley to the left of the cathedral. 'Ice cream!'

'But we've only just eaten.'

Sofia marched toward the vendor. 'You don't understand; I have been craving ice cream for weeks.'

There were two flavours, vanilla and chocolate; Sofia ordered one of each.

'I have no room,' protested Fernando.

'Nonsense, a stomach always has room for ice cream.' She shrugged. 'I studied to enter medical school, remember?'

She removed a coin from her bag, and the vendor looked at Fernando for permission to accept it. Sofia's glare nearly melted the ice creams.

'Does a woman's money not carry the same worth as a man's?'

The vendor blushed and accepted the coin before relinquishing the cones. Fernando and Sofia licked their ice creams as they walked a lap of the cathedral before heading back to the hotel. She nodded to his cone.

'How is the chocolate?'

'It's good.'

'Let me try.'

She pulled his hand toward her and took a mouthful. 'Mmm, *delicioso*.' She offered her cone to him. 'Try the vanilla.'

Fernando hesitated before leaning down to lick it.

'Well?'

It was smooth and creamy. 'It's good.'

Sofia laughed.

'What?' he asked.

'You are a man of few words. I mean, look at where we are.' She nodded to the bustling street ahead of them. 'We're walking through León, eating ice cream, on our way back to a luxurious hotel.'

'Pablo shouldn't have done that.'

She rolled her eyes. 'He wanted to do something nice for his friends. What's so wrong with that?'

'It's a waste, though.'

'Perhaps. But when Pablo is an old man, he'll still remember his night in León with his friends and forget the cost of the hotel.'

'It's not just the money, though; he's wasting his life.'

'How so?'

'He walks across Spain to become a writer, yet how many times have you seen him actually write?'

'Perhaps he's simply drawing inspiration.'

'Or maybe it's because he's not a writer – he's a dentist.'

'But what if he doesn't want that?'

'Then he's wasted his past five years at university.'

'It's better than wasting decades pretending to be someone he is not.'

'But Pablo can have a good life as a dentist – he'll earn

lots of money and raise a family.'

'What if he doesn't want those things?'

'Have you forgotten his tales of chasing the women of Granada?'

'Sometimes people say what others wish to hear.'

'And sometimes, people are too scared to admit who they really are.'

Sofia stopped and glared at him.

'What?' he asked.

She snatched his ice cream and marched to the nearby rubbish bin.

'What are you doing?'

She threw both cones into the bin and glowered defiantly. 'I've lost my appetite.'

She walked on, and Fernando hurried after her.

'Sofia, what's wrong?'

'Nothing.'

'What did I say?'

She wheeled around and stabbed her finger toward him. 'Pablo is braver than you'll ever know. He's not the one running from who he really is.'

The truth of her annoyance had been revealed.

'I had to change my name,' he said. 'I didn't have a choice. I was being hunted.'

'Once, perhaps, but you don't have to keep lying – not to us, and not to yourself. You can be Tito Hernández again. Don't you want to return to your brother with the same name he knew you by?'

'It's just a name.'

'It's who you are.'

'Not anymore!'

A table of locals stopped speaking and stared. He

lowered his voice.

'Tito Hernández doesn't exist anymore; not the name, or the things he did in the war.'

'Whatever happened in the war, it wasn't your fault. You don't have to keep punishing yourself. Walking through La Puerta Santa is pointless if you won't forgive yourself.'

They walked the rest of the way in silence. Once inside the hotel, Fernando walked Sofia to her door.

'*Buenas noches*, Sofia.'

She opened her door but didn't turn to face him. '*Buenas noches*, Fernando.'

The name sounded bitter from her lips.

Later, amid his bed of soft sheets and pillows, sleep eluded Fernando. He wrestled with Sofia's questions, unable to answer why he was so hard on Pablo. Was he jealous of the boy's seemingly endless opportunities, knowing such things had been inaccessible to him? Perhaps it was because Pablo reminded him so much of Emilio. Fernando's drowsy mind drifted to Sevilla. Sofia was right: he couldn't return to Emilio as Fernando Morillas. But the boy his brother had known had died in the war. As his eyelids finally grew heavy, his final thoughts were of Sofia's hand on his as she reached to taste his ice cream.

The click of the hotel room's door being unlocked woke Fernando. Light crept beneath the bedroom's drapes, and Thomas was asleep in the room's other bed. Was Pablo only returning to the hotel now? Fernando's question was answered by the low murmurings of two men outside. Fernando leaped to his feet. How had the Guardia Civil found them? He pulled on his shirt and moved to the door. He paused to consider a possible escape, but this time, there wasn't one. He swung the door open; the two men standing in their hotel room were not soldiers. One was middle-aged, with grey curly hair, dark skin and a neat moustache. He wore a charcoal suit. The other had a similar moustache but was younger and taller; his mop of curly hair was dark.

'Who are you?' asked Fernando.

The older man glared at him. 'Where is he?'

'Who?'

'Don't be clever with me,' said the older man. 'Pablo – where is he?'

Fernando immediately imagined the boy's misdeeds from the previous night. Had Pablo propositioned the younger man's wife, or the older man's daughter? Both scenarios were plausible.

The door to the master bedroom opened.

'Father, what are you doing here?' asked Pablo, pulling on his shirt.

'I should be asking you that question.' The man looked ready to explode. 'Last night, I received a telephone call from some hotel in León. They tell me some kids are impersonating me, waving around some cheque with my signature on it. They're about to call the police when I suddenly realise the only people with access to my chequebook are your mother and my two sons.'

'Father, I can explain.'

'You're damn right, you'll explain. I want to know

exactly how my misfit son – who is supposed to be on a pilgrimage – is stealing money out of my pocket and spending it at luxury hotels.'

'I didn't steal.'

The door to the second bedroom reopened, and a bewildered Thomas emerged. Pablo's father threw up his hands with rage and glared at his son.

'You are supposed to be walking to Santiago to cleanse yourself.' He pointed an accusing finger toward Fernando and Thomas. 'Not gallivanting across Spain and wasting my money on sordid nights with strangers.'

'They're not strangers; these are my friends.'

'Friends?' The old man scoffed. '*Sí*, I know all about your friends. You're sick, Pablo. Get your things; we're going back to Granada.'

'What?' The boy caved. 'I can't. I need to keep walking to Santiago.'

'Like hell you are.' The old man pointed to the younger man he'd arrived with. 'Your brother and I have driven here through the night to fetch you. You're coming home with us.'

'But I'm not finished.'

'Yes, you are. All of this: the Camino, this nonsense about becoming a writer, your little friend Jamie. All of it is finished.'

The suite door edged open, and Sofia appeared in the doorway.

'Another of your so-called friends?' Pablo's father shook his head. 'At least this one's a woman. I hope she cost less than the room.'

'Watch your mouth, old man,' said Fernando, stepping toward him.

Pablo's brother moved forward to intercept him. 'Or what?'

Fernando locked onto the brother. 'Or you and your father will need to perform one another's dental work.'

Pablo placed his hand on Fernando's shoulder. '*Jefe*, it's alright. Leave it be; I'll do as he says.' Tears shimmered in the boy's eyes as he made for the bedroom.

Fernando glared at Pablo's father.

'You're wrong about Pablo.'

The old man laughed. 'What do you know of my son?'

'That he's a decent man.'

'Decent?' Pablo's father spat out the word like a fishbone. 'My son is a drunkard and a deviant. He thinks life is a *fiesta*; he runs from hardship; he always has. And if you haven't learned that already then you're as stupid as he is.' He turned to Pablo, who'd stalled in the bedroom's doorway. 'What are you waiting for? Get your things.'

'I do know your son,' continued Fernando. 'I've walked with him every day since Lourdes. We endured more on the Camino than most. There were many times we thought about quitting but Pablo always kept us going. Your son is brave, *señor*.'

'And what do you know about bravery?'

'I served alongside men who later had medals pinned to their chests. If asked, I'd favour your son by my side over any of them.'

Pablo looked up with slippery cheeks as Fernando continued.

'There's a bravery in following your heart instead of the advice of others.'

When Pablo's father eventually spoke, his voice was calmer.

'I'd like to speak to my son now – alone.'

Fernando looked to the boy, who nodded his permission. Thomas and Fernando gathered their bags and shoes from the second bedroom and joined Sofia in the hallway. Pablo's brother closed the door behind them, and the pilgrims walked down the stairs to the hotel lobby. The concierge grinned smugly beneath his silly moustache.

'Not staying another night?'

They sat on a bench outside the hotel and waited for Pablo. Half an hour passed before the boy emerged. Pablo's father and brother walked to a car parked opposite the hotel while the boy walked over to their bench. They stood up to meet him.

'I'm sorry,' said Pablo, an uncharacteristically embarrassed look upon his face.

'You've got nothing to apologise for,' said Sofia. 'It's our fault; we shouldn't have let you spoil us with a surprise like that.'

The boy's face fell. 'You didn't enjoy it?'

'Of course we did. The hotel was incredible.'

His smile returned. '*Sí*, it was good, no?'

'What did your father say?' asked Fernando.

'He says I need to work in his clinic for the rest of the summer to pay off the hotel bill.' The boy sighed heavily. 'I'm sure he'll have more to say to me on the drive back to Granada.'

'Drive back to Granada?' asked Sofia.

'*Sí*, I'm going home.'

'Is that what you want?'

'Not really, but what can I do? I came to the Camino searching for answers, but perhaps *jefe* and my father are right: maybe I'm just a dentist after all.'

'Maybe not,' said Fernando.

The boy looked confused. 'But you said I was wasting my time on the Camino.'

'*Sí*, I know, but…' Fernando shook his head. 'Wasting five years is better than wasting the rest of your life, no? Besides, who says it's been a waste? Perhaps all of this will make a good book someday.'

Pablo's eyes sparkled. '*Sí*, a modern-day *Don Quixote*, no?'

'"Destiny guides our fortunes more favourably than we could have expected."'

The boy's mouth fell open. '*Jefe* – you listened to my Cervantes quotes, after all?'

Fernando shrugged. 'You offered me little choice.'

Pablo's father honked the car's horn.

'I should go,' said the boy. He embraced Sofia, kissing each of her cheeks twice. 'Don't let *jefe* make you miserable, okay?'

'I promise,' she said, giving him a teary smile. Pablo turned and hugged Thomas, slapping the Englishman enthusiastically and gripping his shoulder.

'It's up to you now, Thomas: you must walk to Finisterre and burn your clothes while looking out over the Atlantic Ocean.'

Without understanding a word, Thomas simply smiled and nodded. Pablo finally turned to Fernando.

'I'm sorry, *jefe*.'

'You've got nothing to be sorry for.' He hugged the boy. '*Adiós, amigo*.'

'*¿Adiós?* The boy pulled away and wagged a finger. 'This isn't goodbye. You'll only be in Sevilla, no? We'll see one another soon. *Hasta luego*.'

Another blast of the car horn, and Pablo hung his head.

'This is going to be a very long drive.' He slung his bag over his shoulder and tramped toward the car.

Sofia placed her hand on Fernando's shoulder as they watched it pull away.

'I hope his father isn't too hard on him.'

The car disappeared around the corner.

'It must be cruel being a parent,' said Fernando.

'Why?'

'Parents only seem to want their children to grow into good people, so they invoke all of the rules they followed when they were young. But when their child disobeys those rules yet still grows into an even better person, they must feel incredibly foolish.' He shook his head. 'Why would anyone choose to endure that?'

Sofia laughed.

'What?' he asked.

'It's too bad you never wanted a family of your own.' She leaned in and kissed his cheek softly. 'I think you'd have made a good father.'

CHAPTER 20

The Camino was quieter without Pablo. Although Tom hadn't ever understood what Pablo was saying, he'd grown accustomed to the Spaniard's incessant chirping. The day's walk from León had been long, yet relaxed; even Fernando had stopped looking over his shoulder for Guardia Civil trucks in the distance. The relative peace gave Tom little comfort, though; his undistracted mind returned to thoughts of a life marooned in the past. Every step they took brought him closer to the Time Gate at Monte del Gozo. While he felt confident the wormhole led back to the future, he still had no way of knowing which Holy Year he'd be sent to. How could he be sure he wouldn't be propelled to the year 3010 instead of 2010?

The fact Tom had been sent back to 1954, the exact time Ana's grandfather had walked the Camino, could not have been a coincidence. This suggested that wormholes transported people to Holy Years of personal significance. It was a reach, of course. Tom could have easily argued 2004 was a year of consequence, whereby he could have travelled back to the European Cup quarter-final and told David Beckham not to take his ill-fated penalty kick against Portugal. But this latest theory suggested the wormhole at Monte del Gozo would send him to his Holy Year – 2010. He realised his hypothesis relied on hope more than science, but it was the only chance he had left. He wished he could ask Sir Walter's opinion, but the knight's trail had grown cold. As the afternoon sun dipped ahead of them, Tom couldn't dispel the notion Sir Walter was now behind them, not in front. Perhaps he should stop for a few days in one of the towns and wait for the knight?

A long, stone bridge led across a river to the town of Hospital de Órbigo. As they crossed it, Tom noticed a series of multicoloured tents on the riverbank below. A crowd had gathered around two riders on horseback.

'What are they doing?'

Sofia passed the question to Fernando.

'*Justas*,' he replied.

Sofia scrunched up her face. 'Sorry, Thomas. I do not know this word in English. It is the sport the knights play.'

Tom watched as the riders were each given long poles.

'Jousting.' He smiled. 'It's a jousting tournament.' If ever there was a place to find a medieval knight, this was it.

Across the bridge, the pilgrims seemed to have travelled back in time: locals dressed in chain mail drank merrily from bejewelled goblets; a band played 'Greensleeves', with one man playing a lute, while a woman plucked away on a harp. Two children battled each other with wooden swords.

'Fernando says it's a local *fiesta*,' said Sofia. 'He thinks we should check for vacancies in the *albergue*. If there are none, we will walk to the next town.'

Tom pointed to the jousting field on the riverbank.

'I'm going to look for Sir Walter. I'll meet you back here in a little bit.'

He wandered toward the crowded field by the river. The two men on horses were each dressed as knights. One wore a gleaming suit of black armour with a crimson cape draped over his shoulder; his opponent sat on his horse at the opposite end of the course. Somewhere in the crowd, a bugle blew a fanfare. A marshal, dressed flamboyantly in an emerald velvet jumpsuit, walked to the middle of the field with a long flagpole. He rested the flag's tip on the railing at the centre of the course. Once both knights had given their final salutes, the crowd hushed, casting an eerie silence over the riverbank. The marshal lifted his banner and the elated spectators roared. Both knights kicked the ribs of their horses and charged forward; the thundering of the horses' hooves reverberated through Tom's body. As the knights neared each other, their lances lowered to their opponent's chest. The crowd held their breath and braced for the impending impact. A sickening crash of wood was followed by the echoing clang of metal. The black knight's lance catapulted his opponent backward out of his saddle and down onto the dirt. The crowd erupted into raptures, and the dark knight saluted them triumphantly before riding back to a crude wooden stand near the middle of the course. A familiar figure rose from his seat and applauded the victor. Tom's heart quickened.

'Sir Walter!' He pushed his way through the mob. 'Sir

Walter!'

The knight squinted down from the dais into the crowd; his pale eyes twinkled with recognition.

'Ah, Tom Anderson.' The old man excused himself from those around him and walked down the steps to Tom. 'I almost didn't recognise you with your wee beard.' Sir Walter clasped his hand upon Tom's shoulder. 'I heard what happened in Carrión. I'm sorry I was not there, lad.'

'It's alright. We're safe now.'

'Thank the Lord. But where are your companions?'

'Finding beds for us in the *albergue*.'

The knight shook his head. 'There'll not be a single available bed, not during the tournament. I'll see to your lodging. 'Tis a wee place on the town's outskirts, but it serves a hearty trout soup.'

They walked up the hill, back toward the town.

'What is this festival, anyway?' asked Tom.

''Tis the annual jousting tournament. Come and look.' Sir Walter led Tom back to the bridge, and they stopped halfway across it. 'In the fifteenth century, there was a Leónese knight, named Suero de Quiñones, who was in love with a maiden named Leónor de Tovar. Suero and his nine champions challenged the knights in the surrounding lands to a jousting tournament to win her favour. He promised his lady he'd break three hundred lances for her.'

'Did he?'

The knight chuckled. 'Nay. After breaking more than one hundred and fifty, the tournament was called in Suero's favour. He married the lady a year later, only to be killed by one of the knights he defeated years after that.' Sir Walter pointed to a series of plaques decorating the length of the bridge. 'Those there plaques bear the names of Suero's nine champions, and each year, the town stages a jousting tournament to honour them. The town invites me to adjudicate.'

'You've never entered?'

The knight's laugh boomed. 'Heavens no, lad. That would hardly be fair, now would it?'

The mention of Sir Walter's origins was the segue Tom needed.

'I've been thinking about how to get us home.'

Sir Walter's face grew serious. 'Oh?'

'Well, remember how we were worried about the Time Gates sending us back or forward to the wrong Holy Year?'

'Aye.'

'I think it might depend on the specific person travelling through it. So, if I pass through the Time Gate at Monte del Gozo, I should travel forward to the Holy Year of significance to me – 2010. Likewise, when you walk through the gate at Saint-Jean, you should return to your own Holy Year – 1193.' The theory sounded even more preposterous aloud.

Sir Walter didn't respond.

'You think I'm crazy, don't you?' asked Tom.

'Not crazy, no.' He sounded like a professor trying to explain why he'd failed a student from his class. 'But I've walked the path from Saint-Jean to Bayonne twice this year already and several times in the Holy Year of 1948. Why did I not pass through your Time Gate then?'

'The Time Gate is located directly on the train tracks. Perhaps you missed it.'

'Aye, perhaps.' The knight sounded even less

convinced than he looked. He pointed to the bridge. 'Do you know how many pilgrims cross this bridge on their way to Santiago every year?'

'In 2010, hundreds of thousands walk the Camino.'

'Precisely. Now, tell me: were you alone on your train to Saint-Jean?'

'No, it was full.'

'Yet, none of the other passengers travelled back to 1954 with you?'

'No, but... they mustn't have passed through the Time Gate.'

'Are the trains of the future so large that one man might pass through the Time Gate while another does not?'

'No.'

'So you see what I'm saying, don't you? Why didn't anyone else pass through the Time Gate?'

The question knocked the wind out of Tom. He steadied himself on the bridge's railing, dizzy with the realisation his theory had failed to answer the most crucial question: why hadn't anyone else travelled back in time?

'I'm stuck here,' he murmured, clenching his eyes shut to trap his tears. 'You're right, I've been spending all my time trying to find a way home, but I've never even worked out how I got here.' Hope leaked out of him. 'There's no reason to any of this.'

'I never said that, lad.' Sir Walter rested a hand on Tom's shoulder. ''Twas no accident we travelled to this time. We were chosen.'

'By who?'

'Who else?'

The knight nodded up to the sky, and Tom slid his

face back into his hands.

The knight fixed him with a curious stare. 'You're not a God-fearing man, lad?'

'No.'

'Yet you walk the Way of Saint James?' Sir Walter shook his head. 'I suppose not every lamb in the field sees the shepherd who watches over it. There is still much in this world which remains a mystery to me, but I'm certain of one thing: if your Time Gate really sent me here, Tom Anderson, it shall remain closed until I fulfil my quest.'

'What's your quest?'

'The same as it's ever been, lad. I'm a knight of the Templar Order; I took an oath to protect people from evil and tyranny. Do you really think it was a coincidence God sent me to the Xacobeo amid mankind's darkest hour?'

'1943?'

Sir Walter had been transported to a time where Hitler had Europe in a stranglehold.

'But the Second World War ended in 1945. Why didn't the Time Gate re-open for you in 1948 or 1954?'

'Because I've not yet fulfilled my quest. Look at the country you've walked across; you've seen the evil Franco's regime propagates.'

Tom recalled the terrified faces of the locals of Carrión and the bowed heads in Burgos Cathedral.

'I believe your Time Gates open and close for those souls chosen to complete a task. I've walked these caminos for over a decade to fulfil my oath. And maybe, one day, when I walk beyond Saint-Jean, a great storm of cloud and ash will carry me back to my wife and sons. And my quest will finally be over.' The knight smiled forlornly into the distance before pinning Tom with an intense stare. 'But you've asked the wrong question, lad.'

'What do you mean?'

'You shouldn't be asking what my quest is.' He stabbed a finger into Tom's chest. 'What is your quest, Tom Anderson?'

Fernando couldn't sleep. The day after the jousting tournament, the pilgrims had walked to Astorga – a crossroad of several different caminos – and the *albergue* was filled with the rustling of an influx of pilgrims. But it wasn't the fidgeting and snores of his new neighbours that had kept him staring up at the ceiling. It was his thoughts of Sofia.

It was true; he'd never been in love. As a boy in Sevilla, he'd been more interested in chasing a football than girls. And there'd been nothing romantic about his transactions with the women who'd worked the old quatres of Cádiz or Casablanca. After arriving in Huelva after the war, Fernando had intentionally kept to himself. His eyes had searched for undercover Guardia Civil agents, not the women in their summer dresses. Love hadn't been a luxury he'd deserved.

He sighed and rolled onto his other side. Any thought of a life with Sofia was pointless; it was too late. He was walking to Santiago for redemption, not love. He closed his eyes and re-attempted sleep. His tired mind betrayed him by replaying Sofia's words from the night they'd held each other in Carrión.

'Don't leave me again. I thought I'd lost you.'

Fernando woke to the sound of the other pilgrims coughing and banging their way out of the *albergue*. He slid down from his bunk. Thomas was already getting dressed.

'*Buenos días*,' whispered the Englishman, one of the few phrases he'd mastered.

'*Buenos días*.'

Fernando, Sofia and Thomas spent their morning climbing the valley, passing through semi-abandoned villages whose locals watched silently from the windows of their crumbled homes. The Camino eventually returned to the road, and after crossing the river via the Puente de Pañote, ascended into a pine forest. They'd soon be entering the Camino's final region – Galicia – and would trade the relative flatness of the past two weeks for the mountains once more. When they arrived in the village of Rabanal, it was only mid afternoon. Fernando pointed to an *albergue* opposite the church.

'We should sleep here tonight.'

'Already?' Sofia looked up at the sun, which was still directly overhead. 'It's still early, no?'

'*Sí*, but it's a strenuous climb to the Cruz de Ferro.' Fernando pointed to the mountain looming over the town. 'It will be better in the cooler temperature tomorrow morning.'

'Well, you've convinced me.' Sofia wiped the sweat from her brow. 'I'll tell Thomas.'

The village of Rabanal was small and pretty, with rows of identical stone houses adorned with flower boxes filled with pink and white petunias. The woman at the *albergue* welcomed them with a toothless grin, her dark skin as cracked as the building's mudbrick walls.

'There are evening prayers at the monastery,' she said as she stamped their *credencials*. 'Dinner will be served at five o'clock.'

Sofia found her way to the female dormitory while Fernando and Thomas were reunited with their noisy roommates from Astorga in the men's room. Thomas and Fernando used the extra hours of sunlight to wash their clothes before meeting Sofia in the dining room for dinner. The three ate their stew quietly, listening patiently to the other pilgrims brag about how quickly they intended to reach Santiago. After dinner, Sofia and Fernando walked to the monastery for evening prayers while Thomas retired to his bed.

The monastery was tiny. They sat in the last remaining seats in a congregation primarily of pilgrims. Four monks, dressed in flowing black gowns, entered and walked to the altar. They smiled warmly and blessed the pilgrims before celebrating the Liturgy with a Gregorian chant. Fernando closed his eyes and listened to their Latin words hum mournfully against the church's rounded stone ceiling; the music calmed his thoughts. Afterwards, he and Sofia strolled back to the *albergue*. The sun had now set, leaving a burnt-orange ribbon across the horizon. As the first of the night's stars twinkled in the navy sky above, Sofia turned to Fernando.

'The service was beautiful, no?'

'*Sí*, Thomas will be disappointed to have missed it.'

'I doubt it.'

Fernando frowned. 'What do you mean?'

She looked around to ensure they were alone. 'He doesn't believe in God.'

'Thomas? Why do you say that?'

'He told me in Burgos.' She looked embarrassed to be revealing his secret. 'It's peculiar, though, no?'

'*Sí*, but not the most peculiar thing about him.'

'You don't really think he's from the future, do you?'

'No.'

'You think he's lying?'

'I didn't say that.'

'So what, then? He doesn't seem crazy to me. And what about the device he used in Carrión – the telephone? You saw what it could do; it saved you. How do you explain it?'

'I can't.' Fernando shrugged. 'The truth is, I don't know what to think.'

'Nor me. Thomas believes there is a path to the future on a mountain outside Santiago.'

'Then we shall take him there and see for ourselves.'

They walked in silence for a moment before Sofia turned to face him.

'What about you?' she asked. 'How long will you stay in Santiago?'

'Not long.' They'd spoken little about what would happen after they arrived at their destination. 'And you? After your work in the orphanage, will you return to Valencia by bus or train?'

'I'm not going back to Valencia.'

'What do you mean? Where are you going?'

'I'm going to England.' She must have seen his shock. 'I was accepted into Oxford; I'm going to study to be a doctor.'

He stopped and turned to her. 'You passed the entrance examination?'

She gave an embarrassed smile.

'Sofia, that's wonderful.' Fernando wanted to hug her. 'Why didn't you tell us?'

They began walking again.

'I wasn't certain I'd accept.'

'Why wouldn't you? It's a scholarship, no? They'll pay for everything?'

'*Sí* – the first year, then it's conditional on my grades. And it doesn't pay for my travel to England.'

'So this is why you are working in the orphanage over the summer, to earn money for your ticket?'

It all finally made sense.

'The only other person who knows I won the scholarship is Hector,' said Sofia.

'Your parents don't know?'

'I didn't tell them, in case I didn't go.'

'Why wouldn't you?'

'It's not easy to pack up your entire life and live abroad.' She looked uncomfortable. 'Oxford is so far away; I won't know anyone.'

'You'll make friends.'

She stopped and looked at him again. 'Have you ever been to England?'

'Me?' He laughed. 'Never.'

'They say it is stunning.' She bit her bottom lip. 'Perhaps you could visit me? We could visit London together. You still owe me an ice cream, no?' Her shy laugh came and went. 'What do you think?'

Fernando froze; he'd never wanted something so much in his entire life.

'I can't,' he eventually said. 'I'm sorry.'

'I understand.' She smiled, even as her eyes glistened. 'It was just an idea; it's fine if you don't want to.'

'I do want to, it's just...' How could he possibly explain? 'I have to meet Emilio.'

'*Sí*, of course.' She steeled herself and met his eye again. 'I understand, really.'

They reached the *albergue* without another word; every footstep inched the blade of their silence deeper into his chest.

'*Buenas noches*,' she said softly before disappearing inside.

Fernando let her go; there was nothing else to say. He leaned against the wall and lit a cigarette, puffing a cloud of tobacco up toward the grinning crescent moon. He'd known every additional day spent with Sofia made their inevitable parting more difficult, but he'd imagined they'd have more time together. Santiago was still another week away, and her invitation had startled him. She'd been brave enough to say the words he'd only dreamed of speaking. Yet now, she'd been left to think he didn't care about her. The thought smouldered in his chest like a hot coal. He finished his cigarette before walking into the *albergue*; everyone else had gone to bed. He walked down the hallway to the girls' dormitory and gently knocked.

'Sofia?'

No answer. Fernando rested his ear against the door and could hear her muffled sobs on the other side. He opened the door and walked in, finding her alone.

'Sofia...'

'Fernando, no!'

Her eyes were wide with tears and dread. Free of her uniform, Fernando's gaze fell to the swollen belly protruding beneath her nightgown.

'Turn around,' she shrieked, snatching her robes and

clutching them against her body.

Fernando twisted around and closed his eyes. What had he just seen?

'I-I-I'm sorry,' he stammered. 'Forgive me.'

'Why are you here?' Her screams were blood-curdling. 'You shouldn't be in here.'

'I know, I was just…'

He was frozen. Unsure if he should stay or go, his mind flashed back to Sofia's stomach. It must have been a mistake. The girl's bawling forced him back around. Sofia's entire body shook beneath her robes as she wailed into her hands. He closed the door and edged toward her.

'Sofia? I don't understand what's happening.'

'What do you mean?' She looked up at him, her tear-smudged face now a confusion of grief and rage. 'You saw.' She pressed her robes flat against her round belly. 'I'm pregnant, Fernando.'

It wasn't simply a bump; her stomach bulged against the gown's tightened fabric.

'I don't understand. How can you be pregnant? I mean…' He clutched for any of the questions rattling through his mind. 'When is the baby due?'

'Three weeks.'

'Three weeks?' He felt dazed. 'You've been pregnant all this time? W-Why didn't you tell us?'

'Because it was none of your business. This was my problem to deal with, not yours.'

All the mountains they'd climbed over their weeks together, all those scorching hot days. 'But you shouldn't be walking, not in your condition.'

'My condition? I'm pregnant, not a leper. And I hadn't planned on walking. If Padre Price hadn't been a drunken fool, I'd already have been in Santiago.'

'We will find someone to drive you.' More questions spiralled through his head and out from his lips. 'Who is the father?'

Sofia's stare became molten, and tears evaporated on her hot cheeks. 'What, now you think I'm just some whore who opens her legs for any passing man?'

'That's not what I meant.'

'Hector's the father.' She clutched her stomach. 'This baby is why we fought; it's the reason he fled back to Barcelona. He doesn't want anything to do with it.'

'What about your parents? They should be here with you.'

'My parents?' She scoffed so hard tears spilled down her cheeks. 'It would kill them to know their unmarried daughter had fallen pregnant.' She shook her head defiantly. 'No, this is my problem to fix alone.'

'You're not alone.'

'Of course I am.'

'You're not.' He stepped toward her. 'I'm here.'

She scanned his face for a moment before edging closer and finally collapsing into his chest. 'Oh, Fernando – what am I going to do?'

She shuddered against him, and he steadied her head against his. 'It will be alright. I'll help you.'

'You can't tell anyone,' she whimpered between her sobs. 'Promise me you won't tell anyone.'

'I promise.'

He held her tight, his mind already planning their next steps. First, they'd have to walk back to Astorga for a bus – it was the nearest town of any size. They could tell Thomas that Sofia was feeling unwell; the Englishman would likely be pleased to arrive in Santiago earlier. How had she expected to work at the orphanage? They'd need to find another way to pay for her ticket to England. And how could she attend classes while tending to her baby?

He must have tensed, for Sofia pulled away from him. 'What's wrong?' she asked.

'The orphanage in Santiago.' The words didn't want to leave his mouth. 'You're not going there to work, are you?'

She bowed her head, and the room fell silent.

'Are you?' he repeated, this time firmer.

When Sofia eventually spoke, her voice was weak. 'There was nothing else I could do. Hector wanted nothing to do with the baby, and my parents would never support me; I'd be raising the baby alone. What kind of life is that for a child? No grandparents, no father.'

'It will have a mother.'

'It's not enough.' Her eyes gleamed with tears. 'With me, the child will only know struggle. This way, the baby will have a chance of a normal life.'

'In an orphanage?'

'It won't stay there for long. When I telephoned, the nuns said there are always good families unable to have a child of their own.'

'And where will you go?'

'To Oxford.'

'You've already decided.'

Her brow hardened. 'You make it sound like I chose this. I didn't choose to fall pregnant to a man who hid his marriage from me.'

'Hector is already married to another?'

'*Sí* – for two years.' Her voice shimmered. 'I didn't

choose any of this.'

Part of him wanted to hold her, but a deep gash reopened within him. 'You're choosing to abandon your baby, Sofia; you're running away like my mother did.'

Her eyes widened like a caged bull's. 'Don't you dare judge me, Fernando – or is it Tito?' Hot tears spilled down her cheeks. 'You, of all people, don't get to lecture me; you've spent your entire life running.'

'*Sí*, but I never abandoned a baby.'

He could see his words had pierced her – Sofia's tears bled freely – but what he'd said couldn't be unspoken.

'I thought I could trust you,' she sobbed. 'But you're no different than anyone else. No, you're worse – you lied. You tricked me into thinking you actually cared.'

He ignored the small voice screaming within him to tell Sofia he did care.

'Get out,' she whispered.

His feet felt fastened to the floorboards.

'Get out!'

Her scream summoned footsteps and voices into the hallway. Fernando paused before turning and leaving. The door closed behind him.

CHAPTER 21

When Sofia woke the following morning, the *albergue* was quiet as a morgue. She walked down the hallway and found Thomas, alone at the dining table.

'Where is Fernando?' she asked.

'He's gone.' He almost looked guilty. 'When I woke up, his bed was empty, and his boots and bag had disappeared.'

'Did he leave a note?'

Thomas shook his head.

She sat opposite him and poured herself a cup of coffee. She pressed her fingers firmly around the mug.

'What's going on?' asked Thomas.

She searched the cup's spiralling contents for a believable lie, but none appeared.

'I'm pregnant.'

He looked surprised but didn't exhibit Fernando's

disgust. Instead, he listened patiently as Sofa explained Hector's treachery and the truth of her journey to Santiago. When she'd finished recounting her fight with Fernando, Thomas placed his hand on her arm. His pale eyes were free of judgement.

'I'm so sorry, Sofia.'

'Why? None of this is your doing.'

'No, but I should have stopped Fernando.'

'You could not have known he would leave us. Anyway, it is better he is gone – for him and for me. This is how it is supposed to be.'

Thomas looked ready to speak but seemed to change his mind, shaking it from his brow.

'So, what will you do now?' he eventually asked.

'What else can I do? I will continue to Santiago.'

'You can't keep walking; you're pregnant.'

'Thomas, I've been pregnant the entire time you have known me, and we have walked hundreds of kilometres.'

'What about a bus? We're much closer to Santiago now; it will be cheaper than before.'

'No – every last cent I have will go to the orphanage for the baby. Santiago is a week away, and the baby arrives in three. I can make it.'

Thomas scanned the table as if searching for an alternative solution. He eventually shrugged. 'Then we'll walk to Santiago together.'

When they left the *albergue*, Rabanal was still shrouded in fog. It felt odd walking without Fernando – as if they were both missing a limb. Outside the town, the Camino rose steeply, and Sofia was soon dripping with sweat.

'Shall we stop for a rest?' asked Thomas.

'If we stop every time I run out of breath,' she said

between gasps, 'the baby will arrive in Santiago as a toddler.'

Thomas didn't ask again. Aside from her wheezing, they struggled up the mountain in silence, and her mind wandered. In some ways, she was relieved her secret had been uncovered. The only thing worse than being pregnant had been hiding it from everyone. Aside from Hector, no one else had known. Even Sofia hadn't known in the beginning.

She'd been so busy – preparing for her entrance examination while still working at the hospital – she hadn't noticed she'd missed her period. It was only after she'd vomited one morning that she'd suspected something was amiss.

'What did you eat?' her mother had asked.

'Nothing,' Sofia had said. 'It's that smell.'

'What smell?' Papa had asked.

'It's like warm, salty, rancid milk. You don't smell it?'

'No.'

Sofia had tentatively sniffed her father, and her throat had immediately filled with bile. She'd hurtled back to the bathroom and vomited into the basin again. Her parents had followed, and her mother's eyes had narrowed.

'What's wrong with you?'

'It's Papa – he stinks of rotten fish.'

'Your father has stunk of rotten fish every day of your life; it's never made you throw up.'

'Leave her be,' her father had said. 'She's allowed to vomit in peace.'

'Well, if she's sick, then we'll get sick too.'

Her father had shrugged. 'She probably just caught something from one of her patients.'

'What if she is pregnant?'

'You can't catch that at a hospital.'

That morning, Sofia had ridden her bicycle to a doctor on the other side of town who attended a different church to her family. The sign above his clinic's door had said he was a paediatrician.

'Well, it's not really my specialty,' the doctor had said, removing his mask. 'But you're undoubtedly pregnant; I'd estimate you're almost nine weeks.'

Sofia had burst into tears, and the doctor had offered a sympathetic handkerchief. After composing herself, she'd cycled to the hospital and lured Hector out to a park behind the hospital.

'You're pregnant?' he'd asked, staring at her in shock. 'You're sure?'

'*Sí*, I'm sure.' She'd told him about her morning sickness and the visit to the doctor. 'He said I'm already nine weeks.'

'But we were so careful.'

'Not careful enough.' Precautions had always surrendered to passion. 'What do we do now?'

Sofia had been terrified, but Hector had placed his hands reassuringly on her cheeks and looked deeply into her eyes.

'Now, we get married and start a life together.'

'Married? We haven't even met each other's parents.'

'We will.' He'd got down on one knee and had taken her hand in his. 'You'll have to wait for a ring, but will you marry me, Sofia Lozano?'

She'd nodded, sending happy tears over the tracks of her earlier sad ones, and they'd kissed. It had been her most perfect memory.

Hector had said they shouldn't tell anyone at first; news of a junior doctor getting a nurse pregnant would cost them their jobs. Instead, he'd suggested the first thing they should do was arrange for their parents to meet and learn about their engagement; news of the pregnancy could follow. Hector had organised for his parents to travel to Valencia, but a day before their visit, he'd rushed back to Barcelona; his father had suffered a heart attack. A few days later, Hector had telephoned Sofia at the hospital, saying he needed to remain in Barcelona.

'For how long?' she'd asked.

'Not long – just until Papa has regained his strength; another week, two at the most. I'll return to you as fast as I can, my love.'

After three weeks, Hector still hadn't returned. Every time she'd spoken to him on the telephone, he'd offered the same response about his return.

'Soon, my love, soon.'

Eventually, the strain had become too much.

'We need to tell our parents,' she'd said one time, gripping the telephone anxiously. 'Mama is getting suspicious.'

Hector's annoyed voice had crackled down the line.

'You'll forgive me if I'm more concerned about my father's health than some damn dinner.'

She'd hung up the telephone feeling guilty and alone. A seed of doubt had started to grow inside her. And her mother had begun asking about Sofia's other growing seed.

'Why do you insist on hiding underneath all of these cardigans?' Mama had moaned. 'You're twenty-seven years old, not sixty-seven. No man will marry a woman he cannot see.'

With her mother's suspicions aroused, and her father's scent causing her to dry retch, Sofia had spent more time at the hospital: working in the days and studying for her examination in the evenings. Any spare time had been spent in the bathroom; her bladder had been perpetually squeezed.

Months passed, and Hector still hadn't returned. Sofia's tummy and breasts had continued to bulge, forcing her to wear evermore clothes, draping herself in uniforms that might have passed as curtains. Her knees and feet had started to ache under the strain of her extra weight. Small flights of stairs had become mountains, and her ankles had slowly disappeared. Thankfully, her studies had distracted her from Hector's absence and her body's betrayal. She'd been well into her second trimester when, along with a handful of other hopeful applicants, she'd eventually sat the Oxford entrance exam in the local university's library.

Things had then got worse. Without the need to study, Sofia had stopped spending her evenings in the hospital. Her mother's relentless barbs about her daughter's ballooning weight had culminated in reduced dinner portions.

'No man will marry a woman he cannot lift, Sofia.'

Hector had telephoned Sofia sporadically at the hospital; his father's condition had improved marginally, but there'd still been no definable date for his return to Valencia. Sofia had thought of asking him whether she could tell her parents about their engagement and the baby but hadn't wished to add further to Hector's troubles. Her daily tasks had seemed to take twice as long. She'd occasionally caught the other nurses whispering behind her back, either feeding rumours Sofia was pregnant or relishing the fact she'd grown fatter than them. One day, when Sofia had felt especially pregnant, she'd threatened to shave off Sister Ophelia's lustrous mane of curls if she didn't stop her sniggering. The following morning, Sofia was called into the matron's office and handed a crisp yellow envelope. She'd opened it, expecting her termination letter. But, instead, it had contained a telegram.

Dear Miss Sofia Lozano,

Thank you for recently sitting the entrance examination for the Moore-Wilton scholarship.

We are delighted to announce you are this year's recipient, with a fully funded scholarship (including lodging), to study Medicine at Oxford University, commencing September 1954.

We will send you more information in the coming weeks, but until then, congratulations and good luck with your forthcoming studies.

Sofia had travelled to Barcelona the following day. Wishing to surprise Hector with the good news, she'd acquired his address from her friend in the hospital's office. Stepping from the bus, Sofia had visited La Rambla and bought a bouquet of red carnations for Hector's mother. Sofia had practically skipped up the stairs to their family's apartment, nestled within the bohemian streets of Gràcia. But when she'd knocked, a woman had answered.

'*¿Sí?*'

At first, Sofia had thought it might have been Hector's

sister. But then she'd remembered, he didn't have any siblings. And when Hector had appeared in the doorway with a small boy tugging at his leg, Sofia had known. She'd turned and run back down the stairs, leaving their doorstep littered with tear-dampened petals.

Her third trimester had been hell: it hadn't been the unrelenting aches and pains ruining her body; instead, it had been the impending doom growing within it. Every kick from the baby had reminded her of the unavoidable shame she'd soon bring down upon her family.

Hector had eventually shown up, loitering outside the hospital after one of her shifts. He'd fed Sofia the tragedy of his loveless marriage, which had been arranged by his parents whilst he'd been studying in England.

'I don't love her, Sofia.' He'd fallen to his knees and finally produced the ring he'd promised. 'I only love you.'

His empty proposal had been drowned out by Mama's eternal warning, which had rung through Sofia's mind like cathedral bells after a wedding: Men could not be trusted – ever. Sofia would not be mistaken again. She took the ring but sent Hector trudging back to his wife and child. A week later, Professor Calatrava announced Doctor González had resigned to spend more time with his family in Barcelona. She'd never felt so alone or foolish.

Sofia had briefly wanted to keep the baby. She'd considered writing to Oxford to defer her scholarship, at least until the child was older. But how could she ever hope to study medicine and raise a child? In someone else's care, the baby could have a decent life. Alone, Sofia would have never been a good mother. Yet, she'd still had a chance of one day becoming a good doctor.

The problem had been where to take the baby –

Valencia had no secrets. The arrival of a baby in the orphanage, coupled with Sofia's sudden disappearance to England, would have pointed to a single conclusion. Her parents would never have survived the secret's stain. Plagued by guilt and incredibly swollen knees, Sofia had waddled into the Iglesia de San Juan del Hospital to seek guidance from the only person left to ask. She'd eased herself down onto her knees and had clasped her hands together. Christ's anguished face had looked down at her from above the altar.

'Dear God, please forgive me for my sins,' she'd whispered, 'for I know I have made many.'

She'd murmured each of her transgressions and begged His forgiveness before explaining her unsolvable predicament.

'I cannot raise a child alone, but I'm not strong enough to leave it behind. Where am I to send this baby, Lord?' She'd clasped her swollen hands together tightly. 'Please send me a sign of what I'm to do. I beg you, I am at your mercy. Help me, Lord.'

'Señorita Lozano?'

The voice had echoed down from the cathedral's vaulted ceiling. Sofia had opened her eyes, expecting a vision of God, but instead found their family's priest – Padre Cabanes – standing before her.

'Señorita Lozano? Is everything alright?'

'*Sí, Padre.*' Sofia had wiped her eyes dry and stood up. 'I was only praying.'

'I spoke to your mother yesterday, and she told me your secret.'

'My secret?' The baby had kicked. 'I don't have any secrets; my mother is mistaken.'

The priest's cherubic face had fallen. 'Well, that is terribly disappointing. Your mother said she'd found some English books in your room, and I'd hoped to enlist your help. A friend of mine, an English priest, is searching for an interpreter along the Camino.'

'The Camino de Santiago?'

'*Sí*, he's here for the Xacobeo – delivering sermons in cities between here and Santiago.'

Sofia had listened to Padre Cabanes explain the itinerary, and she'd rested her hand on her tummy. Even a secret as big as hers couldn't travel across Spain, could it?

'He has a driver, but he needs a translator. You'd be home by August. He won't pay you, but your board and meals would be covered, of course.'

She'd hastily done the calculations: the baby was due in the third week of July. It would be tight, but it could work.

'Well?'

Padre Cabanes and the statue of Christ had both stared at her, awaiting her response.

'*Sí*, Padre. I can help.'

Sofia and Thomas finally crested the mountain they'd spent the morning climbing. Thomas pointed ahead.

'Look.'

She followed his outstretched finger toward a tall wooden post on a mound of stones. A tiny iron cross stood upon it – the Cruz de Ferro.

When Pablo had first mentioned the Iron Cross in Navarra, Tom had imagined an imposing steel crucifix, casting an enormous shadow across the Spanish countryside. The reality was underwhelming. They walked up a mound of rocks toward the wooden pillar; many of the stones bore handwritten messages.

'What are these?' he asked.

'People carry rocks from their home villages across the Camino. Sometimes they write messages or things they wish to leave behind.'

They were standing on people's regrets.

Tom had been wrestling with his own regret on the ascent up the mountain. He'd heard Fernando and Sofia argue the night before – everyone in the *albergue* had. When Fernando had slipped out at dawn, Tom had known it was the betrayal that would haunt Tito sixty years later. Rather than stopping it, Tom had simply lain in his bed, wrapped in a blanket of relief. History would play out as it was meant to. He could still be with Ana. But a spark of guilt had caught aflame within him when he'd faced Sofia at breakfast. Not only was she now alone, but she was also pregnant.

'Did you bring a rock?' asked Sofia.

Tom patted the tiny thigh-pocket he'd stored the stone Pablo had given him in Navarra; it was empty.

'I must have lost it.'

'Then lay something else down. Something which is holding you back, and you no longer need.'

Tom sifted through his bag; there was nothing redundant within. He reached into his pocket and pulled out his phone; drained of battery, it was as worthless as the rocks beneath his feet. He stared at its lifeless screen and remembered the day he'd proudly unboxed it in front of Ana. It had felt so special to own something others coveted. What would his Camino have been like if he'd walked it in 2010? How many of the previous month's spectacular valleys and sunsets would have been watched through his phone's camera? Would he have slept in villages based on the Wi-Fi quality instead of the tiredness of his legs? In London, his phone had been the last thing he looked at before falling asleep and the first thing he held when he woke up.

'I wish you held me in bed as much as you do your phone,' Ana had often teased. Now, at the foot of the Cruz de Ferro, he wondered if it had been a joke at all. Tom had always said his phone connected him to the world, but after three weeks without it, he realised it had kept him from it.

'Are you alright?' asked Sofia.

A voice of reason guided his dead phone back into his pocket and not beneath the pile of rocks.

'Yeah, I'm fine.'

Mobile phones wouldn't arrive for another thirty years; entire generations were still destined to endure telephones attached to briefcases before using iPhones. He pulled his wallet from another pocket and searched for some other keepsake to leave behind. He thumbed through his redundant euros and credit cards; his eye fell on a folded piece of paper protruding from a side pocket. He took it out and unfolded it, a historical document dated sixty years in the future.

'What is that?' asked Sofia.

'It's the letter I wrote to Ana's grandfather, asking for his blessing to marry her.'

'What does it say?'

He hesitated before handing it to her. Sofia began to read before looking up.

'You wrote it in Spanish?'

'I used Google.'

'*Goo-gull?*' She frowned.

'I had it translated.'

She returned to the letter. When she was finished, she passed it back to him.

'It is very romantic, Thomas. Ana is lucky.'

'Her grandfather didn't think so.'

'Why do you think he gave you the test to walk to Santiago?'

Tom briefly debated saying he didn't know, but he'd told Sofia enough lies today. 'He believed I was too sensible, that I thought my way through life, rather than living it. He said he wanted Ana to marry a man who lived his heart, not his head.'

'Then why did you not want to continue to Santiago?' she asked.

Tom scoffed. 'Have you forgotten about the time travel?'

'No, before that. That day by the riverbank, you said you'd already decided on the train not to continue.'

She was right; he had.

'I suppose I came to my senses; I couldn't just trek across Spain on a whim. I had a job in London, I had responsibilities. If I was going to walk the Camino, I needed time to plan it. People can't simply drop everything for love.'

'Why not?'

'Because I'd have lost my job for one.'

'And do you love this job more than Ana?'

'Of course not.'

'Then why did you choose it over her?' She pointed to the letter. 'The man in that letter said he would do anything for Ana.'

'You sound like her grandfather.'

She didn't respond; her unanswered question hovered between them.

'Perhaps I'm just not that man,' he eventually said. 'Maybe I'll never be him.'

The admission hurt to say aloud.

'I sometimes wonder if Ana would be happier with someone else. Someone who didn't overthink things, someone who lives in the moment. She could have anyone; she deserves to be happy.' He looked away and dabbed at his eyes.

Sofia waited a moment before asking her next question.

'How did you two meet?'

'I'd missed my train to London for a football match, so I'd decided to go to a friend's dinner party instead. Ana was a classmate of the host and came to dinner because her lecture had been cancelled. We sat next to one another and began talking about Spanish football. We've been together ever since.' He shook his head in disbelief. 'I once calculated there was a 0.002 per cent chance of us ever meeting; our relationship was a mathematical anomaly.'

'Or perhaps divine intervention?'

'God doesn't matchmake.'

'Fine – if not God, then destiny.'

'There's no data to suggest either of those exist. It was just probability.'

'There is more to life than mathematics, Thomas. I think this is the point Ana's grandfather was making. Of course it did not make sense for you to drop everything and walk the Camino, but that was the idea, no? Some things do not make sense to the brain but feel right in our hearts. Like you and Ana finding each other at the dinner table. Maybe her grandfather wanted to see you let go of your logic and take a leap of faith.' She pointed to the letter. 'There is still time for you to prove you are the man Ana deserves.'

'I don't even know if I'll see her again. Sir Walter thinks he and I were sent back in time to complete some sort of quest. But it's nearly been three weeks and I still have no idea what I'm supposed to do.'

Sofia offered a sympathetic smile. 'What does your heart say? Do you think you will see Ana again?'

'I honestly don't know.' It hurt to say the words. 'I hope so.'

'Hope is a good start. I will pray for your return to Ana, as long as you promise to remain hopeful.'

Tom looked down at the paper in his hand; it now felt heavy with lies. He bent down and picked up a rock near the base of the Iron Cross. A piece of paper flew out from beneath it and flittered against Sofia's foot. Tom laid his letter on the ground and placed the stone on top. He let his hand linger on the rock, thinking of Sofia's words. His heart told him he'd see Ana again, but how would he return to her? As he stood and stared up to the small cross above him, Tom's heart told him what he must do first.

'Sofia, there's something else I haven't told you.' He didn't face her, not yet. 'I knew Fernando would leave the *albergue*; I could have stopped him. You see, I haven't told you everything about who I really am.'

He turned to confront her, but Sofia hadn't been listening. She was holding the piece of paper that had flown out from beneath the rock. Her face was folded with confusion.

'What is it?' Tom asked, standing behind her.

The tattered slip of paper had something scribbled in Spanish on it. Sofia's eyes shimmered.

'Sofia?'

She flipped the paper over. The other side was a faded black-and-white photograph of two teenage boys, each of them holding a wooden pole over their shoulders.

'Who are they?' he asked. 'Do you know them?'

She remained silent, mournfully staring at the smiling boys in the picture.

Fernando had arrived at the mountain's peak just as the sun crept over the horizon behind him. He kneeled on the stones beneath the Cruz de Ferro and pulled the photograph from his shirt pocket. He'd received it in his last month in Morocco – folded within the only letter he'd ever been sent while in the legion.

Dearest Tito,

Our father is dead. The doctor said his heart succumbed to the alcohol, but I know it was his eldest son's disappearance which finally broke it. A friend swore he saw you in Cádiz in a legionnaire's uniform, but I have no way of knowing if this is true. If it is, and this letter finds you, I beg you to return home. As I write these words, our city braces for war. Spain desperately needs you fighting alongside us, brother, not against us. I pray you'll forgive me for what I've done to you and our family. But above all, I pray you'll return to help us.

Your brother, Emilio

Rumours of a civil war had trailed the letter south from Spain in the following weeks. More tales had blown east from the Canary Islands: an exiled army general – named Francisco Franco – was said to be plotting an insurrection to liberate Spain from its ineffectual Second Republic. At first, Fernando had dismissed it as the idle gossip of bored soldiers, but in July 1936, trucks had arrived at the base. A few days later, Fernando's unit had marched onto waiting boats in the port of Casablanca.

The trip across the Strait of Gibraltar had taken most of the night. The ship's deck had been slippery with sea-spray and vomit. When they'd eventually docked in Cádiz, the soldiers had been ushered into trucks with their flaps pulled down. As they'd blindly ridden toward battle, the men had theorised their likely destination.

'Córdoba and Granada have already fallen,' one man had said.

'My brother says there's fierce fighting in Jaen,' offered another.

Fernando had suspected they'd been bound for the Costa del Sol, but when they'd finally dismounted, his chest had caved in.

'Welcome to Sevilla,' a sergeant had bellowed, as the legionnaires had been herded into the city's famous cathedral in the Plaza del Triunfo. Guardia Civil officers had hovered in the shadows, murmuring to the assembled priests. An army officer, wearing a crisp olive-green uniform, had waited for the dishevelled legionnaires to take their places among the church pews. Next to him, a blackboard – the type used in a classroom – had held an enormous map of the city.

'Three days ago, the chief of the frontier police arrested the commanding officer of the 6th regiment of the army, stationed here at the San Hermenigildo barracks.' The officer had smacked a cane against the map, landing directly on the third fairway of Fernando and Emilio's golf course from years earlier.

'We have since detained the chief of the *policía* and assumed control of the town hall and the telephone exchange. Yesterday, the trade unions ordered a general strike, and the factory workers have withdrawn into the industrial districts of La Macarena and Triana – here and here.'

Fernando had never seen a map of Triana. The streets' layout had looked familiar, but the faces and smells of the neighbourhood had all been absent.

'Your mission will be to subdue the unionists and communists, who've established strongholds in several of the factories.'

'How many of them are there?' one man had asked.

'No more than two hundred.'

'Soldiers or civilians?'

'Does it matter?' someone had called out.

The room's laughter had sent a chill down Fernando's spine. When the briefing was over, the legionnaires had marched toward the river. A Guardia Civil guardsman had welcomed them at the Puente de Isabel II.

'The communists have snipers covering this entire bridge,' he'd said. 'You'll have to wait.'

A brutish Catalonian with a shaved head and rotted teeth, named Ortiz, had eye-balled the guard.

'We came here to fight, not wait.'

Two Guardia Civil trucks had soon arrived. Their tailgates had dropped, and a stream of women and children had emerged. The drivers had ushered them toward the bridge, and the guardsman had turned toward the legionnaires.

'Keep your formations tight on the bridge; ensure there's a woman or child on either side of you at all times.'

Whether the snipers had really existed or not, the legionnaires had crossed the river without a single shot fired. The only sounds had come from the children, crying as they'd clutched to their whimpering mothers. Across the bridge, the legionnaires had discarded their human shields and fanned out through the streets. Fernando had stumbled behind his comrades up the Calle San Jorge as if in a dream. His rifle had hung limply by his waist as he'd passed the deserted buildings of his childhood. At the end of the street, they had come to a boarded-up factory with machinery barricading its gates. The stained words of 'Vega & Sabina' had remained on the brick where the sign had once stood. Fernando had intuitively walked toward the gates when gunfire had erupted from a window above.

'Get down,' Ortiz had screamed, tackling Fernando to the ground. 'Are you trying to get yourself killed?'

The bald-headed Catalonian had sprayed the factory's façade with gunfire before waving Fernando toward the gate. 'Let's go.'

Ortiz had clambered up the machinery, and into the factory, Fernando mindlessly followed. Footsteps had run across the floor above them, and the two legionnaires had walked up the stairs. They'd crept down the hallway; the lunchroom where Fernando and his father had once eaten their lunches had looked like an abandoned museum. A blur of movement from the offices ahead had been followed by more gunfire. Ortiz and Fernando had dived into an alcove as bullets shredded the plasterboard around them.

'We're pinned down,' Ortiz had roared.

Suddenly, there'd been a dull metallic thud on the floorboards; the two soldiers had watched the familiar pine-coned shape of a grenade wobble toward them. Instinct had taken over. Fernando had dived toward the grenade and flicked it back down the hallway toward its origin. The metal ball had bounced off the wall and spun like a top into one of the offices. A deafening explosion had rocked the building. Ortiz had stormed out of the alcove and toward the office, his rifle raised to his shoulder. Fernando had numbly followed him through the smoke and into the office, now a mess of loose papers and smouldering furniture. Ortiz had lowered his rifle and grinned at Fernando with teeth like tombstones.

'You lucky bastard.' Ortiz had nodded to the corner of the room. 'Not so lucky for these poor wretches, no?'

Fernando had looked through the dissolving smoke to a pair of crumpled bodies on the floor. Ortiz had run back to the stairs.

'Come on, let's join the others.'

Fernando had remained frozen; his rifle had clattered to the floor as he stared down at the bodies. One of them had been a gangly teen, not yet twenty. The other was…

'No, no, no… No, Emilio, please, no.' Fernando had collapsed to his knees in front of his brother's shredded body. 'Wake up, Emilio, please wake up.'

The boy's eyes had stared lifelessly up to the ceiling. Fernando had shaken him, praying Emilio was merely shell-shocked by the explosion, but the boy's head flopped back – dead. Fernando had peeled back his brother's shirt to reveal a mass of shrapnel embedded into the boy's bloody chest.

'Please, God, no. Please.' He had cradled his dead brother in his arms and rested his chin on Emilio's head. Fernando's tears had rolled down his cheeks onto his brother's blood-spattered face. 'Please, God, save him. What have I done?'

One of Fernando's tears fell onto the photograph, and he wiped it away from his brother's face. Proudly holding his makeshift golf club, the picture of Emilio's glowing smile had long been Fernando's most-prized possession.

'I'm sorry, brother.' Still on his knees, Fernando stared up at the Cruz de Ferro towering above. 'I should have been by your side. I should have never left you. I wasn't as brave as you. I wasn't as strong.'

Emilio had died as he'd lived: passionately fighting for what he believed to be right. In contrast, Fernando had spent his life running. Even now – almost twenty years later – Fernando still couldn't bring himself to return to Sevilla to reclaim his name and pay for his sins. Fernando had never had his brother's strength.

He reached into his bag, took the fountain pen Pablo had given him from the hotel, and turned the photograph over; the pen's tip hovered as he searched for worthy words.

He eventually wrote one final promise to his brother, which he knew he couldn't break. Fernando turned the photograph back around and kissed his brother one last time before lifting a rock and placing the picture beneath it. The stone was now one more plea of forgiveness at the base of this sombre crucifix. And beneath it was Fernando's final act of cowardice before his pain could finally end.

CHAPTER 22

Sofia hadn't spoken since the Iron Cross, only deepening Tom's guilt. As they walked in silence, he thought back to the photograph of the boys and pondered its handwritten message. He knew it involved Fernando, but nothing more. While Tom's head told him Fernando's departure was necessary for Ana's survival, he found himself searching the landscape ahead for the Andalusian and recalled Diego's words in Santiago.

'Tito says after he left, he always looked back for the girl in the distance, but she never appeared.'

While their morning had been spent climbing, their afternoon was an endless descent. Tom had dreaded the steep climbs of the Pyrenees, yet here in Galicia, after three weeks of walking, his cardio had noticeably improved. Now, he loathed the sharp descents; his knees ached with each jolting step down the mountain. He still couldn't believe Sofia was doing this at full-term. He occasionally cautioned her when they came to a particularly steep part of the Camino. Embarrassingly, he was the one who usually tripped while she sturdily continued. Physically and emotionally drained, the two of them arrived in Ponferrada at sundown. The *albergue* was in the centre of town, off the Plaza Virgin de la Encina. A friendly-faced woman stamped Tom's *credencial* while talking to Sofia in Spanish.

'She says the other pilgrims have already eaten,' said Sofia. 'But she will prepare some stew for us in an hour. She also says there is a famous Templar castle by the river. I'll ask her for directions.'

While Sofia rested, Tom followed the directions to a spectacular medieval castle dominating the river. He walked toward a familiar figure sitting alone on a grassy bank below the castle's gate.

'I thought I might find you here,' said Tom.

Sir Walter looked up from stuffing tobacco into his pipe. 'Ah, Tom Anderson. How are ye, lad?'

Tom collapsed onto the grass next to the knight. 'Exhausted.'

The Scotsman offered a grandfatherly smile. 'Aye, the descent from Manjarín is arduous but the hardest is now behind ye.'

'Somehow, I doubt that.'

The knight took a speculative puff before lifting a bushy grey eyebrow. 'Trouble with the Andalusian, lad?'

'How did you know?'

Sir Walter nodded to the road below. 'I saw your companion walk past a couple of hours ago.'

Tom should have been happy Fernando was so far

ahead of them, yet something felt amiss. Sir Walter must have noticed.

'And what's at the root of your dim mood, lad?'

'Sofia is pregnant.'

'Aye.'

'You knew?'

'I'd suspected. The poor lass was wearing every garment she owned in the height of summer.' The old man puffed his pipe. 'The Andalusian is the father?'

'No, but…' Tom threw up his hands. 'It's complicated.'

'Love always is,' chuckled the knight. 'But why does his parting afflict you?'

'Because I know what his life becomes.'

The knight frowned. 'How do you mean?'

'Fernando is my girlfriend's grandfather. I think he's the reason I was sent back here. In the future, the older Fernando told me his greatest regret in life was abandoning a girl he met on the Camino. That girl is Sofia. I think my quest is to make sure they end up together.'

'This is welcome news; you've found your quest. We can leave at first light and catch up to your friend. If we reunite the pair, the Time Gate at Monte del Gozo shall open, enabling your return home.'

'It's not that simple. Fernando is supposed to marry someone else – a woman named Esmerelda. They're meant to have a son, who will eventually have a daughter named Ana.' Tom saved the knight from the tangled knots of the timeline. 'If I fulfil my quest, and Fernando and Sofia are allowed to remain together, Ana will never exist. She'll be lost forever. That's why I didn't stop him from leaving.' Unexpected tears sprang to Tom's eyes. 'I saw how much he regretted leaving Sofia, but…' He choked on the guilt.

'I just lay in bed and let Fernando leave.'

'You did it to protect the woman you love.'

'I know it was the logical decision to save Ana, but it felt wrong inside here.' He tapped his chest. 'Now, I can't shake the feeling that it's all my fault.'

'The future is determined by a much higher power than you, Tom Anderson. You can't control what will transpire half a century from now.'

'But what if I can? What will happen to Sofia and her baby? I knew the right thing to do, but I didn't do it.'

'If there's one thing a decade on the Camino has taught me, it's our past sins cannot be undone; they can only be atoned for.'

Sir Walter's eyes lingered on the horizon, and Tom stopped to consider the knight's story.

'How did you did you do it – being marooned in the future, hundreds of years from your family?'

'Aye, it has not been easy.' A cloud of sorrow passed over Sir Walter's face before his knowing smile returned. 'But there are good things too. To see the ideals the Templars fought for, still intact today; to know our sacrifice wasn't for nowt.' He nodded toward the castle. 'I still remember arriving here soon after the castle was built. Ponferrada was an important sojourn on the Camino back then.'

'Is this why you visit the Templar sites, to be closer to home?'

'It helps. There's so little left of the Templars now. After King Philip's purge of the thirteenth century, the order was dissolved. They accused us of treason and devil-worshipping and took our lands and titles.'

'The thirteenth century?' Tom frowned. 'But you're from 1193; that's in the twelfth century, isn't it?'

'Aye, you're right – it is.' Sir Walter fumbled his pipe. 'But I've read over the texts in your libraries and seen what becomes of the order.' The knight's eyes shimmered. ''Tis not natural for a man to outlive his family, Tom Anderson.'

They sat in silence, looking west to a setting sun veiled behind the dark clouds on the horizon.

'So, where are you walking tomorrow?' Tom eventually asked.

'Well, that depends, lad. Where are you and the lass headed?'

'You'll join us tomorrow?'

'I'll walk with ye to Santiago.'

Tom must have looked stunned, for Sir Walter laughed.

'Don't look so surprised, lad. I've told you the Templars aid those who walk the Way of Saint James. And if I'm no mistaken, a pregnant lass and a man lost in time more than constitute pilgrims in need.' The knight nodded to the horizon. 'Besides, 'tis a storm coming tomorrow, I fancy.'

When Sofia had agreed to be Padre Price's interpreter, the notion of travelling across Spain with an Englishman had seemed odd. Yet here, leaving the town of Triacastela, Sofia found herself travelling alongside two men from Britain.

'*Buen Camino*, Santo Gutierre,' called out a group of smiling locals in the square. The knight greeted them warmly, embracing and kissing the cheeks of each. Thomas smiled wryly.

'He's famous.'

It was true. They'd received similar receptions in every village they'd passed since the knight had joined them in Ponferrada three days earlier. And while Santo Gutierre was eccentric, it had been a blessing to walk the Camino with someone who knew its every inch. They'd been welcomed into people's homes in each village, offering them food and water. More importantly, Santo Gutierre had ensured Sofia had frequent access to a toilet.

He had said there were two paths to the city of Sarria: a shorter route over the hills or a flatter, longer trail past the monastery of Samos. As they passed the mountain to the east, Sofia was relieved they'd chosen the latter path. After a few hours, they arrived at the monastery. Santo Gutierre nodded to a shady tree by the square.

'Ye can rest here. I'll fetch us some more water.'

Sofia pointed to the scaffolding encasing the monastery. 'Are they repairing it?'

'Aye, a fire tore through it a few years ago. They're still rebuilding most of it, but the chapel is open.'

Sofia visited the church alone. The cool, musty air within offered a welcome relief from the humid afternoon. She crossed herself and walked down the aisle to a pew in the middle of the empty church. She groaned as she lowered herself down to the prayer cushion. The sighing face of Christ hovered above the altar, surrounded by angels and cherubs. She clasped her hands together.

'Dear God, please forgive me for my sins. It has been several weeks since I last prayed. *Gracias* for sending Santo Gutierre to protect us on the path to Santiago. Grant us the strength to continue our journey, and please lead

Thomas home to Ana.'

She omitted any mention of time travel.

'Guide Pablo on his own path. Give him the strength to be true to himself and to follow his heart.' Her thoughts drifted back to Valencia. 'Keep my father safe from the ocean's wrath and that of my mother. Lord, please forgive Mama for her sins, so one day, she might find it in her heart to forgive her daughter's mistakes.'

Sofia's eyes drifted to a cherub floating behind Christ's skeletal body. She clenched her moist eyes together.

'And please look after the baby. Send it a mother who will give it all the love I never could.' She gripped her hands so tightly together, they throbbed. 'And a father who will protect it, Lord. Please, God, I beg you. Bless this baby with parents who will love and protect it. Amen.'

She wiped her eyes and prepared to stand when her mind returned to the words written on the back of the photograph.

Emilio, may God forgive me, so I might see you in heaven and tell you how sorry I am. I'll see you soon, my brother –
Tito

Sofia bowed her forehead to her folded hands.

'And please protect Fernando, Lord – I'm begging you. I know he thinks everything is lost, and he thinks there's no hope, but… tell him whatever happened to his brother wasn't his fault.' Tears leaked onto her knuckles. 'He thinks he doesn't deserve to be happy; he thinks he doesn't deserve to live. Just protect him, I beg you. Show him his life still means something. Show him people need him; tell him I still need him.'

Her tears poured out of her, dripping down to the tiled floor. When there were none left, she creaked back up onto her feet, entirely empty. Back at the tree outside, Santo Gutierre welcomed her with a pear.

'Sarria is only two hours away.'

Back on the dusty road, Sofia's thoughts drifted to Fernando, wondering how far ahead of them he was. She imagined foolish fantasies of leaving the baby somewhere in Santiago where Fernando might find it. Like a little baby Moses, lying in a wicker basket on the River Nile. She imagined Fernando lifting the child into his arms and raising it as his. Fernando wouldn't abandon the child; he'd have to save it. That's what he did – he rescued people. Perhaps the baby would save him too.

Her thoughts were interrupted by a sudden rush of warm dampness on her skirt. At first, Sofia thought she'd finally wet herself. But when she looked down at her sopping uniform, her eyes widened with panic. After studying for her entrance examination, she'd learned the medical term was amniorrhexis – the rupturing of the amniotic sac during pregnancy. It usually occurs spontaneously at the beginning of labour. Most people referred to it as 'breaking the water'.

Regardless of its name, Sofia was going into labour. The baby was early.

Sofia crushed Tom's hand in hers as they waited for Sir Walter to return. As soon as her waters had broken, the knight had run to the nearest town for help. A vehicle eventually approached, veering from the road toward them. The mud-spattered pick-up truck jolted to a halt, with Sir Water behind the wheel.

'Come on, lad, get her into the back.'

They must have looked a peculiar sight: Tom, and a tearful Sofia, sat in the tray of a truck driven by a man dressed as a Templar knight.

'Breathe,' Tom said, reciting the only advice he'd remembered from films about childbirth. 'Breathe.'

Sir Walter handled the car surprisingly well for a medieval knight, and they reached Sarria quickly. But rather than a hospital, they pulled up at a farmhouse. A balding, middle-aged man with pock-marked cheeks hurried out of the house, followed by a stocky woman in an apron.

'This is Enrico and his wife, Luciana,' said Sir Walter. 'Enrico is a physician.'

The couple helped Sofia out of the truck and into their home. Tom followed them inside, dropping his and Sofia's bags next to Sir Walter's on a table. They hurried down the hallway to a rudimentary medical surgery at the rear of the house. Luciana eased Sofia onto a bed while Enrico threw an apron over himself and washed his hands in a sink. He fired off instructions over his shoulder in Spanish. Sir Walter pointed to the hallway.

'Get some towels from the cupboards, lad.'

Tom returned with an armful of towels. Luciana pointed to a chair next to the bed.

'*Aquí.*'

He placed them down just as Sofia cried out his name. 'Thomas!'

'I'm here, I'm here.'

He stood beside her, and she gripped his hand.

'I'm scared, Thomas. The baby is early; something is wrong.'

'No, everything is alright.' He brushed her hair from her sweaty brow. 'These people are going to take care of you and your baby, okay?'

Sofia screamed in pain. Enrico and Luciana rushed over, now garbed in gloves and masks. They rattled off more instructions in Spanish. Sir Walter eased Tom away from Sofia.

'Give them space to work, lad. Go and wait in the front room.'

'Are you sure?' He didn't want to leave her.

'Aye, there's nowt you can do. I'll call you if we need you.'

Tom gave a parting look toward Sofia before eventually returning to the house's front room. He sat on the couch; the sitting room's eerie silence was punctuated by the ticking of a clock on the mantle. After a few torturous minutes, Tom rose to his feet and paced. Needing a snack for distraction, he reached for his bag and inadvertently knocked Sir Walter's leather satchel to the floor. The flap opened, and the bag's contents scattered over the floorboards.

'For fuck's sake.'

He leaned down and picked up the knight's Bible and tobacco tin, placing both back into the satchel. The last item was a newspaper clipping. Noticing it was written in English, Tom unfolded it and read.

THE PRESS AND JOURNAL
ABERDEEN, THURSDAY, 22 APRIL 1943

SEVERE RAID ON N.E. SCOTLAND TOWN
Number Killed, Two Churches damaged, Houses Wrecked

Several fatalities and severe casualties resulted from a devastating air raid on the north-eastern Scottish city of Aberdeen last night.

Most of the damage and casualties were caused in working-class districts. At least two churches were damaged, fires were started in several parts of the town and dwelling-houses were wrecked.

By the roar of the engines, it was apparent that the raiders were coming in low, and a couple of flares preceded the crump of bombs. Succeeding planes made their run across the town, a little above roof-top height, and through the noise of the guns came the whistle of the bombs and then the explosions.

One stick of bombs fell across one of the poorer quarters and others on industrial premises. Two big bombs fell together in a narrow back street, knocking several houses askew and burying the inmates under debris. Around the fires, most of the other bombs were dropped, but sticks fell elsewhere.

A.R.P. personnel, police and N.F.S. worked courageously while the planes were still overhead, rescuing people trapped under debris and shepherding the large numbers who were rendered homeless into rest centres.

Tom re-read the masthead – 1943 was the same year Sir Walter had arrived. A smaller headline at the bottom of the page called to him.

UNIVERSITY PROFESSOR'S TRAGIC LOSS
It has emerged one of the errant bombs in the raid struck and destroyed a house on King St, the home of a prominent university professor, killing all inside.

It is believed Professor Walter Samuels was not in the house during the bombing, currently leading a research team in Spain. But the bodies of Professor Samuel's wife, Edith, and their two sons, Richard (12) and Arthur (10), were recovered from the rubble by members of the N.F.S.

Professor Samuels is the senior lecturer of medieval history at Aberdeen University and Scotland's eminent authority on middle-age history, publishing several works on the Crusades and the Knights Templar.

Professor Samuels has been notified via telegram, and arrangements for his return have been made.

The world shook. The article was accompanied by a photograph. It was an old-fashioned black-and-white photograph, the type found in a museum or a history book. It was a family portrait: two young boys seated in front of their parents, all of them focusing on some distant point to the left of the camera's lens. The woman wore a dress, and her hair was curled and pinned like the women in old films. Each of her sons wore a collared shirt and a pair of braces; their light hair was neatly brushed to the side. The younger boy held a toy car, while his older brother's bow tie was slightly askew. Their father was wearing a three-piece suit and tie, his greying hair was neatly slicked to the side and he was cleanly shaven. The family all wore the same solemn expression, except for the man – who bore a familiar twinkling grin. Tom's stomach churned. He read the picture's accompanying caption.

The Samuels family – Walter, Edith, Richard and Arthur. Aberdeen, 1942.

Tom inspected the portrait. With his clean-shaven chin and shorter hair, the man was almost unrecognisable. But as Tom looked closer, he was sure. The man in the photograph was Sir Walter.

Hours might have passed – or minutes – Tom couldn't tell. Footsteps in the hallway eventually distracted him from the newspaper clipping in his hands.

'Well, the contractions have subsided, for now, lad. Sofia is asleep. Enrico and Luciana want us to…'

The old man froze, staring at Tom's discovery.

'What's that, lad?'

'Maybe you can tell me.' Tom thrust the article toward the impostor. 'Is this you?'

Sir Walter stared at the picture, his eyes wide with fear. 'Please be gentle with that, lad.'

'After everything you've done to me, you're worried about a fucking article?' The room turned red. 'You lied to me!'

'I didn't—'

'Yes, you did! You're not a Templar knight; you're a fucking history professor.'

'I can explain.'

'Explain?' Tom nearly choked on the word. 'Explain how you led me across Spain, letting me think you were a time traveller as well? Is that how you amuse yourself? By taking advantage of others' misfortune?'

'No, I just—'

Every word from the old man was like gasoline.

'You were just bored? So you thought it would be amusing to lie to someone who needed your help. Maybe I should tear this clipping into a thousand pieces. How would you like that? As repayment for the way you've ripped my life apart.'

The old man clasped his hands together. 'Please, son, I know you're upset – but please.' His eyes were transfixed on the photograph. 'It's all I have left of them.' Tears brimmed in Sir Walter's pale eyes.

The photograph slipped from Tom's fingertips and floated to the floor like a feather. The old man collapsed to his knees to rescue it. He smoothed its creased edges against his chest.

'I'm sorry, lad. I didn't mean to lie to you.' His voice was paper-thin.

The unconquerable knight had transformed into a pitiful old man, and Tom's fury evaporated. The clock on the mantle counted their shared sorrow.

'Why did you lie to me?' Tom eventually asked.

Sir Walter rose to his feet. He carefully folded the article back into his Bible before meeting Tom's eye.

'It wasn't just you, lad; I lied to everyone. After the accident, I was lost.'

'You were in Spain when it happened?'

'Aye, I was here.' Sir Walter rose to his feet and ran a hand over his tired face. 'Our project was exploring the role of the Templars during medieval pilgrimages. The war had engulfed the rest of Europe, but Franco had kept Spain neutral. The university had warned us against coming.' His voice cracked. 'So had Edith.'

The old man smeared his eyes with the back of his hand.

'I still see them; I have the same dream every night. I'm in my office at the university, and I hear the air-raid sirens. I run outside, fetch my bicycle and ride home to them as fast as I can. The streets are all abandoned. I can hear the whistling sounds of the bombs falling from the sky, followed by the roar of the explosions around me. There are flames and ash everywhere.'

Tom recalled the knight's tale of riding his horse through the storm in Santiago.

'When I arrive home, I run into the house and up the stairs. I call to Edith and the boys, but no one answers.'

His pale-blue eyes dripped tears. 'I find them all asleep on our bed; the boys look so peaceful, like angels. And for a wee moment, the air-raid sirens go silent, and all is quiet.' A sad smile rested on Sir Walter's lips. 'And then I wake up.'

'You didn't return to Scotland?' asked Tom.

'Nay – without them, there was no reason to go.' He took a deep, steadying breath. 'No, when the courier handed me the telegram atop Monteo del Gozo... something broke inside of me, lad. My students tried to have me return for the funeral, but...' He shrugged. 'I couldn't. I tried, but... I couldn't. So I just left everything behind and walked. I wasn't even conscious of where I was headed; 'twas as if I'd been in a trance. Then, a few weeks later, I arrived back in Saint-Jean.' He shook his head, seemingly unable to believe it himself. 'And with nowhere else to go, I turned around and walked back to Santiago. That was eleven years ago.' He smiled his disbelief. 'I've not stopped walking since.'

'But why did you pretend you were a Templar knight?'

Sir Walter's cheeks turned pink. 'That wasn't my idea. The Spanish had always called me Gutierre – the closest name to Walter. After a few years of helping people along the Camino, some joked I was a saint. Santo Gutierre was the nickname the locals bestowed upon me – the British drifter who wandered between the Templar sites along the Camino.' He shrugged. 'But I suppose, as the years passed, I realised the Camino gave me purpose. Much like the Templars, I found solace in aiding people. So I allowed my hair and beard to grow, and I eventually changed the clothes I wore. A family from Toledo gifted me a sword.' He shrugged. 'The joke eventually became my truth. I never knew things would go as far as they did.'

He rested his hand on Tom's shoulder and fixed him with a look of sincerity. 'I'm sorry I've betrayed your trust, Tom. All I can ask is that you forgive me.'

Tom was numb. As if his insides had been scooped out of him and placed in a box. 'You were my only hope of getting home.' Saying the words aloud made his voice tremble. 'What am I supposed to do, now?'

Footsteps hurried down the hallway, and Luciana appeared. She pulled down her mask.

'*Perdón, pero la muchacha quiere hablar con el inglés.*'

'Sofia is asking for you,' said Sir Walter.

Tom followed Luciana back to the surgery. Sofia lay on the bed, covered by a sheet. She reached for Tom.

'Thomas, I need you to do something for me.'

He walked toward her and held her hand. 'Of course – anything.'

She clasped his hand tightly. 'I need you to find Fernando.' She stared fiercely into his eyes. 'Bring him back to me.'

CHAPTER 23

Tom left at first light. Sir Walter had offered to join him, desperate to atone for his sins, but Tom had needed to be alone. He walked all morning without rest. His brain screamed at him to stop, to allow Fernando to walk toward his destiny. But this inner voice was drowned out by Sofia's tear-filled pleas.

'Fernando is not walking to Santiago for forgiveness, Thomas; he is walking there to die.' She'd squeezed Tom's hand and looked pleadingly into his eyes. 'Promise you will bring him back to me; promise you will save him.'

Before Sofia could further explain, another wave of contractions had arrived. Luciana had pushed Tom out of the room again. Whatever Sofia's meaning, her terror had been genuine.

Tom arrived in the village of Mercadoiro at noon. Employing his handful of Spanish phrases on the locals, he deduced Fernando had passed two hours earlier. Tom quickened his pace, hopeful he could catch up to the Andalusian in the town of Vilachá.

Clouds sagged overhead and a light fog clung to the path. Tom came to a crossroad and followed a scallop shell along a well-trodden path to the right. Vilachá should have been half an hour away, but an hour later, Tom arrived at an unmarked road. Where was the village? He'd continued on, but no town ever arrived. The brooding clouds finally opened, lashing Tom with sheets of rain. With the sickening feeling he'd taken a wrong turn at the crossroad, Tom turned back. He battled the wind and rain back up the hill and inspected the scallop shell nailed to the crooked wooden post. Tom had assumed the shell's natural arrow-shape pointed to Santiago, but now he wasn't sure.

He examined the other two paths. The one veering to the left was the second most prominent, while the way directly ahead was nothing more than a trickle of dirt. He searched for boot prints on both, but if there'd been any, the mud had now swallowed them. Tom squinted behind him for approaching pilgrims, but the storm had kept them indoors. He stared at the post and glowered at the scallop shell, as if the harder he stared, the more likely it would reveal the path to Santiago. After three weeks blindly following Fernando, Tom hadn't learned to decipher the scallop shells himself. He remembered Sir Walter talking of the shell's grooves converging at its base signalling the way to Santiago. Did that mean Tom should follow the faint trail ahead? The path to the left looked twice as travelled. Or perhaps the path to the right had been correct after all, and he'd simply needed to walk a little further. Why had people chosen a scallop shell as a marker, anyway? Why couldn't there just be the yellow arrows he'd been promised? This was ludicrous.

The rain hammered harder, and Tom wanted to erupt. How could he be so fucking stupid? He might never catch Fernando before Santiago. And if Sofia was right, and Fernando really was walking the Camino to die, Ana would never be born. Tom could have saved her but hadn't – all because of this ridiculous scallop shell.

'Fuck!'

His scream thundered across the empty fields, echoed by a silent fork of lightning. He slammed his boot against the post, hurtling the sign back into the mud. Belated thunder rumbled as the scallop shell mockingly pointed up to the sky. He marched toward the scallop shell and smashed his foot down upon it.

'Fuck!'

Pain seared up his leg; Tom fell backwards onto the ground and clutched his foot. The rock hidden beneath the sign looked like one of the cobblestones from the original Roman path. He'd unknowingly driven his boot down into it with full force. The rock hadn't pierced the boot's sole, but Tom's entire leg felt numb. He looked to the heavens; the cold rain drummed down onto his face. If his foot was broken, Ana was gone forever.

Adrenaline seeped from his body. After spending his entire month scheming and planning his way back to Ana, Tom had failed. His stupid theories about Holy Years and wormholes had all been worthless; he was never returning to 2010. He began to sob. He'd been so preoccupied with reaching Santiago, he'd neglected how to read the signs along the way.

He closed his eyes and pictured Ana: the glint in her eye when she smiled; the freckle above her left eyelid; the ferocity of her laugh. Had he ever really told her what she meant to him? Or had it been like the Camino? Had Tom been more preoccupied with where their relationship was headed rather than enjoying the quiet moments they'd shared together? He'd give anything for the chance to spend a weekend with her, doing nothing. As the rain tumbled harder, he let his body sink into the surrounding mud and imagined himself being enveloped by it, submerged completely and lost forever. If Ana didn't exist, why should he? An odd calmness arrived, as if he'd eventually surrendered to an unfinished crossword. Tom's tears stopped, and he waited for the mud to rise.

When Tom opened his eyes, the sky was a brilliant, rich blue. And if the man standing over him was an angel, the paintings in the cathedrals had all been inaccurate.

'*Hola, señor.*' The young man had a handsome face with olive skin and a wispy moustache. He wore a pair of overalls and carried a tin of paint. '*¿Estás bien?*'

The stranger helped Tom to his feet. Pain shot up Tom's leg, but he gently shifted his weight onto his injured foot, relieved to discover it wasn't broken. The painter eyed him curiously.

'*¿Estás bien?*'

Tom nodded. '*Sí*, I'm *bien*. Do you know where the Camino is? Err, *dónde está el Camino?*'

The painter looked from Tom down to the broken scallop shell. He rested his paint tin on the ground and used a nearby rock to hammer the signpost back into the soil. Next, he took a brush from his belt and dipped it into his paint. When the man had finished painting, he stood up and pointed to the indistinct path ahead.

'Santiago.'

Tom stared at the sign with disbelief. Upon it, the man had painted a simple yellow arrow.

The sagging clouds over the Camino had kept the other pilgrims indoors. Fernando enjoyed the solitude. He and the others had met very few pilgrims on their days walking through Navarra and La Rioja. Yet here in Galicia, the Camino was swarming with them, each asking a different combination of the same five questions.

'Where are you from?'

'Where did you begin the Camino?'

'How many days have you been walking?'

'Which village are you aiming for tonight?'

'Have you ever walked the Camino before?'

Fernando avoided eye contact, merely murmuring '*Buen Camino*' as he passed. He would arrive in Santiago in three days; new friendships were pointless.

The path climbed up yet another Galician mountain before descending into a mist-filled valley. Shrouded in fog, he nearly missed a scallop shell at a crossroads outside Vilachá but eventually arrived at Portomarín, just as the heavens opened. Fernando briefly considered waiting out the storm in the tavern, but its windows were fogged with the hot breath of other travellers. He walked on, gnawing on the last of his bread as he started the climb to Gonzar. The rain finally eased when he arrived in the town. A dog trotted out from its shelter to sniff him, and Fernando scratched its head. A blood-curdling scream rang out through the village.

'Help! Somebody help me!'

Fernando ran toward the sound of the screaming woman, following her shrieks through the town's empty streets. Rounding a corner, he came upon a young woman staring up at the roof of a house covered in scaffolding. He rushed toward her.

'*Señorita*, what's wrong?'

The girl, who would have been no older than twenty-one, pointed to the house's door. 'He's locked me out. Help me break it down.'

'Why, what's happening?'

'It's my fiancé, Carlos; he's upstairs.'

'Is he in danger?'

'Once I'm inside, he will be.' The girl hammered her fists against the door and howled up at an open window above. 'Carlos Figueroa, you coward. Come down here and face me. I know all about your little slut from Vilachá; I know everything.'

A man's petrified face emerged from the window. He was likely in his mid twenties, but the patchy moustache on his face made him appear younger.

'Rosalía, lower your voice. Everyone can hear you,' he hissed.

'Oh, I'm sorry.' The girl's apology dripped with sarcasm. 'We wouldn't want the entire town knowing that Carlos Figueroa is a lying dog.'

'I never lied,' pleaded the boy.

'No? Then who are you building this house for?'

'You, my sweet!'

The girl stamped her foot. 'That's not what I heard. I heard you're to marry the daughter of Vilachá's mayor.'

'That's not true!'

'No? So their family isn't eating dinner with yours tonight?'

The boy's face fell.

'Aha – so you admit it.' She threw an accusing finger up at her fiancé. 'Well, if this house is for you and your tramp, I'll help you finish it.' She walked over to a cart filled with tins. 'What colour shall we paint the door?' She pried open a can with a screwdriver. 'Aha, yellow – the perfect colour for a coward, no?'

'Rosalía, please!' cried out the boy, but it was too late.

The girl carried the tin toward the house and swung it; a wave of yellow paint splashed against the front door. She tossed the canister to the ground.

'Not bad,' she said, dusting off her hands and surveying her work. 'Not bad at all. Now, let's do the windows.' Rosalía walked back to the cart and selected another tin.

Suddenly, the paint-spattered door flew open and Carlos ran out.

'Rosalía, let me explain.'

She pointed the screwdriver toward the boy's throat. 'Talk quickly.'

'It's true. My parents want me to marry Sylvia.'

'Sylvia?' She spat on the ground. 'She even sounds like a whore.'

'But I don't want to marry her. It was my mother's idea; she had another vision.'

Rosalía's nostrils flared. 'I should have known. Who was it this time? Saint Christopher? Saint Mark?'

Carlos' eyes fell to his feet. 'No, Saint Mateo visited

her last week as she hung out the bedsheets. He said God wanted her son to marry the daughter of Vilachá's mayor.'

'How fortunate God takes such interest in your romantic affairs, Carlos.' Her scowl was volcanic. 'And did you remind your mother that you're already engaged?' Rosalía held up her left hand and pointed to an engagement ring.

'No, she hasn't forgotten.' Carlos sighed. 'She asked me to retrieve Abuela's ring from you.'

Rosalía aimed the screwdriver at Carlos' neck and walked toward him. Fernando stepped between them.

'Everyone stay calm. We can resolve this without bloodshed.'

'It's too late for that.' Rosalía's eyes flooded with tears. 'Carlos and his mother have already killed me. All that is left is to finish the job. *Adiós*, my love.' She turned the screwdriver toward her heart.

'Rosalía, no!' Carlos fell to his knees and clasped his hands together. 'I'm begging you, my sweet, drop the screwdriver.'

'*Sí*, put it down,' urged Fernando. 'We'll find a solution.'

Carlos nodded furiously. 'He's right, Rosalía – listen to him.' Suddenly, the boy frowned. 'Wait, who are you?' He looked at his lover. 'Is this a new suitor, Rosalía?'

The girl flipped the screwdriver's tip back toward the boy. 'You're accusing me of being unfaithful? How dare you. I'm not the one—'

'I'm no one,' interjected Fernando. 'Just a pilgrim destined for Santiago. I heard screaming, so I ran to help.'

'No one can help,' moaned Rosalía. 'The whole town believes his mother's cursed visions, even Padre Ramirez.

If she says Saint Mateo wants her son to marry the little hussy from Vilachá, then everyone will expect it.'

'She can't help it,' stammered the boy. 'Mama says her gift is a curse.'

'Oh, please.' Rosalía tossed the screwdriver back onto the cart. 'Your mother's visions are as fake as her damn teeth. She only wants you to marry into a rich family.'

'You think she lied?'

'Of course she lied. Have you never noticed how your mother's visions always seem to bring her good fortune? Like the time Saint Luke told her the well in your garden is a spring of holy water?'

'That's true, though. Padre Ramirez uses the water for Holy Communion.'

'Of course he does. Every time your mother has one of her damn visions, the cardinal visits here from Madrid. Why would he travel to this godforsaken village otherwise? No one can compete with your mother's visions, Carlos. Especially not me.' Her slender shoulders collapsed. 'Your mother has never approved of you marrying the baker's daughter.' She buried her face in her hands. 'We'll never be together.'

Carlos wrapped his arm around Rosalía's shoulders and rested his head against hers. 'Tell me what to do, and I'll do it. I'd do anything for us to be together.'

'There's nothing, Carlos. We'd need a miracle.'

The boy turned to Fernando. '*Señor*, you're a pilgrim – there must be a great many places along the Camino where miracles occur, no?'

'*Sí*, I suppose some people have seen miracles along the Way, but—'

'Where?'

Fernando wished he'd never spoken, but the boy looked desperate. 'Well, the people of Lourdes have claimed to see visions of the Virgin Mary.'

Rosalía looked up from her hands. 'You were visited by the Virgin?'

'Not me. The miller's daughter says she saw an apparition of the Virgin on the city's lake. But this was one hundred years ago.'

Rosalía looked excitedly at her fiancé. 'Carlos, you must travel to Lourdes.'

'Me?'

'*Sí* – perhaps you'll be visited by the Virgin Mary too.' The girl smeared her eyes dry. 'And perhaps she'll send you a message: that if you marry the baker's daughter, good fortune and prosperity will be enjoyed by the townsfolk of Gonzar.'

The boy frowned. 'You think Mother Mary wants me to marry Alejandra?'

'*Jesucristo, dame fuerzas.*' Rosalía shook her fist up to the heavens. 'You handsome idiot. The baker's other daughter.'

Realisation flashed upon the boy's face. '*Sí*, I understand. Perhaps Mother Mary will tell me that I must marry you?' Suddenly, the boy looked uncertain. 'But, Rosalía, my mother has these visions; I don't.'

Rosalía took his hands in hers and stared deeply into his eyes. '*Sí*, but don't you think, if you truly love me and pray very, very hard on the walk to Lourdes, you might be blessed to have a vision of your own?' She squeezed his hands harder. 'I mean, you do love me, don't you, Carlos?'

'*Sí*, of course.'

'And your mother has these visions; perhaps they are

hereditary, no?'

'*Sí*, it's possible, I suppose.'

'You suppose? Or you are certain? I don't think anyone will believe you if you're not certain.'

He nodded, this time more assuredly. '*Sí*, I am sure Mother Mary will visit me. And when I return, I will tell my mother the Virgin said I'm to marry you, instead of Sylvia.'

'Not just your mother. You'll tell the entire village: your family, your friends and, especially, Padre Ramirez.'

'*Bueno*. So tomorrow, I shall start my pilgrimage to Lourdes.'

'Tomorrow?' The word seared the girl. 'Your parents are meeting the mayor's family tonight, no?'

'*Sí*, but—'

'But nothing – you must leave now. Unless, of course, you secretly wish to marry your tramp from Vilachá after all?'

'Of course not, it's simply…'

Rosalía slid a hand to her hip, and the boy shook his head.

'It's nothing. As always, my angel, you're right. I will leave at once.' He turned to Fernando. 'How far is Lourdes, *señor*?'

'A month's walking; it's in the south of France.'

The boy looked ill. He turned to his fiancée. 'Rosalía – my tulip – perhaps I could walk to Santiago and be visited by Saint James instead.'

'Santiago is only two days' walk from here. I doubt Saint James would visit a man who has only walked for two days. Besides, no one has a higher authority than the Virgin Mary; she's a part of the Holy Trinity, no?'

'This is true. But... it will be two months until I return, no?'

Rosalía took the boy's hand in hers. 'And I shall count the days until I'm once again within your warm embrace, my love.'

Carlos nodded glumly. 'Then I shall leave now. Will you tell my family where I have gone?'

'Of course.'

Rosalía pressed herself against her lover, and the couple kissed. After eventually parting, Carlos extended his hand to Fernando.

'*Gracias, señor*, for bringing my Rosalía back to me.'

'*De nada*. Take care on the path to Lourdes; the path up to Mercadoiro is poorly marked.'

'Carlos, perhaps you can help.' Rosalía picked up a tin of paint and a brush. 'Paint some more scallop shells along the way to guide the pilgrims down the mountain.'

'Scallop shells?' The boy swallowed. 'My two-month pilgrimage would now take three, my sweet.'

Rosalía folded her arms. 'Well, if you're not grateful to our new friend for rescuing our marriage...'

'No, I am, I am.' Carlos took the tin of paint from her and rested it by his feet. Using the tip of the brush's handle to pry its lid off, he dipped the bristles into the paint and drew a simple yellow arrow on the cobblestone. 'How's that?'

'*Bueno*.' Fernando nodded.

Carlos gave Rosalía one final kiss before picking up the tin and paintbrush and starting his pilgrimage to the beginning of the Camino Frances. Fernando and Rosalía watched the boy stop briefly to paint another yellow arrow next to the church before continuing his journey out of town.

'He must really love you,' said Fernando. 'To drop everything and walk across the country to marry you.'

Rosalía shrugged. 'A man would walk across a country without hesitation for the love of his life, no?'

Tom followed the yellow arrows all the way to the town of Gonzar. He approached a group of locals to ask whether they'd seen Fernando, but they seemed to be arguing. A well-dressed girl sat on the steps of a nearby house and wept. Further along, Tom passed a dried puddle of yellow paint; there were no more arrows after that.

He arrived in Ventas de Naron at dusk. A farmer said he'd seen Fernando pass five hours earlier. With the light dying, Tom accepted the man's offer to sleep in his barn. Tom's unscheduled detour, and subsequent breakdown at the crossroads, had cost him hours. But he could still catch Fernando before Santiago; there was still hope.

The next day, he set off before sunrise and followed the ghostly shape of the Camino, shimmering under the setting full moon. When he reached Ligonde, the sun had finally risen, and by Eirexe, the Camino was dotted with pilgrims starting their day's journey. One of them said they'd seen Fernando the previous evening and thought he might have stayed in the next town. Tom walked faster, ignoring his throbbing foot. Tom missed Fernando in Palas de Rei by two hours and only one in San Xulián. He was closing in. The rest of the morning was a blur, jogging along the Camino and passing Galician villages, seemingly each with an x in its name. Eventually, with the sun at its peak, he arrived in the larger town of Melide and walked into a crowded restaurant to rest his foot and find something to eat.

It was lunchtime, and the rows of tables were filled with mostly men, shouting over one another between mouthfuls of beer and food. Tom hoped his scallop shell might earn him a plate of whatever he smelled wafting from the kitchen. A group of locals were crowded around an old-fashioned wireless sitting on the edge of the bar. Tom took a seat, and a waiter reluctantly left the radio and walked toward him. No older than sixteen, the waiter's surly face hid beneath a pair of thick dark eyebrows.

'*¿Sí?*'

'*Hola.*' Tom awkwardly raised the shell hanging by his chest. '*¿Pan y agua, por favor?*'

The waiter scrunched his face up. '*¿Qué?*'

'I'd like some food, please.' Tom listed the foods he knew in Spanish. '*¿Pan? ¿Queso? ¿Huevos?*'

'*Sí.*' The waiter scribbled something on his pad. 'I bring you food.'

'You speak English?'

The waiter held his fingers an inch apart. '*Un poco.*'

'Have you seen a pilgrim pass through here today?'

'This the Camino – many pilgrims.'

'He's a tall Andalusian.'

'You mean, him?'

Tom's eyes followed the waiter's finger to a solitary figure sitting at the bar; it was Fernando. Tom stumbled to his feet and walked toward the bar, leaving the bewildered waiter behind.

'*Hola*, Fernando.'

The Spaniard looked stunned.

'Thomas, *¿qué estás haciendo aquí?*' The Spaniard searched the bar. '*¿Dónde está Sofía?*'

'Sofia is in Sarria. She's with a doctor. With *el médico*.'

'*El médico?*'

'She's okay. She's gone into labour. The baby came early. *El bebé es...*' Tom tried to think back to his stalled Spanish lessons. '*... temprano.*'

'*¿Está bien, Sofía?*'

'*Sí*, Sofia is okay. She's safe. *Bien*.'

Fernando seemed to understand, and his concern transformed to confusion.

'*¿Entonces, por qué estás aquí?*'

'I'm here because... Sofia asked me to find you.' Tom had been so focused on catching up to Fernando, he hadn't considered what he'd say if he ever did. 'Sofia needs you. *Sofia te necesita.*'

'*¿Por qué?*'

Explaining this in English would have been hard enough, but doing it in Spanish was impossible. Just then, the waiter arrived and placed a plate of food on the bar in front of Tom.

'*Pulpo.*'

Tom stared at the plate's contents: boiled octopus on a bed of fried potatoes sprinkled with paprika. It was the same dish Tom had tried in Santiago. His neck hairs stood up, and he stared at the waiter.

'Diego?'

'*¿Sí?*' The waiter's head tilted. 'You know me or something?'

It was him: the tuxedo and belly were missing, but the

kid had the old waiter's bushy eyebrows.

'Your name is Diego; you work here in the summers. Your uncles fish for octopus, and your aunts cook it.'

The younger Diego's eyes narrowed. 'How you know that?'

A man by the radio yelled in Spanish, and Diego shrugged.

'I have to go, man.' He pointed to the radio. 'They need me to translate the game for them – it's BBC radio.'

Tom grabbed his arm.

'Wait, I need you to translate something for me.' He nodded to Fernando. 'To him.'

The young Diego glanced at the clock behind the bar and sighed. 'Fine, what do you want me to say?'

'Tell him Sofia wants him to return to Sarria…'

'Who is Sofia? His wife?'

'No.'

'Girlfriend?'

'No, they're not together yet.'

'Then why she want him to return?'

'Can you translate it or not?'

The kid's bushy eyebrows lifted. 'No need to be grouchy, man. I'm only trying to help, no?'

'I'm sorry.' Tom reset. 'Tell Fernando that Sofia asked me to bring him back to Sarria. She's worried about him.'

Diego spoke to Fernando, who shook his head.

'*Es mejor si me quedo aquí…*'

'He says he should stay here,' translated Diego. 'He says things will work out better for everyone if he walks to Santiago alone.'

'It won't. Tell him I've seen how his life unfolds and leaving Sofia is the biggest mistake of his life.'

Diego frowned. 'You are talking too fast, man. It sounds like you seen the future or something. How you know all this?'

Tom paused to think of a different explanation, but there wasn't one. It felt like the ultimate breach of the butterfly effect, but there was no other choice.

'I'm from the future.'

Diego exploded into laughter and slapped Fernando's shoulder. '*Tu amigo dice que es del futuro. ¿Está loco, no?*'

When Fernando didn't laugh, Diego looked confused. 'Is a joke, no?'

'It's true. How do you think I knew your name or the fact you work here with your aunts and uncles in the summers?'

Diego crossed his arms. 'You saying you know me in the future?'

'Yes, we've met.'

'Oh, yeah? Then what year was it, Future-man?'

'2010.'

Diego laughed. 'I'd be dead by then.'

'No, you are living in Santiago, running a café in a square next to the cathedral.'

'I work at Papa's café?' The boy's smug grin slid from his face. 'I'd rather be dead.'

'You're not the reason I was sent here,' said Tom, nodding toward Fernando. 'He is; it's crucial he returns to Sarria with me.'

'Why? Is your friend famous in the future or something?'

'No, he's…' There was no other way. 'In the year 2010, he's the grandfather of my girlfriend, Ana.'

'How do he and I know this Ana even exists?'

'Fernando has seen her.' Tom pulled his phone from his pocket and placed it on the bar. He tapped its dead screen. 'This contained her photograph.'

Diego eyed the phone with suspicion. 'I don't see no photograph.'

'Just tell Fernando the girl in the photograph was his granddaughter – Ana.'

Diego glanced back to the dead phone before finally fulfilling Tom's request. Fernando seemed to ask a question, and the two Spaniards fell into a longer discussion.

'What's he saying?' asked Tom.

'I asked him if he thinks I should take you to a hospital, but he says no.' The boy leaned closer. 'I think you both crazy. He asks if Sofia is Ana's grandmother.'

'No, tell him he marries another woman who becomes Ana's grandmother.'

Diego grinned. 'Well, now I know you're lying.'

'It's the truth.'

'Really?' The boy folded his arms. 'If you say he is supposed to marry another woman, why you want him to go back to this Sofia woman, hmm? What will happen to your girl? She may never be born, no? You have to be lying; otherwise, it makes no sense.'

'You're right – if he returns to Sofia, then Ana may never exist.'

'So why do it then?'

It was the question burning a hole in Tom's gut.

'Because it's the right thing to do.' He took a deep breath in. 'It was a miracle I'd even met Ana in the first place; perhaps there will be another.'

The men around the radio hollered toward Diego, and the boy sighed. 'Fine, I'll tell him.'

Fernando's expression remained unchanged as he listened to Diego's translation; the Andalusian responded with a single question.

'*¿Por qué caminaste originalmente por el Camino?*'

'He wants to know why you walked the Camino.'

'Because of him.' Tom pointed to Fernando. 'He told me he'd only grant me his blessing to marry Ana if I walked to Santiago.' He recalled Tito's exact words. 'A man would walk across a country without hesitation for the love of his life.'

Diego translated this, and Fernando straightened in his seat.

'*¿Por qué dijo eso?*'

'He wants to know why you said these words.'

'They were the last thing he said to me before I left.'

Something about Tom's answer troubled Fernando. When he eventually spoke, his voice was weak.

'He says he doesn't believe your story,' translated Diego. 'He says there is no proof.'

'Proof?' Tom shook his phone before him. 'This telephone saved his life. He knows I'm telling the truth.'

Fernando's eyes slid to the floor. '*Lo siento, Thomas. Mi historia termina en Santiago.*'

'He says his story ends in Santiago.'

The men crowded around the radio banged on the bar and bellowed toward Diego.

'Sorry, Future-man, but the match has started; they need me to translate.' He smiled an apology. 'It is the final.'

'The World Cup Final?'

'*Sí*, Hungary versus West Germany.'

The 1954 World Cup Final between Hungary and West Germany. Tom clutched Diego's arm.

'Wait, tell Fernando I have proof I'm from the future.'

A whistle blasted through the radio's speaker, followed by the crackled roar of the crowd. The locals waved Diego over.

'What proof?' asked the boy.

'I know who wins this football match.'

Diego snorted. 'You don't need to be from the future to know Hungary will win. They smashed West Germany 10 to 3 in the group stages.'

'West Germany wins.'

The boy howled with laughter. 'Of all the shit you've said today, Future-man, this is the craziest.'

'Tell Fernando that he must return with me to Sarria if Germany wins. If I'm wrong, he's free to continue to Santiago.' It was Tom's only chance. 'Please, just tell him.'

'*Vale, vale.*' Diego sighed. '*Guiri loco.*'

He passed Tom's proposition to Fernando, who hesitated before replying.

'He says if you predict the correct score, he will come back with you,' said Diego. 'Your friend is smart; even a broken watch is right twice a day, no?'

Tom knew West Germany won; it was the first of their three World Cups and one of the most famous upsets of all time. He was confident the game hadn't been decided by penalties, but he wasn't certain of the final score. He sifted through the countless hours of football podcasts and YouTube highlights trapped inside his brain.

'West Germany wins, 3 goals to 2.'

It was his best guess and his only chance. Diego passed the counteroffer to Fernando, who eventually nodded. Diego shouted something to the bartender, who slid a couple of frosted mugs of beer down the bar toward them.

'Good luck, Future-man.' Diego slapped Tom's back and rejoined the men hunched around the radio.

The crowd's rolling hum wafted through the restaurant as Tom took a shaky sip of beer. Suddenly, the commentator's shrill English accent pierced the air.

'A good ball from Bozsik finds Kocsis, saved by Turek, but it falls to Puskás, who scores! Hungary score in the sixth minute!'

The locals clapped and hooted, clinking their mugs together in celebration. Diego laughed at Tom.

'Not looking good for you, Future-man.'

Tom avoided Fernando's gaze and eyed the *pulpo*; the thought of eating anything made him gag. Two minutes later, the commentator's high-pitched voice rose again.

'… and now there's been a mix-up, with a dangerous back-pass to the keeper, intercepted by Czibor, who slams it into the empty net! Another goal for Hungary, 2–0.'

The bar exploded in more applause, and Diego rushed over and threw his arm around Tom's shoulder.

'Poor Future-man, looks like you are walking back to Sarria all alone, no?'

The commentary continued.

'Dear, oh, dear. Now, after only eight minutes, the West Germans find themselves needing a miracle here in Bern.'

CHAPTER 24

Sofia reached across and touched the bundle within the bassinet next to the bed. The room's darkness hid her smile as she felt the baby's chest rising and falling beneath the blankets. A knock at the door forced her hand away from the baby.

'*¿Sí?*'

The door creaked open, and a familiar silhouette appeared from the illuminated hallway. She sat upright in the bed.

'Thomas, you're back. What time is it?'

'It's late – almost ten. I'm sorry if you were asleep, but I wanted to see you as soon as I arrived.'

His flat tone betrayed the truth, but she asked anyway.

'You didn't find Fernando?'

Before he could answer, the door opened, and Fernando entered. Her eyes moistened.

'You came back.'

He nodded awkwardly. '*Sí.*'

Silence suffocated the room until the baby stirred. Sofia leaned across and turned on the lamp before scooping the baby against her chest and patting its tiny back. Fernando and Thomas crept closer and smiled down at the small bundle in her arms.

'Is it a boy or a girl?' asked Thomas.

'A boy.'

'He looks well.' He stroked the baby's cheek before looking up at her. 'Is Sir Walter still here?'

'I'm sorry, Thomas. He left yesterday. He did not tell me he was going; otherwise, I would have asked him to wait for you.'

She could see his disappointment.

'It doesn't matter anymore, anyway.' Thomas' tired smile was unconvincing. 'I'll go and set up our beds. I'm glad you and the baby are okay, Sofia.'

She squeezed his hand, and the door gently closed behind him. Sofia faced Fernando.

'Is he alright?'

'He walked one hundred and twenty kilometres over three days; he's tired.' Fernando paused. 'What about you?'

'Still sore, but mostly I've slept; I can't seem to stay awake for longer than a few hours.'

'You've been through a lot.'

'So have you.'

They caught one another's eye; the silence amplified.

'I'm sorry, Sofia. I shouldn't have said the things I said to you. It was wrong to mention my mother. The truth is...' His voice unexpectedly failed; he swallowed and tried again. 'The truth is I was so angry my mother left us,

405

I never stopped to understand why. I'm sure she had her reasons: perhaps it was my father's drinking, or perhaps she wasn't well. Either way, I apologise for how I acted. I'm sorry I left you.'

Sofia placed the baby back within its bassinet and opened the dresser's top drawer. She pulled out the photograph.

'I found this.'

Fernando's cheeks burned crimson. He snatched the picture and tucked it into his shirt pocket. 'I must have dropped it.'

'No, you didn't.'

Their eyes met.

'You blame yourself, don't you?'

An age passed before he spoke; when he did, his voice was softer than the lamplight.

'When we returned from Morocco, they deployed us to Sevilla. We were ordered into my family's neighbourhood, and there was a firefight in a factory.' He swallowed back his tears. 'Everything happened so fast, but I still remember it so clearly: the sound of the grenade rolling toward me; the weight of it in my hand as I threw it away from me.' He shook his head. 'When the smoke cleared, and I saw the body, somehow I already knew.' Two tears raced each other down his cheeks. 'I killed him, Sofia. I killed my brother.'

She wrapped her arms around him and held him against her.

'It was an accident, Fernando, a terrible, terrible accident.' She rubbed her hand over the back of his neck. 'You couldn't have known. It wasn't your fault.'

Sofia stroked his hair and pressed herself against him.

She bit back her own tears as Fernando's freely spilled onto her neck. After several minutes his weeping softened, and he pulled away from her with a glistening face.

'*Lo siento.*'

'You have nothing to apologise for. I can't imagine how hard it's been for you to carry this with you for so many years.'

'All I ever wanted was to talk to Emilio again and tell him how sorry I am. But he was in heaven, and I'll be going to hell. But then I remembered the Xacobeo and how a man's sins are forgiven when he passes through La Puerta Santa.'

'I like to think this is true, Fernando – I do – but killing yourself will not reunite you with your brother. Even if God forgave you for taking your own life, would Emilio?'

'I should pay for what I did.'

'You already have. Killing yourself won't change anything. If you really want to honour your brother, help the people he died fighting for.'

'I'm not like him; who could I ever help?'

'You help everyone, Fernando. You carried Thomas through the streets of Pamplona when he was punctured by the bull. You defended Pablo against his father in León. You were prepared to die for all of us in Carrión. Don't tell me you can't help people – I've seen you do it every day I've known you.' She pointed to the baby, now soundly asleep in its cot. 'Do you think this baby would really be here if you hadn't rescued me from the mud outside Logroño?'

'You didn't need rescuing.'

'Yes, I did.' She squeezed his hand. 'Sometimes people need rescuing, Fernando – it doesn't make us weak.'

He stared down at the baby. 'He's so small.'

She allowed herself to look too. '*Sí*, he was early, but Enrico said he is strong.'

'Like his mother.'

Sofia let go of Fernando's hand, turning back to the bed. 'I'm not his mother.' She began smoothing down the sheets; she didn't know why.

'So you're still going to the orphanage?' he asked.

'*Sí*, Enrico will drive us to Santiago tomorrow. The sooner, the better.'

'And then?'

'And then nothing.' She pulled the sheets tight. 'I'll go to England.'

'Is that what you want?'

'Oxford University is Europe's best university; I'm fortunate to receive a scholarship.'

'*Sí*, but it's not what I asked. You hadn't told me you'd been awarded the scholarship because you still hadn't decided whether you would give up the baby. Am I right?' He stood behind her and placed his hands on her shoulders; his hands felt rough on her bare arms. 'Sofia, look at me.'

She plumped a pillow. 'The baby will find a proper family in Santiago; he'll have a better life than I could give him.'

Fernando's voice was close but gentle. 'Sofia – please, look at me.'

She turned and faced him.

'Do you really want to give your baby up?'

Her trembling lip betrayed her. 'I can't study medicine and raise a baby at the same time.'

'Write to the university; ask to delay your start.'

'I can't go back to Valencia with a baby; my family will be disgraced.'

The baby stirred, and she lowered her voice again.

'Even if I wanted to keep it, there's nowhere for me to go.'

'What about Santiago?'

'Santiago?' She frowned. 'I don't know anyone there.'

'Neither do I.'

She tried to read his face. 'What are you saying?'

'I'll stay with you in Santiago. I'll help you look after the baby.'

'Don't just say that, Fernando. You don't have to rescue me.'

'I know, but...' He looked embarrassed to say it. 'Maybe you and the baby could rescue me. I mean, maybe—'

She didn't let him finish; she simply threw her arms around him.

'We can rescue each other,' she whispered before leaning up to kiss him.

He pulled her against him and kissed her deeper; she tasted her salty tears on his lips. The baby stirred again, filling the room with its hungry cries once more. Sofia pulled herself from Fernando's embrace and lifted the baby from the cradle. Fernando stepped closer and brushed his finger against its tiny cheek.

'Do you want to hold him?' she asked.

'I don't know how.'

'I'll show you.' She passed the baby to him, guiding one of his hands to the baby's bottom and the other behind its head. 'That's it.'

She stepped away and laughed; Fernando was rigid.

'You are allowed to breathe; you won't break him.'

He blushed, looking down at the little parcel in his arms. The lines of concentration on his forehead eventually faded into a smile.

'What's his name?'

'I hadn't given him one; it didn't feel like it was my place.'

Fernando leaned down and whispered to the child. 'Well, that's okay, *chico*, we'll find you a name.'

She walked next to Fernando and rested her head on his shoulder. They stared down at the boy together.

'*Sí*, we'll find you a good name, little one,' said Sofia, stroking one of the baby's tiny fingers. 'This is Fernando; he's going to help look after you.'

'No, my name is Tito.' He leaned down and kissed the baby's forehead. 'And we will all look after each other.'

Sofia nearly cried, but her baby beat her to it. The short-lived tranquillity was destroyed again.

'What did I do?' asked Tito, looking as if he'd knocked over an expensive vase.

There was a knock at the door, and Luciana appeared.

'Sounds like someone is hungry, no?' Luciana rescued the baby into its mother's arms and ushered Tito toward the door. 'Let's give Mama some privacy.'

Tito looked reluctant to leave.

'Get some rest,' said Sofia. 'I'll see you in the morning.'

She waited until the door was closed before sitting on the bed and bringing the baby to her breast. This time, its mouth latched on to the nipple quicker, and she felt the milk begin to flow. She looked down at the boy's tiny face and imagined his name.

'Why are you grinning?' asked Luciana over her shoulder. She led Tito down the hallway to a room that looked more suited to patients than guests. 'Where's your friend?' she asked, pointing to two stripped wire beds.

Enrico appeared.

'The English boy is making the beds up in the barn.'

'The barn again?' Luciana clucked her tongue at her husband. 'Are they cows? They will sleep in the house. Go and fetch him; I'll make up the beds.'

'I'll go,' said Tito. He walked out of the house and saw the barn on the far side of their yard. 'Thomas,' he called out.

There was the faint glow of lamplight from within but no response. Tito walked toward the barn, expecting to find the Englishman already asleep. Tito still didn't know what to make of Thomas' claims in Melide – was the girl in the photograph really Tito's granddaughter? When the Englishman had uttered Rosalía's exact words, something had shifted inside Tito. So when the Hungarian player had been called offside in the dying minutes of the match, and Thomas' predicted scoreline had come true, Tito had begun to wonder: what if Thomas was telling the truth?

He pushed the barn door open. 'Thomas?'

The Englishman was standing in the middle of the barn, perfectly still.

'What's wrong?'

He walked toward him, and Thomas' widened eyes immediately flicked over Tito's shoulder. The barn door creaked closed; a familiar raspy voice emerged from behind it.

'*Buenas tardes*, Señor Hernández.'

Tito turned, and Ramos stepped out from the barn's shadows. He looked smaller out of his uniform. Heavy bags hung under his eyes, and his face was covered in a week's growth. He waved his gun toward Thomas.

'Move next to your friend.'

Tito carefully stepped toward Thomas. 'What do you want?'

'I've come for the device. Once I prove your conspiracy, Aznar and Besteiro will be the ones charged with treason.' He nodded toward Thomas. 'Fetch it from him.'

'I don't speak English.'

'Shall we pry the nurse from her bastard child to translate for us?' A cruel smile appeared on Ramos' lips.

Tito turned to Thomas. 'Give him the device.' He pointed to the Englishman's pocket. '*El teléfono* – give it to him.'

Thomas seemed to understand and carefully pulled the telephone from his pocket. Ramos snatched it and stepped back to inspect it. He pressed each of its buttons, but the object remained dormant.

'What's wrong with it?'

'He told us the battery is flat,' said Tito.

Ramos thrust the device toward Thomas. 'Then tell him to find another.'

'He says he can't. He says he doesn't have the right equipment. Just take it and go; you've got what you came for.'

Ramos scoffed. 'What I want is for people to stop pretending we're at peace. My country is riddled with spies and traitors.'

'You're delusional; Thomas isn't a spy.'

'Stop lying!' The gun shook with every screamed word. 'I saw what this machine did in Carrión. It's a military weapon, spreading propaganda.'

'All it did was reveal the truth; you murdered women and children.'

'I did what Spain needed me to do.' Spittle flew from his unshaven lips. 'For twenty years, nobody questioned my methods; they only ever demanded results. But now, in their new Spain, there are rules. Now, they believe the word of a deserter and a foreigner over that of a patriot.' Ramos shook with rage. 'Well, they can try and strip me of my uniform and pension, but they'll never stop me fighting Spain's enemies.'

Ramos waved the gun toward the door. 'Let's go.'

'Where?'

'Inside – the girl will help me get the truth out of him.'

'Leave Sofia out of this,' said Tito. 'She's innocent.'

'Once, perhaps, but you've involved her now. Her blood will be on your hands.' Ramos pushed back against the door; it creaked open. The gun remained locked on them. He took two backward steps out of the barn and into the night. 'Now, you and your friend, follow me – very slowly.'

Tito and Thomas did as ordered, edging toward the door. Ramos took a third step backward and froze, his cruel grin suddenly replaced by a look of shock. He lowered his pistol and slowly stepped back into the barn. Behind him, emerging from the night, was the bearded face of Santo Gutierre.

'Stand back,' the old man said in Spanish.

Tito guided Thomas to the side of the barn, and they watched Santo Gutierre lead Ramos into the centre of the room, the tip of his sword pressed against the brigada's back.

'You're making a mistake, old man,' snarled Ramos.

'It's you who are mistaken, Ramos; drop the gun.'

Ramos hesitated, and Santo Gutierre nudged the blade forward. Ramos' face twisted with pain; the pistol slipped to the hay-covered ground.

'*Muy bien*,' said Santo Gutierre. 'Now turn around, slowly.'

As Ramos began to turn, Tito remembered their night in Carrión. 'Careful, he carries a second pistol in—'

But he was too late. As Ramos turned, his left hand slid within his jacket to the holster at the small of his back. He drew his second pistol.

Bang.

Santo Gutierre tumbled toward Ramos, and the two men crashed to the ground.

'*No!*' screamed Thomas, lunging toward the old man and lifting him clear of Ramos.

Tito dived for Ramos' guns, scooping them up and tucking one into the waistband of his trousers. He aimed the second at Ramos before slowly lowering it.

'H-H-Help.' Blood gushed from Ramos' mouth.

Santo Gutierre's fall had pushed his sword so deep into Ramos that its hilt rested against his chest.

'H-Help me,' he croaked. More blood poured from his mouth over his neck and into the dirt.

Tito leaned down, wrapped his fingers around the sword's hilt and prepared to pull the blade clear. A final gurgled sigh, and Ramos stared lifelessly at the barn's steepled ceiling. Tito released his grip.

'*No, no, no, no.*'

Tito spun around to discover Thomas kneeling over Santo Gutierre. The Englishman had his hand pressed firmly against the knight's neck, but it wasn't enough. The bullet had hit the old man at point-blank range; his white tunic was now as crimson as the Templar cross upon its centre. Thomas looked up with tears in his eyes.

The old man was dead.

CHAPTER 25

They buried Sir Walter the following day. Tom had initially suggested returning the body to Scotland but the others explained this was impossible without involving the police. Instead, Enrico had driven them to his brother's farm, with the knight's tarpaulin-covered body lying within the pick-up truck's tray. The farm was a thirty-minute drive away, a serene patch of paddocks on a mountain overlooking Santiago. When they stepped from the vehicles, a small crowd of twenty awaited them.

'Who are all these people?' asked Tom.

'Luciana says many are from the surrounding villages,' said Sofia. 'Others have walked up the mountain from Santiago.'

Tom and Fernando helped dig the grave before the locals carefully moved Sir Walter from the truck to his final resting place, high above the city he'd spent a decade protecting. Word of the knight's death had swept through the villages, and the crowd eventually grew to over fifty. Some had driven from as far as Burgos to pay their respects. People tossed scallop shells into the grave on top of the knight's body; Tom and Fernando threw theirs in too. Everyone bowed their heads, and Enrico said a few words. Sofia offered to translate Tom's message, but he knew the Spanish words needed.

'*Gracias, Santo Gutierre. Muchas gracias y adiós.*'

As the grave was filled, Tom couldn't help but think of the night before.

'What will they do with Ramos' body?' he asked Sofia.

Her response was cryptic. 'He will disappear, like those he disappeared.'

When the grave was filled entirely, Enrico thrust Sir Walter's sword into the earth next to it. The doctor dangled Sir Walter's scallop shell necklace from the sword's cross-guard, which served as a simple crucifix. Each of the locals crossed themselves as they passed the grave on their journey home. Tom looked out over the valley and down to the city of Santiago. From here, it looked small, unworthy of such a perilous journey.

Sofia joined him, her baby asleep in a wrap against her chest.

'Enrico offered to drive us to Santiago, but I have said we will walk.'

'But what about the baby?'

'He is asleep. After lying in bed for four days, I need a walk. Besides, it isn't far.'

The pilgrims thanked Enrico and Luciana for all they had done.

'*Muchas gracias*,' said Tom, hugging them both.

'*De nada*,' replied Luciana.

Tom looked back at Sir Walter's grave, wishing he could somehow mark its location. He turned to Sofia.

'Can you ask them the name of this place? In case I ever want to return.'

Sofia asked, and Luciana replied.

'Monte del Gozo.'

'It means the Hill of Joy,' translated Sofia.

Tom searched the sky for signs of a brooding storm, but there wasn't a single cloud – let alone a wormhole.

They set off for the final leg of their pilgrimage, their group of three, joined by a fourth. The Camino was busy, filled with other pilgrims' songs and laughter. Tom didn't share the joy or accomplishment he saw on their faces. He'd spent the entire month with Santiago as his North Star: his only way back to Ana. What would he do when he arrived in the city and remained trapped forever in the past? The question loomed larger with every step he took closer to Santiago.

After half an hour, they came to the city's outskirts. The locals were too busy in their days to notice the pilgrims, much less wish them *buen Camino*. The city was different from the one Tom had left a month ago, with none of the souvenir stores or bars touting their 'Free Wi-Fi'. They passed an orphanage, and Tom wondered if it was the same one Sofia had planned to give her baby to. Tom noticed a sign hung in the window: *Trabajo ofrecido – manitas*.

They continued to the city's Old Town and weaved through its narrow streets, catching glimpses of the cathedral's spire before surfacing into the Praza do Obradoiro. The three embraced, each with teary eyes, but likely for different reasons. The clocktower chimed eleven o'clock. Families rushed across to the plaza and into the cathedral, which somehow looked dirtier than it would sixty years later.

'Shall we attend mass?' asked Sofia.

With nowhere left to walk, they followed the last of the stragglers into the cathedral. An usher guided them to a row of pews reserved for pilgrims, far from the fresh-looking locals. The interior of Santiago's cathedral was similar to that of Burgos; the only noticeable difference was a large, silver urn standing by the altar. Tom leaned toward Sofia.

'What's that?' he whispered.

'It is called the *botafumeiro*. It burns incense to mask the smell of the pilgrims.'

The pipe organ began to play, and the congregation stood to welcome the procession. Fernando said something, and Sofia giggled.

'He wants to know if you will deliver a sermon,' translated Sofia.

The three of them laughed, and an usher glared them back to silence.

The mass itself was a sombre affair, lasting for an hour but feeling years longer. When it eventually finished, a group of robed men attached ropes to the *botafumeiro* and hoisted it high above the congregation. Plumes of incense billowed over the pilgrims as the enormous urn swung back and forth. The pungent smell reminded Tom of the Easter masses of his childhood.

After the service, the congregation filtered out of the cathedral. Instead of following everyone back into the square, Fernando led Tom and Sofia up a spiralled set of steps to the crypt. Tom looked at the stone slab which supposedly housed Saint James' remains and his thoughts drifted to Sir Walter. On their way back down, they passed behind a statue of Santiago himself and took turns embracing it. Sofia said it was supposed to bring them good luck, and Tom added it to the long list of statues he'd rubbed or hugged across Europe – all promising the same. After descending the stairs back to the empty cathedral floor, they approached a set of large bronze doors, tinged green with oxidation. Both bore depictions of Saint James and his disciples.

'La Puerta Santa,' said Fernando.

The doors stood open, and Tom recognised the plaza beyond them. It was the same one he and Tito had met in a month earlier. Tom began to walk through the doors but the Spaniards didn't follow.

'What's wrong?' he asked, pointing into the square. 'Shall we go?'

Fernando said something in Spanish and pointed to the rear of the church. Sofia translated.

'We will walk out the way we entered. We will find you in the plaza.'

'You're sure?'

'*Sí*, we are.'

'Okay, *adiós*.'

Fernando clicked his fingers and shook his head. '*No, no es un adiós*.'

Tom realised his mistake. 'Okay, *hasta luego*.'

Fernando nodded, and Tom watched the couple walk back up the aisle to the rear of the cathedral. While he was terrified history would be changed forever, Tom couldn't know precisely what would unfold. Perhaps Fernando was meant to only be with Sofia in this particular place and moment and would still somehow find Esmerelda. Sir Walter had been right: Tom couldn't control the future; he could only do what felt right to him now. Tom hoped he'd find his way home to Ana but realised it mightn't be up to him. He turned and passed through the Holy Doors and into the square.

The midday sun was hot, and the plaza was filled with families. Tom dodged a group of boys kicking a football and walked past the café where he'd sat with Tito a month earlier. Like much of the Camino, it didn't look vastly different to the 2010 version of itself, with the same umbrellas and outdoor seating. He sat on a bench against the wall next to the café and waited for Fernando and Sofia. He closed his eyes and let the hum of the square wash over him – the laughter of the adults and the gleeful screams of their children. Spain sounded different from England. People spoke louder; they laughed more freely. Was this true, or had Tom simply never taken the time to listen to London? Should he travel back to England? Although it had always been his home, there was nothing there for him. In 1954, his parents were children. He'd been so focused on returning to 2010, he'd never considered what a lifetime spent in the past could be like. Sir Walter had mentioned several caminos across Europe and said they'd provided him comfort. Perhaps one of them would do the same for Tom. But which path should he take next? The question went unanswered, interrupted by a peculiar sound.

Bling. Bling.

The sound wasn't extraordinary in itself; Tom must have heard it a million times before. But it was a sound that had no worldly reason for existing in this place. He must have imagined it.

Bling. Bling.

Tom opened his eyes and stood up. He scanned the square for the source of the familiar chime.

Bling. Bling.

He followed it to the next bench along the wall. A teenage girl sat hunched with her back to him. He walked toward her and craned his neck to see the girl's face. Before he could, salsa music exploded from the girl's hands. She lifted an object to her ear, and the music stopped as quickly as it had begun.

'*¿Sí? Sí, en la plaza,*' said the girl, standing up and turning around.

Tom stared at the mobile phone in her hand. Noticing his expression, the girl veered away from him and toward the cathedral. He watched her disappear into the crowd; a syringe of adrenaline thumped into his heart. Was she a time traveller too? He began to follow her when a small boy bumped into him.

'*Perdone,*' called out the boy, racing after a football.

Tom stared at his shirt. It was a Real Madrid football jersey – a common sight in Spain – but it bore the number 9 and Cristiano Ronaldo's name on its back. The pavement rippled, and Tom felt lightheaded. He staggered through the plaza, as if he were walking around a moving ship, and stared at the nearby families. Whereas the men had all been in suits a moment earlier, now they wore jeans and t-shirts. The women, modestly adorned in hats and gloves in the cathedral, now wore summer dresses and tank-tops with thin straps. A girl wore a Metallica shirt, her head completely shaved except for the blonde fringe dangling over her eye. Tom stopped a young man walking past him.

'*Perdone*, what year is it? Err… *¿Que año es?*'

The man scowled at Tom as if he was high before walking away. Tom hurried over to a girl in hiking clothes.

'*Perdone*, do you speak English? *¿Hablas inglés?*'

The girl, who was Tom's age, smiled. 'Sure do – I'm Australian.'

Relief and fear combined; Tom took an extra breath before asking, 'What's today's date?'

'It's the 7th of July, I think. It's kind of hard keeping track on the Camino, isn't it?'

'No, the year; what's the year?'

The girl frowned as if not understanding the joke. 'The year?' she asked. 'It's 2010.'

Tom's knees nearly surrendered, and the girl steadied him.

'Are you alright?'

'I'm fine.' His heart pounded against his shirt, and his eyes shimmered.

The girl gave him a knowing grin. 'Don't worry, I was a bit emotional when I arrived in Santiago too. But I didn't forget the bloody year.'

'Yeah, well…'

'Well done making it to Santiago, though. You did it.' She gave him a reassuring smile before drifting over to a group of hikers posing for a selfie in front of the cathedral.

Tom stared at his surroundings as if her were an abandoned child in a department store. It had been 1954 two minutes earlier; how was he back? He looked to the empty bench he'd been sitting on, half expecting to find himself still asleep on it. Had his walk along the Camino actually been a dream all along? Excitement fluttered within him; maybe Ana was safe after all. This thought was interrupted by the sight of a familiar figure seated at an outdoor table in the square's café. Tom walked over, drawn to them like a magnet.

'*Hola, Tito.*'

Bald-headed and wrinkled, the old man looked up from the table. '*¿Sí?*'

It was him; it was the man Tom had sat opposite at the same table a month earlier. It was Ana's grandfather – Tito.

'*Soy Thomas.*' He patted his chest excitedly. 'I'm Ana's boyfriend. *El novio del Ana, de Londres.*'

The old man's face creased in confusion. '*Lo siento.*'

Thinking his beard might have confused him, Tom tried the phrase again, speaking slower. Tito studied Tom carefully before slowly shaking his head.

'*Lo siento, no te conozco.*'

The words kneeled on Tom's chest, as he suddenly realised what was happening: Tito didn't recognise Tom as Ana's boyfriend because Ana didn't exist. Tom had returned to a future where the butterfly effect had erased her. The ground trembled, and Tom knocked a glass from the table as he tried to steady himself; it shattered into a thousand pieces onto the cement. Tito gripped Tom's arm and helped him down onto the chair opposite him.

'*Agua,*' he yelled toward the bar.

A man shuffled toward them with a glass of water. Tom took a few sips and nodded his thanks up to the waiter. When he saw the waiter's face, Tom's fingers sprang open with shock; the second glass of water slipped to the ground, shattering next to the first.

'*Jesucristo!*' said Diego, before hollering toward a bored

teen hunched over his phone by the bar. '*Paco, levántate de tu trasero holgazán.*'

Tom stared open-mouthed at the waiter. 'Diego?'

The old, tuxedoed version of Diego lifted his grey bushy eyebrows. '*¿Sí?* You know me or something?'

'It's me, Thomas. I was here a month ago. Don't you remember?'

'Many pilgrims come here.'

'No, I wasn't a pilgrim. I was here to ask for Tito's permission to marry Ana.'

Diego and Tito shared a concerned look.

'*Creo que necesitas un médico.*'

'No, I don't need a doctor,' said Tom, understanding enough Spanish to know they thought he was insane. 'I was here a month ago, and you translated for me.'

The two elderly Spaniards murmured to each other before Diego waddled back to the bar. Tom closed his eyes and rubbed his temples. Was he actually having a breakdown? Tito patted his shoulder.

'Everything will be okay.'

Tom opened his eyes. 'What did you say?'

'We will look after you.'

'You… you speak English?'

The old man looked embarrassed. '*Un poco.* I never practise. You are English, no?'

'Y-Yes, I'm from London.'

'*Londres.*' Tito nodded. 'And you finish walking the Camino?'

'Yes – today.'

'Today?' The old man looked impressed. 'Is good. I once walked the Camino when I was your age. Is very long, no?'

'Very.'

Tito's eyes drifted up to the cathedral's spires. 'I meet an Englishman on the Camino. We walked together – him and me. We no talk much. I no speak English, he no speak Spanish.'

The hairs lifted against the back of Tom's collar. 'Your friend... what happened to him?'

'When we get to Santiago, he disappeared. I searched the city for months, but I never found him.' The old man smiled sadly and pointed to the cathedral. 'For years, I come here and watch the pilgrims. I pray one day to see my English friend again.' He tapped his chest. 'This is why I learn the English, no? So if I ever see him, I can finally thank him.'

Tom's lip trembled. 'Thank him for what?'

They were interrupted by Diego, who returned with his phone in hand. He nervously smiled down at Tom.

'The doctor will be here soon, okay?' The waiter slid a packet of cigarettes from his pocket and lit one.

Tito threw his hands up in protest. '*¿Estás fumando?*'

'*¡Porque es una emergencia!*' said Diego.

Tito pointed to the bar. '*¡Ve adentro!*'

'Fine.' Diego threw up his hands and faced Tom. 'He thinks he is so clever because he guessed cigarettes cause cancer. So what? We all have to die sometime, no?' Diego huffed his way back to the bar.

The cathedral's bells announced it was 12:30.

'My wife will arrive soon,' Tito said to Tom. 'We always go to the market together.'

'Your wife? Esmerelda?'

Tito frowned. 'Who is Esmerelda?'

Diego whistled from the bar. 'Hey, old man, the

doctor is here.'

A short, elderly woman walked toward them. She wore a dark pair of trousers with a grey sleeveless top and stylish, black-rimmed glasses; her silver, curly hair was tied up in a bun. She placed her hand on Tito's shoulder.

'*¿Qué pasa?*'

Tito spoke to the woman in Spanish, and she eventually faced Tom. 'You are English?'

'Yes.'

'They told me you fainted. How do you feel now?'

'I'm fine.'

Tito pointed a bony finger toward Tom. 'He just finished the Camino. I have been practising my English with him.'

The doctor leaned down and looked into Tom's eyes. 'How much water have you drunk today?'

'A little, not a lot.'

She glared toward the bar. '*Oye, Diego, tráele un poco de agua.*'

Diego sounded defensive as he shuffled back to the table with a bottle of water. 'I bring a bottle this time; every time I bring a glass, he smashes it. Who's going to pay for all these glasses, huh?'

The doctor took the water from Diego and passed it to Tom. 'Drink.'

Diego returned to the bar, puffing his cigarette. 'You better do as she says, man. She's the boss.'

Tito leaned toward Tom. '*Sí*, this is my wife, Sofia.'

Tom's heart thumped against his chest as he found his friend's face in the old woman's.

'Sofia?'

'*¿Sí?*' Her brow wrinkled with recognition. 'What is

your name?'

'Thomas.'

She covered her mouth in shock and looked down at her husband. '*Es él.*'

'Thomas?' Tito stared at his wife, the confusion on his face lifting to wonder. 'Is… is it really you?'

Tom nodded, his words caught behind the lump in his throat. The old man's mouth sagged open.

'But how? I no understand, you… you look the same. Y-You have not aged. How?'

'I don't know. I wish I could explain it, but I can't.'

Sofia softly removed her hand from her mouth and turned to her husband. 'It was true.' Tears brimmed behind her glasses. 'After all these years, everything he told you – it was all true.'

Tito slowly rose and shuffled around the table; Tom rose to meet him.

'Tito, I don't know how it happened or how I came home. I can't explain it. It might have been…'

Tito threw his arms around him. '*Gracias.*' The old man's frail body shuddered against Tom's. '*Muchas gracias.*'

Sofia removed her glasses and covered her eyes; tears seeped out between her fingers. Eventually, Tito pulled himself free, and Sofia handed him a handkerchief. The old man dabbed at his eyes and blew his nose.

'I'm sorry, but…' He waved away the rest of his words.

Sofia wrapped her arms around Tom, kissing each of his cheeks twice and looking into his eyes.

'He's wanted to say thank you for over fifty years, Thomas. We both have. He told me what you sacrificed to bring him back to me. He's never forgotten it; neither have I.'

'So…' Tom's throat burned as he fought to voice the question. 'So, everything has been undone? Tito doesn't remember me asking for his blessing a month ago?'

'I'm sorry, Thomas.' She placed her hand on his shoulder. 'But we haven't seen you since 1954, not since the pilgrims' mass in the cathedral. We have lived in Santiago ever since.'

Tears now formed in Tom's eyes. Ana wasn't here; she'd never existed in this world. Sofia clutched his forearm and patted his shoulder.

'We are so sorry, Thomas; when I asked you to bring Tito back to me in Sarria, I never knew what it would cost you.'

Tito also wrapped his arms around Tom, the three of them knotted together in gratitude and grief. Eventually, Tom pulled away and wiped away his own tears. He managed to meet Tito's eye.

'Has it been a good life?'

'Not a good life.' Tito's eyes glistened as he shook his head. 'It was *fantastico*. It has been a life filled with love and happiness; my family and I owe it all to you.'

'Your family? How is your son?'

Tito tried to speak but paused. Sofia reached across and took her husband's hand.

'Our son turned out so beautiful, Thomas,' she said. 'So smart and funny and artistic.'

'Did he become a doctor too?'

'No, he became a teacher.' Both of them burst with pride. 'He taught literature and music and was the football team's coach.'

'Married?'

'*Sí*, to a stunning woman named Annabella, and they

had a beautiful daughter.'

'Do they live in Santiago too?'

Tito looked away, and Sofia smiled sadly. 'There was a road accident several years ago. Sadly, our son and his wife were taken from us.'

'I'm so sorry, Sofia.' His thoughts flashed to the accident that took Ana's parents from her when she'd been a little girl. How could the same disaster occur in two different histories?

'You have nothing to apologise for, Thomas. We miss our son and his wife every single day. But without you, we would never have had the joy he gave us.'

Sofia's phone rang, and she lifted it up to her ear.

'*¿Sí? Ya estamos en el café. Hemos conocido a un viejo amigo. Ven a conocernos.*'

She hung up, and Tito waved to someone before clasping his frail hand onto Tom's arm.

'Without you,' said Tito, 'we'd never have our granddaughter.'

A woman in hospital scrubs arrived. She was in her mid twenties and was slim and short; her wavy brown hair was messily tied up in a bun. The girl kissed her grandparents on both cheeks before Tito steered the girl toward Tom.

'Thomas, this is our granddaughter.'

The girl stared at Tito.

'*Abuelo*, you're practising your English?' She turned to Tom. '*Hola*, my name is Ana.' She leaned in and kissed Tom's cheeks.

His heart froze. Tito and Sofia glanced at one another before Sofia performed Tom's introduction on his behalf.

'Ana, this is Thomas. He's an old friend of ours from

England.'

Still unable to speak, Tom could only smile. He studied the girl's face. It was a face he'd woken to for the past five years, one he'd imagined every night for a month. It was her – the flecks of hazel in her dark-brown eyes and his favourite freckle on her upper-left eyelid – it was her. Inexplicably, it was Ana. But how?

'My father's name was Thomas,' said Ana. 'He was named after Abuelo's best friend.' Ana rested her hand on Tito's shoulder. 'Well, shall we eat? I worked a night shift, so I'm starving.' She took a seat and picked up a menu. 'Thomas, will you join us for a meal?'

He paused, utterly adrift. 'I'd like that very much.'

They all sat down, and Ana passed around the menus.

'Have you ever tried *pulpo*, Thomas? It's delicious here. But don't let me force it on you; order what you want.'

Ana waved Diego over to the table; a warm smile replaced the surly waiter's frown.

'Analita, how is my favourite doctor?'

Sofia threw her hands up in the air. 'Hey – you said I was your favourite doctor.'

'I have many favourites.'

Ana turned toward Tom. 'Do you know what you want, Thomas?'

He placed the menu down on the table and smiled at her.

'I do.'

July 2012

Ana looked out to the horizon; it was impossible to see where the ocean stopped, and the clouds began. The wind bit at her, and she zipped her jacket up to her chin. Rocks trickled down the cliff behind her; a baby mountain goat scrambled down a ledge. It glanced at her before continuing down the escarpment. Ana didn't favour the kid's chances of finding something to eat. There wasn't anything here, let alone grass. The name of the town, Finisterre, literally meant World's End.

The goat negotiated its way further down the rocky cliff and stopped to calculate its next step. Some more rocks clattered from the ledge above, and Ana turned, expecting to see the kid's mother.

'I found you.' Thomas scrambled down the slope toward her and nodded to the cloudy horizon. 'So much for the sunset.' He made it to the rocky outcrop she was perched on and leaned down to kiss the top of her head. He held up his knapsack. 'You were right; I left it on the bed.'

'You're terrible with that thing.'

'You have no idea.' He looked at her face, and his grin disappeared. 'Are you crying?'

'It's nothing; it's just the wind.' She wiped her shimmering eyes.

Thomas placed the backpack on the ground. 'Hey, what's wrong?' He gently took her hands. His blue-grey eyes looked bluer with the dark clouds behind him. 'You've been a bit off since we passed Santiago. Are you missing home?'

She dropped her head, immediately embarrassed she was ruining their last night on the Camino. Thomas rested his forehead against hers and wrapped his arms around her. She closed her eyes and pressed her face against his chest. She wished they didn't need to have this conversation.

'I just don't want this to end,' she said.

'The Camino?'

She shook her head. 'I mean this – us – I don't want us to end.'

'Why would you think it would?'

'Because everything ends eventually. I've been looking forward to this trip ever since I've known you, and now it's over. What if we end too, you know? I mean, what if you get sick of me or find someone else?'

'I don't want anyone else.'

'Maybe not right now, but that could change. You could get bored of me.'

'Why would you think that?'

Her shoulders slumped. 'Because you've lived so

much more than me, Thomas. You went to Cambridge and worked in London.'

'Trust me, you could have easily done those things too.'

'*Sí*, but I didn't. I've lived in Santiago my entire life.'

His eyes narrowed. 'Does this have to do with us moving in together or visiting my family for Christmas? Because we don't have to do that.'

'Your sisters will kill me if we cancel our trip.' She took his hand. 'And of course I want us to live together; I hate living in separate apartments. It's just… you've lived with other girls before.'

'I've only lived with one girlfriend and, like I told you, I was a terrible boyfriend. So I'm nervous about moving in together too. I don't want to rush things.'

'Rush things?' She grinned up at him. 'It took you six months to finally kiss me.'

His cold cheeks turned pink. 'I know it was odd how we met, so I just never wanted you to think I'd somehow tricked you into being with me.'

'Tricked?' His Spanish had really improved, but sometimes he still used the wrong word. 'Even if you had, there's no fooling Abuela – she loves you.' She sighed deeply and rested her head on his shoulder. 'You've just seen and done so many things already.'

'None of that matters, though. For the longest time, I cared about all the wrong things – my phone, restaurants, holidays.' He held her hand. 'But being with you is what makes me happy.'

The words were always comforting to hear.

'I suppose I'm just sad the Camino is ending. It sounds silly, but it's safer to keep these things as dreams. Dreams never end.'

'It's not silly; I understand.'

He wrapped his arm around her, and she pressed her face into his chest, sheltering from the sea breeze. The young mountain goat bleated, still alone on the rocky bluff in front of them.

'Do you remember our second day on the Camino?' asked Thomas. 'We'd planned to walk from Roncesvalles to Pamplona, but we both felt tired.'

'You mean how I got blisters and began to cry?'

He grinned. 'Do you remember the name of the village we stayed in?'

'*Sí* – Zubiri. We stayed in the *albergue* by the river, and you showed me the trick with the needle and thread.'

'That's right. And that night, we drank with the locals.'

'And I ate the best steak of my life.'

'We hadn't even planned to stop in that village, yet it's my favourite night of our trip. I think that's what we should do now – not worry about what may or may not happen, just take every day as it comes.'

'Like how we walked the Camino, no?'

'Exactly.'

She placed her hands on Thomas' rosy cheeks and stared up into his eyes. 'Okay, one day at a time.'

'One day at a time.'

She leaned up and kissed him. His lips were warm, but his nose was ice. She wrapped her arms around him and squeezed him tightly.

'*Gracias* for walking the Camino with me. Especially when you've already done it.'

He stroked her hair. 'A friend once told me the same person never walks the Camino twice.'

Rocks tumbled down from the ledge behind them, and the mother goat sturdily climbed down the cliff to her kid. The two goats trod away out of view. Thomas turned to Ana.

'Well, now we've decided we're not breaking up, I have something important to ask you.'

Butterflies awoke in Ana's tummy.

'Tell me, what were your three favourite moments on the Camino?'

Ana's smile hid her surprise and disappointment. She'd never realised how excited she'd been at the thought of Thomas proposing.

'You seriously expect me to only pick three?' She shook her head. 'That's impossible.'

'Come on, let's hear them.'

'Fine.' She took a deep breath. 'These are in no particular order, okay?'

Thomas nodded.

'So one of them was definitely the fountain of wine near Estella.'

He shook his head like a disapproving headmaster. 'The sign did actually say only one bottle of wine per pilgrim.'

'I thought it was water. Whatever possessed monks to build a fountain of wine, anyway?'

Thomas offered an indecipherable grin but didn't respond.

'And my second favourite was probably León.'

'It was very kind of your uncle Pablo to book us into the hotel room.'

'He's a famous poet; it's the least he could do for us. He and Abuelo stayed in the same hotel when they walked the Camino together.'

'And what's number three?' asked Thomas, his face filled with mischief.

'That's easy.' Ana smiled. 'This.'

'This magnificent sunset?' Thomas waved theatrically to the blanket of cloud shrouding the sun.

'Shut up. It's my list, and I choose being here with you at the end of the world.'

'Well, I feel honoured.' He placed his hands on her face and stroked her cheeks with his thumbs. 'I love you, baby.'

'I love you too.'

He leaned down and kissed her; she forgot about the future to enjoy the warmth of his lips. The sun finally dipped beneath the grey veil of cloud and transformed the sky into a mosaic of pinks and oranges. She leaned her head on Thomas' shoulder, and they silently watched the sun slowly plunge into the ocean.

'So, are you ready to do this?' he asked.

Ana lifted her head and eyed him suspiciously. 'You seriously still want to do it?'

'It's tradition.'

'According to who?'

'A friend of mine.' Thomas stood up and looked around before getting undressed. 'Come on, the sun's almost gone.'

She giggled at her crazy Englishman, who was standing on the rockface in nothing but a pair of flip-flops. His tan marks on his body made it look like he was wearing a white bathing suit from the 1920s. He pointed to the knapsack.

'Hurry up. The wind is freezing.'

'*Inglés loco.*' She tossed him the bag and shook her head in disbelief. 'I can't believe I'm doing this.'

Ana stripped off her clothes and stood naked next to Thomas. The two of them cackled like schoolchildren as they snapped off the tags of the new clothes they'd bought at the tourist shop in Santiago. Their outfits were identical: grey tracksuit bottoms and a bright-blue t-shirt with a large yellow arrow under the words 'This way to Santiago'. Thomas surveyed their new outfits proudly.

'Not bad for thirty euros.'

'This is so ugly.'

He piled their old clothes onto the ground in front of them and took out a can of lighter fluid from the bag. As he doused their discarded second skins in accelerant, Ana retrieved the book of matches she'd stuffed into her wallet. Her eyes clung to the faded black-and-white photograph within the wallet's inside pocket.

'I wish you could have known him.' She stroked her thumb over the plastic covering the two boys' smiling faces.

Thomas stood next to her.

'I still can't believe he's gone,' she said. 'I know it sounds crazy, but sometimes I think he lived just long enough to know I'd meet someone like you before he could finally leave Abuela and I.'

'He once told me he wanted you to have someone who cared more about you than they did themselves. Someone who'd walk across Spain for you.'

Tears filled her eyes, and she wrapped her arms around Thomas again. '*Gracias.*'

'For what?'

She didn't answer, and he silently held her and stroked

her hair. The final sliver of sun was extinguished by the sea, and the cold wind blew harder. He gently shook her.

'Come on, let's do this.'

Ana took out the receipt from the shopping bag and lit it with one of the matches. She dropped the burning paper onto the pile of clothes, sending them up in a small ball of flame.

'*¡Olé!*' said Tom jovially.

Ana held Thomas' hand and stared at the fire. With their faces illuminated by the flames, she forgot about the journey they'd just finished and focused on the one about to begin.

AUTHOR'S NOTE

As the time travel suggests, *Once Upon a Camino* is a work of fiction, born during my own pilgrimage across Spain in 2010. It should certainly not be confused with a serious travel guide to Santiago. There are dozens of comprehensive guidebooks for that. Likewise, this book isn't intended as an accurate telling of Spanish history. The Spanish Civil War and Franco's thirty-six-year dictatorship were painfully real; this novel doesn't belong alongside the history books which carefully and accurately document these events. While I've conducted thousands of hours of research to write this book, my perspective will forever be that of an outsider, limited by my own perspective. If you'd like to learn Spain's history, I'd suggest you read the works of authors with primary experience and hearing the history in their own voices.

While I attempted to be as truthful to the past as possible, some liberties were taken throughout. The FIFA

World Cup Final did occur on Sunday, 4th July 1954 and West Germany really did come back from two-nil down to win their nation's first World Cup. But Pamplona's San Fermín festival does not occur in June; it's always held in the first weeks of July. Aberdeen was indeed bombed by the Germans in 1943, but Sir Walter's character and story are entirely fictional. And if there really is a secret trapdoor leading from Eunate's Iglesia Santa Maria into the forest – I never found it.

As to the details of the Camino itself: the path is indeed long, and the mountains are steep. Blisters and epiphanies are not uncommon; I'd recommend packing a needle and thread for the former.

Buen Camino.

This book would not have been possible without the guidance and encouragement of my dear friends – Rowan, Kon and Paolo. Your wise counsel made this story better; your endless encouragement motivated me to finish.

I'd also like to thank my friends and fellow writers from Writers Victoria, whose digital accompaniment on our Zoom sessions got me through the long months of Melbourne's wintry lockdown of 2020.

Enormous thanks to Lauren Finger, editorial extraordinaire. Not only did you polish the very rough edges of my work, but your attention to detail, both in language and story, allowed me to reach a new standard.

Your knowledge of the publishing industry and reassurance throughout made the entire editing process a joy. I'd also like to thank Becca Allen, whose keen eye for detail provided such a thorough final proofread.

I'd be remiss if I didn't thank the companions who accompanied me along my own Camino – Antonio, Pablo (both from Spain), Katie (Australia), Martin (Austria), Steve (Canada) and Daniella (US) – we started as strangers, but after countless hours of walking and talking, we became friends. Buen Camino, amigos.

As always, thanks to my family for always supporting my writing.

But above all else, thanks to my wife, Jenny – who supported me every step of the way. From the moment I first told her the end to the story – at our local Japanese restaurant – her happy tears confirmed my silly Camino time travel story was a tale worth telling. Thanks for always believing in me – always and forever.

ABOUT THE AUTHOR

Matthew is an independent writer from Melbourne, Australia. His first book, *The Devil's in the Detail*, was released in October 2012.

You can find more of his work and short-fiction at www.matthew-s-wilson.com. For other musings, follow him on Twitter at @Matthew_SWilson.

Printed in Great Britain
by Amazon